THE JUPITER MYTH

Lindsey Davis

Century · London

Published by Century in 2002

1 3 5 7 9 10 8 6 4 2

Copyright © Lindsey Davis 2002

Lindsey Davis has asserted her right
under the Copyright, Designs and Patents Act, 1988
to be identified as the authors of this work

First published in the United Kingdom in 2002 by Century
The Random House Group Limited
20 Vauxhall Bridge Road, London SW1V 2SA

Random House Australia (Pty) Limited
20 Alfred Street, Milsons Point, Sydney,
New South Wales 2061, Australia

Random House New Zealand Limited
18 Poland Road, Glenfield,
Auckland 10, New Zealand

Random House (Pty) Limited
Endulini, 5A Jubilee Road,
Parktown 2193, South Africa

The Random House Group Limited Reg. No. 954009

www.randomhouse.co.uk

A CIP record for this book is available
from the British Library

Papers used by Random House are natural,
recyclable products made from wood grown in sustainable forests.
The manufacturing processes conform to the environmental
regulations of the country of origin.

ISBN 0 7126 8044 6 – Hardback

Typeset in Bembo by MATS, Southend-on-Sea, Essex
Printed and bound in Great Britain by
Mackays of Chatham PLC, Chatham, Kent

To Ginny,
Who deserves it

Now look here; you had better not expect half a page of sentimental guff.
If you are a treasure and an inspiration and a dear friend who
has suffered a year of stress, I shall certainly not say so.
This is a British dedication, after all!

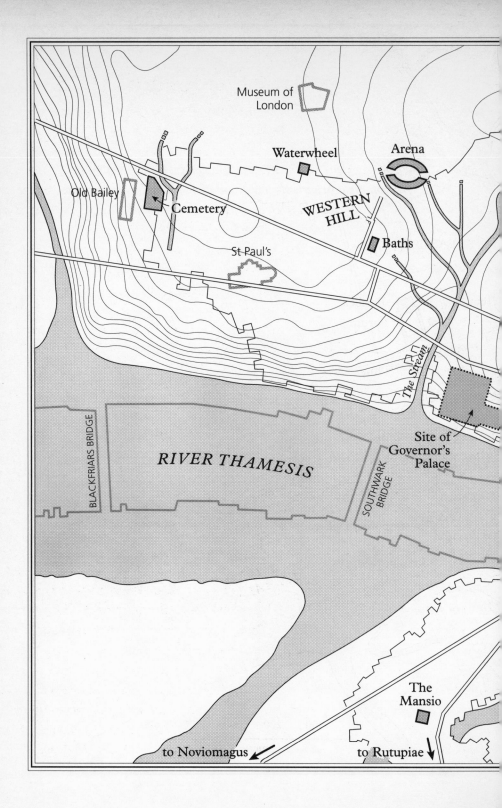

Museum of
London

Waterwheel

Arena

Old Bailey

Cemetery

WESTERN
HILL

Baths

St Paul's

The Stream

Site of
Governor's
Palace

BLACKFRIARS BRIDGE

RIVER THAMESIS

SOUTHWARK BRIDGE

The
Mansio

to Noviomagus

to Rutupiae

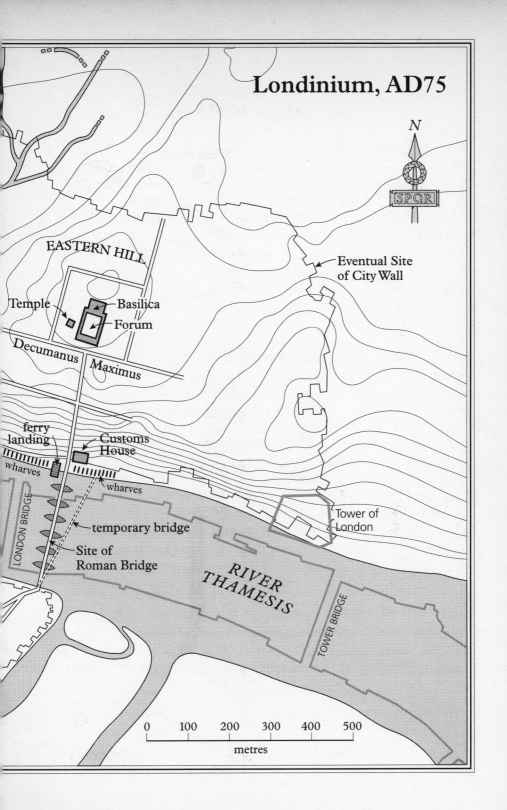

Londinium, AD75

N
SPQR

EASTERN HILL

Temple — Basilica
— Forum

Decumanus Maximus

Eventual Site
of City Wall

ferry landing — Customs House

wharves

wharves

LONDON BRIDGE

temporary bridge

Site of Roman Bridge

Tower of London

RIVER THAMESIS

TOWER BRIDGE

0   100   200   300   400   500
metres

PRINCIPAL CHARACTERS

M. Didius Falco	an auditor on holiday
Helena Justina	companion of his life and heart, poor girl
Maia Favonia	Falco's sister; a widow (heading for trouble)
L. Petronius Longus	a vigiles officer (aiming for Maia)
S. Julius Frontinus	governor of Britain (thinks he runs the province)
G. Flavius Hilaris	procurator of finance (really does run it)
Aelia Camilla	Helena's aunt, his wife (runs Flavius Hilaris)
King Togidubnus	a Roman ally with a mind of his own
Verovolcus	past tense; a British mugging victim
Flavia Fronta	a 'respectable' barmaid, allegedly
Crixus	a disrespectful centurion, who knows it all
Silvanus	another centurion, who should know better
Norbanus Murena	a 'charming' property developer; perhaps a suspect
Popillius	an 'honest' lawyer; definitely suspect
Amazonia	a fighter with a future . . .
. . . *aka* Chloris	trouble from the past
'The Collector'	working at the office; a cowardly pimp
Epaphroditus	a brave baker; in really bad trouble
Albia	a troubled young survivor
Firmus	a sunbather, in the customs service
Amicus	the official torturer
Splice	a different kind of persuader
Pyro	a persuasive arsonist
Children too numerous to mention	especially Julia, Favonia, Marius, Cloelia, Ancus, Rhea and Flavia
Dogs ditto	
Barkeepers, gladiators, crooks, soldiers, slaves and so forth	
A bear	
A tired bee	

LONDINIUM, BRITANNIA
AUGUST, AD 75

I

'I̲T DEPENDS WHAT we mean by *civilisation*,' the procurator
mused.

Staring at the corpse, I was in no mood to discuss philosophy.
We were in Britain, where the rule of law was administered by the
army. Justice operated in a rough and ready fashion so far away
from Rome, but special circumstances meant this killing would be
difficult to brush aside.

We had been called out by a centurion from the small local
troop detachment. The military presence in Londinium was
mainly to protect the governor, Julius Frontinus, and his deputy,
the procurator Hilaris, but since the provinces are not manned by
the vigiles, soldiers carry basic community policing. So the
centurion attended the death scene, where he became a worried
man. On investigation, an apparently routine local slaying
acquired 'developments'.

The centurion told us he had come to the bar, expecting just a
normal drunken stabbing or battering. To find a drowned man
head-first down a well was slightly unusual, exciting maybe. The
'well' was a deep hole in a corner of the bar's tiny back yard.
Hilaris and I bent double and peered in. The hole was lined with
the waterproof wooden staves of what must be a massive German
wine container; water came nearly to the top. Hilaris had told me
these imported barrels were taller than a man, and after being
emptied of wine they were often re-used in this way.

When we arrived of course, the body had already been
removed. The centurion had pulled up the victim by his boots,

planning to heave the cadaver into a corner until the local dung cart carried it off. He himself had intended to sit down with a free drink while he eyed up the attractions of the serving girl.

Her attractions were not up to much. Not by Aventine standards. It depends what we mean by *attractive*, as Hilaris might muse, if he were the type to comment on waitresses. Myself, I was that type, and immediately we entered the dim establishment I had noticed she was four feet high with a laughable leer and smelt like old boot-liners. She was too stout, too ugly, and too slow on the uptake for me. But I'm from Rome. I have high standards. This was Britain, I reminded myself.

There was certainly no chance of anyone getting free drinks now Hilaris and I were here. We were official. I mean *really* official. One of us held a damned high rank. It wasn't me. I was just a new middle-class upstart. Anyone of taste and style would be able to sniff out my slum background instantly.

'I'll avoid the bar,' I joked quietly. 'If their water is full of dead men, their wine is bound to be tainted!'

'No, I'll not try a tasting,' agreed Hilaris, in a tactful undertone. 'We don't know what they may stuff in their amphorae . . .'

The centurion stared at us, showing his contempt for our attempts at humour.

This event was even more inconvenient for me than it was for the soldier. All he had to worry about was whether to mention the awkward 'developments' on his report. I had to decide whether to tell Flavius Hilaris – my wife's Uncle Gaius – that I knew who the dead man was. Before that, I had to evaluate the chances that Hilaris himself had known the casked corpse.

Hilaris was the important one here. He was procurator of finance in Britain. To put it in perspective, I was a procurator myself but my role – which involved theoretical oversight of the Sacred Geese of Juno – was one of a hundred thousand meaningless honours handed out by the Emperor when he owed someone a favour and was too mean to pay in cash. Vespasian reckoned my services had cost enough, so he settled up remaining debts with a joke. That was me: Marcus Didius Falco, the imperial clown. Whereas the estimable Gaius Flavius Hilaris, who had known Vespasian many years ago in the army, was now second only to the provincial governor. Since he did know Vespasian personally, then (as the governor would be aware) dear Gaius was the Emperor's eyes and ears, assessing how the new governor ran the province.

He did not need to assess me. He had done that five years ago when we first met. I think I came out well. I wanted to look good. That was even before I fell for his wife's elegant, clever, superior niece. Alone in the Empire, Hilaris had always thought Helena might end up with me. Anyway, he and his own wife had received me back now as a nephew by marriage as if it were natural and even a pleasure.

Hilaris looked a quiet, clerkish, slightly innocent fellow, but I wouldn't take him on at draughts – well, not unless I could play with my brother Festus' weighted dice. He was dealing with the situation in his usual way: curious, thorough, and unexpectedly assertive. 'Here's one Briton who has not acquired much benefit from Roman civilisation,' he had said on being shown the corpse. That was when he added drily, 'I suppose it depends what you mean by civilisation, though.'

'He took in water with his wine, you mean?' I grinned.

'Better not jest.' Hilaris was no prude and it was not a reproof.

He was a lean, neat man, still active and alert – yet greyer and more haggard than I had remembered him. He had always given a slight impression of ill health. His wife, Aelia Camilla, seemed little changed since my last visit, but Flavius Hilaris looked much older and I felt glad I had brought my own wife and youngsters to see him while I could.

Trying not to show that I was watching him, I decided he did know the dead man at his feet. As a career diplomat, he would also be aware of why this death would cause us problems. But, so far, he was not mentioning his knowledge to me.

That was interesting.

II

'I'M SORRY TO drag you out, sirs,' murmured the centurion. He must be wishing he had kept quiet. He was totting up how much additional documentation he had let himself in for, and had realised belatedly that his commander would give him all Hades for involving the civil powers.

'You did the right thing.' I had never seen Hilaris back off from trouble. Strange to think that this man had served in the army (Second Augusta, my own legion, twenty years before me). He was part of the Invasion force, too, at a time for pragmatic dealings with the locals. But three decades of civic bureaucracy had turned him into that rare high-flying wonder, a public servant who followed the rules. Even rarer, instead of stagnating uselessly out here, he had mastered the art of making the rules work. Hilaris was good. Everyone said so.

By contrast the centurion covered *his* ineptitude by moving slowly, saying little, and doing even less. He was wide-bodied and short-necked. He stood with his feet planted wide apart, his arms hanging loose. His neckerchief was tucked into his armour with just enough untidiness to express contempt for authority, yet his boots were buffed and his sword and dagger looked sharp. He would be the type who sat around, obsessively honing his weapons and complaining about higher officers. I doubted he grumbled at the Emperor. Vespasian was a soldiers' general.

Vespasian would know that the army is stuffed with such characters: not as good as those in charge would like, but sound enough to coast along in a far-off province where the frontiers were fairly quiet and open rebellion was no longer an issue. The legions in Britain carried no dead wood. In a real crisis, something could be made of this centurion.

We had a crisis here. Correctly, the centurion had sensed it. And to be fair, he responded properly. He had noticed the white circle around the dead man's neck where a torque had habitually sat, and he saw the grazes where the heavy twisted metal must have been wrenched off by a thief or thieves. He realised this was serious. It was not the theft itself that made for trouble, but in tribal Britain heavy gold and electrum neck torques were worn only by the rich and well-born. That torque, now missing, was a mark of rank. Persons of status do not usually die shabby deaths alone in taverns, whatever their culture. Something was up. So the centurion had sent a runner to the governor.

Julius Frontinus was in his first year of office here. When the message came, he was eating breakfast during an early morning meeting with his right hand man. We all shared the official residence so I was there too. 'Gaius, go and see if you recognise the victim,' Frontinus told Hilaris, who had been in Britain all those decades and so knew absolutely everyone. Since the governor had previously worked with me on a murder hunt in Rome, he then added: 'Sounds your sort of thing, Falco. You should trot along there too.'

So here I was. I had been dispatched to the crime scene as an expert in unnatural death. But I was a thousand miles from my own patch. How would I know the motive for a local British murder, or where to start looking for the killer? I was on holiday, intending to claim that I had nothing to contribute. My own official mission in Britain was finished; afterwards I had brought Helena to Londinium to see her relatives, but we were pretty well *en route* for home now.

Then when the centurion presented the sodden body, Hilaris went quiet and I too felt queasy. I knew at once that I might have had a direct involvement in how the victim came to be here.

So far, only I knew that.

III

'WONDER WHO HE is?' The centurion nudged the corpse with the side of his boot – avoiding the tip, where he might have touched dead flesh with his big bare toes. 'Who he *was!*' he laughed sardonically.

The dead man had been tall and well fed. The straggles of long hair that clung to his head and neck, tangling in the edges of his woollen tunic, were once wild and red-gold. The eyes, now closed, had been bright with curiosity and used to delight in dangerous mischief. I supposed they were blue, though I could not remember. His skin was pallid and swollen after drowning, but he had always been light-complexioned, with the gingery eyebrows and lashes that go with such colouring. Along his bare forearms fine hairs began to dry. He wore dark blue trousers, expensive boots, a belt with hole-punched patterns into which the plaid tunic was gathered in thick clumps. No weapon was present. Every time I saw him alive, he had worn a long British sword.

He had been always on the go. He dashed around; was full of vigour and crude humour; always accosted me in a loud voice; regularly leered at women. It seemed odd to find him quite so still.

I stooped, picking up the cloth on a sleeve to inspect a hand for finger-rings. One sturdy item in rope-twisted gold remained, perhaps too tight to drag off in a hurry. As I straightened, my gaze briefly caught that of Hilaris. Clearly he could see that I too knew the man's identity. Well, if he thought about it, I had just come up from Noviomagus Regnensis so I would.

'It is Verovolcus,' he told the centurion without drama. I kept

6

quiet. 'I met him officially once or twice. He was a courtier, and possibly a relative, of the Great King – Togidubnus of the Atrebates tribe, down on the south coast.'

'Important?' demanded the centurion, with a half-eager sideways look. Hilaris did not answer. The soldier drew his own conclusions. He pulled a face, impressed.

King Togidubnus was a long-time friend and ally of Vespasian. He had been lavishly rewarded for years of support. In this province he could probably pull rank even on the governor. He could get Flavius Hilaris recalled to Rome and stripped of his hard-earned honours. He could have me knocked over the head and dumped in a ditch, with no questions asked.

'So what was Verovolcus doing in Londinium?' Hilaris mused. It seemed a general question, though I felt he aimed it at me.

'More official business?' asked the centurion meekly.

'No. I would know of it. And even if he came to Londinium for private purposes,' continued the procurator levelly, 'why would he visit an establishment as grim as this?' He now glanced directly at me. 'A British aristocrat laden with expensive jewels is as much at risk of robbery in a hole like this as a lone Roman would be. This place is for locals – and even they have to be brave!'

I refused to be drawn, but left the yard, ducked inside the bar and looked around. As wine bars go this lacked charm and distinction. We had found it halfway down a short, narrow alley on the sloping hill just above the wharves. A few crude shelves held flagons. A couple of windows with iron grilles let in some light. From its filthy straw-strewn floor to its low shadowy rafters the bar was as lousy as bars can get. And I had seen some.

I tackled the woman who kept the place.

'I know nothing,' she spouted immediately, before I could ask her anything.

'Are you the owner?'

'No, I just wait at table.'

'Did you summon the centurion?'

'Of course!' There was no of course about it. I didn't have to live in Britain to know that if she could have hidden this crime, she would have done so. Instead, she had worked out that Verovolcus was bound to be missed. There would be trouble and unless she made it look good today, the trouble would be worse for her. 'We found him this morning.'

'You never noticed him last night?'

'We were busy. Lot of trade in.'

I gazed at her calmly. 'What sort of trade was that?'

'The sort we get.'

'Can you be more specific? I mean –'

'I know what you mean!' she scoffed.

'Sinful girls, after sailors and traders?' I threw at her anyway.

'Nice people. *Businessmen!*' Nasty forms of business, I bet.

'Had this man been drinking here last night?'

'Nobody can remember him, though he could have been.' They should remember. He must have been of a higher class than any regulars, even the nice businessmen. 'We just found him left here with his feet waggling –'

'Excuse me! Why were his feet waggling? Was the poor sap still alive?'

She blushed. 'Just a manner of speaking.'

'So was he dead or not?'

'He was dead. Of course he was.'

'How did you know?'

'What?'

'If only his feet were visible, how did anyone know his condition? Could you have revived him? You might at least have tried. I know you didn't bother; the centurion had to pull him out.'

She looked thrown, but carried on gamely, 'He was a goner. It was obvious.'

'Especially if you already knew that he was crammed down the well last evening.'

'I never! We were all surprised!'

'Not as surprised as he must have been,' I said.

8

There was nothing more to be gained here. We left the centurion to shift the body for safe keeping until the Great King was informed. Gaius and I emerged into the alley, which was used as an open drain. We picked our way past the daily rubbish and empties to what passed for a street. That was dingy enough. We were on terraced ground below the two low gravel hills on which Londinium stood. The area was right down near the river. In any city that can be bad news. The procurator's two bodyguards followed us discreetly, frontline soldiers on detached duty, fingering daggers. They provided reassurance – partially.

From the badly cobbled lane that connected this enclave to larger, perhaps less unfriendly vicinities, we could hear the creak of cranes on the wharves that lined the Thamesis. There were pungent smells of leather, a staple trade. Some towns have regulations that tanneries have to be out in the country because they reek so badly, but Londinium was either not that fussy or not so well organised. Attracted by the river's proximity, we walked there.

We came out among new warehouses with narrow fronts at the river's edge, running back from their tight-packed unloading berths in long secure storage tunnels. The river embankment was fringed with these, as if it had been planned. A great wooden platform, of recent construction, provided a landing stage and a bulwark against the spreading tide.

I stared at the river gloomily. The Thamesis was much wider than the Tiber at home, its high tide width more than a thousand strides, though at low water it shrank to a third of that. Opposite our wharf were reeded islands, which would become almost submerged at high tide, when for miles all up the estuary the Thamesis marshes would flood. Roads from the southern ports arrived over there on the south bank, conjoining at a spot where ferries had always crossed the river. There was a wooden bridge coming across from the main island, at a slightly odd angle.

Standing beside me, the procurator clearly shared my melancholy mood. Death and misty grey riverbanks produce the same effect. We were men of the world, yet our hearts ached.

Oppressed by our surroundings, I felt unready yet to address the Verovolcus death. 'You mended the bridge, I see.'

'Yes. Boudicca used it to get at the settlement on the south bank – then her troops made a good attempt to put it out of action.' Hilaris sounded dry. 'If this one seems rather strangely aligned, that's because it isn't permanent.' Clearly the bridge issue amused him. 'Falco, I remember the post-Invasion bridge, which was intended to be for purely military purposes. It was just decking on pontoons. Later the supports were made permanent – but it was still wood, and we pulled it down. It was decided a decent stone bridge would signify permanence in the province, so this one was built.'

I joined in the satire. 'You said this isn't permanent either?'

'No. The permanent bridge will come straight across to link up with the forum; people arriving will have a splendid view, directly across the river and up the hill.'

'So when is the permanent bridge planned for?' I asked, smiling.

'About ten years' time, I'd say,' he told me gloomily. 'Meanwhile we have this one, which you could call the permanent temporary bridge – or the temporary permanent bridge.'

'It's off-set so while you build the final version alongside, you can maintain a crossing point?'

'Correct! If you want to cross now, my advice is, use the ferry.'

I quirked up an eyebrow. 'Why?'

'The bridge is temporary; we don't maintain it.'

I laughed.

Hilaris then fell into a reflective mood. He enjoyed giving history lessons. 'I remember when there was nothing here. Just a few round huts, most of them across the water. Orchards and coppices this side. By Jove it felt desolate! A civilian settlement struggled into existence after Rome invaded. But we were then away out at Camulodunum, the Britons' own chief centre. It was bloody inconvenient, I can tell you. Our presence caused bad feeling too; in the Rebellion that was the first place lost.'

'Londinium had enough by Nero's day to attract Boudicca's energy,' I reminisced bitterly. 'I saw it . . . Well, I saw what was left afterwards.'

Hilaris paused. He had forgotten that I was here in the Icenian Rebellion – a youngster, marked for life by that grim experience. Evidence of the firestorm remained to this day. Memories of corpses and severed heads churning in the local waterways would never die. The whole atmosphere of this place still upset me. I would be glad when I could leave.

Hilaris was in Britain then too. I was a ranker, and in a disgraced legion; he a junior official among the governor's élite staff. Our paths would not have crossed.

After a moment he went on, 'You're right; the bridge will change things. The river used to form a natural boundary. The Atrebates and Cantii roamed to the south, the Trinovantes and Catuvellauni to the north. The floodplain was no man's land.'

'We Romans were the first to deploy the corridor, making the river a highway?'

'Before we put in decent roads it was the best way to move around supplies, Marcus. The estuary is navigable way up to here – and in the early days ships were more secure than trundling goods across country. They can float up on one tide, then back on the next. After the Rebellion we made this the provincial capital and now it's a major import base.'

'New city, new formal administrative centre –'

'And new problems!' said Hilaris, with unexpected feeling.

What problems? Did he already know what we were dealing with? It seemed a cue to discuss the Briton's death.

'Verovolcus,' I admitted, '*might* have been in that district close to the river because he was trying to arrange transport to Gaul.'

I made no overt link to the *problems*. Whatever that was about could wait.

Hilaris turned his neat head and considered me. 'You knew Verovolcus' movements? Why was he going to Gaul?'

'Exile. He was in disgrace.'

11

'*Exile!*' Some people would at once have asked me why. Ever the pedantic administrator, Hilaris demanded, 'Have you told the governor that?'

'Not yet.' I had no option now. 'Oh, I like Frontinus. I've worked with him before, Gaius, and on confidential matters too. But you're the old lag in this province. I was more likely to tell you.' I smiled, and the procurator acknowledged the compliment. 'It's a stupid story. Verovolcus killed an official. His motives were misguided, he expected royal protection – but he had misjudged Togidubnus.'

'You exposed him.' A statement, not a question. Hilaris knew how I worked. 'And you *did* tell the King!'

'I had to.' That had been far from easy. Verovolcus had been the King's close confidant. 'It was tense. The King is virtually independent, and we were in his tribal centre. Imposing a Roman solution was not easy. Fortunately Togi wants amicable relations, so in the end he agreed that his man had to disappear. Murder's a capital crime but that seemed the best I could ask for. From our angle, I felt I could sanction exile rather than a public trial and an execution. Sending Verovolcus to Gaul was my bargain for us all keeping the affair quiet.'

'Neat,' Hilaris agreed, ever pragmatic. Britain was a sensitive province since the Rebellion. Tribal feeling might not tolerate a respected king's henchman being punished for murdering a Roman official. Verovolcus did it (I was confident of that) but the governor would have hated having to dole out a death sentence to the King's right-hand man and if Frontinus was publicly lenient he would look weak, both here and back in Rome.

'Verovolcus agreed on Gaul?'

'He wasn't keen.'

'Londinium was not allowed as an alternative?'

'Nowhere in Britain. I would have made Londinium formally off-limits if I had ever thought Verovolcus would turn up here.'

'And the King?'

'He knew Gaul was better than the standard desert island.'

'But with Verovolcus killed in a Londinium bar instead, the King may well turn rough,' Hilaris observed glumly.

'Bound to,' I said.

He cleared his throat, as if diffident. 'Will he suspect that you arranged this death?'

I shrugged.

No stranger to the ways of undercover agents, Flavius Hilaris turned to stare at me. He was blunt: 'Did you?'

'No.'

He did not ask whether I would have done so, if I had thought of it. I chewed a fingernail, wondering that myself.

'You said Verovolcus killed someone,' suggested Hilaris. 'Could his drowning be some form of retribution, Marcus?'

'Unlikely.' I was fairly sure. 'There is nobody with an interest. He killed the architect, the project manager for the King's new palace.'

'*What?* Pomponius?' As financial procurator, Hilaris ultimately signed off the bills for the King's palace. He would know who the architect was – and that he had died. He would also have seen my situation-review afterwards. 'But your report said –'

'All it had to.' I sensed a slight awkwardness, as if Hilaris and I answered to different masters over this. 'I was on site to clear up problems. I put down the architect's death as a "tragic accident". There was no need to start a scandal by saying Togi's man had killed him. The King will rein in his people and the crime won't recur. A substitute is running the site, and running it well.'

Hilaris had let me talk him through it, but he remained unhappy. The report we were discussing had been addressed to the governor, but I sent my own copy to Vespasian. I had always intended to give a more accurate statement to the Emperor later – if he wanted to know. Killing the story might help him preserve good relations with his friend the King. I did not care. I was paid on results.

The results Vespasian wanted were to stop a glut of wild expenditure on a very expensive building site. He had sent me, nominally a private informer, because I was a first rate auditor. I had discovered a feud between the King as client and his officially appointed architect. When it flared up, with fatal results, we found ourselves left with nobody in charge of a multimillion-sesterces scheme – and chaos. Verovolcus, who had caused this mess, was not my favourite Briton. He was damned lucky that Gaul was the worst punishment I devised for him.

'Did Pomponius have relatives?' Hilaris was still fretting away at his retribution theory.

'In Italy. He had a boyfriend in Britain who was rather cut up, but he's working on the site. We beefed up his responsibilities; that should keep him quiet. I can check he has not left the area.'

'I'll send a messenger.' If Hilaris was overruling me it was tactful – so far. 'What is his name?'

'Plancus.'

'Did Verovolcus act alone?'

'No. He had a crony. A site supervisor. We arrested him.'

'Present location?'

Thank the gods I had been conscientious about tying up ends: 'Noviomagus. The King's responsibility.'

'Punishment?'

'That I *don't* know –' Now I felt like a schoolboy who had neglected his homework. Flavius Hilaris might be my wife's uncle but if I had bungled, I would be slated. 'Mandumerus had had only a secondary role and he was a local, so I let Togidubnus deal with him.'

'Mandumerus, you say.' Hilaris picked me up at once. 'I'll find out.'

I let him run with the line. In the long term, I could bunk off to Rome. Rome might give me a grilling, but I was up to it. Hilaris would live with the legacy of this tavern slaughter as long as he stayed in Britain. The royal connection was awkward enough. In addition, one of the Hilaris family's private homes stood in Noviomagus, just a mile from the King. Poor Uncle Gaius had been handed a personal 'bad neighbour' quarrel, if nothing else.

'Marcus, you don't think Togidubnus himself has punished Verovolcus in this way?'

'What a terrible thought!' I grinned. I liked Hilaris, but the devious minds of bureaucrats never cease to amaze me. 'The King was annoyed at the man's hot-headed action – but more annoyed with me for finding out.'

'Well, we are a step ahead of him so far.'

'I hope you are not suggesting a cover-up!' I offered satirically.

At that, Flavius Hilaris looked genuinely shocked. 'Dear gods, no. But we do have some grace to find out what happened – before the King starts slamming us with ballista bolts.' The use of a trooper's term from this quiet, cultured man reminded me there was more to nice, stylus-pushing Uncle Gaius than most people noticed.

I foresaw what was coming. 'You mean, *I* have time to do it?'

'Of course.' He beamed at me.

I sighed. 'Well, thanks.'

'Didius Falco, we are exceptionally lucky to have you here!'

Oh yes. This was a very familiar situation, one that clients had exploited in the past: I was implicated. I had made the victim leave his home ground, and though I told myself it was not my fault he ended up dead in a strange bar, I felt guilty. So I was stuck.

IV

'OH JUNO! I thought we had left all that nonsense behind,' my sister Maia complained. All my sisters were renowned for despising my work. Maia might be a thousand miles from home, but she kept up Aventine traditions. 'Marcus! Britain may be a small province in the rump of the Empire, but does everything that happens here have to be related to everything else?'

'It is rather unusual to be drowned in a wine barrel,' said Aelia Camilla mildly.

'What barrel?' scoffed Maia. 'I thought the man was shoved down a well?'

'Same thing. Wine is a hugely popular import. From the River Rhenus area in Germany it often comes in enormous wooden casks which then make good well-linings at a small cost.'

Aelia Camilla, the procurator's wife, was a calm, intelligent woman, the unflappable mother to a bunch of fearsomely bright children. Like her husband she was both more competent and much more approachable than she appeared. The self-sacrificing pair had been born to represent the Empire abroad. They were wise; they were fair. They embodied noble Roman qualities.

That did not make them popular with colleagues. It never does. They did not seem to notice, and never complained. Expertise in the British situation buoyed them up. Under a different emperor they might well have dwindled into oblivion. Under Vespasian they flourished surprisingly.

The slight friction between Aelia Camilla and my favourite sister Maia was a sadness to Helena and me. Being mothers several times

16

over was not enough in common to create warmth. Maia — fashionable, pert, angry and outspoken — was a different type. In fact, Maia shone in a different sky from most people. That was her problem.

This scene was taking place after lunch. Everyone official lived at the procurator's residence since the governor's palace was not yet built. Life abroad is communal. Diplomats are used to that. Lunch occurred without the governor; Frontinus took a tray in his office. (Whereas he hosted dinner, which was always formal, and rather a trial.) So now the procurator and his wife were eating gritty bread and travel-weary olives with just the four adults of my party. The couple were hospitable. When they first insisted that I bring Helena Justina to visit, they knew we were with our two baby daughters — although not that I was also accompanied by my moody sister, her four lively children, two excitable pet dogs, and my grumpy friend Petronius. Luckily Helena's two squabbling brothers and a loud nephew of mine had stayed behind in the south to go hunting and drinking. They could turn up any minute, but I had not mentioned that.

Hilaris, to whom I had promised more details (while hoping to avoid it), lay on a reading couch apart, apparently absorbed in scrolls. I knew he was listening. His wife was speaking for him, just as Helena would often question my own visitors — whether I was present or not. The procurator and his lady shared their thoughts, as we did. He and I were parties to true Roman marriage: confiding to our serious, sensitive womenfolk things we never even told our masculine friends. It could have made the women domineering — but females in the Camillus family were strong-willed in any case. That was why I liked mine. Don't ask me about Hilaris and his.

Petronius Longus, my best friend, did not approve. Still, he was a misery these days. Having come out to Britain, either to see me or my sister, he had travelled to Londinium with us but apparently just wanted to go home. At present he was hunched on a stool looking bored. He was starting to embarrass me. He had never

17

been anti-social or awkward in company before. Helena thought he was in love. Fat chance. At one point he had been after Maia, but they now rarely spoke.

'So, Marcus, Verovolcus was in trouble. Tell us about what happened to the architect,' Aelia Camilla prompted me. She behaved informally for a diplomat's wife, but she was personally shy and I had yet to deduce even which of her two names she preferred in private use.

'Confidential, I'm afraid.'

'Hushed up?' Helena's aunt leapt in again. Her great dark eyes were impossible to avoid. I had always found it difficult to play the hard man in her presence. While seeming gentle and bashful, she screwed all sorts of answers out of me. 'Well, we are all in government service, Marcus. We know how things work.'

'Oh – it was daft.' As I gave in, I sensed Helena smiling. She loved to see her aunt get the better of me. 'A clash of ideas. The King and his architect were daggers drawn and Verovolcus took it upon himself to defend his royal master's taste in an extreme way.'

'I met Pomponius,' Aelia Camilla said. 'A typical designer. He knew exactly what the client should want.'

'Quite. But King Togidubnus is now on his third major refit to the palace; he has strong opinions and is very knowledgeable about architecture.'

'Were his demands too expensive? Or did he keep making changes?' Aelia Camilla knew all the pitfalls of public works.

'No, he just refused to accept any design features he hated. Verovolcus bore the brunt; he was supposed to liaise between them, but Pomponius despised him. Verovolcus became just a cipher. He did away with Pomponius so a more amenable architect could take over. It sounds stupid, but I think it was the only way he could reassert his own control.'

'It casts interesting light on the British situation.' Helena was seated in a wicker chair, her favourite type. With her hands folded over her woven belt and her feet on a small footstool, she could have been modelling memorials for submissive wives. I knew better. Tall, graceful and grave, Helena Justina read widely and kept up with world affairs. Born to bear and educate senatorial children, she was giving culture and good sense to mine. And she kept me in hand. 'Representing progress we had the Great King: an ideal provincial monarch – civilised, keen to be part of the Empire, utterly go-ahead. Then there was Verovolcus, his closest aide, still at heart a tribal warrior. Murdering the Roman project manager was repugnant to the King, but Verovolcus honoured darker gods.'

'I never dwelt on his motives,' I admitted. 'So was it really just an artistic feud that blew up out of proportion – or more political? Was Verovolcus expressing barbarian hatred for Rome?'

'How did he react when you confronted him with the crime?' asked Aelia Camilla.

'Spat fury. Denied it. Swore he'd get me.'

'Just like any cornered suspect,' Helena observed. Our eyes met. Communal discussions made me ill at ease. I would much have preferred a private boudoir exchange.

'So, Marcus, let me understand you,' her aunt pressed on intensely. She moved against the embroidered cushion at her back, so her bangles shivered and gold flickers freckled the ornately coffered ceiling. 'You told Verovolcus he would not be tried for the murder, but must go into exile. The punishment for a Roman would be exclusion from the Empire'

'But for him I suggested Gaul.'

We all smiled. Gaul had been part of the Empire for longer than Britain, but we were Romans and for us even Gaul was backwoods territory.

'He could have sailed straight to Gaul from Novio.' From his couch, Gaius' thoughtful voice proved me right: he had been listening in.

'True. I assumed he would.'

'Would riding off to Londinium seem less obvious to his friends? Less shameful, say?' Maia enjoyed a puzzle.

'Or was he heading somewhere else?' Helena tried. 'No, if you pick up transport in Londinium it always goes across to Gaul. He gained nothing by coming here.'

Petronius spoke, dour as a bad-tempered oracle: 'There is nowhere beyond Britain. The only way is back!' He hated Britain.

So did I. I played it down while I was the procurator's guest. Hilaris had been in Britain so long he had lost his nostalgia for the real world. Tragic.

'If Verovolcus came to Londinium,' mused Aelia Camilla, 'would he have had to hide?'

'From me?' I laughed. So did rather too many of my friends and relatives.

'He thought he was a fugitive, though in fact,' Aelia Camilla said demurely, 'you had not told the governor!' I tried not to feel guilty. 'Verovolcus didn't know that. So he might have skulked in that bad district to lie low?'

'What's the bad locale, Falco?' asked Petronius. A professional question. At home, he was a member of the vigiles.

'A bar.'

'What bar?' At least he had revived and taken an interest. Petro was a big, active man, who seemed cramped in smart indoor locations. He could have relaxed on a padded couch with lion's head feet as I did, but he preferred to ignore what passed for comfort here, hugging his knees uncomfortably and scuffing the striped woollen rugs with his sturdy paramilitary boots.

I felt an odd reluctance to tell him about the crime scene. 'A black little hutment at the back of the wharves.'

'Whereabouts, Falco?' His brown eyes quizzed me. Petronius knew when I was stalling for some reason. 'How did you get there?'

'You don't mean you want to take a look?'

'Take the road down from the forum, bear left, and go into the worst alleys you see,' explained Hilaris. 'It was called the Shower of Gold – incongruously. There was a dim painting on the outside wall. Did you notice that, Falco?' I had not. The hovel had hardly been the kind of place where Jupiter would flash in through a

20

window disguised as a shower of gold – or anything else – to reach the arms of a lady friend. The waitress we met would surely repel divinities. 'What's your interest, Lucius Petronius?' Hilaris then asked. He spoke politely, but I reckoned he regarded Petro as an unknown quantity who should be watched.

'Nothing at all.' Petro lost any interest he had had. Apparently.

'Out of your jurisdiction.' I said it sympathetically. Petro was missing Rome.

He gave me a bitter, rather ambiguous, smile. He even missed his work, it seemed. Maybe his conscience was pricking. I had still not extracted how he managed to bunk off on leave for a couple of months. I knew he was between postings, but his very request for a transfer off the Aventine would have used up any goodwill from his old vigiles tribune. The new one, presumably, just wanted Petro on the squadron-house bench as soon as possible.

'Any bar is a good haven for Lucius Petronius!' My rude sister was scathing. They had been bickering since Petro had reached us, bringing her children to rejoin her. He had done her a favour – not that Maia thought so.

'Good idea,' Petronius smacked back, jumping up and sauntering to the door. Once I would have headed after him, but I was a good husband and father these days. (Well, in public, I mostly managed to look like one.) Helena sucked her teeth anxiously. Maia shot Petro a superior look. By accident or on purpose, he slammed the door as he left.

The procurator and his wife tried to avoid showing how weary they were of their visitors' guests squabbling.

I closed my eyes and pretended to doze off. It fooled no one.

V

'I USED TO believe,' Helena complained to me privately later, 'Lucius Petronius and Maia were each trying to decide what they wanted. Sadly, I think they know now – and it's not each other.'

My sister and my friend both had tragic histories. Petro, once seemingly respectable, domesticated, and kind to tabby kittens, had plunged into a crass affair. He had strayed from home before, but this was with a gangster's wife, which was disastrous. Even his tribune became touchy about it, and his wife divorced him. Silvia took his daughters away to Ostia, where she now lived with a low-grade seasonal street-food seller; she had humiliated Petronius as much as possible.

Maia, equally settled apparently, had then been widowed. This situation is often to be welcomed, though even the deadbeats and wastrels my sisters married were rarely eaten by arena lions in Tripolitania after a trial for blasphemy. Few families on the Aventine could boast of so much excitement and we were trying to keep the dishonour quiet, for the sake of Maia's children. Lying about it no doubt added to her sense of isolation. She had made other mistakes too. Bad ones. She made a fool of herself with Anacrites the Chief Spy, for one thing. That was a situation we could not talk about at all.

'I thought they just needed time,' Helena sighed.

'Oh they may yet be prodded into close proximity – but you'll need to use a long stick.' Petronius Longus was a big lad, and my sister could be volatile.

'Better not to interfere, Marcus.'

'Right.'

If the bad thing about staying in an official residence was constant smalltalk, the good was that on the occasions Helena and I did sneak off alone, we were *entirely* alone. Nux, my dog, was scrabbling outside the door now, but we could pretend to ignore her. Our two little daughters, along with Maia's children, were safe in the custody of Aelia Camilla's nursery staff. Even our hopeless nursemaid had been absorbed and put to some use; I dreamed that she would stay there when we left.

'This is fine,' I said, stretching lazily. 'What we need is a house with so many rooms that nobody can find us, and cohorts of obedient staff, trained to walk about in silence, sponging away all trace of children's mashed-up food with tolerant smiles.'

'They have a Greek steward who can play the tibia.'

'The double flute! We could get one. We wouldn't need a new nursemaid if we had him to put the babies off to sleep with his tootling.'

'This one certainly soothed you into nodding off last night!' scoffed Helena.

'He's a rotten player. Anyway, I confess I had a drop too much to drink with Petro before dinner. I was trying to cheer him up.'

'You failed then, Marcus.'

'Lucius Petronius is not a happy boy.'

'Well he should be! He's going to the bad, isn't he? He chose to do it,' Helena said crisply. 'He damn well should enjoy it.'

'Going bad was good fun when I tried it. I don't know why he's so incompetent . . .'

'Hasn't found the right rope-dancer yet.'

Helena was referring to an old girlfriend of mine. She had never even met the woman, but she never let me forget that she knew of my colourful past.

To retaliate, I closed my eyes with a smile of supposed blissful reminiscence. A mistake, of course. My thoughts really did stray in the wrong direction. Helena knew that. She whacked me with a cushion, right at the spot where my stomach was digesting its unsatisfactory British lunch.

Petronius had in fact now ceased to be a social embarrassment. He completely disappeared. He left me a rudely worded note to say he was going off alone. He did not say he was leaving the province, nor did he give me any clue where to contact him. I checked discreetly with the procurator's staff: Petro had been seen leaving the governor's residence, wearing what my prissy slave informant described as a *very* dirty tunic. (So at least he was not off screwing some carrot-haired woman he had left behind to marinade ten years ago.) I found all his usual clothes, still in his pack, under the bed in the guestroom he had occupied. When Petro went to the bad, he threw himself into it in sordid style.

I tried not to feel envious.

In Rome, I would have assumed he was on vigiles surveillance and thought nothing of it. Here, a continent away from his official patch, that explanation could not apply. For him simply to vanish without discussion troubled me; I wondered if he were even more unhappy than I had noticed.

Maia was less sympathetic. 'Now you know how Helena feels when you just stay out and don't tell her why,' she reproved me. 'Still, he's a man. He is thoughtless and selfish. That's all we can expect.' She had dumped him, so presumably she did not care, but her children had grown enormously fond of Petro on their long trip across Europe together; they were giving their mother a bad time, mithering over where he was. Maia had no answers – a situation that never suited her.

'Am I to set him a place tonight at dinner, I wonder?' asked Aelia Camilla, more anxious and puzzled than annoyed. She was a decent woman.

'No, don't. In fact,' scoffed Maia, 'don't set him a place even if he suddenly comes back!'

Petronius did not return.

VI

ABANDONED BY PETRONIUS, that afternoon I settled down to work. Being asked to investigate the Verovolcus case would keep me trapped in Londinium even longer than I wanted, but I could not refuse the procurator and governor.

The governor, for one, thought it amusing to see me lumbered. Sextus Julius Frontinus was in his forties, a dedicated ex-consul whom I had met a couple of years before in Rome. We had worked together to solve a cruel series of female fatalities. Most consuls stink; he seemed different and I took to him. Frontinus had all the makings of an old-time Roman in power: soldierly, cultured, intrigued by administrative problems of all kinds, decent, absolutely straight. He had asked for me by name as his trouble-solver on the Togidubnus palace audit. My success there made me even more popular.

'If anyone can decipher what happened to the King's crony it's you, Falco.'

'Honeyed words!' I never treated men of rank with fake respect. If my manner seemed abrasive, that was tough. Frontinus knew I would do a good job; I had a fair idea what this crime was about, and I was blunt: 'My guess is, Verovolcus skulked up to Londinium hoping to escape notice. He wanted to stay in Britain. Then he cut across some locals at the bar. The hothead tried to lord it. They took exception. Someone tipped him arse-up in the cask-lined waterhole. While he was gurgling – or just before they plunged him in – they took the chance to pinch his torque. They scarpered. Any officer on your staff with local knowledge should track them down. Find the torque and it should convict them.'

'Nice theory,' retorted the governor, unmoved. 'I can accept that. Now prove it, Falco, before Togidubnus hears the tragic news and gallops here with sparks flying.'

He was very down to earth. He must have been chosen for Britain because the Emperor thought him both efficient and adaptable. I knew from talking to him already that he had a heavy programme ahead. In the three years he would administer Britain, Frontinus was planning to Romanise the province completely. He was about to embark on a major military expansion, with a big campaign against the untamed western tribes, then perhaps a further campaign in the north. In the stabilised interior, he wanted to establish ten or twelve new civic centres, self-governing *coloniae*, where the tribes would be semi-autonomous. Londinium, his winter headquarters, was to become a full municipality and a major works programme would aggrandise the place. If all this came off, as I thought it would, Britain would be transformed. Julius Frontinus would haul this marginal, barbarian province properly into the Empire.

Britain was a hard posting. It took its toll on every grade. Flavius Hilaris had taken over the financial role after his predecessor, the Gaul who restored order after Boudicca, died in harness. The governorship had a worse history. Suetonius Paullinus had been formally reported to Rome for incompetence. In the Year of the Four Emperors, Turpilianus was ousted by his military legates who then – unthinkably – ran Britain as a committee. Petilius Cerialis, the immediate past incumbent, had a history of ludicrous errors; he had acquired the job only because he was related to Vespasian.

Frontinus would do well. He was both active and conciliatory. But the last thing he needed while he found his feet was a tricky situation with a dead British notable. 'This has the potential to turn bad, Falco.'

'I know, sir.' I used my frank and trustworthy gaze. That was a look I had once kept for women, and still employed with creditors.

Frontinus may well have noticed I was a devious double-dealing toad, but he tolerated that. My next question was a fair one: 'Flavius Hilaris mentioned some administrative problems. Any chance I can be told what's up?'

'Better ask him. He has it all at his fingertips.' The governor took the classic way out. It was impossible to tell whether he even knew about these problems.

I asked Hilaris. He now seemed unable to remember having mentioned them.

Right. Thanks, lads! You mighty legates of Augustus sit tight in your frescoed headquarters dealing with dispatches, while I barge off into the mire.

Why did I always opt for clients who tried to conceal dirty situations? I spent more time investigating the people who hired me, than dealing with whatever they had asked me to investigate.

As usual I refused to let my secretive employers have their way. If there was mud on the marble, I was perfectly able to step in it by myself. Then everyone would have to endure the mess.

VII

FIRST I TRIED the centurion.

I thought I would pick him up at the fort. Easier said than done. First I had to find it. I remembered a wood and turf enclosure, hurriedly thrown up after the Rebellion, just east of the forum. We had used it to protect survivors as much as anything. When I found the site, it had clearly been abandoned years before.

There had never been legions permanently stationed in the capital; they were always needed forward, to guard the frontiers. Thirty years after its conquest by Rome, Britain still kept four active legions – more than any other province. It was out of proportion and stupidly expensive. It showed Rome's fears, after our near-overthrow by Boudicca.

If there were five hundred soldiers in Londinium, that was pushing it, but they ought to be decent quality. The legions took turns to send men back to the capital on detached duty. In a frontier province even the walking wounded and duffers who had annoyed their legate should be capable of guarding the governor and his staff, impressing visitors, flashing swords in the forum, and patrolling the docks. They had to live somewhere. Information from a passer-by took me right the other side of the forum, across the stream that divided the town, and down the Decumanus, the main street. I ended up on some remote thoroughfare, way out by the amphitheatre, a tedious hike. There I found a mess. The western hill had been taken over by whatever units were stationed here to guard the governor, and since the governor rarely stopped in the capital long, they lived in chaos. It was worse than a

28

marching camp – no proper defences and individual groups of barrack blocks all over the show.

I found my man. He was annoyed at being rooted out but agreed to come and play. I took him for a drink. He could pretend to his mates that I needed specialist advice in private. And in private, I might seduce him into revealing more than he should.

He insisted on taking me to a bar the soldiers liked. By the time we arrived I knew his name was Silvanus. I offered wine, but he preferred beer. 'That Celtic muck is fermenting in your belly, Silvanus!' I joshed. Pretending to be friends with a man I despised was a strain. 'You'll end up like some fat pink Celt.'

'I can handle it.' They always say that. He would never look pink, in fact. My banqueting guest was a swart southerner; he had arms clothed in dark hairs like a goatskin rug and was so coarsely stubbled he could have removed paint from woodwork with his chin.

'I've drawn the short straw on that barrel killing,' I said gloomily. That made him laugh, the lazy bastard. It meant he would not have to bestir himself; he liked seeing me suffer too. The laugh was openly unpleasant. I was glad I did not have to work with him.

I kept the beer flowing his way. I stuck with wine, surreptitiously diluting it with extra water when Silvanus wasn't looking.

It took half a bucketful of beer to soften him up enough to start talking, then another half to slow him down on how he hated the climate, the remoteness, the women, the men, and the piss-poor gladiatorial games.

'So Londinium's acquired its own dinky amphitheatre? If I may say so, it's a bit cut off out here – and aren't arenas usually near the fort? Mind you, I wouldn't say you had anything that I would call a fort!'

'There's to be a new fort, to stop fraternising.'

'As if anyone would! So how do the lads like the arena?'

'It's rubbish, Falco. We get puppy fights and pretty girls in armour.'

'Saucy stuff! Sex and swords . . . How lucky you are!' We drank. 'Tell me what the mood is around here nowadays.'

'What mood?'

'Well, I was last in Londinium when Boudicca had done her worst.'

'Fine old times!' Silvanus gloated. What a moron. He cannot have been here then. Even a man as dense as this would have had sorrow etched into his soul.

If he asked me what legion I served in, I would lie. I could not face it if this lightweight learned I had been in the Second Augusta. My tragic legion, led at the time by a criminal idiot, abandoned their colleagues to face the tribal onslaught. Best not to think what a currently serving centurion would make of that.

Nor was I intending to ask Silvanus which outfit he graced. The Twentieth or Ninth, perhaps; both did fight Boudicca and neither would be friends of mine. These days Britain also had one of the patched-together new Flavian units, the Second Adiutrix. I ruled it out. Silvanus did not strike me as a man from a new legion; he had old lag written all over him from his scuffed boots to his scabbard, which he had customised with tassels that looked like bits of dead rat. At least I knew he did not belong to the dire, gloating Fourteenth Gemina. They had been relocated to Germany to reform their habits, were that possible. I had met them there – still pushing people around and pointlessly bragging.

'This place should never have been rebuilt.' Silvanus wanted to carp about the town; it stopped me brooding about the army anyway.

'Disaster has that effect, man. Volcanoes, floods, avalanches – bloody massacres. They bury the dead, then rush to reconstruct in the danger area . . . Londinium never had any character.'

'Traders,' Silvanus grumbled. 'Wine, hides, grain, slaves. Bloody traders. Ruin a place.'

'Can't expect high art and culture.' I spoke slowly and slurred my words like him. It was coming quite easily. 'This is just a road junction. A huddle of industries on the south bank, a couple of cranky ferries coming across. North side, a few low-rise stinking warehouses . . . everything about it tells you it's nothing.'

'The end of the road!' exclaimed Silvanus. Slurred by a drunken centurion, it sounded even more unappealing than when Petronius had complained.

'Does that give you problems?'

'It's a bugger to police.'

'Why's that? The natives seem docile.'

'When not dropping each other down wells?' His voice cracked with mirth and I felt my hackles rise. I had known Verovolcus, even if I had not liked him. Silvanus failed to notice my expression. He was enlarging his theories. I told myself that was what I wanted. 'This place is a draw to scum, Falco.'

'How come?'

'Every chancer who has lost himself or wants to find himself.'

'Surely it's too remote for dreamy-eyed tourists?'

'Not for inadequates. Every tosspot with a warped personality. When they've tried all the other dead-end provinces, they sniff the wind and waft up here. No money, no likelihood of work, no sense.'

'It's cold and inhospitable – drifters surely don't like that?'

'Oh sun and seduction are not for losers. They yearn for empty open spaces, they want to endure hardship, they believe suffering in a wilderness will expand their lives.'

'So they seek out the mist on the edge of the world, among the legendary woad-painted men? And now you have a wild-eyed population of ragged people in shanties – feckless, rootless characters who may go off pop.'

'Right. They don't fit.'

'Are any running from the law?'

'Some.'

'That's fun.'

'Joyous.'

'So here they are – looking for a new start.'

'Butting up against the innocent British who only want to sell shale trays to visitors. All the British want to see arriving here are importers of dodgy wine that's passing itself off as Falernian. And now,' exclaimed Silvanus, who was close to passing out, which in theory was what I needed, 'we are starting to get the others.'

'Who are those?' I murmured.

'Oh these people know exactly what they're doing,' he burbled.

'These are the ones to watch, are they?'

'You get it, Falco.'

'And who are they, Silvanus?' I asked patiently.

'The ones who come to prey on the rest,' he said. Then he lay down, closed his bleary eyes, and started snoring.

I had made him drunk. Now I had to sober him up again. That's because the theory is wrong. When you bring a witness to the point of passing out, he does not know he is supposed to tell you all before he quits – he just goes ahead and drifts into oblivion.

This drinking hole was a colourless, chilly, hygienic establishment, provided for the soldiers. Britons, Germans, Gauls, don't naturally have a street life with open-air foodshops and wine bars. So this bar was Rome's big gift to a new province. We were teaching the barbarians to eat out. When soldiers arrived in new territory, the army would at once send someone to arrange recuperation areas. *'I want a good clean room, with benches that don't tip over, and a working dunny in the yard . . .'* No doubt the local commander still came along every month to taste the drink and check the waitresses for disease.

It had the usual bleak facilities. Bare boards, scrubbed white-wood tables from which vomit could be easily cleaned and a three-seat latrine out the back, where constipated inebriates could sit for hours, being maudlin about home. It stood near enough to their barracks for them to scuttle home easily once they were rat-arsed. It was years since I had glugged poison in a bar like this, and I had not missed the experience.

The landlord was polite. I hate that.

When I asked him for a bucket of water, I was led to the well. We were on much higher ground than at the Shower of Gold, and must be some way above the water table. The landlord confirmed there were no springs in this part of town. This time the well-head was an evil pile of stones, green with decades-old algae. Wriggly things dimpled the surface of the water and mosquitoes flitted among the stones. If Verovolcus had been upended here, he would have suffered nothing more than a sinister hairwash. We trailed a bucket sideways and managed to get it half full.

'This the best you can do?' I had had a bad experience with a well last year in Rome. I was sweating slightly.

'We don't get much call for water in the bar. I fetch it from the baths when I have to.' He did not offer to do so now.

'So where do the baths obtain their supply?'

'They invested in a deep shaft.'

'I see that wouldn't be economical for you – how are your lats swilled out?'

'Oh washing-water trickles along there eventually. It's fine except when they have a big celebration for a centurion's birthday . . .'

I refrained from imagining the effects on his latrine of thirty big legionaries who had eaten bowls of hot pork stew, all with extra fish-pickle sauce, after eighteen beakers of Celtic beer apiece and a fig-eating contest . . .

I threw the water over Silvanus.

Several buckets more and we reached the cursing stage. I was cursing. He was just lolling weakly, still in truculent silence. Some informers will boast about their efficient use of the 'getting-them-drunk-so-they-tell-you-stuff' technique. It's a lie. As I said, witnesses pass out too soon. Often it's not even the witness who becomes incapable, it's the informer.

'Silvanus!' Shouting was the only way to get through. 'Wake up, you bundle of jelly. I want to know, have you had regular trouble around the Shower of Gold?'

'Stuff you, Falco.'

'Offer appreciated. Answer the question.'

'Give me a drink. I want a drink.'

'You've had a drink. I'll give you another when you answer me. What's going on behind the wharves, Silvanus?'

'Stuff you, Falco . . .'

This routine continued for some time.

I paid the bill.

'Leaving?' enquired the landlord. 'But he hasn't told you anything.'

He was never going to. 'It will keep,' I answered breezily.

'What's this about then?' He was nosy. It was worth giving him a moment.

I eyed him up. He was a bald smarmer in a very blue tunic with an unnecessarily wide belt. I tried to maintain a steady stare. By that time I was so bleary myself I could not have intimidated a shy scroll-mite. 'Trouble at another bar,' I hiccuped.

'Serious?'

'A visitor from out of town was killed.'

'That's nasty! Who copped it?'

'Oh – a businessman.'

'Trying to muscle in on a racket,' suggested the landlord knowingly.

'In Britain?' At first I thought he was joking. The landlord looked offended at the insult to his chosen locale. I modified my disbelief by whistling. 'Whew! That's a turn-up. What are you suggesting? Protection? Gambling? Vice?'

'Oh I don't really know anything about it.' He clammed up and began wiping tables. He moved around Silvanus fastidiously, not touching him.

'Do you get problems up here?' I asked.

'Not us!' Well they wouldn't. Not at a semi-military bar.

'I see.' I pretended to drop it. 'You from these parts?'

He winced. 'Do I look like it?' He looked like a pain in the posterior. I had thought so even before I was drunk. 'No, I came across to run this bar.'

'Across? From Gaul?' So he was part of the great swarm of hangers-on that moves in the shadow of the army. It worked to mutual advantage, when it worked well. The lads were entertained and provided for; native people found livelihoods in supply and catering, livelihoods that would have been impossible without Rome. Once, this man would have lived all his years in a clump of round huts; now he was able to travel, and to assume an air of sophistication. He was earning cash too. 'Thanks, anyway.'

I could have provided a larger tip for him, but he annoyed me so I didn't. Anyway, I hoped I would not have to come back.

I propped up Silvanus against a wall and this time I did leave.

VIII

So NOW I knew there were rackets.

It had taken most of the afternoon to extract information I would rather not have stumbled on. To achieve that, I had drunk myself into a condition where it was best not to follow up that kind of clue.

I was just sober enough to realise this. One swig more, and it could have been fatal.

It was a good idea not to transport myself straight home like this. Not to the fluted halls of a procurator's riverview residence. I did not care what the highly placed personnel thought, but my wife and my dear sister were a different prospect. Both Helena and Maia had seen me drunk before, and both could deliver ripe speeches on the subject. I felt rather tired, and unwilling to hear a reprise. I needed a bolthole for sobering up. Rome was stuffed with nooks where I could spend an hour chatting with amiable companions while my head cleared. Londinium offered nothing suitable.

So what kind of entrepreneur would seriously move in on a town like this? Only a stupid one.

I was a city boy. I did what we do. I went to the forum. The first part of the walk was downhill. That helped. After crossing the stream where Boudicca's hordes had cast the severed heads of murdered settlers, it was back uphill. A mistake, I felt.

Romulus had more idea of where to place a forum. In Rome, after quaffing away a lunchtime, you can stumble off the Palatine or Esquiline, riotously unstable, and have to go no further. Down in the valley of the Sacred Way you can lie on ancient pavements, gazing up at stupendous temples and statue-decked civic buildings, knowing you are at the heart of things. Collapse neatly and you will be left alone, drooping in a long shady portico or steadying your back against some mighty Carrara column that may have propped up that noble boozer Mark Antony. Basilicas and sanctuaries line a mile-long stretch of glory, where centuries of thoughtful generals and princes have thrown up triumphal arches; the dense shade protects the somnolent from the unyielding sun's blaze. Nearby fountains and basins offer cool water to the badly parched. In extreme situations, there is the ultimate rescue: at the Temple of Isis, loose women will offer to take you home for a lie down.

So far, Londinium offered only a four-sided enclosure with a silent basilica. Stores, shops and offices stood empty on the other three sides. A colonnade was deserted. Outside the perimeter stood the spanking shell of a solitary temple. That's all. At least there was no sun.

I sat on a bollard, breathing hard. It was early August. While I was drinking with Silvanus there must have been a prolonged heavy rain shower. It was over now, and the day was warm enough to be comfortable in open shoes and a short-sleeved tunic, but the shine of water had been shrinking off the cambered roads as I walked here. Of the few people I passed, some thoroughly depressed folk were still standing in doorways as if sheltering. Fine drizzle drifted in the air. Agitated gusts of wind blustered around the buildings. The sky was a uniform grey and even in the late afternoon the light seemed to be failing gloomily. It was typically Britain, and it made my heart ache for the endless, bright, scented summer days of home.

Julius Frontinus had tried to impress me with talk of long-term expansion in the civic area. According to him there was a master-plan which allowed for tacking on new forum facilities piecemeal as the town grew in size and expectations. I did not believe it. From where I sat in this deserted hilltop amenity, damp and low in spirits, there seemed no point in any of us being here. We

Romans had come in the hope of mining precious metals; as soon as our belief in Britain's riches died, we should have given up. The worst legacy of the tribes' rebellion was that we now felt chained by blood and grief to this pitiful, uninteresting, miserable territory.

I was still tipsy, but I went home anyway. My sister took one look at me then held her peace. How sensible.

Helena was closeted in our private suite, playing with the children. Julia, our two-year-old, spotted my demeanour with those great dark eyes that missed nothing, and decided simply to observe proceedings. The baby, now five months, was lying in Helena's lap throwing her limbs in all directions; she continued, gurgling, lost in her own gymnastic world while her elegant mother dodged the worst kicks and tickled body parts that asked for it. This was, in effect, how Helena Justina had always dealt with me.

'Say nothing about my state.'

'I shall not comment,' Helena replied calmly.

'Thanks.'

'Been working?'

'Right.'

'Got nowhere?'

'Right.'

'Want a nice kiss and a bowl of food to take the nasty wine away?'

'No.'

She stood up and came to kiss me anyway.

Somehow the baby, Favonia, ended up being passed into my arms, then when I sat in Helena's half-round wicker chair, little Julia scrambled in there with me too, and lay smiling up at me. This left Helena free to stroke my hair soothingly, knowing I could not shake her off without harming the children. I growled. The baby may not have understood quite what she was at, but all three of my supposedly subservient females giggled at me. So much for being the top god in the household shrine. As in most families, patriarchal power held no meaning. Eventually I gave in to the onslaught of comfort, and just slumped glumly.

Helena left me long enough to settle, then said quietly, 'You do not like Britain.'

'You know that, love.'

'Marcus, is this situation dangerous to you personally?'

'Someone killed a man. That's always bad.'

'Sorry!' When Helena was so reasonable, it cut like a reproof.

'I'm upset.'

'I know.'

We left it there. Later, after the children had been collected by staff from the nursery, when she thought I was up to the pressure, Helena told me how things had progressed that day here. We were supposed to be dressing for dinner, though neither of us had made a start.

'The governor has sent a dispatch rider to King Togidubnus. Frontinus decided it is best to admit what has happened. The hope is, this will be the first the King hears of it. The murder will be explained the way it sounds best – well, sounds least bad – and the messenger can try to judge whether the King knows something he should not.'

'The King is not involved. I won't have that!'

'No, Marcus. So what do you think Togidubnus will do?'

'Turn up here, in an angry mood. Noviomagus is sixty Roman miles, plus. One day's journey for an imperial post rider – if he chases. But he won't; this is not war or the death of an emperor. So the King will know about the murder by tomorrow evening, say –'

'He won't set out in the dark,' Helena said.

'So at first light in two days' time he'll be on his way. He may be an old man, but he's fit. I need to supply answers, not by tomorrow but soon after.'

'Oh Marcus, that's not long enough.'

'It will have to be.'

I had no appetite for passing dainties on silver platters tonight. I did start to change my clothing, but I had more on my mind than a cultural soirée. Helena watched, not moving. She commented that there was little investigation I could carry out at this time of the evening. I answered that I needed movement. I needed results. I could do what I should probably have done this afternoon. I could revisit the Shower of Gold. I had no plan of how to tackle this, except that if they had changed the barmaid from the one I met, I would go in incognito.

'You will stand out as a Roman,' Helena remarked.

'I am a master of disguise.' Well, I had a scruffy tunic and a worn cloak.

'Your skin is olive and your haircut screams Rome.' My mad tangle of curls only said I had forgotten to comb them, but she was right in principle. My nose was Etruscan. I had the bearing of a man who had been given legionary training, and the attitude of the city-born. I liked to think that even in other parts of the Mediterranean my sophistication stood out. Among fair-skinned, blue-eyed, lackadaisical Celtic types there was no hiding me.

Helena by now was rootling in her own clothes chest. 'They will be expecting more officials –' Her voice was muffled, though not enough to hide a note of excitement. 'Any Roman male alone will stand out as far too obvious.'

'This is where I need Petro.'

'Forget him.' Garments were being thrown in all directions. 'With Petronius you just look like an official who has brought back-up. Trust me,' Helena cried, popping back upright and immediately dragging her patrician white dress up and over her head. I thought briefly of hauling her straight into bed. 'You need a girlfriend, Marcus!'

And I had one. No further explanation was required. Luckily there were staff to look after our children. Fired up with excitement, their noble mother was coming with me.

IX

'FRESH OFF THE boat!'

'Exactly the look.' I was unperturbed by Helena's hilarity. 'And smell!' I added, dipping my head to sniff: laundry damp – and whatever of me the Noviomagus washerwoman had failed to remove.

My tunic was a heavy, coarse-weave, dirty rust-coloured thing – gear I had packed to use on a building site. Over it I had a travelling cloak with a pointy hood, that gave me the look of a woodland deity. One who was not very bright. As well as a hidden dagger down my boot, I wore another openly; its scabbard hung on my belt alongside a money pouch. Add a trusting look, tempered by crotchety tiredness, and I could be any tourist. Ripe to be conned by the locals.

Helena had stripped off all her normal jewellery, leaving only a silver ring I once gave her. She then put on a pair of large, surprisingly trashy ear-rings. If these were some old lover's gift she did right to ditch the swine. More likely, they were a present from one of her mother's attendants. Her muted clothes were her own, and might have revealed her status, but she had hitched them up awkwardly and trussed them under her bosom with a complete lack of grace. She looked as if she possessed neither closet slaves, nor hand mirror, nor even taste. She was no longer herself. Well, that was fun for me.

Don't get me wrong. This was foolish and dangerous. I knew it. Two excuses, legate: One, Helena Justina, daughter of the senator Camillus, was a free woman. If she wanted to do something I could not stop her, any more than her noble father ever had. Two, she was right. As part of a couple, I would be much less conspicuous.

Add to that, we were both bored silly with being well-mannered visitors. We yearned for stimulus. We both enjoyed shared adventures – especially when we sneaked off without telling anyone, and when we knew if we *had* told them, they would all disapprove hysterically.

We slipped out of the residence. Our departure was spotted, but when staff gave us a second look we just kept going. There was no point borrowing Aelia Camilla's carrying chair. It would draw attention to us. We could manage on foot. Wherever we were going in this town would be close enough to walk.

I was getting my bearings. Londinium had not been developed by addicts of Hippodamus of Miletus and his structured gridiron street plans. It never grew from a major military base, so it lacked form and it lacked town walls. Instead of a four-square pleasing pattern, the T-shaped development followed one line across the river then sprawled untidily in two directions, with houses and businesses ribboning along important roads. There were very few developed plots behind the few main streets.

On the north bank, two low hills were divided by several free-flowing freshwater streams. Industrial premises had been sited along the banks of the main stream. The forum stood on the eastern hill, and most of the new wharves lay at the foot of that particular high ground. Beyond, on the western hill, there must be houses amidst perhaps further commercial premises, and I had seen what looked like smoke from bath-house furnaces. Apart from major imports and modest exports operating from the wharves, this was a town of potters and tanners. Even amongst the houses, empty spaces were farmed. I had heard livestock as often as the marsh birds or the gulls following traders' ships.

A straight arterial road led downhill from the forum, direct to the river. There it passed a landing-stage for ferries and what would one day be the bridge-head. Crossing at forum level was what passed for the main road, the Decumanus Maximus, with a secondary east-west highway halfway down to the river. Helena and I took that road for a short while and crossed the forum approach.

The patchy development continued. Residential plots had sometimes been rebuilt with new brick houses, or otherwise left as blackened patches of burnt ground. It was almost fifteen years since the Rebellion, but recovery was still slow. After the tribes' massacre, a few escapees must have returned to claim their land but many had died without descendants – or with descendants who could no longer bear the scene. The authorities were reluctant to release land that appeared to have no owner. A land registry had existed, which prevented a free-for-all. There was plenty of space here anyway. Taking the decision to sell off plots where whole families had died would be sorry work. So it might be decades before all the gaps in these stricken streets were filled.

Helena took my hand. 'You're brooding again.'

'Can't help it.'

'I know, darling. One day all trace of what happened will vanish. It would be worse if everything had been made good immediately.'

'Insensitive,' I agreed.

'One of the saddest things I ever heard,' Helena mused gently, 'is how the governor raced here to assess the situation, just before the furious tribes arrived. He knew he had insufficient troops and would be forced to sacrifice the town to save the province. So he closed his ears to pleas, but allowed those who wished to accompany him and the cavalry. Then, we were told afterwards, "those who stayed, because they were women, or old, or attached to the place were all slaughtered". Some people *were* attached to Londinium, Marcus. It made them stay to face certain death. That's heart-rending.'

I told her they were idiots. I said it gently. What I thought was worse, but she knew that. There was no need to be coarse.

Looking around, as we searched to rediscover the sad bar called the Shower of Gold, it seemed perverse for anyone to feel sentimentality for this town. The community had no aediles to oversee street cleaning or repairs. A few far-from graceful porticoes offered red-tiled roofs, not so much for shade as storm protection. Lights were a luxury. In a couple of hours I would be getting out of here fast.

'Is that the place?' asked Helena.

'You've never been here,' I muttered.

'No, but I can read a signboard, darling.'

I peered at the crude fresco, with its vague representation of light streaming through a tip-tilted window. The paint had weathered so much I was surprised Hilaris ever spotted the name. We went in. The lintel was low slung. Most customers must be midgets with rickets.

The serving girl, whose short legs I remembered, was missing. The taverner himself stared at us as we entered. He seemed to wonder what we wanted, coming in his bar, but that's regular. It happens in Rome too. To serve the public requires a special type: unwelcoming, obtuse, inaccurate with coinage, and very deaf when called. Some informers are no better equipped. But most do have good feet. His were embossed with corns and he had at least one toe missing. I could see this because there was no counter; he just perched on a stool.

We found our own table. Easy – there was only one. Since we were supposed to be a couple travelling, Helena took the purse from me, and went to order. I sat and smiled, like a man who could not manage foreign currency and who would drink more than he was used to, if his wife let him loose.

She dropped the fresh-off-the-boat routine immediately and chose her own approach. 'I don't think we'll have wine today. I hear yours suffers from interesting additives!'

'What do you mean?'

'Bodies.'

'Word gets round,' replied the landlord dourly.

'So what happened?'

'Nobody saw.' He spurned gossip. It could have been for the sake of his establishment, had it any reputation to protect.

'We just had to come and see the scene . . . Have you any fresh fruit juice?' Even I winced. Helena was forgetting she was in Britain.

'We only serve wine.' Her request was out of place, but he held back any sarcastic riposte. Too sophisticated – or just too much effort.

'Oh we'll risk it!'

'Nothing wrong with our wine. The man drowned in the well,' the dour fellow corrected her.

'Oh! Can we see the well?' she demanded excitedly.

He gestured to the yard door, pushed a jug at her, and left us to our own devices.

Helena went out to peer quickly down the well, then came back to our table with the jug.

'Cups, darling?' I teased, playing to a non-existent audience, but the landlord had brought them, with over-obvious efficiency. 'Thanks, legate!' I poured and tipped a cup to him. He gave me a brusque nod. 'Sorry,' I murmured sympathetically. 'You must be sick of sightseers.'

He made no comment, only sucked a blackened tooth. He went back to stand in silence among his amphorae in a corner, staring at us. I would normally have tried chatting with other customers – but there were none. And it was impossible to talk to Helena while the man was listening.

Now we were stuck. Stuck in a dark drinking hole that lacked atmosphere: a small square room with a couple of seats, about three shapes of wine flagon, no snacks evident, and a man serving who could crack marble with his stare. Once again, I wondered why ever Verovolcus, a happy soul who was oppressively con-vivial, would have come here. The woman this morning had sworn nobody knew who he was or remembered him. But if tonight's effort represented normal trade, it would be impossible to

45

forget. The landlord must have had time to count the stitches on Verovolcus' tunic braid.

He would certainly remember me, right down to the fact that I had forty-seven hairs in my left eyebrow. Uncomfortable, we drank up and prepared to leave.

With nothing to lose, as I paid him I bantered, 'The Shower of Gold – I wish I had Zeus popping in at the window in a heap of cash! He could sleep with anyone he liked.' The landlord looked bemused. 'You named your winery after a myth,' I pointed out.

'It was called that when I came here,' he snarled.

As we reached the doorway, people emerged from a dark passage that seemed to lead upstairs. One was a man who slipped straight out past me, adjusting his belt-buckle in a way that was all too recognisable. He must be desperate; his companion was the bar-room waitress. She was as ugly as I remembered. The squat little monster chinked a couple of coins into the petty cash bowl and the landlord hardly looked up.

Servicing customers could be part of a waitress' duties, but usually the girls looked better. Not good, but better. Sometimes quite a lot better.

She had seen me. 'My girlfriend wanted to see the crime scene,' I told her apologetically.

'We're going to charge for tickets,' snapped the waitress. To the landlord, she added unpleasantly, 'He was here with the nobs this morning. Has he been asking more questions?' There was no need to warn him; he knew how to refuse to co-operate. She rounded on me again. 'We told you what we know, and it's nothing. Don't come again – and don't bother sending your pals.'

'What pals? I sent nobody.'

Both waitress and landlord were now a little too truculent. We took the hint and left.

'Was that a waste of time, Marcus?' Helena asked demurely.

'I don't know.'

Probably.

'So what shall we do now?'

'Use a trick of the trade.'

'Like what?' asked Helena.

'When you learn nothing in the first wine bar, try another one.'

X

F INDING ANOTHER WAS difficult. As a kindness to my lady I
tried working back uphill, towards what passed for better parts
of town. No luck. 'Better' was a misnomer anyway.

We were forced to head back down towards the river, at one
point even emerging on to a planked wharf. Nothing was moving
on the water; we were right by a ferry landing point, yet it seemed
a lonely spot. We retreated hastily. Up the next steep entry we hit
a row of shops. Most seemed to sell either pottery or olive oil, the
oil in the great round-bottomed Spanish amphorae Helena and I
knew well from a trip we had made to Baetica. Wine seemed a
scarcer commodity on public sale, but there was evidence that
everyone in Londinium had access to the fine golden oil from
Corduba and Hispalis. If everyone had it, presumably the stuff was
sold at a reasonable price. Then from a street corner we spotted a
small brown-tinged bay tree; half its leaves had been shredded by
moths and its lead shoot was broken, but it seemed to serve the
same advertising purpose as greenery outside any foodshop in the
Mediterranean.

As we arrived, a waiter or the proprietor stepped out of doors
and spoke to a bundle who was scavenging on his frontage. He was
not abusive, but she scuttled off. I took it as a good sign that he
repelled vagrants. We went inside.

Warmth hit us: bodies and lamps. It was much bigger and better
lit than our first venue. A wine list had been chalked up on a wall,
though there was nothing I recognised. The man who served us
made no reference to the list, just offered red or white, with the

extra option of beer. Helena, still in character, thought it would be fun to try British beer. Petro and I had done that in our youth; I asked for red. I wanted a water jug as well. With a head still sore from this afternoon, I was going gently. The waiter managed not to sneer. Roman habits were clearly not new to him.

This time we sat quiet, relaxed as we waited for our drinks. We gazed around. Both waiters here were thin, slight, hollow-cheeked, hardworking types with balding crowns, glossy black face hair and lugubrious eyes. They did not look British, more likely from Spain or the East. So here was another establishment staffed by migrants. Who knows how many miles they had travelled, humping their possessions, their hopes and their past history, to end up running a cheap bar that lay on the other side of everywhere. Their customers represented a shifting population too. Some were traders by their appearance: tanned, competent businessmen locked in conversations in twos and threes. None looked like Britons. The locals skulked at home. Places of entertainment in this town were catering for outsiders. As long as that continued, the province could hardly be civilised. It would just be a trading post.

Nearest to us was a man who reminded me of Silvanus' claim that Londinium was attracting oddballs. He was wrapped in many layers, with old rope for a belt around coarse trews, his skin ingrained with dirt, his hair lank and straggly.

'Want a doggie?' he demanded, as Helena made the mistake of watching him feed titbits to a lean cur at his feet. The dog looked disgusting and whined unhappily.

'No, we have one already, thanks.' I was relieved that we had locked Nux in the bedroom before we came out. Pupped in an alley, Nux had moved up in the world when she adopted me, but she still liked making playmates of mongrels with bad characters.

'This boy's very smart.'

'No, really. Ours is already a handful.'

He dragged his stool nearer, scraping it sideways on two legs. A leech, who had found new victims. 'British dogs are magic,' this dire parasite claimed proudly. Was *he* British, or just loyal to the commodity he hawked? Unlike other customers here, I thought he could be genuine. Which poor tribe did he belong to? Was he some unwanted lag kicked out of the enclosure by the Trinovantes, or a reprobate shoved off a hillfort by fastidious Dubonni? In any culture, he would be the long-lost grisly uncle, the one everybody dreads. At Saturnalia, or the tribes' equivalent, they no doubt spoke of him and shuddered, looking quickly over their shoulders in case he came limping home up the trail sucking grass in the huge gap between those awful teeth . . . 'I sell as many as I can get, easy. Marvels. If you, fine lady, bought one of these –' A clawlike hand crept into the neck of his lowest undertunic, then scratched slowly. The dog at his feet, raddled with sarcoptic mange, joined in. Most of the fur was gone from its haunches; you could see every rib. For both of them the scratching was unconscious and continual. 'I guarantee you'd get your money back four or five times over, selling it again in Rome or some big place.'

'That's wonderful. Still, no thank you.'

He paused. Then tried again gamely. 'He'll be perfect if your husband hunts.'

'No, he doesn't hunt, I'm afraid.'

'Sure?' She was sure. So was I, damn it. A city boy, I would rather go to the races any day.

The filthy salesman nodded at me secretly. I was being blamed for Helena's resistance. 'Bit of a tight-arse, is he?'

Helena smiled at me, considering. I smiled back. Then she told her new friend. 'Maybe. But I love him. He thinks he's a man of the streets; don't disillusion him.'

'Illusions!' warbled the dogman loudly. 'We all need illusions, don't we?' Other customers glanced our way, pitied us for being trapped, then buried their snouts in their beakers. 'Cherish your illusions, queenly one – lest the dark gods steal you to Hades unfulfilled!'

He was crazy. On the other hand, he could deal in abstract

concepts and multi-syllable definitions. I groaned. Did we have that gruesome icon, a man once wealthy, a man of intellect and background, who had fallen on hard times? Had he and his poetic soul been brought low by inadequacy of character, bad financial luck – or drink?

No, he was low grade; he just liked selling dogs. He thought he would make a fortune passing off his lame, wormy hounds to dumb Romans. He hoped he might even sell one to Helena and me. Tough luck, dog-sharp.

Two men came in. The one in front was short and solid, the other was leaner and kept looking round. They were known to the proprietors. They disappeared with the senior waiter through a curtain to some inner recess. I heard raised voices. A short time afterwards the two men emerged and left, unsmiling, walking rapidly. The waiter came out. He muttered briefly to his companion. Both looked hot and angry.

Most customers failed to notice. It was all quite discreet.

Helena had watched me watching them. 'What do you think that was?'

'Market gardeners selling parsley.'

'Protection rackets? Money-lenders?' Helena thought along the same lines as me. 'Do you think the owner paid them?'

'Difficult to tell.'

'If he did, he did not want to – and he made his feelings known.'

'If he paid up, fruit, those bagmen won't care about his attitude.'

'And if not?'

'Presumably they will be back – to ensure he changes his mind.'

We were speaking in low voices, ignoring the dogman. He knew enough to leave us to our confidential talk. Maybe he listened. It made no difference to me. If there were heavies leaning on shop owners, the sooner the better for them to learn that someone was checking up on them.

The waiters went around the tables, busying themselves. They served the dogman and several others automatically, so those must be regulars. This seemed a place to pick up local atmosphere, so we lingered. I accepted a refill and snacks. Helena was still progressing slowly through her beer; she would not admit to a mistake, though my guess was she did not care for it. The waiter expected her to leave half the beaker, but she would finish. Then she would say thank you very nicely when she left.

Helena Justina might be a senator's daughter, but she was my kind of girl. I grinned and winked at her. She belched modestly.

I leaned back and grabbed olives from a bowl on a table behind me. The titbits may have been communal. I acted as if I assumed so, and got into conversation with the two men sitting there. They were negotiators, shifting supplies north for the army; then they took cattle hides south. The first part was profitable, they told me; the hides only acted as ballast, filling their ships with flies. They had thought about transporting slaves instead, but there were too many problems. I joked that they should go into partnership with the dog trader – at which point the conversation died.

Helena had been watching the scavenger we saw earlier. That whey-faced skinny mite had now sneaked back inside; this time the waiters let her alone. Whenever customers departed, she wafted like a sylph to their table then devoured any food they left. There was rarely drink. One man leaned towards her and asked something; she shook her head. It may have been a sexual approach or he could just have asked if it was raining out of doors.

Nothing much seemed to be happening, so next time our beakers were empty I paid up and we took off. Outside the streets were growing very dark. The temperature was balmy, though nowhere near as hot as Rome would be on an August night. There was no street life, just mosquitoes to smack. They had learned to head into town from the marshes at dusk for a bloody feast. Something had nipped my ankle badly and Helena kept imagining they were dancing in her hair.

Helena took my arm to steady both of us as we walked. It took some time to find another bar to crawl to. In Rome there would be a food shop counter on the street every few yards, and probably an inside drinking den on every block. You would not have to keep stopping to shake pea-grit from your shoes either. Londinium had paved roads, but most of its back alleys were rough under foot. The town was built on gravel and brick earth. There were plenty of tile and brick kilns, and the old wattle and daub huts were being replaced with timber and brick dwellings. But I was yearning to walk on great warm slabs of Travertine.

I needed a pee too.

Not finding a venue that offered hygienic facilities, the issue was sorted in ways you need not know.

'What about me?' grizzled Helena. The perpetual beef of a woman on holiday in a strange town. I was the paterfamilias. My role was to find her somewhere. Like most holiday husbands, I had made my own arrangements and now lost interest. This aspect of the situation was pointed out to me.

'Are you desperate?' They always are. Still, we sorted that too, once she was desperate enough. We found a dark place and I stood on guard.

'That's true love,' she thanked me gratefully.

The next time we ventured into what looked like a wine bar, it turned out to be a brothel. They had a table and two chairs outside, as enticement and camouflage, but once we stepped indoors we knew. We saw little sign of activity, but there was every appearance that business was good. As soon as I spotted the teenage scrubbers at the ready, white faced in their drop-necked frocks and glass bead anklets, we backed out with polite smiles.

The madam did look British. All over the world, this is the first trade to develop when civilisation hits the backward barbarians. Widows, for one, are quick to catch on. Widows and unmarried mothers who have to call themselves widows. This one had a direct manner and tired professional eyes. She had probably serviced soldiery outside Roman forts long before she set up here in the town.

Maybe the house of love gave us ideas. Not long after that, Helena and I stopped on a street intersection, moved close and kissed. It was a long tender kiss, not lustful, but full of enjoyment.

We were still locked together in this friendly fashion when we noticed an odd smell. I realised traces of smoke in the air had been bothering me for a few moments. We broke off, walked on quickly, and found there was some night life in Londinium after all: a bakery was on fire.

XI

I N ROME, A crowd would have gathered. In Londinium, only a
few curious shadows lurked on the dark fringes of the street.
Occasional bursts of flame lit their faces briefly. One overhead
window creaked open and a woman's voice laughed, 'Someone's
had an accident! The dough dump's copped it . . .'

I wondered what to do. There were no vigiles here, ready to
whistle for colleagues to start a bucket line; no esparto mats; no
siphon engine with a full water tank to dump on the blaze.

The building was well alight. You could see it was a bakery
because the frontage doors were open; beyond the red-hot
counter, two full-height ovens showed up inside, open-mouthed
like ancient gargoyles. The flames were not coming from the
ovens, however, but leapt all around the walls. Perhaps a spark in
a fuel store had started this.

I grabbed at a spectator. 'Is anyone inside?'

'No, it's empty,' he answered, quite unconcerned. He turned
on his heel and walked away, joining a companion ten strides from
me. They glanced back at the bakery then one slapped the other
on the shoulders; they were both grinning as they walked off. I
recognised them then: the two heavies who had angered the
waiters at our second wine bar. It was not the moment to pursue
them. But I would know them again.

As if they had waited for the pair to leave, people now began to
rally and to douse the fire. It took some doing. I helped sling a few
buckets. Someone must be fetching them from a well – another
re-used wine barrel? As we worked, one of the folding doors came

away from its moorings and crashed down in showers of sparks. That should not have happened; it must have been damaged. Deliberately? It landed right up close to a group of panicking dogs, who had all been lashed to a pillar on individual strings. They kicked up a racket, frantic to escape. The door continued burning so it was impossible to approach the dogs. I tried, but they were too scared and they snarled too viciously.

One plunging hound had its coat on fire now. That caused him to yank his head ever more violently, trying to free himself. The others became yet more alarmed as he clambered on top of them.

'Marcus, do something!'

'Hades – what?'

Someone ran past me, jerking my dagger from its sheath at my waist. I yelled. The slight figure darted in among the dogs, heedless of their teeth, and slashed at some master cord tying them to the pillar. Instantly they were off. Their rescuer still clutched hold of a central knot and was towed nastily along the rough ground. The group of barking canines raced two ways around another pillar, tangled crazily, then were apprehended by a man I recognised as the dirty dog-seller. He grabbed the ties and took over. I cannot say his presence soothed the animals, but he was strong enough to hold them as he bent to inspect them for damage. Their barks subsided into whines.

Helena had gone to the rescuer; it was another familiar face: the pathetic scavenger. The dogman showed her no gratitude. He kicked and beat his hounds into submission, looking as if he would as soon kick and beat the girl too. She had been badly grazed through her rags and was crying. Averse to publicity, he soon went off into the darkness, muttering, leaning back against the undertow, amidst a swarm of struggling hounds.

I retrieved my dagger from where it had fallen to the ground in the chase, then turned back to help with the fire again. I found we had professional help: some soldiers had arrived.

'The bakery's beyond saving – just protect the premises each side!' They dealt with matters briskly, seeming unsurprised by the blaze. Well, fires are commonplace in towns and cities. I had already observed that oil was readily available. Lamps and stoves are always a danger.

'Lucky you turned up,' I complimented the officer in charge.

'Yes, wasn't it?' he returned. Then I felt their arrival was no coincidence.

Silvanus was not leading this troop; he probably still nursed a sore head from our drinking bout, and anyway they were the night patrol. Regulars on this patch, who clearly expected trouble. Detachments had orders to check these streets at intervals. Businesses might be attacked at any time. Weighing in to help the public had become routine.

Was it routine to stand by and let a blazing building go up, while ostentatiously protecting nearby premises? Were the military tiptoeing around the racketeers? They would only do that if they were heavily bribed.

Of course nobody would acknowledge what was going on. 'Rogue spark,' decided the officer. 'No one at home to notice.'

Why was nobody at home at live-in business premises? I could work that out. Somewhere in this town lurked a baker who had rashly stood out for his independence and now knew his livelihood was doomed. He must have made some gesture of defiance – then he wisely ran.

Rackets usually operate in specific areas. Bars were one thing; if a bakery had been threatened it was highly unusual. If all the shops, in all the streets, were being targeted, that was real bad news.

The soldiers were pretending to take names and addresses of witnesses. It would be for the secret service lists, of course. Anyone who cropped up on a military rota too often (twice, say) would go down as a disruptive element. Britons seemed to have learned about that; the sightseers melted from the streets. That left me and Helena. I had to tell the boys in red who we were. Ever so politely, we were offered a safe conduct straight back to the procurator's residence: we were being shifted out of there.

Once, I would have objected. Well, once I would have given a false name, kicked the officer in the private parts and legged it. I might even have done it for practice tonight, had I not had Helena with me. She saw no reason to make a run for it. Senators' daughters are brought up to be trusting with soldiers; though rarely caught up in a street interrogation, when it happens they always say at once who their daddy is, then expect to be escorted to wherever they want to go. They will be. Especially the good looking ones. A senator's daughter with a hare lip and saggy bust may simply be told to move along, though even then they probably call her madam and don't risk pinching her bum.

'I say we've had enough excitement for one night. Helena Justina, these kind men are going to see us home.'

The quicker the better: Helena wanted to nurture the bleeding, weeping scavenger. 'She's hurt. We can't leave her.'

The soldiers gathered and watched me react. They knew that the hunched, whimpering creature was a street vagrant. They knew that if Helena took her in, we would be infected with fleas and diseases, lied to, betrayed on every possible occasion, then robbed blind when the skinny scrap finally upped and fled. They knew I foresaw all this. They refrained from grinning.

Helena was crouching on her knees beside the mite. She glanced up directly at the soldiers, then at me. 'I know what I am doing!' she announced. 'Don't look at me like that, Falco.'

'Know the girl?' I murmured to the officer.

'Always around. Supposed to be a survivor of the Rebellion.'

'She only looks a teenager; she must have been a babe in arms.'

'Ah well . . . So she's a walking tragedy.' I knew what he was saying.

I tried not to seem frightening. The girl cringed anyway. Helena was talking to her in a low voice, but the girl just shuddered. Apparently she spoke no Latin. I had not heard her talk at any time, in any language. Maybe she was mute. Another problem.

The officer, who had followed me over, offered helpfully, 'They call her Albia, I believe.'

'Albia!' Helena tried firmly. The girl refused to recognise the name.

I groaned. 'She has a Roman name. Neat trick. One of us – orphaned.' She was little more than a skeleton, her features unformed. She had blue eyes. That could be British. But there were blue eyes all across the Empire. Nero, for instance. Even Cleopatra. Rome was damn well not responsible for *her*.

'This is a poor little Roman orphan,' the officer sympathised, digging me in the ribs.

'She looks the right age.' Flavius Hilaris and Aelia Camilla had a daughter who was born close to the Rebellion: Camilla Flavia, now radiantly fourteen, all giggles and curiosity. Every young tribune who came to this province probably fell for her but she was modest and, I knew, very well supervised. This waif looked nothing like Flavia; her pitiful life must have been quite different.

'It really does not matter whether her parentage was Roman,' Helena growled up at me through gritted teeth. 'It does not even matter that she was left destitute by a disaster that would never have happened if Rome had not been here.'

'No, sweetheart.' My tone was even. 'What matters is that you noticed her.'

'Found as a crying new-born in the ashes after the massacre,' suggested the officer. He was inventing it, the bastard. Helena stared up at us. She was smart and aware, but she had a huge fund of compassion. She had reached her decision.

'People always adopt babes who are plucked alive from disasters.' Now it was me speaking. I too had a dry edge. Helena's scornful gaze made me feel dirty but I said it anyway. 'The wailing newborn lifted from the rubble is assured of a home. It represents Hope. New life, untouched and innocent, a comfort to others who are suffering in a stricken landscape. Later, unfortunately, the child becomes just another hungry mouth, among people who can barely feed each other. You can understand what happens next. A cycle sets in: neglect leading to cruelty, then violence and the most corrupt kinds of sexual abuse.'

The girl had her head down on her filthy knees. Helena was

very still. I leaned down and touched Helena's head with the back of my knuckles. 'Bring her if you wish.' She did not move. '*Of course!* Bring her, Helena.'

The officer clucked quiet reproof at me. 'Naughty!'

I smiled briefly. 'She takes in strays. She has a heart as big as the world. I can't complain. She took me in once.'

That had started in Britain too.

XII

I T FELT AS if we had been out for hours. When Helena and I
returned, the procurator's residence was aglow with lamps. The
house had an after-banquet feel. Although Hilaris and his wife ran
their home quietly, while the governor was living with them they
readily joined in the grim business of overseas diplomacy. Tonight,
for instance, they had been entertaining businessmen.

Helena went to see her new protégée lodged somewhere secure,
with her wounds salved. I threw on a better class of tunic and
searched for sustenance. Wanting to tackle Hilaris and Frontinus
about the local situation, I braced myself and joined the after-
dinner group. There were still platters of figs and other treats
remaining from the dessert course that had concluded the meal we
missed. I piled in. The figs must be locally grown; they were just
about ripe, but had no taste. A passing slave promised to find me
something more substantial, but he never got around to it.

My hard day in the watering holes of Londinium had left me
jaded. I kept a low profile. I had been introduced as the
procurator's relative, a detail which the other guests found pretty
uninteresting. Neither the governor nor Hilaris gave away that I
was an imperial agent, nor said I was charged to investigate the
Verovolcus death. They would not mention the death at all, unless
the subject came up, even though it must be the most exciting
local news.

The diners were now sitting up on their cushioned couches,
moving around to meet new people as the portable food tables
were removed and this gave us more space. When I arrived, they

continued their conversations, expecting me to join in as and when I could, or to sit tight meekly.

I can't say being a hanger-on appealed to me. I would never make a happy client to any patron. I wanted status of my own, even if it was a status people despised. As an informer I had been my own man; I had lived like that too long to change. Gratitude never came easy. I owed nobody anything, and I paid no tributes socially.

The guests were a type I don't care for: merchants looking to expand their markets. They were newcomers, or relative new-comers to Britain. Calling on the governor was meant to smooth their path. Of course encouraging trade was part of the job for Frontinus. But tonight he kept talking about his plans to go west with the army: he was pleasant, but his heart lay in engineering and military strategy. He made it plain that he had spent part of this year establishing a big new base on the far side of the Sabrina Estuary and that he was preoccupied with going back to oversee a push against the unconquered tribes; so we were all lucky to have caught him on a brief return to the capital. Normally, he would only be here in the winter.

I wondered if the governor's frequent absences on campaign contributed to lawlessness.

When I went to extract Silvanus from his barracks, I had gained the impression there was a standard vexillation stationed there – part of a particular cohort or possibly small detachments from each of the legions. Officially they were the governor's bodyguard, his equivalent of the Praetorian Guard nannying the Emperor. This was not because madmen were likely to make assassination attempts. Attendant soldiery was part of the panoply of govern-ment. Whenever Julius Frontinus rode off to the scene of the action, most of those troops must go with him. Only a remnant of his guard would stay behind to do routine policing work.

I would put this problem to Frontinus. He was no fool, and far from vainglorious. He did not require every available legionary to be glued to him to promote his standing. Nor was the army his sole interest. He would deal with civil projects even-handedly, so Londinium's security would be attended to. If we needed extra manpower here, I could probably persuade him to supply it.

He had four legions in Britain; there was some slack to play with. The south and east had been consolidated and part-Romanised years ago. Pinning down the west was the subject of current attention. Unfortunately the north too had become a problem. Once the Brigantes, a major Rome-friendly tribe, had formed a large buffer zone, but under Frontinus' predecessor that famously changed. It was a story of scandal, sex and jealousy: Queen Cartimandua, formidable and middle-aged, fell heavily for her husband's much younger spear-carrier. The lovers tried to take over. The outraged husband took against that. Torn loyalties plunged the once-stable Brigantes into civil war. Celebrity folly is fun, but not when the resulting strife loses Rome a good ally.

Cartimandua had been apprehended, no doubt amidst many raucous jokes from the legionaries, but our alliance with the Brigantes crumbled. Frontinus or whoever succeeded to his post would have to square up to this: more military commitment, new forts, new roads, and perhaps a full-scale campaign to bring the wild northern hills under Roman control. Maybe not this year or next year, but soon.

Despite that, prudence dictated a reassessment of how the settled regions, including Londinium, were run. The troops ought to provide law and order cover; some of the lads would have to be withdrawn from biffing barbarians' heads. There was no point in the army pushing out in all directions, if chaos raged behind them. That was damned dangerous. Boudicca had shown all too clearly the risks of disaffection in the rear.

'You're quiet, Falco!'

Frontinus called me over. He was talking to two of the most interesting guests, a glassmaker from the Syrian coast and a general trader, another easterner, a Palmyrene.

'Jove, you're both adventurous – you couldn't have travelled much further across the Empire!' I knew how to be gracious when I bothered. Frontinus slipped away and left me to it. He must have heard their stories already. The glassmaker had found the competition in the famous Syrian workshops too much for him; he intended to set up in Londinium, train a few staff to blow down tubes and snap off multicoloured rods, and get up a British production line. Since glass is so delicate this seemed a better prospect than importing over long distances. Some fine quality goods would undoubtedly continue to be brought from Tyre, but this man did seem to have chosen a province that could accommodate a new trade.

The general import man just liked travel, he told me. A few hints led me to think he might have left quarrels behind him. Or perhaps some personal tragedy made him want a new start; he was old enough to have lost a treasured wife, say. He found Britain exotic and untried and was willing to negotiate any commodities that were in demand. He had even found a girl, a Briton; they were planning to settle . . . So if my theory was right, he was a second-time romantic, choosing new happiness in a changed environment.

In another situation I would have been fascinated with these far-flung travellers – especially the fellow from Palmyra, where it so happened I had been. But neither appeared to be 'preying' on this province in the way Silvanus had complained about. They had found avenues to explore, but that was to their credit. They posed no threat. They would be earning a living, providing sought-after goods, and offering the local people welcome opportunities.

The fact was, my questions would not be answered here. These were the wrong kind of men – far too legitimate. As usual, it was my task to delve among the dirtier layers of humanity. I would not find my culprits cosying up to the governor. Racketeers never register their presence openly.

I could be wasting my time anyway. However bad the scene shaping up behind the Londinium waterfront, it might be irrelevant to the Verovolcus killing. I did not even know that

Verovolcus had run up against any extortionists. It was just a hunch.

Aelia Camilla was leaving the party. To her husband, she merely signalled her intention to withdraw. She and Gaius were traditionalists; they shared a bedroom, without doubt. Later, they would exchange opinions of tonight's party, discussing their guests. They would probably note my late arrival and speculate where I had been all day.

On me, now a nephew by marriage, Aelia Camilla bestowed a few words and a goodnight kiss on the cheek. I told her briefly about Helena's scavenger (it seemed wise; by tomorrow the girl might have laid waste to the household).

Aelia Camilla pulled a face. But she made no complaint; she was loyal to Helena. 'I am sure we can cope.'

'Please don't blame me for this.'

'Well, you do want a new nursemaid, Marcus.'

'But I would rather place my children in the care of someone who has known a happy life.'

'This girl may have one,' disagreed Helena's aunt. '– If Helena Justina takes to her.'

I sighed. 'Helena will turn her around, you mean?'

'Don't you think so?'

'She will try hard . . . Helena makes it her business. She turned me.'

Then Aelia Camilla gave me a smile of enormous sweetness, which to my surprise seemed genuine. 'Nonsense! Marcus Didius Falco, she never thought there was anything about you she needed to change.'

It was all getting too much for me: I went to bed myself.

XIII

NEXT DAY, 'HELENA'S wild girl' quickly became an object of attention for the children in the house. Mine were too young to take much interest, though Julia was seen toddling up to stare. She was good at that. She came and stared at me sometimes, with an expression of private wonder that I preferred not to interpret.

It was Maia's bunch and the procurator's darlings who adopted Albia. Their interest was almost scientific, especially among the girls, who solemnly discussed what was best for this creature.

Clothing was found. 'This dress is blue, which is a nice colour, but the dress is not too expensive to look at,' Maia's Cloelia explained to me gravely. 'Then if she runs away back to her life, she won't attract the wrong kind of attention.'

'She eats very quickly,' little Ancus marvelled. He was about six, himself a faddy little boy who was always in trouble at mealtimes. 'If we take her food, she eats it straight away, even if she has only just had something.'

'She has been starved, Ancus,' I explained. 'She never had a chance to push her bowl away and whimper that she hates spinach. She has to eat what she can get, in case there is never any more.'

'We don't make her have spinach!' Ancus answered quickly.

Flavia, the procurator's eldest, was talking to the girl. 'Does she ever seem to understand you, Flavia?' I asked.

'Not yet. We are going to keep speaking to her in Latin and we think she will learn it.' I had heard the children naming household items as they towed Albia around with them. I even heard the eloquent Flavia describing me: 'That man is Marcus Didius, who married our cousin. His manner can be abrupt, but that is because he has plebeian origins. It makes him uncomfortable in ornate surroundings. He is more intelligent than he lets on, and he makes jokes that you don't notice until half an hour afterwards. He does work that is valued by the highest people, and is thought to have as yet under-explored qualities.'

I failed to recognise this creature. He sounded grim. Who in Olympus had Flavia been listening to?

It was difficult to say what the scavenger made of it. She had been plunged into this enormous residence, with its painted frescos, polished floors and high coffered ceilings, full of people who never screamed abuse at each other, who ate regularly, who slept in beds – the same bed every night. It was possible that her original parentage entitled her to some of those things, but she knew nothing of that. It seemed best not to suggest it. Meanwhile the girl must have wondered, as others of us did, how long her stay in the residence would last.

The slaves were contemptuous of course. A street foundling was lower even than them. They at least had a point of reference in the family who owned them. They were well fed, clothed, housed, and in the Frontinus and Hilaris ménages they were treated with kindness; if ever freed, they would legally join their owners' families, on pretty equal terms. Albia had none of those advantages, yet she was nobody's property. She represented in the worst degree the adage that the freeborn poor live far less well than slaves in wealthy households. This cannot have comforted anyone. If the children had not been making such a pet of the creature, she would have had a hard time of it from the slaves.

The household ointments were not healing her grazes. Maia's children muttered among themselves about whether it was ethical to invade Petro's room and borrow something from his medicine chest. It was famously well stocked. 'Uncle Lucius forbade us to touch it.'

'He is not here. We can't ask him.'

They came to see me. 'Falco, will you ask him for us?'

'How can I do that?'

Crestfallen, Marius the elder boy explained, 'We thought you would know where he is. We thought he must have told you how to contact him.'

'Well he didn't tell me. But I can look in his box. Because I am an adult –'

'I have heard that doubted,' stated Cloelia. All Maia's children had inherited a rude trait, but apparently dear Cloelia was being merely factual.

'Well, because I am his friend then. I shall need the key –'

'Oh we know where he hides the key!' Great. I had known Petronius Longus since we were eighteen and I had never spotted where he stashed that key. He could be very secretive.

When I went to his room, we were all disappointed; his medicine chest was missing. I checked around more carefully. There were no weapons left behind either. He would never have left Italy without a decent armoury. It must be quite some drinking bout he was indulging in, if he took a full chest of remedies and a sword.

I went out later, on observation back in the riverside area. Marius came with me. He was tiring of the endless nurture of Albia. We both took our dogs for a walk. 'I don't mind if you sell Arctos!' Maia yelled after Marius. She must have heard about that dogman Helena and I encountered. 'Your pup's big and strong; he would make a lovely investment for somebody. Or a good meat stew,' she added cruelly.

A stalwart boy, Marius pretended he had not heard. He loved his dog and appeared fairly fond of his mother; brought up by my strict sister and her slapdash drinking husband, he had long ago learned diplomacy. At eleven, he was turning into a caricature of a good little Roman boy. He even had a small-sized toga my father had bought for him. Pa had totally neglected the rites of passage of his own sons – mainly because he was away from home with his paramour. Now he thought he would treat his grandsons traditionally. (The polite ones, that is. I had not noticed him spoiling the gutter tykes.) I told Marius he looked like a doll; I made him leave the toga at the residence. 'We don't want to stand out as foreign prigs, Marius.'

'I thought we had to teach the Britons how to live like proper Romans.'

'The Emperor has sent a judicial administrator to do that.'

'I haven't seen such a man.' Marius was a literal boy, who tested everything.

'No, he's out and about in the British towns holding citizenship classes. Where to sit in a basilica; what bodyparts to scrape with your strigil; how to drape your toga.'

'You think if I parade about togate on the streets of Londinium, I'll be laughed at.'

I thought it a possibility.

Being inconspicuous was difficult with Arctos and Nux dragging at their leads. Arctos was a boisterous young beast with long matted fur and a wavy tail, whose father we had never traced. My dog Nux was his mother. Nux was smaller, madder, and much more proficient at nosing in filthy places. To the locals both our pups were piteous. Britons bred the best hunting dogs in the Empire; their speciality was mastiffs, so fearless they were a good match for fighting arena bears. Even their lapdog-sized canines were tough terrors, with short stout legs and pricked up ears, whose idea of a soft afternoon was to raid a badger set – and to win.

'Is Nux going to help you track a criminal, Uncle Marcus?' Nux looked up and wagged her tail.

'I doubt it. Nux just gives me an excuse to wander about.' I then thought it worth trying: 'Marius, old pal, did Petronius say anything to you about what he was up to, before he went off?'

'No, Uncle Marcus.'

The boy made it sound convincing. When I stared at him, he looked me in the eye. But even in Rome, a city crammed with the world's worst confidence tricksters, the Didius family had always bred a special brand of sweet-faced liars.

'You grow more like your grandfather every day,' I commented, to let him know I was not fooled.

'I hope not!' quipped back Marius, pretending to be one of the boys.

We spent a couple of hours trailing round the downtown district, with no luck. I discovered that the baker whose business burned down was called Epaphroditus, but if anybody knew where Epaphroditus had his bolthole, they were not telling me. I tried asking about the Verovolcus killing, but people pretended they had not even heard that it happened. I found no witnesses who had noticed Verovolcus in the locality while still alive; nobody saw him drinking in the Shower of Gold; no one knew who had killed him. Finally I mentioned (because I was growing desperate) that *there might be a reward*. The silence continued. Evidently the judicial administrator had failed, in his citizenship classes, to explain how Roman justice worked.

We found a booth that passed for a pie-stall and treated ourselves. Marius managed half of his, then I helped him finish, making up for my lack of grub yesterday. He had slathered his pie in fish pickle sauce from the encrusted communal jug at the stall. I would have done the same at eleven, so I said nothing.

'All these people you have been talking to seem rather law-abiding and dull.' Most of my nephews had a dry wit. 'You would think a man head-first down a well would cause more fuss.'

'Maybe murders occur more often here than they should, Marius.'

'Well maybe we should nip off out of here then!' Marius grinned. Among my nieces and nephews I was viewed as a clown, though one with a hint of danger attached. His face clouded. 'Could we get into trouble?'

'If we upset someone. You can get into trouble anywhere if you do that.'

'How do we know what to avoid?'

'Use good sense. Be quiet and polite. Hope that the locals have been paying attention to the section about manners in their toga-folding lessons.'

'And always keep an escape route when entering an enclosed area?' Marius suggested.

I raised my eyebrows at him. 'You have been listening to Lucius Petronius.'

'Yes.' Marius, who was quiet by nature, hung his head for a moment. Bringing four young children all across Europe to their mother, Petro must have resorted to strict drill, for everyone's safety. In Maia's offspring he would have found intelligent listeners, keen to learn when plied with army and vigiles lore. 'Lucius Petronius was good to be with. I miss him.'

I wiped my mouth and my chin with the back of my hand, where the pungent fish pickle had dripped from his pie. 'So do I, Marius.'

XIV

W E WERE NOT the only ones missing Petronius. A letter had arrived for him from Rome.

Flavius Hilaris had the letter, and he made the mistake of mentioning it to me when we were all at lunch. 'If anybody sees your friend, it would be helpful to say I have this –'

'Is it from a lover?' demanded young Flavia, unaware of the ripples her remark caused. With Petronius there were quite a few women in that category. Most were long in the past as far as I knew. Many would be too easygoing to correspond; some probably could not write. Petronius had always had the knack of staying on good terms with the flighty ones, but he also knew how to break free. His liaisons meant little; they ran their course, then usually petered out.

'His exciting love, the gangster's wife perhaps,' jeered Maia. Petro's stupid affair had been no secret anywhere on the Aventine. Balbina Milvia did try to stick, but Petro, with his domestic life in tatters and his job threatened, had shed her. He knew that dallying with Milvia had been very dangerous.

'A gangster!' Flavia was greatly impressed.

'Please, all of you be serious.' Hilaris was more pinched than usual. 'This letter comes from the vigiles. It is written by a tribune, Rubella. But it is passing on a message to Petronius from his wife.'

'Ex-wife.' I did not look at my sister.

As I said it, I realised that aspects of this letter, which clearly bothered Hilaris, were odd. He would deny that his province practised censorship of correspondence, yet he had obviously read the letter. Why not simply hang on to it until Petro reappeared?

Why was the letter from a tribune? Arria Silvia could write if she wanted to bother – unlikely, given the state of things between them; but she would hardly ask Petro's superior to pass on her usual complaints about their three girls growing out of their clothing and how the slump in sales of potted salads caused her new boyfriend problems . . .

Neither could I imagine any vigiles tribune, especially the hard-bitten Rubella on the Aventine, scribbling a fond note to wish Petro a wonderful holiday.

How did Silvia know he was in Britain, anyway? How did Petro's *tribune* know? If he were taking leave, he would consider his destination his own business.

'Give the letter to me, if you like,' I offered.

Hilaris ignored my offer to take custody of the scroll. 'It was forwarded by the Urban Prefect.'

'Official channels?' I stared. 'The Prefect is so close to the top, he is virtually hung on the belt of the Emperor! What in Hades is going on?'

He bent his head, avoiding my eyes.

'What's up, Gaius?'

'I *really* don't know!' Hilaris was frowning, and sounded slightly annoyed. He had given his working life to Britain and he expected to be kept informed. 'I thought you knew, Falco.'

'Well, I don't.'

'Someone has died, Marcus,' interrupted Aelia Camilla, as if imposing sense on us. So her husband had been sufficiently perturbed to discuss the letter's contents with her.

'I didn't know Petronius had much family.' Helena glanced quickly at me. He had some flat-footed relatives in the country, whom he hardly saw. An aunt in Rome. He did have contact with her, but who gets letters from estranged wives sent urgently half across the world – about an aunt? His Auntie Sedina was elderly and overweight; it would be no surprise if she passed away.

Helena must have read in my face a reflection of her own fears. 'Oh not one of his children!' she burst out.

Aelia Camilla was upset. 'I'm afraid it is worse — it is two of them.'

Everyone was horrified. The message from the tribune was curt bureaucracy: L. Petronius Longus was to be informed with regret that two of his children had succumbed to the chickenpox.

'*Which* two?' Helena demanded.

'It does not say —' Hilaris at once faced a barrage of female anger.

'You must send a signal urgently,' his wife commanded. 'We have to be able to tell this poor man which of his daughters has survived!'

'Are they all daughters?'

'Yes, he has *three* daughters; he speaks of them very fondly. Gaius, you cannot ever have been listening.'

Maia, my sister, had remained silent, but she met my eyes with horror. We knew that Petronius had been laid up with the chickenpox himself, no doubt caught from his children, as he travelled here through Gaul. All of Maia's brood had it at the same time. Any of them might have died. If it had been Petro who succumbed, the four young Didii would have been stranded. Maia would have been bereft. I saw her close her eyes, shaking her head slightly. That was all the comment she could ever make.

I was aware of her eldest, Marius and Cloelia, watching us with their eyes wide. We adults avoided looking at them, as if talking amongst ourselves conferred some kind of privacy.

Thinking of the three Petronius girls, those of us who knew them were stricken. All three had always been delightful. Petro had been a solid father, romping with them when he was at home, but insisting on regular discipline. They were his joy: Petronilla, the sensitive eldest, a father's girl who had taken her parents' separation harder than the rest; sweet, neat Silvana; adorable round-faced barely school-age Tadia.

We were realists. To bring three children into the world was the Roman ideal; to keep them alive was rare. Birth itself was a risk. A whisper could carry off an infant. More precious children died at less than two years old than ever marked the formal passage out of infancy at seven. Many slipped away before ten and never entered puberty. The Empire was filled with tiny tombstones, carved with miniature portraits of toddlers with their rattles and pet doves, their memorials full of exquisite praise for best-loved, best-deserving little souls, snatched away from grieving parents and patrons after lives of heart-rending brevity. And never mind what the damned jurists say: Romans make no distinction between boys and girls.

In an Empire whose business was the army, far-reaching trade and administering lands overseas, many a father lost his children in his absence too. To be one of many would not make it easier. Petronius would blame himself, and he would suffer all the more because he heard this news a thousand miles away. Whatever past troubles had happened between him and Arria Silvia, he would have wanted to support her, then to comfort and reassure his remaining child. He would think it important to preside at the tragic funerals of the lost two.

The worst was, knowing this and knowing that *he* did not know.

It was too much. I left the room quietly, finding my way by instinct to the nursery. There I sat on the floor among the miniature chairs and walking frames, holding my own two warm little treasures tight. My mood must have affected them; Julia and Favonia became subdued, letting me embrace them for my own comfort.

Maia came in. Only one of hers was in the nursery. Marius and Cloelia had disappeared; the eldest were allowed out if they promised to be careful. Ancus, a quirky soul, had decided he was tired and put himself to bed for a siesta. Rhea was here alone, crawling round on a rug, playing some long-winded epic game with a set of pottery farm animals. Maia did not touch her youngest daughter, just sat on a chair, hugging her arms around her own body, watching.

After a long time, my sister asked me, 'Do you think he knows?'

'What?'

She explained patiently, 'Do you think someone else has already told him, and he has gone back home without informing us?'

I knew why she asked. That would be just like him. Speaking about his loss would be too painful, and he would be angered by fuss. While others flapped and increased his anguish with well-meaning hysteria, he would want to move, fast.

But I also knew how Petronius would have gone about it. Every debt settled up. Then the swift, scrupulous packing. Each boot-strap, tunic and memento neatly positioned in his luggage roll. He might take himself off, but it would be evident that he had packed up and gone home.

'He still doesn't know. He is here somewhere. I am certain.'

'Why?' demanded Maia.

'All his gear is in his room.'

Well, all except the stuff he would need if he was doing something dangerous.

Maia breathed harshly. 'Then you have to find him, Marcus.'

I knew that. The only problem was, I had no idea where to start looking.

XV

H OW COULD I work?
          Yesterday had been arduous. Today started well, but from lunchtime, with its dreadful news, everything fell apart. All anyone wanted was to go into huddles to discuss this shock. The only person who talked sense, in terms I recognised, was Helena.

'Petronius may be anywhere in town, or he may even have travelled away. Don't waste energy, Marcus. He will resurface when he's ready. In the meantime, what's lost?'

'From his point of view, nothing,' I agreed sombrely.

'Silvia and the poor surviving child won't be expecting anything from him yet. Once he knows, he will rush home to them.'

'Right. Better let him finish whatever he's up to.' He would need a free mind to cope. If he had swanned off with some woman, this would be the wrong moment to break bad news; he would feel guilty for ever. If he was drinking, better let him sober up.

'And whatever,' Helena asked narrowly, 'can he be up to here in Britain, anyway?'

'No idea.' She glared at me. 'Honest, sweetheart; I really have no idea.'

We both sank into reverie. After a long time, Helena said, 'He has only been gone a day.'

A day and a night. Somehow I did not expect to see him back in the near future.

I had to do something. He would not thank me for this, but I did it anyway. I drew up a missing-person sheet that Frontinus could issue to the legionaries.

L. Petronius Longus, Roman male of thirty-four years, freeborn; good height; serious build; brown hair; brown eyes. If subject spotted, observe and notify governor's office. Do not approach or arrest subject. Do not insult, beat up, or otherwise maltreat subject. If forced to make your presence known, urge subject's immediate contact with the governor's office and withdraw.

Do not inform subject his heart is about to be broken, lads. Leave it to the old cliché, the appropriate quarters. This filthy task is detailed to his best friend.

I did go out to look for him. I wandered about all afternoon. All I found were Marius and his dog, peering shyly into bars. I took them home. On the way we ran into Maia and Cloelia. They claimed they were out shopping. I took them home too.

As we arrived back at the procurator's house, a swirl of horsemen and a carriage rattled up to its stately portico. That was all I needed: King Togidubnus had wasted no time and had already arrived. Since I still had no information or explanations on who had drowned his disgraced retainer, I was the one who would probably catch most of the crud the King threw – plus anything else Julius Frontinus added, hoping it would seem any lack of progress on the case was not *his* fault.

Part of me did not care. A trousered killer had been killed himself and if it started a war, well at the moment I quite felt like a good war with somebody.

There is a special atmosphere in official buildings when a political crisis starts.

At one level everything continued as normal. Aelia Camilla ran her household quietly, showing by only the faintest frown that she anticipated difficulty in keeping mealtimes properly. The governor, the procurator, various officials, and the agitated King, were all in conference behind closed doors. Efficient slaves came and went, carrying scrolls or refreshment trays. They were keyed up with excitement; there was a sense that routine business would be overridden. The diary was being scrapped: meetings that had been fixed for weeks were cancelled or hastily rearranged. Dispatch riders and signallers were held at the ready. Arriving messengers were grounded in a side-room and crisply advised that they would have to wait because of the flap. Local officers and officials were summoned in a hurry; escorted in; then they left again in double-quick time, most looking as though they had somehow been caught out.

Nobody said what was happening. This was top grade secret, with triple wax seals.

I myself was never called in. It suited me. And I understood: the governor was trying to appease the King before we admitted how little progress we had made.

On the cusp of afternoon and evening, Flavius Hilaris appeared briefly.

'How's it going?'

He smiled wryly. 'Could be worse.'

'Could be better?'

He nodded, looking tired. 'Frontinus and I are dining the King strictly in private this evening. Out of respect for his grief.' And to keep him incommunicado for a while longer, no doubt. 'He has seen the body –' I had not been aware that people had emerged for an undertaker's visit. I wondered if the corpse had been brought here. 'The governor has agreed that a cremation may be held tomorrow; in the circumstances very discreet. I shall go, as a friend and neighbour of the King. Official representation is ruled out, in view of Verovolcus' disgrace. It will just be Britons from his home district.'

'Want me to attend?'

'Frontinus thinks not.' Luckily I never believed that myth about murderers turning up to watch when their victims are being dispatched to Hades. Few murderers are that stupid.

'It's a funeral Roman-style?' I asked.

'Pyre and urn,' Gaius confirmed. 'The King is fully Romanised.' He saw my face. 'Yes, I know it's not *his* funeral. But he is Roman enough always to take charge!' I liked this man's enduring quiet humour.

I wondered what ceremony Verovolcus would have chosen for himself. Did he see himself as this much in tune with Rome? I doubted it. Would he really have opted for cremation in a haze of scented oils – or would he want to be buried with his severed skull between his knees, among his weapons and rich grave goods?

'And what kind of grief is the King showing, Gaius?'

'He knew Verovolcus from childhood. So despite whatever has happened, Togidubnus is depressed. He's threatening to send his own boys in to scratch around for information.'

'No harm in it,' I said. 'I've done every possible initial check for witnesses. Let the Britons go over everything again if they wish. They may stir up something – or if not, at least Togidubnus may then believe we did our best.'

A senior clerk came to speak to him. Gaius had to go. He paused only to warn me that a formal meeting with the King had been arranged for me tomorrow morning. (I guessed I would also be called to a pre-meeting with Gaius and the governor at the crack of dawn, as they panicked over what I might say.) Then he asked if Helena and I would assist his wife in entertaining guests from the local community who were to dine here tonight. More earnest importers: I was not enthralled, but cancelling their invitation would cause too many questions and somebody ought to play host. I told the weary procurator he could rely on us.

Aelia Camilla could have managed the dinner single-handed. As a diplomat's wife she was well used to such events, and probably used to supervising them when Gaius was suddenly called away. But Helena and Maia were already dressing to help her, and she welcomed their support.

I would become the male host, virtually a diplomatic role. It was a major shift upwards for an informer. It meant a clean-shaven face and a toga. It also meant I had to be pleasant, even though being pleasant did not suit my mood.

80

My presence was poor compensation for guests who had hoped to meet senior men: men whose interest would advance their careers in Britain. Not much of a stand-in! But Aelia Camilla assured them they would get a second chance with the genuine gold knobs.

'Thank you, dear Marcus, for filling the gap so bravely.' She was a decent woman. Like Helena, she was by nature shy of strangers, though perfectly competent when social duty called. Both would have chosen to be traditional matrons shunning public appearances, though if anyone had *instructed* either to sit out of sight behind a curtain, both would have shot off barbs like an army of Parthians. Tonight they and Maia had lashed on extra jewellery, taken great care with the face paint, and braced themselves to exude warmth towards our guests.

These were the usual ungrateful hogs in search of a free meal. We had a couple of loud Gallic wine importers from some Aquitanean fleece-those-guzzlers guild, and an extremely nervous Briton who wanted assistance in finding markets for exporting live oysters; he said he would have brought samples but it was out of season. Then there was a quiet businessman whose exact role I must have missed, though he seemed quite at home in ambassadorial surroundings. He knew not to pick his nose. The rest strode into the residence as if forgetting it was essentially a private house, then stared around, so I checked the comports and counted the cups. Anyone would think their taxes had paid for the place. Whereas if I knew anything (and I did), their devious accountants had set up sly tax avoidance schemes.

I indulged in some fun with this conversation topic, to repay the wine importers for their crass attitudes. I let the Gauls confide all their accountants' cunning advice, then dropped in that I had been the Emperor's Census tax investigator. 'Off duty tonight!' I beamed, a swimmingly benevolent official host. I made the reassurance sound as insincere as possible.

Helena stared at me suspiciously, then came over and swapped seats. Now I was looking after the oyster man. He did not have an accountant. I gave him some sensible hints about acquiring one if he was to trade long-distance successfully. The tricksters in the Roman fishmarkets would run rings around any amateur who sent his wares blind to the Emporium. 'You need to use a negotiator. If their own percentage depends on it, they will ensure you get the right price.'

'They do seem very expensive.'

'But what's your alternative? Are you intending to escort every barrel of seawater all the way to Rome personally? You'll lose a lot of time that way, and then what? There is no guarantee you'll find the best bidder once you get there. The retailers will all swear to you that Romans only want traditional Lucrine oysters, then when they've bought yours up cheaply they'll sell them on as exotics from Britain at a massive profit: *their* profit, not yours!'

'But I would like to see Rome.'

'Then go, my friend. Go once, for pleasure. While you are there, fix yourself up with a product negotiator. You will cover his fees, believe me. Without help, you'll go bankrupt among the Emporium sharks.'

He thanked me profusely. Maybe he even trusted me. Maybe he would do it. From across the room, Helena gave me an approving smile to which I returned a courteous salute. The oyster man was pale and grey himself, gnarled like his own produce. I wrote my home address on a tablet, grinned, and said that was where he could send a free barrel if he found my advice helpful. It might work. He might grasp the give and take of rewards and bribes that made Roman commerce interesting. Or perhaps I had just trained him to be as tight-fisted as most traders.

For the dessert course we all moved outside into the garden. It was a warm night. Surprisingly so for Britain, though I remembered that they did have summer for about a fortnight here. This must be it. They had no way of dealing with the heat; all the bath houses either kept their water piping hot as usual, or let it go stone cold. Nobody closed their window shutters in daylight, so houses became stifling. And when dining in the open air, there were only benches; no one owned a proper exterior dining room with permanent stone couches or a shell-decorated nymphaeum.

I moved to sit beside the final guest, the quiet one. We explored a bowl of dates. They had come a great distance and needed picking over.

'I think I'd say that these don't travel well! I'm your substitute host. Marcus Didius Falco.'

'Lucius Norbanus Murena.' He was trying to place me.

'Your relaxed confidence at a formal dinner implies you are from Italy?' *I* was determined to place *him*. He had three names. That means nothing. I had three names myself yet I had spent much of my life scratching for the rent.

He was in his forties, maybe a little older; heavy, but he kept fit. He spoke well, with a lack of accent. There seemed to be enough money to kit him out in decent cloth; I think he had arrived here togate. This was not required in the provinces (where most locals did not even own a toga), but for visiting a residence it was good manners. His neat hair, beardless chin and manicured fingernails all spoke of acquaintance with a decent set of baths. With a strongly angled jawline, dark eyes, combed-back thick straight hair, I suppose he could be called handsome. You would have to ask a woman that.

'I'm from Rome,' he said. 'And you?'

'Rome too.' I smiled. 'Has tonight's set-up been explained? Due to the sudden arrival of an important British king, we are unexpectedly deprived of the governor and procurator. We're in the proc's house, as the gov still needs to build one grand enough; that lady in the embroidered gown is Aelia Camilla, your efficient hostess, wife of Hilaris. They are old British hands. She will ensure you are put on a future invitation list, with a chance to meet the notables.'

'And what is your role?'

'I'm family. Brought my wife to see her aunt.'

'So which is your wife?'

'The elegant Helena Justina.' I indicated her as she chatted pleasantly to the two dreadful Gauls. She loathed this kind of occasion, but had been brought up not to mock the concept of duty. She looked graceful and composed. 'The tall piece in refined white.' I had a suspicion that Norbanus had leered at Helena. I had noticed that she glanced at us, then straightened her stole around her shoulders with an unconsciously defensive air; I recognised unease in her.

Maybe I misread the mood. 'Ah yes; your wife very kindly saw me through the appetisers.' Norbanus spoke with a light inflexion of good humour. He was cultured and urbane. If such men prey on people's wives, they don't do it openly, and not at the first meeting, nor with husbands watching. For intelligent adulterers – and I felt he was intelligent – keeping husbands in the dark is part of the fun.

'Her noble mother trained her up as a helpful table companion.' I joined in the quiet satire. 'Helena Justina will have been responsible for setting you at ease, asking questions about your journey to Britain, and how you find the climate here. Then no doubt she passed you on to the stroppy madam in red, for the main course and polite enquiries about whether you have family and how long you intend your visit to last. My sister,' I added, as he switched his gaze to Maia.

'Delightful.' Maia had always been attractive. Men with an eye instantly fixed on her. As her brother, I had never been sure how she did it. Unlike Helena and her aunt, Maia tonight wore little jewellery. They both moved in fine ripples of gold, even out here at twilight where only small lamps swinging in rose bushes caught the filigrane beads in their bracelets and necklaces. My sister's drama came naturally; it came from her dark curls and the flashy ease with which she wore her trademark crimson. I felt no surprise when Norbanus asked politely, 'And is your sister's husband here?'

'No.' I let a beat of time elapse. 'My sister is widowed.' I was tempted to add: she has four demanding children, a furious temper, and no money. But that would be over-protective. Anyway, she might find out, and that temper of hers scared me.

'So, what line are you in, Falco?'

'Procurator of the Sacred Geese at the Temple of Juno.' My ghastly sinecure did have some uses. It nicely gave the impression that apart from a dubious role cleaning out augurs' hen-coops, I was a feeble man of leisure who lived off his wife's money. 'What about you?'

'You may not like this!' He had an honest charm. Mind you, I was no follower of honest charm. 'I am in property.'

'I have lived in rented apartments!' I returned, mentally scratching out 'honest'.

'I don't do domestic tenancies. Strictly commercial.'

'So what is your field, Norbanus?'

'I buy up or build premises, then develop them into businesses.'

'A big organisation?'

'Expanding.'

'How discreet. Still, no canny businessman reveals details of his balance sheet!' He only smiled politely, nodding in reply. 'What brings you to Britain?' I tried.

'Sniffing the market. Looking for introductions. Maybe you can tell me, Falco. This is the big question: what does Britain want?'

'Every damned thing!' I laughed gently. 'And first you have to explain to them how much they do want it . . . The natives are still being tempted down from hilltop villages; some have only just come in from their round huts. You start by telling them that buildings should have corners.'

'Gemini! It's more of a backwater than I thought.' We were by now on friendly terms – two suave Romans among the naïve barbarians.

I remembered that my job as a stand-in was to generate enthusiasm for this potholed byway. 'Optimistically, if the province stays Roman, the potential must be enormous.' Julius Frontinus would have applauded my two-faced bluff. 'Anyone who finds himself the right trading niche could make a killing.'

'You know the province?' Norbanus seemed surprised.

'Army.' Another useful cover; all the better for being true.

'I see.'

A slave brought us warm water and towels so we could rinse our hands after eating. The subtle hint broke up the party. Well, the Gauls might never have noticed that it was time to leave, but they were bored anyway. They bumbled off, discussing drinking-dens for a late night fling, with barely a nod to us. The British oysterman had already vanished. Norbanus bowed over the scented hands of the Three Graces in our goodbye line-up. He did thank Aelia Camilla and Helena perfectly civilly. It was to Maia that he stressed how much he had enjoyed the evening.

'Maia Favonia, good-night!' Interesting. Maia moved in a small circle and rarely used her full two names. I wondered how Norbanus knew them. Had he made a special effort to find out? Had I been jumpy, I might also have asked why.

I saw the guests off the premises. I made it look like a courtesy, rather than a ploy to ensure they stole nothing.

Exhausted, I was longing for my bed. It was not to be. As I returned down a corridor of offices, I saw the centurion from last night's watch patrol hanging around.

XVI

‘WAITING TO BE seen by someone?’
    ‘There’s been a development in the Longus case.’ The centurion explained his presence only reluctantly.

‘Petronius Longus is not an undesirable and it is not a case, centurion. What’s the development?’

I was about to have trouble. I knew this type. His normal manner was a mixture of fake simplicity and arrogance. For me he saved a special sneer on top. ‘Oh, are you Falco?’

‘Yes.’ The bakery fire was only last night; he cannot have forgotten meeting me.

‘It was your name on the information sheet?’ My description of Petronius had gone out from the governor’s office, but Frontinus was not name-proud and he had let it carry my signature.

‘Yes,’ I said again, patiently. He did not like me, by the sound of it. Well I had some doubts about him. ‘And what’s your name, centurion?’

‘Crixus, sir.’ He knew I had him now. If I carried any weight with the governor, Crixus was stuck. But he managed to stay unpleasant: ‘I don’t quite remember what you said you were doing in the downtown area last night, sir?’

‘You don’t remember because you didn’t ask.’ His omission was an error. That evened things up between us. Why was he so bothered? Was it because he now realised I was not just some higher-up’s domestic hanger-on, but someone with an official role that he had misinterpreted?

‘So; you mentioned a “development”, Crixus?’

'I came to report it to the governor, sir.'

'The governor's in conference. There's a flap on. I signed the sheet; you can tell me.'

Crixus reluctantly backed off. 'There may have been a sighting.'

'Details?'

'A man who resembled the description was observed by a patrol.'

'Where and when?'

'On the ferry-deck by the customs house. A couple of hours ago.'

'*What?* And you are only just here to report?'

He feigned a crestfallen look. It was sketchy and brazenly fake. This man wore his uniform smartly but in manner he was like the worst kind of dreary recruit who can't be bothered. If he had succeeded in seeing Frontinus, I dare say things would have been different. Double standards are a bad sign in the military. 'The info sheet made no mention of urgency.'

'You knew its status!' It was too late now.

The centurion and I were fencing quite toughly. I wanted to extract what he knew, whilst instinctively withholding as much as possible about Petro or myself. For some deep reason I did not want Crixus to learn that Petro and I were close, that I was an informer, or that he worked for the vigiles.

'Finish your report,' I said quietly. In my time in the legions I had never been an officer, but plenty of them had pushed me around; I knew how to sound like one. One who could be a right bastard if crossed.

'A patrol spotted a man who fitted the details. As I say, he was at the ferry landing.'

'Crossing over?'

'Just talking.'

'To whom?'

'I really couldn't say, sir. We were only interested in him.' In the ten years since I left the army, the art of dumb insolence had not died.

'Right.'

'So who is this person?' asked Crixus, with an air of innocent curiosity.

'Same as everyone who comes here. A businessman. You don't need to know more.'

'Only I don't think he can be the right man, sir. When we asked, he denied that his name was Petronius.'

I was furious and let the centurion see it. 'You *asked*, when the sheet said "don't approach"?'

'Only way we could attempt to discover if he was the subject, sir.' This idiot was so self-righteous I barely refrained from hitting him.

'It's the right man,' I growled. 'Petronius Longus loathes nosy questions from stiffs in red tunics. He generally claims to be a feather-fan seller called Ninius Basilius.'

'That's rather peculiar, sir. He told us he was a bean-importer called Ixymithius.'

Thanks, Petro! I sighed. I had plucked a known alias of his from my memory – the wrong one. Any minute now, Crixus would decide it was a fact of note that the subject worked under cover using several false identities. Then the centurion would be even more nosy. If I knew Petro, he was just being rebellious; he had instinctively stiffened up when a strutting patrol apprehended him. On principle, he would lie to them. At least it was better than questioning their parentage, telling them to go to Hades in a dung cart, then being thrown in a cell.

'You're going the long way round to admitting that he gave you the slip,' I warned. 'The governor will not be pleased. I don't know why you're playing silly beggars over this. The poor man has to be told some bad news from home, that's all. Frontinus has a past acquaintance with him; he wants to do it personally.'

'Oh well, next time we'll know he's the one. We'll pass the message to him, never fear.'

Not now. Not if Petro saw them coming again.

XVII

King Togidubnus' long-term friendship with Vespasian went right back to when Rome first invaded Britain; Togi had played host to the legion which the young Vespasian had spectacularly led. That was over forty years ago. I had seen the King much more recently and when we had our meeting the next morning we were comfortable together.

To look at, he was clearly an elderly northerner, his mottled skin now papery and pale, his hair faded from a reddish tribal shade into a dusty grey. On any formal occasion he dressed like Roman nobility. I had not deduced whether any rank conferred on him actually entitled him to the broad purple stripe on his toga, but he called himself a 'legate of Augustus' and he wore that stripe with all the confidence of a senatorial bore who could list several centuries of florid ancestors. Most likely, Togidubnus had been selected young, brought to Rome, educated among the various hopeful hostages and promising princelings, then replaced on a throne to be a bulwark in his home province. After thirty years the Atrebates seemed only a little less backward than any other British tribes in the Romanised area, while they and their king were unquestionably loyal.

All except the dead Verovolcus. He had killed a Roman architect. Mind you, hating architects is legitimate. And the one Verovolcus took against had held opinions on spatial integrity that would make anybody spew.

'We meet again, in sorry circumstances, Falco.'

I adjusted my pace to fit the King's sober grandeur. 'My pleasure at renewing our acquaintance, sir, is only marred by the grim cause.'

He sat. I stood. He was playing the high-ranked Roman; he could have been Caesar enthroned in his tent, receiving rebellious Celts. I was entirely subordinate. Anyone who works for clients expects to be a treated like a tradesman. Even a slave who employed me as an informer would take a high-handed attitude. The King was not even hiring me; nobody thought that necessary. I was doing this job as a duty, for the good of the Empire and as a favour to family. Those are the worst terms ever. They don't pay. And they don't give you any rights.

I ran through what I knew and what I had done about it. 'To sum up: the most likely scenario is this: Verovolcus came to Londinium, perhaps intending to hide up here. He went into a bad location by chance and paid a tragic penalty.'

The King considered it for a moment. 'That explanation would suffice.'

I had expected furious demands for retribution. Instead the Togidubnus response could have come straight from one of the deviously slick offices on the Palatine. He was trying to contain the damage.

'It would suffice for the *Daily Gazette!*' I said harshly. Rome's official Forum publication loves scandal in the lowbrow columns that follow its routine lists of senate decrees and calendars of games, but the *Acta Diurna* is produced by official clerks. The *Gazette* rarely exposes uncomfortable truths in politics. Its wildest revelations involve lurid sex in the aristocracy – and then only if they are known to be shy of suing.

One bushy grey eyebrow flicked upwards. 'But you have doubts, Falco?'

'I would certainly like to investigate further . . .'

'Before you commit yourself? That's good.'

'Let's say, whoever dunked Verovolcus in the well, we don't want a repeat.'

'And we do want justice!' insisted the King. In fact 'justice' would have put Verovolcus in the amphitheatre here, as lunch for starved wild beasts.

'We want the truth,' I said piously.

'My retainers are making more enquiries.'

The King was glaring defiantly but I merely replied, 'The more that district is shaken up, the more we show that violence won't be tolerated.'

'What do you know about the district, Falco?'

'It's a grim area at the back of the unloading and storage wharves. It's full of small enterprises, mainly run by migrants, for the benefit of sailors on shore leave and transient import/export men. It has all the disadvantages of such districts in any port.'

'A colourful enclave?'

'If that means a hangout for tricksters and thieves.'

The King was silent for a while. 'Frontinus and Hilaris are telling me that what happened to Verovolcus was probably provoked by him, Falco. They say that the perpetrators would otherwise only have robbed him.'

'His torque is missing,' I agreed, letting caution sound in my voice.

'Try and find the torque, Falco.'

'You want it back?'

'I gave it to him.' The King's expression showed nostalgia and regret at the loss of his long-term friend. 'Will you recognise it?'

'I remember.' It was unusual: fine strands of twisted gold, almost like knitted skeins, and heavy end pieces.

'Do your best. I know the killers will have vanished.'

'You are right to feel cautious, but it's not entirely hopeless, sir. They may one day be exposed, even perhaps when arrested for some other crime. Or some small-time criminal may turn them in, hoping for a reward.'

'They tell me it is a bad area, yet murders are infrequent.'

I felt the King was working up to something. 'Frontinus and Hilaris know the town,' I commented.

'And *I* knew Verovolcus,' said the King.

A slave entered, bringing us refreshments. The interruption was annoying, even though I for one had not had breakfast. Togidubnus and I waited patiently in silence. Maybe we both knew Flavius Hilaris might have sent the slave to observe our meeting for him.

The King made sure of privacy and dismissed the slave. The boy looked nervous, but left the offerings on a carved granite side table.

After he went out, I myself sawed off slices of cold meat and gave us each a dish of olives. While the King stayed on his silver-backed couch, I went to a stool. We munched the soft white breakfast rolls and sipped water, no longer speaking. I pasted my ham to my roll with chick-pea dip. He wrapped a slice of meat around a hard-boiled hen's egg.

'So what did Frontinus and Hilaris tell you I would want?' asked the King eventually.

'I've had no opportunity to receive instructions, sir.'

'What – no briefing?' He looked amused.

'I was out walking this morning.' This was true. I had gone to the forum early, where I chalked up graffiti on a wall saying *'LPL, contact MDF: urgent'*. I had no great hopes. Petronius was unlikely to hang around that dreary spot. I risked murmuring frankly, 'I expect our two great men are sweating shit!' The King chuckled even more. 'But you and I, sir, don't need a briefing before we communicate.'

Togidubnus finished his egg and wiped his scrawny old fingers on a napkin. 'So what do you really think, Marcus Didius?'

I noted the more informal nomenclature. I chewed up an olive, dumped its stone in a dish, and told him. 'I am still puzzled why Verovolcus went to that place. I have noticed an organised racket in the vicinity, though I have not been able to show any link, I admit.'

'Are you saying that officials deny that this "racket" exists?' demanded the King.

'No.' They had managed to avoid *admitting* it, but they were diplomats. 'Civilisation brings much good, but you know it brings bad as well. I have no idea what criminal activities occurred when the tribes ran Britain from hillforts, but every society has its bandits. We bring you the city and we bring city vices. More complicated, perhaps, but all based on fear and greed.' Togidubnus made no comment. If he really had been brought up in Rome and had ever walked the Golden City's teeming streets, he had seen at first hand the worst of organised grief and extortion. 'Did Verovolcus hate Rome?' I asked.

'Not particularly.'

'But you said you "knew" him. You meant something by that.'

'He liked to be in the thick of any action, Falco. Being my liaison officer never quite suited him, but nor was he the type to sit on a farm watching cattle graze.'

'Meaning?'

'He would not go into exile meekly.'

The King rose, went to the side table, inspected a flat bowl of cold fishes, tried one, decided against, and took another roll with some ready-sliced venison. That kept him busy, chewing bravely, for some time. I sat and waited.

'So what *do* you want to tell me, sir?' I asked, when I was fairly sure he could get words out again.

He screwed his up lips, his tongue struggling with a shred of trapped venison in his back teeth. I pecked at breadcrumbs on my tunic. 'He was not going to Gaul, Falco.'

Togidubnus had spoken in a low tone, which I matched: 'He meant to stay here in Londinium? Did he have friends here?'

'No.'

'Any means to live?'

'I gave him some money.' That came out fast: conscience money. Whatever Verovolcus had done, his regal master had felt responsible for him.

'Did he say anything, sir, about coming here?'

'Enough.' The King set aside his empty watercup.

'He spoke to you?'

'No, he knew I would have had to stop him.'

I filled in the story myself: 'Verovolcus told his friends he was sneaking off to Londinium, not going to Gaul. He knew there was an expanding crime scene and he boasted that he would be part of it?' The King went so far as to nod. The rest was inevitable: 'If there are rackets, and he tried to muscle in – then whoever runs the show here must have refused him an entry ticket.'

They had done it in the classic style too: a striking death, which would attract public notice. A death that would serve as a warning to any other hopefuls who might consider invading the racketeers' turf.

XVIII

SEEING HILARIS AT one end of the corridor as I emerged, I
bunked off the other way. I wanted space; I had to reach
decisions. Did I take this further in person, or hand the whole
packet over to the authorities?

I knew what was making me hesitate. Acknowledging there
were rackets, and in a province where the Emperor had once
served with distinction, was politically inconvenient. I thought
they were likely to drop the case.

Music and the sound of voices drew me to a salon. The
womenfolk were listening politely to a blind harpist. He was ill-
shaven and expressionless, with a sullen, even pugnacious, young
boy crouched at his feet, presumably to lead him around. He could
play. I wouldn't have walked far to hear him, but his technique
passed. It was background music. Bland, melodious pattering that
allowed people to talk over it. After a while you could forget the
harpist was there. Maybe that was the point.

I nudged up against Helena on a couch. 'What's this? Are we
auditioning him for an orgy tonight or taking culture a bit far?'

'Hush! Norbanus Murena has sent him on loan to Maia. Such a
kind thought.'

'What prompted that?' I sounded like an ungracious brute.

'I remember us talking to him last night about music.'

'*Maia* was?' I managed not to laugh.

Helena biffed me gently with the back of her wrist. 'No, I think
it was me, but you can't expect a man to remember things
properly.'

I frowned. 'Did you like Norbanus?' I trusted her instincts with people.

Helena paused, almost undetectably. She may not even have known that she did so. 'He seemed straight, decent and ordinary. A nice man.'

I sucked my teeth. 'You don't care for nice men.'

Helena suddenly smiled at me, her eyes soft. I swallowed. One of the things I had always loved about her was her brutal self-awareness. She was eccentric; she knew it; she did not want to change. Nor did I want her to be a conventional matron with narrow vision and appalling friends. 'No,' she agreed. 'But I'm a grouse, aren't I?'

The harpist twiddled to the end of a tune. We clapped demurely. 'How long have we got him for?'

'I think, as long as Maia likes.'

'Olympus! That's a cheat. Making up to a woman by giving her a necklace, at least she gets to keep the jewels. This way, Norbanus takes his harpist back at the end of his flirtation and meanwhile Hilaris has to feed the swine. I don't suppose Maia suggested she must ask her head of household for permission?' I saw myself as Maia's head of household – not that she ever did.

'No, Marcus.' Helena looked pained, though not at the joke about my status; she thought my suggestion was rude. 'Are you insisting she send him straight back? That would be an unkind rebuff. It's just a loan. No one but you would see any harm in it.'

Exactly.

'We are pushed into accepting the loan,' said a quiet voice. 'That is why Marcus hates it.'

I looked back over my shoulder. Hilaris must have followed me here. He was now standing behind us and listening. I consulted him in an undertone: 'Norbanus. One of your visitors last night. In property. Likes women, apparently. Gets his wicked way using flashy loans and gifts.'

'I met him; I found him intelligent and well-mannered.' Hilaris paused. I could not tell whether he approved of those qualities, or

97

of property speculators generally. Perhaps not. 'Uneasy?' he murmured in a low tone.

I was, for some reason. 'Why do I feel pressurised, Gaius?'

He dropped his hand on my shoulder for a moment, and muttered, 'I'm sure you are over-reacting.'

'My sister can look after herself,' I said, as if that was it.

'Then let's keep the musician for a while, if Maia wants to do so.' The choice was his; it was his house. 'Do you have a moment, Marcus?'

He wanted to discuss my meeting with the King. Well, it was his province too. And if there was a problem, it was his problem.

Walking down a painted corridor, vaguely heading for an office, we held a short, efficient discussion. Hilaris now acknowledged that Londinium had been targeted by extortionists. He said it happened everywhere, and that the provincial staff would address it as a normal law and order issue. I would continue to work on the Verovolcus death.

He was a brilliant bureaucrat. It felt as if we had just devised a communiqué on major issues. Nothing substantial had changed, however.

'I'm glad we are of one mind,' said Flavius Hilaris in his diplomatic mode.

'I'm glad you think so,' I replied, an informer still.

'We shall beat this menace,' he maintained.

He smiled and I did not. As I say, nothing had changed.

The establishment might convince itself that social corruption was a force it could combat in practical ways, denouncing it with edicts. That baker, Epaphroditus, who made a stand but then fled in the face of certain retribution, knew the truth.

'There's another thing, Gaius – you've put the military on to the streets at night, but don't get too complacent. I won't say anyone at that shambles you pass off as a fort has been co-erced – but you need to monitor them carefully.'

Hilaris looked startled. 'The commander is an excellent officer –'

'Really.' I gave him a glance that said Frontinus needed to pep up the commander.

'I'll make a note: Falco recommends acquiring a decent fort – with a disciplinarian in charge! How is it, my dear Marcus, that when you are around, we always start with a small problem – or even no problem – then end up facing major chaos?'

'You had the chaos all along,' I said. 'I only exposed it.'

'Thank you!' replied Hilaris, with a rueful grin.

Then we turned a corner and met a different kind of riot.

Albia, Helena's wild girl, had just hurled a vase and smashed it.

Hilaris and I had popped up like stage ghosts through a trapdoor; it caused an abrupt silence. Children, some my host's, some Maia's, one mine, froze and waited for the worst. Hilaris and I only paused because we were each hoping the other father would weigh in like a good Roman disciplinarian.

He cleared his throat and asked what was going on Gingerly; I picked up a broken shard of fine turquoise coloured glass. The smashed vase had come from a new display in a room whose door stood open; the manufacturer we met at dinner last night had given samples as presents to Aelia Camilla. I plucked at the tunics of Julia and the Hilaris girl, Gaia, who were standing nearest to the breakage, shaking out the little girls' garments to clear off any sprayed glass needles. I motioned all the children to step back from the broken fragments on the black and white mosaic.

Flavia told her father quietly that Albia had wanted to go to the kitchen for food. Aelia Camilla had given orders against this. Yesterday there had been a row over missing raisins; Albia had devoured a full platter intended for the official evening dinner. It had messed up the dessert menu, annoyed the cook, and then Albia had of course been sick. Today the children had tried to explain that she must wait until lunch, but she took it badly.

'Albia doesn't understand,' Flavia said.

I looked at the scavenger. 'Oh, I think she does.'

Albia and Flavia must be about the same age. Albia was smaller, skinnier of course, and stubbornly expressionless. I saw no reason to think her any less intelligent than the fine-featured Flavia.

Albia had glanced at me once, then looked away, deliberately staring at the ground. Just before the vase broke there had been screaming – wilful, unrestrained fury and noise, hysteria that even my little Julia would be ashamed of. I gripped Albia by the shoulders. Through the blue dress, I could feel the bones as I turned her to face me. Her pale face and thin bare arms were still badly grazed from when she rescued the dogs. Cleaned up, she had a washed-out look, with bloodless skin. Her hair was light brown, her eyes bright blue – that dark blue colour most prevalent here in the north. But her unformed young features seemed familiar in style. I guessed she might be half British and half Roman.

'She doesn't understand!' squealed little Rhea defensively. Albia's mouth was pressed in a tight line, as if to emphasise that.

'Even a dumb bunny could understand!' I growled. 'We took her in: she lives by our rules. Aelia Camilla will be very hurt that her beautiful glass has been broken. And on purpose, Albia!'

The girl stayed mute.

I was losing ground. With every second I seemed more like a cruel master threatening a troubled victim.

'Are you going to make her be a slave?' demanded Gaia breathlessly. What had brought that on? It might be what the wild girl feared, but if she wouldn't speak, how had she told the children? I sensed conspiracy.

'Certainly not. And don't tell her that I will. She's not a prisoner of war, and nobody sold her to me. But listen to me, Albia – and the rest of you mark what I'm saying too! I will not tolerate wilful damage. One more piece of destruction – and it's back on the streets.'

Well, that told them. M. Didius Falco, tough bastard and Roman father. My own tiny daughter's eyes were wide with amazement.

Hilaris and I walked on together. By the time we reached the end of the corridor, we heard another crash. Albia had defiantly smashed a second piece of ornamental glass. She did not even make a run for it but waited, chin up, while we walked back.

I had given my ultimatum: there was no escape. So Flavius Hilaris, procurator of Britain, found himself left with the task of quietening seven weeping children. I had been going out into the town anyway, so I went at once – and I took Albia. With my hand heavy on her shoulder, I marched her back to the alleys she came from. I did not pause to let myself think what a typical middle-rank swine I had become.

Nor did I dare tell Helena.

XIX

=======

THE SCAVENGER ACCEPTED her fate in silence. I took her to a food shop, one I didn't recognise. It must be a daytime-only place. I sat her in a corner outside, in a short row of small square tables on the pavement, delineated by dry old troughs of laurel in the Mediterranean style. I bought some food, since she was perpetually hungry, and told the owner to let her stay there if she caused no trouble. It was coming up to lunchtime but the caupona was quiet. I noted the name: the Swan. It was opposite a knife-seller. Two shops along was a more louche-looking wine bar, with a flying phallus sign between two enormous painted cups, called the Ganymede.

'Wait for me here, Albia. I'll be back again later. You can eat and look around. This is what you came from. It's what you will go back to, if that's your choice.' The girl stood beside the table to which I had propelled her, a thin, beaten figure in her borrowed blue dress. She looked up at me. Perhaps by now she was more miserable than morose. 'Don't fool around,' I told her. 'Let's get it straight. I know you can talk. You haven't lived on the streets of Londinium all your life without learning Latin.'

I left without awaiting a response.

It was a hot day. The sun baked down almost as warmly as in Rome. People staggered through the narrow streets, huffing. In some places a pantiled portico created shade, but the habit of Londinium traders was to fill the porticoes with impedimenta: barrels, baskets, planks and oil amphorae found handy storage on what should be the pavement. You walked in the road. As they had no wheeled vehicle curfew here, you kept an ear out for approaching carts; some natural law made most creep up behind unexpectedly. Londinium drivers took the line that the road was theirs and pedestrians would soon jump if bashed into. Calling out an early warning did not occur to them. Calling out abuse if they narrowly missed you was different. They all knew the Latin for 'Trying to commit suicide?' And some other words.

I was walking to the docks.

In the heat the wooden decks that formed the wharves stank of resin. There was a lazy midday siesta feel. Some of the long ware-houses were secured with chains and mighty locks. Others stood with their huge doors open; whistling or wood-sawing sounded from the bowels, though often nobody was visible. Shipping had been packed along the moorings, sturdy merchantmen that could brave these violent northern waters. Occasional long-haired, bare-chested men fiddled about in bumboats, looking at me suspiciously as I passed. I tried polite greetings but they seemed to be foreigners. Like all harbours, this long strip of water bobbed with apparently deserted vessels. Even in daylight the ships were left to creak and lightly bump each other in isolation. Where does everyone go? Are captains, passengers and matelots all asleep on shore, waiting to disrupt the night with knife fights and carousing? If so, where in Londinium were the crammed lodging houses in which all the merry sailors snored away until the evening bats came out?

Waterfronts have a special seediness. I buffed one shin against the other, trying to deter small, unbelievably persistent flies. A haze hung over the distant marshes. Here everything was desiccated by the heatwave, but the river had patches of rainbow oiliness, in which ancient rubbish floated among greasy bubbles. In what seemed to be dead water, a log end thumped against the piles. A slow tidal current was carrying debris upriver. If a bloated corpse had suddenly broken the surface, I would not have been surprised.

★

No such thoughts troubled the customs officer. In his time he had probably fished out floaters – drowned bodies – but he remained as perky as they come. He operated out of a customs house near one of the ferry landings, a porticoed stone building that would stand at the bridgehead once the bridge was built. His office was crammed with dockets and note tablets. Despite the chaotic appearances, whenever someone came to register a cargo and pay their import tax, they were dealt with calmly and speedily. The clutter was under control. A young cashier presided over boxes of different currencies, working out the tax percentage and taking the money with panache.

Lulled by unaccustomed sunshine, the officer had basked too much without his tunic. He was a big fellow, running to fat. His rolling flesh had originally been pallid, as though he was a northerner by birth; now it was striped with raw pink sunburn. He winced and moved stiffly, but took his punishment philosophically.

'You need to organise some shade,' I warned.

'Oh I like to enjoy the sun while I can.' He eyed me up. He could tell I was not nautical. Well, I hoped he could. I do have standards.

'Name's Falco. I'm looking for my good friend Petronius Longus. Somebody said he was seen down here yesterday, talking to you.' There was no reaction, so I carefully described Petro. Still nothing. 'I'm disappointed then.' The customs officer steadily blanked me. Nothing for it: 'He's an elusive character. I bet he told you, "If anyone comes asking for me, say nowt".' I winked. The customs officer winked back, but this jolly fellow with the red shiny face may have reacted automatically.

I slipped him the proverbial coin that loosens tongues. Though a public official, he took it. They always do. 'Well if you do see the man who wasn't here, please tell him Falco needs to speak to him urgently.'

He gave me a cheerful tilt of the head. I was not encouraged.

'What's your name?'

'Firmus.' We were on moneyed terms. I thought it fair to ask.

'Handy to know. I may want to list your sweetener in my accounts.'

He opened his palm and looked at the coins. 'This is business, then? Thought you said he was a friend?'

'He is. The best. He can still go on expenses.' I grinned. Conniving always makes new pals.

'So what business are you in, Falco?'

'Government food regulations,' I lied, with yet another friendly wink. 'In fact, I'll ask you, Firmus: some of the hotpot hawkers up back of the stores seem to be having trouble. Have you seen any evidence of the local bars being threatened?'

'Oh no, not me,' Firmus assured me. 'I never go to bars. It's home straight after work for a Chicken Frontinian and an early night.'

If his habits were so abstemious, I was surprised he put on so much flab. 'Frontinian has too much aniseed for me,' I confided. 'I like a good Vardarnus. Now Petro, he has disgusting taste. He's happy as a sandflea sitting down to braised beets or beans in the pod . . . What's the word on the docks about that Briton dead in the well?'

'He must have upset someone.'

'Anybody suggesting who he upset?'

'Nobody's saying.'

'But everybody knows, I bet!'

Firmus gave me a knowing head tilt, indicating assent. 'Lot of questions about this stuff lately.'

'Who's asking? Long-haired Britons from the south?'

'What?' Firmus looked surprised. The team King Togidubnus had sent out could not yet have worked this part of the wharves.

'Who then?' I drew up short. 'Surely not that old friend of mine, the one you haven't seen?' Firmus made no reply. Petronius must have given him a bigger sweetener than I did. 'So what would you have told this invisible person, Firmus?'

'It's supposed to be out-of-towners,' said Firmus, almost matter-of-factly, as if I should know it already. 'I mean a *long* way out of town. There's some group taking an interest in the Londinium social scene.'

'Where do they hail from? And who's the big meatball?'

'What?'

'The man in charge.' But Firmus clammed up. Even though he had been enjoying the attention as he held forth as the expert on the local situation, something now proved too much for him.

He might know the answer to my question about who ran the rackets, but he wasn't going to tell me. I recognised the look in his previously friendly eyes. It was fear.

XX

I WALKED BACK past the warehouses and into the unpromising interior streets where the racketeers seemed to operate. I had agreed with Hilaris: this happened everywhere. Yet that big-time frighteners would try taking over the commercial outlets in *Britain* still seemed unlikely.

There was so little here. Retail outlets selling staples: carrots, spoons and firewood bundles, mostly in rather small quantities. Oil, wine and fish-pickle sauce, all looking as if their crack-necked amphorae, with dusty bellies and half the labels missing, had been unloaded from the boat several seasons before. Dim eating houses, offering amateur snacks and piss-poor wine to people who hardly knew what to ask for. One obvious brothel that I saw yesterday; well, there must be more of those. A respectable husband and father – well, a husband with a scathing wife who missed nothing – had to be careful how he looked for them. What else? Oh look! Between a sandal-seller and a shop full of herbal seeds (*buy our exciting borage and caress away care with curative coriander!*) here was a placard scrawled up on a house wall which advertised a gladiatorial show: Pex the Atlantic Thrasher (*really?*); the nineteen times unbeaten Argorus (clearly some old frowsty fox whose fights were fixed); a clash of bears; and Hidax the Hideous – apparently the retiarius with the niftiest trident this side of Epirus. There was even a furious female with a cliché name: Amazonia (advertised in much smaller letters than her male counterparts, naturally).

I was too grown-up to be lured by nasty girls with swords, though they might be sensational for some. Instead, I was trying to remember the last time I had any borage that was more than mildly interesting. Suddenly I became aware of excruciating pain. Somebody had jumped me.

I never saw him coming. He had slammed my face against a wall, pinioning me with such brutal force he nearly broke the arm that he had twisted up my back. I would have cursed, but it was impossible.

'Falco!' Hades, I knew that voice.

My fine Etruscan nose was squashed tightly against a wall that was so deeply rough-cast it would imprint me for a week with its hard pattern; the daub was bonded with cow dung, I could tell.

'Petro –' I gurgled.

'Stop drawing attention!' He might have been bullying some thief he had caught fingering women's bustbands off a laundry drying line. 'You sapheaded blunderer! You interfering, imbecilic rat's bane –' There were more hissed insults, all meticulously spittable, some obscene, and one I had never heard before. (I worked out what it meant.) 'Get this, you flakewit – leave it, or I'm a dead man!'

He released me abruptly. I nearly fell over. When I staggered round to tell the swine he had made himself quite clear enough, he had already gone.

XXI

I WAS HAVING a frustrating time: when I retraced my steps to the Swan, Albia had disappeared too.

'Went off with a man,' the proprietor enjoyed telling me.

'You should be ashamed if people are using your bar as a pick-up point. Suppose she was my darling little daughter and you had let her be dragged off by a pervert!'

'But she's not your darling, is she?' he sneered. 'She's a street child. I've seen her around for years.'

'And was she always with men?' I asked, nervous now about what type of bad influence Helena had imposed on the children at the residence.

'No idea. Still, they all grow up.'

Albia was fourteen, if she really was an orphan of the Rebellion. Old enough to be married off, or at least politely betrothed to a poxy tribune, if she were a senatorial brood mare. Old enough to get pregnant by some layabout her father hated, if she were a plebeian needed in the family business. Old enough to be wise in ways I could not think about. Yet she was childishly slight, and if her life had been as hard as I suspected, she was young enough to deserve a chance, young enough to be capable of being saved – if she had stayed with us.

'She'll be at it all over the forum soon, even if she's a virgin now.'

'Sad,' I commented. He thought I had cracked. And I did not like the way he watched me walk away down the street.

★

I had no plan when I set off walking, just a need to get out of there. I felt there were too many eyes watching me, from people in doorways or even people unseen.

I had gone about three streets. I was starting to be aware that there was more activity in Londinium than most Romans would expect. All the regular commodities were sold. The dark little shops were open in the day; life in them just had a duller pace than I was used to. Buyers and sellers lurked inside, just as they always did; even when the sun was so hot that I was sweating after fifty strides, people here forgot they were allowed to sit out in the open air. Otherwise I felt at home. In the daily markets, selling fresh veg and sad-eyed dead game, the traders' shouts were vibrant and their wives' jokes were coarse. The men could have been tricky barrow boys around the Temple of Hope back home in the Tiberside Vegetable Market. The stench of old fish scales is the same anywhere. Walk your boots across a newly sluiced butchers' street, and the faint odour of animal blood will haunt you all day afterwards. Then pass a cheese stall and the warm, wholesome waft will draw you back to buy a piece – until you are sidetracked by those remarkably cheap belts on the stall next door that will fall apart when you get them home . . .

I turned my back on the belts eventually (since I would not be caught dead in brick red leather). Mooching into a shop full of jumbled hardware, I was trying to work out how I could carry back home with me ten stupendously good value, but heavy, black pottery bowls. Despite a generous discount offered by the pleasant shopkeeper, I said no and I started to inspect some interesting skeins of hairy twine. You can never have too much hairy twine around the house and he assured me it was the best goat's hair, neatly twisted, the skeins only going for a song because of over-production in the goat-hair-twine making trade. I loved this tempting hardware emporium, where next I spotted a quite hilarious lamp. It had naked young ladies either side of the hole, looking over their shoulders to compare the size of their bottoms –

No chance to linger. I happened to glance out of doors and there were the two enforcers strolling past the shop.

The amiable seller caught the direction of my glance so I muttered, 'Know those two?'

'Splice and Pyro.'

'Know what they do?'

He smiled bleakly. Pyro obviously set the fires, while Splice must have some painful speciality on which I would not speculate.

In two heartbeats I was out of there and dodging after them. Informers learn not to load themselves up with shopping, just in case of such emergencies.

I held back as the pair walked unconcernedly. I had recognised them at once: Splice, the short, well-built one, who probably did the chat and the brutality, and his leaner chum Pyro, who stayed on guard or played with flame. Splice had a square face decorated with two intriguing old scars; Pyro sported dirty beard-shadow and a speckled crop of moles. A snipper who knew how to wield steel had given them fine Roman haircuts. Both had muscled legs and arms that must have seen some nasty action. Neither looked like a man to argue with about the outcome of a horse race.

Watching from behind, I could sum them up from how they walked. They were confident. Unhurried but not loitering. A bulge under Splice's tunic hinted that he might be carrying swag. Once or twice they exchanged words with a stallholder, light greetings in passing. These men behaved like locals who were old faces about the district. Nobody showed much fear; they were an accepted part of the scenery. People almost seemed to like them. In Rome they could have been typical spoiled wastrels: everyday adulterers who avoided work, lived with their mothers, spent too much on clothes, drink and brothel bills, and dabbled with the sordid end of crime. Here, they stood out as Romans because of their Mediterranean colouring; they both had facial bone structure that was straight off the Tiber Embankment. Maybe that hint of the exotic attracted people.

They had melded in, apparently very fast and without effort. Londinium had accepted extortion as easily as it accepted mist every morning and rain four times a week. That was how the rackets worked. The enforcers arrived in a place and made out that their methods were a normal part of the high life. People could sniff money when near them. Moneyed bastards will always attract sad people who yearn for better things. These thugs – they were no better – soon acquired status. Once they had beaten up a few stubborn customers, they carried another smell too: danger. That also has a perverse attraction.

I saw it all working when they led me right back where I came from earlier, straight past the Swan to the other caupona, the Ganymede. They were well known to the waiter, who came out at once and chatted as he laid their table, a private one set slightly apart from the rest. It was lunchtime and a lot of people were calling for a hasty bite, but the enforcers were able to take all the time they liked over whether they wanted olives in brine or in aromatic oil. Wine came automatically, probably in their special cups.

Pyro went inside, perhaps to visit the latrine, more likely to stash the money from their morning round. I had obviously found their operating base. Here, Splice and Pyro were openly holding court. Male visitors came and went constantly, like cousins at a Greek barber's. On arrival there would be formal standing up and handshakes. The two enforcers then got on with their lunch, rarely offering hospitality, rarely being bought drinks. The point for everyone was to make contact. They were businesslike and even abstemious; they ate stuffed pancakes with simple side salads, no sweetmeats, and their wine flagon was the small size. The visitors would sit and gossip for a respectable period, then leave after more handshakes.

I saw no sign that Splice and Pyro were being brought bribes or payments. People just wanted to register respect. Just as in Rome a great man holding public office will receive clients, supplicants and friends in the formal rooms of his pillared house at set hours every morning, so these two lice allowed fawners to assemble at their table on a daily basis. Nobody handed out presents, though it was evident that this was a favour-exchange. On one side, reverence was being offered in a way that made me bilious; on the other, the enforcers promised not to break the supplicants' bones.

Passers-by who did not choose to stop and grovel used the far side of the road. There were not many.

I had positioned myself outside a booth selling locks. Unfortunately, as I pretended to peruse the intricate metalwork, I was standing in full sun. Only I could land myself a job in a province famous for its chilly fog on the one week in a decade when the heat would make a sand lizard faint. My tunic had glued itself to my body right across my shoulders and all down my back. My hair felt like a heavy fur rug. The inner soles of my boots were wet and slippery; a boot-thong that had never given trouble before had now blistered my heel raw.

While I stood there, I was pondering a complication: Petronius. Had I been working alone, I would have returned to the procurator's residence to request a posse to arrest Splice and Pyro and search their base. I would then have held the thugs incommunicado for so long that some of their victims might be reassured enough to speak out. The governor's enquiry team, his rough *quaestiones,* could meanwhile have played with the enforcers, using their nastiest instruments of coercion. The interrogators, who must be bored out here, were trained to persist. If Splice and Pyro felt enough pain and found their isolation too terrible, they might even scream out the name of the man who was paying them.

It seemed a good solution. But I could still hear those terse words from Petronius: *leave it, or I'm a dead man.*

Whatever he was doing, we had been wrong to suspect flirtation or debauchery. He was working, the devious hypocrite. He was under cover somehow. On what? The Verovolcus case had clearly intrigued him, though I failed to see the draw myself; I was puzzled by it, but I was only pursuing the issue out of loyalty to Hilaris, Frontinus and the old King. Petronius Longus had no such ties. I had no idea why Petro should get involved. But if he was watching these two bullies, I would not move against them before consulting him. That was a rule of our friendship.

I was still fretting over this when a passer-by who did not know the local respect system came tripping along: my sister Maia. What was she doing? Unaware of the two enforcers, she walked straight past the Ganymede on their side of the street. That meant I had no chance to warn her off, or ask why she was here. Wanting to stay unobtrusive, I could only watch.

Maia was striking to look at, but she had grown up in Rome. She knew how to pass safely through streets full of obnoxious types. Her walk was quietly purposeful and although she looked briefly into every shop and food place, she never met anyone's eye. With her head and body wrapped in a long veil, she had disguised her private style and become unremarkable. One man did lean over a rail and say something to her as she passed – some mutt who on principle had a try at anything in a stola – but as my fists balled, that chancer was treated to such a savage look he shrank back. He certainly knew he had encountered proud Roman womanhood.

Mind you, my sister's self-possessed disdain could itself attract attention. One of the men with Splice and Pyro stood up. At once Pyro spoke to him and he sat down again. Maia had by then gone past the Ganymede.

Nice thought: that the enforcers had a noble regard for women! But they just left women alone to avoid attracting the wrong public notice. Gangs who work through fear understand, if they are efficient, that normal life should be allowed to flow through the streets unhindered. Some even go so far as to batter a known rapist or threaten an adolescent burglar, as a sign that they represent order, men who will protect their own. This implies they are the *only* force of order. Then the people they are threatening feel they have nowhere to turn for help.

They had finished their lunch. They stood up and left. As far as I saw, there was no attempt to offer them a bill. Neither of them left money anyway.

I followed them around for the early part of the afternoon. From place to place they went like election candidates, often not even speaking to people, just making their presence felt. They did not appear to be collecting. That would be better done after dusk. More worrying, and the wine bars would have more cash in the float.

Soon they returned to the Ganymede and this time went indoors, no doubt for a good Roman siesta. I gave up. I was ready for home. My feet were taking special care to remind me how many hours I had been out walking. When I saw a small bath house, the feet headed that way on their own. I stopped them when I spotted Petronius Longus already on the porch.

I was desperate to talk to him. I wanted to discuss the gangsters, and I had to tell him of his children's deaths. But I took his warning to heart.

So far he had not noticed me. I stood still, in what passed for a colonnade – hardly what Rome would know as a grand arcade. Petro made no move to enter the baths, but stood talking to a ticket-man who had come out for air. They seemed to know each other. They looked up at the sky as if discussing whether the heatwave would persist. When new customers drew the gateman indoors, Petronius settled down on a small bench outside as if he were a fixture at the baths.

This street had a slight curve and was so narrow that by crossing over to the other pavement I could walk up close, keeping tight against the wall, without Petro seeing me. His back was slightly turned in any case. A neat bank of cut furnace logs, nearly four feet high, was stacked – blocking the pavement of course – on the bath house boundary. This made the road almost impassable but formed a tiny free area outside the premises next door. The baths were unnamed, but the neighbouring hovel had a painted sign with red Roman lettering, calling itself the Old Neighbour. I passed the open door and saw a dark interior whose purpose was undetectable. It looked more like a private house than a commercial property, despite the sign.

Whatever it was, it offered me a handy broken stool on which to lower my tired body only a few feet from Petronius; now I could try to attract his attention. It would have been ideal, but just as I dropped out of sight preparing to cough loudly, I saw my damned little sister again, approaching from the other direction. She stopped dead just as I had done. Then being Maia, she threw back her stole and marched straight up to Petronius, who must have seen her coming. I huddled up to the furnace logs. If this was a romantic assignation, I now had no way to leave without giving away my presence.

But my sister's manner had already told me that Petronius was not expecting her. Maia had had to brace herself to come and speak to him, and I knew why.

XXII

'LUCIUS PETRONIUS!'
    'Maia Favonia.'

'You want to tell me to get lost?'

'Would it work?' Petro asked drily. Maia was standing, facing my way. I had to keep down low. Luckily she was not tall. 'Maia, you are not safe here.'

'Why; what are you doing?' That was my sister all over: crisp, blunt, brazenly curious. Part of it came from motherhood, though she had always been direct.

'I'm working.'

'Oh but surely the vigiles have no jurisdiction in the provinces!'

'Exactly!' Petro broke in harshly. 'Shut up. I'm out of bounds. Nobody must know.'

Maia lowered her voice, but she would not let go. 'So were you *sent* here?'

'Don't ask.' His mission was official. Well, the bastard kept that quiet! I heard my own intake of breath, more angry than surprised.

'Well, I'm not interested in that. I have to talk to you.'

Then Petronius changed his tone. He spoke quickly, in a low, painful voice: 'It's all right. You don't have to tell me. I know about the girls.'

I was so close I could sense Maia's tension. That was nothing to the emotion I could sense in Petronius. Somebody local came walking up the road. 'Sit down,' muttered Petro, clearly thinking that by standing in front of him, agitated, Maia was attracting attention. I thought I heard the bench legs scrape. She had done as he said.

After the man had passed, Maia asked, 'How long have you known?' The acoustic had changed. I had to strain to catch what she said. She was more obviously upset, now that it was out in the open. 'Did a letter reach you?'

'No, I was told.'

'Marcus found you?'

'I did see him earlier.' Petronius was talking in staccato sentences. 'I didn't give him a chance. I suppose that's why he's been searching for me.'

'We all are! So who did tell you?'

Petro made a small sound, almost laughter. 'Two little boys.'

'Oh no! Not mine, you mean?' Maia was angry and mortified. I felt no surprise. Her children had been fretting over where their hero was; they knew about the tragedy; they were an outgoing group who readily took independent action. Petronius stayed silent. Maia finally said ruefully, 'So much for telling them not to bother you . . . Oh I am so sorry!'

'They caught me right out . . .' Petronius sounded remote as he began to talk, in the way of the bereaved, needing to recite how he had learned his dreadful news. 'I had already spotted Marius. He was sitting on a kerbstone, looking depressed. Ancus must have wandered away from him and he saw me —'

'Ancus? Ancus told you?'

Petro's voice softened, though not much. 'Before I could growl at him to scarper, he ran up. I just thought he was pleased to see me. So when he climbed up on the bench, I put an arm round him. He stood here and whispered in my ear.'

Maia choked slightly. I was stricken myself. Ancus was only six. And Petronius would have had no idea what was coming. 'You were never supposed to hear this from children.'

'What difference does that make?' Petronius rasped. 'Two of my girls are gone! I had to know.'

Maia let his outburst quieten. She, like me, must be worried what young Ancus had blurted out, because she made sure Petronius was given the details properly: 'This is it, then. You have lost two; we were not told which, stupidly. People are trying to find out for you. Chickenpox. My guess is that it happened shortly after you left Italy. The letter didn't say.'

'I must have caught it myself when I said goodbye to them. I infected yours,' admitted Petronius. 'I blame myself . . .'

'They survived.'

'*I* survived.' He was not the type to say he wished he had died instead, though it sounded close. 'Just so I would have to live with this!'

'You will, Lucius. But believe me, it's hard.' My sister, who like most mothers had seen a child die, spoke bitterly. There was a silence, then Maia repeated, 'I am sorry about the boys.'

'It was all right.' Petronius was not interested in her apology. 'Ancus told me, then Marius arrived and they sat down one each side of me and stayed there very quietly.' After a while he added, forcing some kindness into his voice, 'And now you are sitting with me quietly.'

'I lost my first daughter. I know there is nothing else I can do for you.'

'No.' I had rarely heard Petronius so defeated. 'Nothing.'

There was quite a long silence.

'Do you want me to leave?' Maia asked him.

'Are you ready to go?' From his hostile tone, I guessed Petro was hunched motionless, staring ahead bleakly. I had no idea what Maia was doing. I had never seen my sister comfort the bereaved. Especially someone she had at least briefly wanted in her bed. That no longer seemed relevant – and yet she had persisted in the search for him. It was the old Didius affliction: she felt responsible. 'I have to do this mission,' Petronius explained, in a well-mannered, meaningless tone. 'I may as well finish. There's nothing else for me.'

'You do have a daughter left!' snapped Maia. 'And there is Silvia.'

'Ah, Silvia!' A new note entered Petro's voice. He showed some feeling at last, though it was not clear whether his ruefulness was a comment on his ex-wife, himself, or even Fate. 'I think she may want us to get back together. I already detected it when I saw her at Ostia. That boyfriend she took on is a loser, and now –' It poured out, then he stopped himself. 'Now we have a child to console.'

'So what do *you* want?' Maia asked him quietly.

'I can't do it! That's the past.' He would know how many men had decided to stand firm in such a manner, only to be dissuaded. Pain and conscience were lined up to entrap him. His surviving daughter's tearful face would haunt him.

'Then Silvia has lost out all round.' I was surprised my sister could be so fair. It had even been she who had reminded him that Arria Silvia needed him.

'You think I should?' Petronius demanded brusquely.

'I won't tell you what I think. This is for you. But –' Maia had to add – 'don't make a mistake out of guilt.'

Petronius gave a small snort of acknowledgement. If it helped him make his decision, he was not revealing his thoughts. He had always been tight over his personal life. When we shared a tent in the army, there were things he could not hide from me, but since then I had had to guess. He kept his feelings to himself; he thought restraint would help. Maybe that had in fact contributed to problems when he was living with Arria Silvia.

Maia must reckon she had done all she could. I heard movement. She must have stood up again. 'I'll go now.' He said nothing. 'Take care.'

Petronius stuck to the bench but he must have looked up. 'So, Maia Favonia! I understand the boys. But why did you come?'

'Oh . . . you know me.'

Another short bark of humourless mirth came out. 'No,' replied Petronius, his voice blank. 'I don't know you. You know damn well that I wanted to – but that's all over, isn't it?'

My sister left him.

When Petronius leapt up abruptly and went inside the baths, I prepared to leave too. I should have gone after him. He was suffering. But explaining my presence would be too difficult. I had never wanted him to join up with my sister, nor her with him, but I was troubled by the scene I had just overheard.

As I stood undecided, a third party intervened.

'*Please!*' A sudden muffled whisper almost evaded me. 'Please, Falco!' I was in no mood for intrusions. Still, hearing your name somewhere you don't expect it always makes you react.

I stepped out into the road and looked up. Above me, at a window in this dump that was called the Old Neighbour, I saw Albia's white face. She did not need to explain she was in bad trouble. And she was appealing for me to get her out of it.

Now I myself was trapped. I had never heard Albia speak before. She was clearly terrified. I had brought her out on to these streets today. Helena Justina had promised her refuge, yet I put the girl back in danger. There was nothing for it. I had to enter this dark, no doubt unfriendly house and fetch her. The old Didius affliction had kicked in again. Albia was my responsibility.

XXIII

THE MOMENT I set foot across the threshold, I knew what the house was. The entrance corridor was still empty. A small shabby side table, holding the door open, impeded my path. Somewhere to leave your hat − if you wanted it stolen. On it a cracked and filthy dish dared to request gratuities. There were none. Not even the usual broken *quadrans* to give people the right idea. Only some joker's present of a rusty nail.

The front of the house must have been designed as a shop, but the Roman-style folding doors on the frontage were jammed closed and seized up. I glanced in through an archway. It was untenanted and used only for storage of rubble and old horse bedding. Whatever went on here would go on upstairs. Cautiously I moved down the interior passage towards a shadowy stair flight going up into darkness. Underfoot was a pressed earth floor. I knocked into a piece of broken furniture. Part of a cupboard. I was treading slowly, so I had time to steady it at the cost of a wood splinter in my right palm. I managed to muffle the noise. Above, there must be at least a couple of rooms. That would be standard for a live-in shop. Though I listened, I could gain no sense of how many occupants might be there.

The stairs were wooden. As I climbed, they swayed and creaked as if the house was unsound. Dirt made this ramshackle property seem old, though it could not predate the Rebellion. Good going: derelict after ten years. The roofspace must be low; heat had been absorbed all day through the building fabric, so I moved upwards into a stifling, airless atmosphere. The first loft-like space formed an antechamber, definitely used for the purposes I feared. Though the pallets on the floor were unoccupied, a faint sexual smell told its story. I tripped over a lamp, unlit of course. Anyone who wanted to inspect his bedmate would have to pay for extras. I bet no-one bothered. The only light filtered up from the stairs; there were no windows.

I could hardly breathe. Commerce here must be rapid. To call it a brothel would be a linguistic outrage. This was a doss to which rank street-whores brought their undiscriminating marks. It was a toss-up which party in the grim couplings would be the rougher character, and whom cheated who the most. I knew there would be violence. I could believe there had been deaths. I had to pray there was no pimp asleep now, with his arms around an amphora and a large knife to hand. He would see me before I was aware of him.

By feel, I discovered two doorways. I worked out which one gave on to the room with the window where I had glimpsed Albia. The door had been wedged on the outside, locking her in. I was not surprised.

Quietly I removed the heavy wooden stave that held the door closed. Even more gently, I pushed my way in. Light filtered through the window but I could hardly see where she was. She had cowered in a tiny ball, even though she knew I was coming. I assumed she trusted me, yet terror had her paralysed.

I gave a low whistle. 'Come on. You're safe. Be quick.' It was like freeing a trapped sparrow. First the creature froze, then it made a desperate bolt for the light. 'Shh!'

The girl had fled right past, barging her way between me and the doorpost. She had already spirited herself down the stairs. I let her go. As I turned to follow, the other door burst open. There was suddenly more light, a frightfully smouldering lamp, held aloft by a three-foot-high old baggage with ferocious bad breath and a vicious snarl. I think it was female, but I felt like a hero who had woken some foul mythical beast. 'What do you want?'

'I came for a girl,' I answered honestly. I pulled the door to behind me, as if Albia might be still inside. 'I saw her looking through the window.'

'Not that one.'

'I like them young.'

'Not her!'

'Why not?'

'She's not trained.' Well, that was a relief, mainly.

'I can handle her.'

'I said no!'

The old woman was ghastly. A huge round face with features slammed on as if by a bad potter after he'd had too much to drink with his lunch. Flabby white arms, tremulous fat in the body, oily grey hair. Her flat dirty feet were bare. On a cord at her waist hung a bulging purse. She was wrapped in layers of grimy rags, their stiffened cloth twisted like cheese wrappings all around her body. This swaddling seemed to have trapped in dirt, flea droppings and smells. She was marinaded in filth. And the evil madam oozed with redolence of her foul trade.

'Why not?' I insisted. 'What's so special about that one?'

'The Collector only brought her in today.'

'Who's the Collector? I'm sure he's reasonable. Can I speak to him?'

'Gods, where were you spawned? He won't see *you*. Get out,' she ordered.

Pretending to be a polite innocent, I replaced the heavy wedge that had held the door. 'Can I come back later?'

'No!' yelled the human fungus.

Knowing I still had to find the girl, I refrained from any retort and left quietly.

Albia was in fact waiting. As I came out half suffocated into the pleasant air, she whimpered. She had not been visibly beaten though they had stripped her; she shivered in a torn undergarment, yet was clutching the blue dress the Hilaris children had found for her, now folded into a tight parcel which she gripped to her bony chest. Her only possession in the world. Her first decent experience. Maybe the sole reason why she did trust me.

I nodded her to come with me. We moved to the porch of the bath house, where I paused to clear my lungs; I need to cough heavily or I would retch.

'You stink, my girl.' I had been in the brothel for only a moment, but I felt I stank myself. I could wait. There was a decent baths back at the residence, but I needed to make Albia presentable before I returned her to Helena's care. I had to do it for my own sake. 'We're going home. It's over now. Better get cleaned up first.'

Petronius was lounging beside the attendant's booth. Since he was on watch, I ignored him; that was the rule.

It was men's hour at a one-sex-at-a-time baths. There was no way I could send Albia through, and I was certainly not taking her. I persuaded the attendant to give me sponges and a bucket of warm water then we put the girl in the changing room to wash herself. There were no customers in there at the lockers and at least it saved me having to worry about her slipping away through a back entrance.

'If she steals any clothes –'

'She won't.' She had her prized blue dress.

A bench ran around the vestibule where tickets were sold. Two young women were seated there, massaging almond oil into their fingernails. They were respectably dressed, with shiny, well turned-up hair and good postures, yet they gave the impression they were prostitutes. Girlfriends often sit around in pairs, dressed alike, of course, so maybe I slandered them. They seemed to be hanging around on spec, but did not make a pitch even while I was idly awaiting Albia. After watching my negotiations in silence, they both stood up and left.

I walked back out on to the porch again, giving Petro the chance to stroll out quietly after me.

'What's going on?' he murmured.

'Helena's protégée.' We stood side by side, looking at the street, and spoke matter-of-factly as if we were strangers exchanging polite words while one of us waited for a friend. 'I have something to tell you, Lucius.' I had to pretend not to know about Maia. 'It's about your family –'

'Skip it. I know.'

'Ah . . . We're heartbroken for you. They were lovely girls.'

Petronius said nothing. I could feel him enforcing tight self-control. In the end he muttered, 'So what brings you here?'

I could play it that way. I wanted his advice. 'I think I've just barged into a child prostitute racket.'

'You stole that girl out of the brothel, Falco? That could be foolish.'

'Helena is sheltering the sad scrap. She was mine in the first place.'

'Tell them that! Did they see you?'

'Afraid so. They call it the Old Neighbour. I just met the old neighbour's mummified grandmother.'

'She'll make a vicious enemy,' Petronius warned.

'I can handle it. You've noticed her?' His reply was a grunt. 'Who's the Collector?' I asked.

Petronius gave me a sharp look. 'Pimp who collects new bait.' He paused. 'Dangerous.' After a moment, he told me the full rubric. 'You know how it works. They prey on vulnerable girls. The Collector's on the streets picking them up. Takes them in, rapes and batters them, makes them believe they are worthless, pretends they have no option, fits them up in some drab hole and then works them to death. Only management profit. The punters are charged, overcharged, and robbed. The old bag keeps the new flesh in her filthy claws until it's submissive then the pimp runs the girls until they drop.'

I exclaimed angrily. I tried convincing myself Albia had not been part of this trade previously. When they kidnapped her she knew what was coming, but she took her chance to appeal for help and I got to her just in time.

'So,' I demanded slowly. 'Longus, my old mucker, are you on observation over the vice game?'

'I am on obbo,' he agreed tersely.

'Vice?'

'Vice. And everything else.'

'Do I dare to ask how come?'

'No, Falco.'

'Did you join the Ostia cohort?'

'Doesn't work that way. The Ostia vigiles are not a separate cohort. Ostia is covered by out-stationed members of the Rome regulars; the cohorts provide them on rotation. I'm still with the Fourth.'

'So is it Rome or Ostia that has taken an interest in Britain?' I asked drily.

'Both, Falco.'

'And the governor does not know?'

'I believe not.' Petro's note of uncertainty was rhetoric. He knew all right.

'You are not supposed to be here. What are the vigiles up to, stretching their arm overseas? And secretly?' It must be a secret. If the Prefect of Vigiles asked permission to send men here, the answer would be negative. The army dealt with everything in the provinces. The governor held sole authority; Frontinus would be outraged by this sly manoeuvre. Even supposing Petro's superiors had sent him – and I assumed they had, since they knew where to write to him – if he were caught here working they would disclaim any knowledge of the mission. Arrest would be the least of his problems with Frontinus. 'I'll ask again, you reprobate: how come?'

Petronius was standing with his arms folded. I could sense a new dark mood in him yet he was still himself. Big, generally placid, shrewd, capable, dependable. A pity about his rebuff to my sister, in fact. A shame about her previous rebuffs to him.

'You're playing the muscle at this bath house?' I guessed. 'But that's a cover?'

'I'm looking for someone,' he admitted. 'Maybe two men. We know one came out to Britain for sure, and the other's gone missing from Rome. There are henchmen involved too, but the operation is to catch the big pair.'

'You're talking about a major gang?'

127

'Yes, real bastards. They caught attention in Ostia, though Rome is their base. We think they have targeted Britain as a new regional market. They have put managers in place, a whole development team, and it looks as if the leaders are currently over here setting things up. So I'm here too.'

'You and how many?'

'Me,' he said. 'Just me.' I shivered; maybe he did too.

'Pigshit, Petro.' At that point I did turn and look at him. 'This is a doomed errand.' Petronius Longus, a man of quiet intelligence, did not disagree. 'I am with you if you want,' I then commented. He could respond, or dump my offer.

'Your presence in this godforsaken province,' Petronius confirmed ruefully, 'was the sole benefit when I took the job.'

'Thanks for that.' I stared back at the street again. 'I suppose I must not say you could have bloody well told me.'

'That's right,' returned Petro. 'Don't say it.'

Who knows what he was thinking, the rogue? At least he seemed pleased that we were now talking. I was pleased myself.

'Why you, though?' I asked.

'I know Britain. And it's personal.' I was surprised. Petronius Longus was more self-collected normally. 'I want to get one of the principals.' His voice was dark. 'I've been watching him for a long time.'

'And there's another out here?'

'New partner. A man we have never identified. We know he exists, but he has kept his face hidden. I'm hoping to put a name to him while I'm here. He should be visible – a Roman setting up an elaborate crime network of a type that never existed in Britain before.'

'And what about the one you want?'

'He could be anywhere – but I believe he's here with his partner.'

'And who is he?'

Petronius thought of telling me, then for some reason kept his own counsel. My work had rarely ventured into the gangland

128

world; presumably the name would mean little. 'So long as it's not bloody Florius this time.'

'What a joker you are, Falco!' Petronius clapped my shoulder and then smiled sadly. Florius had been the useless husband of his ill-chosen young lover, Milvia. Milvia came from the worst background. Her dead father had been a major racketeer; her mother still was. If anything, she was more criminal than the father. Florius, her pathetic husband, didn't count. For Petro, little Milvia was in the past – and we let the subject drop.

'Are you living here?' I asked, jerking my head at the baths.

'No. Across the river. There's a mansio.' An official travel lodge. 'It's not bad. I can see who comes and goes into town.'

'How do I find it?'

'Don't show yourself there, Falco.'

'No I won't – but tell me how to find it anyway.' We were almost joshing in the old way.

'Go over by ferry and it's obvious.'

'I'll remember not to do that.'

'Good. I won't see you then!'

Albia came out. Her idea of cleaning up was feeble but she had replaced her dress, which covered much of the grime. The brothel odours seemed to cling. There was nothing more I could do about that.

Petronius returned indoors. I led Albia back up the narrow street, ducking into the colonnade to be less noticeable. A mistake. Suddenly the witch from the Old Neighbour leapt out at us from a doorway. She had her talons into Albia before I could react.

The girl squealed. It was a scared noise, but filled with resignation. She had been a victim all her short life. Rescue had seemed too good to last.

Disgust thickened my throat again. As the old woman madly tried to drag the girl back to her stinking house, I grabbed some brooms from a besom stall. I don't normally attack grannies but this hag was outrageous and I know when to break rules. I beat at the short, overweight figure, thrashing her furiously while I yelled to Albia to escape.

No good. She was too used to cringing, too used to taking punishment. The cathouse-keeper was hauling her along, partly by one arm, partly by her hair. At the same time, the old woman had managed to disarm me of my brooms. As they scrabbled on the pavement outside a vegetable shop, I began to pelt the kidnapper with anything I could grab: cabbages, carrots, neatly tied bundles of hard asparagus. Albia may have been struck by a flying brassica by accident; she was screaming much louder now.

Time to stop being squeamish. The madam snarled, showing rotten teeth and a wine-stained gullet. I've looked down prettier throats on blood-dripping boarhounds. I jumped on her, got my arm around her neck and pulled her head back while I let her feel that I was now wielding my knife. She let go of Albia. Albia's screams only increased.

An elbow jammed me in the privates with the force of a demolition ram. Heels kicked backwards at me with agonising power as the other elbow took my breath away in a vicious waistline battery. Both hands came back and tried to pull my ears off. Then she gripped me with both legs and fell forwards, her great weight toppling me over too.

I tried to roll sideways. She had all the initiative. I was flummoxed by this huge bundle of stinking fat. My legs were pinioned together by her treetrunk thighs. The knife was some-where under us, not achieving much. I wanted Albia to fetch Petro, but when in the company of racketeers I still had to pretend he and I were strangers. If the girl had only made a run for it I could have gone limp and wriggled free, but I knew she was still nearby, capering in distress. I could hear her strangled little cries.

Deadlocked, the woman and I struggled breathlessly. I had overcome my diffidence about her age and sex. It was like fighting a rank slug that had heaved up from some black lake at the gates of the underworld. As we flailed, her rags loosened so odd ends hung off like long branches of a Stygian weed. She bucked and jerked. I was flung around, but clung to her, digging in my nails. I stabbed one boot into a calf, hard enough to break bone, but I met only flesh and she just growled angrily. Filthy hair strands were whipping in my eyes. I nutted her skull. I don't know what it did to her, but it hurt me.

Suddenly my right arm slipped free. I had lost my knife, but I grappled the woman harder. I pulled her up by the shoulders, then banged her face down on the ground, once, twice, and three times. We were lying in the gutter so I was bashing her against the kerb. I could hear my own grunts of effort.

Without warning the situation changed. Other people had arrived. Abruptly I was pulled away, receiving a barrage of pummelling to subdue me. I saw the old woman being dragged backwards up the road, held by her splayed legs. It was her turn to scream; this was rough handling. After being hauled off her, I had been thrown headlong, though I had recaptured my knife. No use: a booted foot trod briskly on my wrist and pinned it down. There was another foot on my neck, applying just enough pressure to threaten breaking it. I lay still.

'Get up!' I can recognise female authority. I scrambled to my feet.

'What's happening?'

'Don't talk!' That old cliché.

I still had my knife; no attempt was made to remove it from me. No attempt was made by me to use the thing, either – not with a pair of swords pricking right through my torn tunic into my back and a third weapon glittering directly in front, aimed upwards at my heart.

I already knew what to expect; I had heard the voices. A glance around confirmed the worst. Albia had vanished. The old woman was lying out cold, dumped near the brothel. And I was being captured by an efficient gang of well-dressed, dangerously armed young girls.

As they marched me away with them, I saw Petronius Longus on the bath house porch. He was watching my removal with a faint sardonic grin.

XXIV

THE HOUSE TO which I had been taken by the women gladiators seemed small, but I sensed there were quite a few occupants. The room where they dumped me was almost dark. By now it was evening. Faint domestic sounds and smells suggested people were occupied with dinner. No food was brought to me. For informers, starvation was the curse of the job.

They had not bound me, but the door was either bolted or jammed. I stayed calm. Well, so far. No violence had been done to me after the capture. These women were fighters, but they killed professionally – for the winner's purse. If they had brought me here for a reason, it did not seem to be a reason that required me to be dead.

All the same I was wary. They *were* fighters, and there were a lot of them.

When they had reached the entertainment stage of their evening, where some diners might have called up tumblers, witty dwarves or flautists, they had me fetched. The house was stylish. It must contain a dining room; I thought longingly of leftovers. But they were waiting to amuse themselves with me in a small colonnaded garden. I walked there through quiet corridors on level tesserae. From somewhere came the evocative scent of smoking pine cones, used in arena ritual. From somewhere else a maddening hint of sautéed onion, used merely to torture hungry men.

My captors leaned gracefully on the pillars, while I stood centrally like a disgraced child. If they noticed my stomach rumbling, these girls ignored it, proving that gladiators are immured in cruelty. I must have made a sorry spectacle: grimy and bruised, depressed, puzzled, smelly and exhausted. Such qualities are normal in my trade, but a group of female fighters might not see it as colourful. They belonged to a class that was legally infamous, debarred from all rights in society. Informers may be reviled, a subject of satire whose bills never get paid, yet all the same, I was a free man. I was entitled to vote, to cheat on my taxes and to bugger my slaves. I hoped these women on the edge of society would not envy that too much.

I was uneasy for another reason. All men know from puberty that females in the arena are balls-grabbing sexual predators.

To look at, they hid this aspect courteously. Although the two I had first spotted at the baths had had the air of loose women waiting for customers, when relaxed at home the entire group – five or six here currently – seemed like woodland nymphs with nothing on their minds beyond perfecting scurrilous echoes. Laundered white gowns; endlessly combed long hair; manicured toes showing in beaded indoor slippers. You might discuss poems with these beauties – until you noticed their arrogance, their muscles and their healed scars. They were oddly mixed. Tall or tiny, blonde or ebony: good box office variety. One stood out: a girl who thought she was a boy, or a boy who thought he was a girl.

I wondered at first why they were not slung up in chains in a gladiators' barracks. How could they afford to run a pleasant and sizeable house? Then I worked it out. Yes, untried colleagues would be in thrall to seedy *lanistae* in the training schools, but these had achieved independence. These were the successful fighters. The unsuccessful were dead.

'Are you planning to let me go?' I asked them meekly.

'Amazonia's coming.' It was an extremely tall, lean Negress who addressed me first.

'Who's that?'

'You'll find out.'

'Sounds ominous.'

'So be afraid! And who are you?'

'Didius Falco is the name.'

'And what do you do, Falco?' Heavy innuendo made me blink. Or was the innuendo all in my mind? Setting aside the urge to joke that I was just a time-waster who played around with girls, I told them straight: that I worked for the governor and was investigating the Verovolcus death. It seemed best to be honest. They might already know who I was.

They exchanged glances. I could not tell whether it meant they were impressed by my social standing, or whether the name Verovolcus was significant.

'How does it feel to be rescued?' sneered a sturdy brunette.

'It stinks.'

'Because we are women?'

'I didn't need help. I was holding my own.'

'Not from where I was standing,' she exclaimed, laughing. They all chortled. I grinned. 'Well, fair enough, ladies. Let me thank you then.'

'Turn off the charm!' exclaimed the boy who thought he was a girl (or the girl who thought she was a boy).

I merely shrugged at him (or her). 'Do you know what happened to the teenager who was being dragged off by that hag?'

'She's safe.' A neat Greek-style blonde chipped in. She had a nose straight off an Athenian temple peristyle but sounded as common as a harbour whelk-picker.

'Don't frighten her; she's endured enough today. She was under my wife's protection –'

'Then you should have left her with your wife, you pervert!'

Now I was beginning to understand why they had grabbed me: this tough sisterhood had been defending Albia. That was fine – but it was unclear whether they saw me as a victimiser. 'I never tried to make her a child prostitute. I wanted to get her out of it.'

Maybe they realised that. (Maybe they didn't care.) The Greek put her foot up on a balustrade, revealing lengths of superb, wellpumiced leg through an unsewn skirt. The action, apparently unconscious, made me consciously gulp. 'She's with us now.' This would be tricky to explain to Helena.

'Well think again, is my advice. Albia is not a slave. Turning a free citizen into a gladiator unlawfully is serious. You could all end up being butchered with the criminals.' That was the morning event in an arena, when convicts were put to bloody punishment: slash and smash with no reprieve. Each winner goes straight into another fight and the last man is slaughtered by the ring-keeper on the sodden red sand. 'Besides,' I tried, 'You've seen her — she's totally unsuitable. She has neither the build nor the body. I can tell you too, she has no speed, no fighting intelligence, no movement finesse —'

As I ladled on the flattery, from somewhere behind me came an ironic burst of clapping. A voice cried loudly, 'Oh why don't you just add that she has flat feet and bad eyesight and her boobs get in the way?'

Rome! The accent, the language and the attitude plunged me straight back home. Familiarity socked me in the empty gullet. I even felt I knew the voice.

I turned. I had lasted long enough in the confrontation so far to be feeling quite relaxed. That was about to change.

'Amazonia,' one of the girls to my left informed me. At least these tough maidens were polite. When they had finished battering thick wooden posts with practice swords, someone must sponge the sweat off them and put them through an hour of gentle etiquette.

When my eyes found the newcomer, I was stunned. Wide apart brown eyes gazed at me playfully. Amazonia wore white like the others, setting off dark and sultry skin. Her hair was pulled up on the top of her head then fastened in a two-feet-long snaky ponytail; flowerbuds decorated the fastening. I was expecting some haughty and humourless group leader, who had plans to humiliate me. I found a little treasure with a flexible body, a warm heart and a deeply friendly nature. Was this instinctive male recognition of a good bedmate? No. I already knew this woman. Dear gods, at one time in my dubious past I knew her rather well.

She had changed her career since I last saw her, but not much else, I guessed. There were extra fine lines around the eyes and an air of hardened maturity, but everything else was just as I remembered, and as I remembered it was all in the right place. A flash of her eyes said that she remembered everything too. She was a Tripolitanian rope-dancer. Believe me, she was the best rope-dancer you have ever seen, a shining circus acrobat – and equally good at other things. There was no way I would ever be able to explain this chance meeting to Helena.

If the so-called Amazonia was surprised to see me, I doubted it. She must have been listening for a while. Maybe she had known exactly what pitiful captive she was coming to inspect. 'Thank you for looking after him. Everyone – this is Marcus! He's not as gormless as he looks. Well, not quite. Marcus and I are old, old friends.'

I fought back feebly. 'Who thought up the *nom de guerre*? *Amazonia*? Hello, Chloris.'

She did blush. Someone else tittered, though quietly. I could sense their respect. She was clearly their leader – well, I would expect that; there was a time she could have led me through the flowery meadows all the way to Elysium.

'It's been a long time, Marcus darling,' the girl I knew as Chloris greeted me, with a rapacious smile.

Then I felt the deep-down fear of a man who has just met an old girlfriend who he thought was just a memory – and who finds that she's still after him.

XXV

'WELL, WELL! THIS is such a treat!' she beamed. 'Missed me?'

'Why; did I know you or something?' she joked.

'Never noticed that I'd gone,' I riposted stalwartly.

'Oh, I left you, Marcus darling.' If she wanted to think that, fair enough. 'The person I was really leaving was your evil old mother.'

'Now then, my mother's a wonderful woman and she was extremely fond of you.'

Chloris gazed at me. 'I don't think so,' she said, sounding dangerous. Here we go, I thought.

I had been led off to a private bower, strewn with very expensive animal skins. Mostly well crushed, I regret to say. Chloris had always liked plenty of places to loll. Whenever she dropped to a reclining position, her intention was not restful. This room had seen plenty of the action she loved, if I was any judge.

It was stunningly painted with much drama: dark red walls, punctuated with black details. If you dared to look closely, the illustrations featured violent myths where unhappy people were torn asunder or tied to wheels. These pictures were mostly tiny. I did not disturb myself too much by looking at the wildly plunging bulls and maddened victims; it was rash to take your eyes off Chloris.

'What's happened to the teenager?'

'Run off again.' At least Chloris was never a girl to engage in subterfuge. That was the trouble in the old days: she had always

137

liked Ma to know *exactly* what was going on. My mother was shocked, since I wisely never told her anything.

'You let the girl leave?' I showed my annoyance. 'Look, if any of you spot her again, will you haul her in, please? She's an urchin in trouble. Name's Albia. I don't want any harm to befall her.'

'She will probably run straight back to the brothel, little idiot.' Chloris was unfortunately right, I guessed. 'What's your interest, Falco? Is she a witness in your case?'

'The drowned man?' I had not thought of it, though it was possible. Albia had scavenged around the Shower of Gold; she might well know something. 'I never even asked her. No, my wife took her in.'

'Your *wife*?' Chloris shrieked. 'What – some poor bag finally moved in with you? Do I know her?' she demanded suspiciously.

'No.' I was certain of that.

'What's she called?'

'Helena Justina.'

'Helena is Greek. Is she a slave?'

'Only if her noble papa has been telling very big lies for twenty years. He's a senator. I went respectable.'

I knew what kind of raucous reaction that would cause.

When Chloris stopped laughing, she wiped the tears from her eyes. Then she was off again, helplessly. 'Oh, I just can't believe it!'

'Believe it,' I ordered levelly.

My tone stopped the hysteria. 'Don't go pompous on me, Marcus love.'

I gave her a grin. It was fake. Just like a lot of things had been in our relationship. It would be tactless to say I was married now because once she had dumped me, I had at last found true love. Chloris, a demonstrative girl, would probably throw up.

'What about you? What's all this?' I asked.

'I knew how to use a sword.' In her circus act Chloris had had them as balancers, when she was not waving parasols or feather fans. Males in the audience had liked the *frisson* of the swords, though most preferred the fans because it looked as if she wore nothing underneath. I happened to know – because she had told me – she wore leather undergarments to prevent rope burns anywhere sensitive. Her motto was: keep your equipment in good order. I expected she still followed that. 'I wanted a change when I ditched you, darling. I took up fighting professionally. I knew the organisers already; they soon took me seriously. I'm good!'

'You would be.'

A gleam lit her face, half boasting, half invitation. She scrabbled upright on the quicksand of furs then began working off her boots – high, tightlaced items with hard soles for kicking and thick thongs for protection. With her near-transparent feminine white drapery the contrast was unsettling. That had always been the attraction: a petite girlish figure on someone unexpectedly strong. As she wriggled her bare toes, I began to sweat with erotic recollection. Chloris owned feet that were trained to grip ropes and trapezes; she could use them to curl fiercely around pretty well anything . . .

'Tell me about your British set-up.'

'Ooh, Marcus. It sounds as if I'm under investigation.'

'Just curious. Why here of all places?'

'Britain? I heard about it enough from you. We formed a team specifically to come out here. Plenty of bored men, with few outlets for entertainment. Perfect spot. A brand new arena. Best of all, no built-in male gladiator groups, hogging the action and ganging up to stop us working.'

'Who's your fixer, your lanista?'

'Stuff that!'

Wrong question. I should have known. Chloris had always been independent. Being prey to managers, who were ignorant of her skills and who stole the appearance fees, had annoyed her in the circus life too. Having a trainer was really not her style.

'We can train ourselves,' she said. 'We practise every day, and observe each other's progress. Women are damned good analysts.'

'Yes, I remember you used to spend a lot of time analysing what was wrong with me . . . You lead the team?'

'Analysing your faults was too exhausting, darling!' she interposed.

'Thanks. You are the leader?' I repeated doggedly.

'We don't have a leader. But I brought the group together. They listen to me. They know I have the best balance and fitness. And I can do two styles – *retiarius* and *secutor* – plus I'm working up Thracian too.'

I whistled. Not many male gladiators could offer three fighting styles.

'Want to try me out?' she beamed.

'No. I've been thwacked enough for one day.'

'Yes, mummy's boy has made himself all tired and grubby with the fat lady . . . Come here and I'll make you feel better.' Chloris stretched, limbering up for an hour's hard workout on me. The mere thought was dispiriting.

She meant it. She thought that I wanted what she wanted, as women do. You could make a philosophical treatise out of it but I was too preoccupied with staying out of reach. 'Look, I'm appalled to be so feeble, but I'm far too hungry, Chloris. I'm no use to you. I just couldn't concentrate.'

'Oh you haven't changed.' She thought I was teasing. Dangerously, she enjoyed the thought. 'It's make up your mind time!'

'Oh Chloris, surely you're not going to say, *it's screwing me or eating?*'

'Sounds a good choice!' She jumped up and came for me. There was no time even to gulp before she was winding herself around me as only an acrobat can. If I had forgotten what that felt like, memory soon surged back. '– So which is it, darling?' she chortled.

I sighed with what might pass for polite regret. 'Look, I'm absolutely starving. May I have some dinner, please?'

Chloris punched me in the kidneys, though it was a loose, wild swipe that only did partial damage. She flounced from the room. I collapsed, sweating. Then, as I had thought she would, she had a tray sent in to me. I chose my old girlfriends pretty well. There had never been malice in Chloris.

'Later!' she had promised meaningfully as she strode off.

O Mercury, patron of travellers – either get me out of this, or just smite me dead so I don't know that it's happening! In Rome I was Procurator of the Sacred Geese and Chickens. *O Mercury, never let Chloris discover that!* Now I myself was a soft little pullet in my cage, being fattened up. I munched dutifully. I would need my strength.

You don't mix it with a gladiator. Besides, she was a wonderful armful and I certainly knew it. Once I would have let myself be persuaded without a struggle. There was too much at stake now. I had moved on – way, way into another life. Face to face with what was expected from my old self, I felt awkward. I had loyalties nowadays; I had new standards. As Petronius Longus had said to Maia earlier, once you make huge decisions you cannot go back. The shock is the way other people fail to see how much you have altered. After the shock comes the danger. When those people think they know you inside out, you start to doubt yourself.

She must be impatient. I had barely eaten my solitary victuals when a couple of the women came for me.

'Ah Heraclea, he's looking worried again?'

'Yes, I'm scared!' I grinned good-humouredly, as if I thought I was being roped in for a themed orgy. Heraclea and her companion exchanged glances, no doubt aware that Chloris had plans. I could not tell how they felt about it but I knew they would not intervene.

'You're in real trouble,' they promised me. Even at that point apprehension of the deepest kind was called for.

When they brought me back to the enclosed garden area, Chloris was waiting for me. She met me with a beaming smile. She wound herself around me, as she drew me into the garden, promising, 'Have I got a wonderful surprise for you, darling!'

It seemed best to accept the promise with a tolerant smile. That was before she led me around a statue to the centre of the group and I saw just how treacherous a promise it was.

The women were all here. They had fallen silent as Chloris brought me into view, waiting to see what would happen. At the last minute, but too late to alter anything, I had heard another very familiar female voice. I had Chloris hanging off my arm and nibbling on my ear, while I wore an expression that can only have looked like pure guilt. Helena was here.

Albia, who was standing beside her, must somehow have found her and said I was a prisoner. Helena would have fearlessly broached a house full of women. She must have rushed here in a hurry, for she had even brought the children. She had come to try to rescue me – but her eyes told me if she had known in advance about Chloris I would have been left to my fate.

'Well *here* he is!' exclaimed Helena Justina, companion of my bed and heart. She used the sing-song voice that is supposed to reassure small children who are anxious in strange surroundings and who fear a parent has got lost. She was a good mother. Neither Julia, who was sitting on the grass, nor the baby in her arms would sense whatever emotions Helena herself felt. I was really lost now and I knew it.

She did look impressive. A tall dark-haired woman, making conversation with these professional fighters as if she moved among females who were outside society all the time. Like Albia at her side, she wore blue but in several well-dyed shades, the material draped around her body with unconscious elegance. Lapis and pearl ear-rings said she had money; the lack of other jewellery added that she need not crudely flaunt her wealth. She seemed confident and forthright.

'Helena, my soul!'

Her dark eyes fixed me. Her voice was carefully tuned. 'Your children were missing you, Marcus! And here you are like Hercules diverting himself among Queen Omphale's women. Do be careful. Hercules was suspected ever afterwards of too much liking for women's dress.'

'I am wearing my own clothes,' I murmured.

Her glance flicked over me. 'So you are,' she commented insultingly.

Arms wide and screaming with glee, Julia Junilla hurtled up to see me. When I picked up my little thunderbolt she devised a boisterous game of climbing head-first down inside my tunic. It was already a gaping neck-hole where the threads had run in mighty ladders and the braid had torn. This was the final indignity. I just stood and let myself become gymnastic equipment for my two-year-old.

'So!' Helena then exclaimed, her gaze resolutely finding Chloris. 'Have you finished with him? Can I take him home?'

'You've married your mother!' Chloris accused me, not bothering to lower her voice.

'I don't think so,' I said. 'I can handle my mother.'

Tired of being choked, I wrestled Julia back upright. For once, she subsided and lay looking out at the women with her curly head on my shoulder in a way that made her pretty cute. Hands reached to pet and tickle her, amidst oohs and aahs.

The situation changed. Chloris was bright enough to see that her companions had been swayed by the sight of us as a family group; breaking us up would do her more harm than good. 'It's been lovely having you, but you had best run along home now, Marcus.'

Chloris walked us to the door. She did her best to sour the situation further. 'Well, he makes good babies, I can see.' It implied that Helena was just my breeding mare. Neither of us took the bait. 'I hope I haven't caused you too much trouble, Marcus, darling,' she said sweetly.

'You were always trouble.'

'And you were . . .'

'What?'

'Oh – I'll tell you next time we're alone.' Helena was seething,

as she was meant to. 'Now off you go, darling . . .' mouthed
Chloris maliciously. 'Don't be too hard on him, Helena my dear.
Men have to follow their willies, you know.'

Helena Justina then pulled off her best effort. Standing in the
street, she said, 'Of course they do.' She smiled. It was polite. It
showed the power of her upbringing. 'That was what brought him
to me.'

Albia had bent to unfasten Nux, who had been left outside tied to
a wooden post. She threw me a scared look, then let the dog drag
her along well ahead of us.

'Thanks for the rescue.'

'I heard you were kidnapped!' Helena retorted. 'If it had been
mentioned that you had become a willing sex toy, I would not
have interfered.'

'Settle down.'

'Who exactly was that, *Marcus darling*?'

'A crowd-pulling gladiatrix called Amazonia.' I came clean. 'In
a previous career she was a circus rope-dancer.'

'Oh *her*!'

'I always had good taste,' I growled. 'That's why I went for
you.'

Helena Justina, with the full power of her breeding, let it be
known that she was unimpressed.

I felt like a man who had just made a choice. That is always
depressing, for some reason.

No wonder I was feeling low. I was now carrying two tired
children through darkened streets whose ambience I did not trust,
alongside an extremely silent wife.

XXVI

I TOOK THE children to the nursery and put them into their cribs myself. This looked like a ploy. I couldn't help that. Their mother rather pointedly opted out.

I found Helena afterwards, just as I expected, on her own. She was seated in a wrap-around chair pretending not to care. That was an act. She was waiting for me to come and find her. I had made hasty preparations. I even bathed rapidly; never have an argument with a woman when you know she is scented sweetly with cinnamon but you really stink. Lest my clean-up look too calculated, I then rushed off to find her barefoot and I forgot to comb my hair. The eager lover, with the endearing tousled look: tonight I had to throw in every lousy gambit.

I lowered myself to a couch, staying upright with an elbow propped on the end arm. 'Want to hear about my day?'

I kept it brief. I kept it factual. Near the beginning, when I described taking out Albia, Helena interrupted, 'You did not consult me.'

'I did wrong there.'

'You are the man of the household,' she commented sarcastically.

I plodded on with the story. She listened, but never looked at me. '. . . At that point the gladiator girls took me into custody by force. The rest you know.'

I sat exhausted. It felt good to be clean and in a fresh tunic. Dangerous too; this was no moment to relax and nod off. I might as well pass out in the middle of making love. A subject I was not too tired to think about – but a pleasure I would not be given tonight.

When Helena finally looked up, I was gazing back at her peacefully. The love in my expression was natural; she should believe that. I had never known anyone like her. I studied her face, every line familiar from that fiercely jutting chin to the heavy, knitted eyebrows. After we came home she had quickly re-done her hair; I could tell from the new arrangement of the knobbed bone pins. She saw me work that out, wanting to hate me for being so observant. She had changed her ear-rings too. The lapis danglers always made her ears sore; she now wore smaller gold ones.

'Want to hear about *my* day?' Ever the fighter, Helena challenged me.

'Love to.'

'I won't bother you with the tedious round of morning and afternoon duties.' Thank Jove for that.

'I am always intrigued by your wide social range, Helena,' I reproved her gently.

'That doesn't sound like you.'

'No, it sounds like a pompous donkey,' I said. 'But this isn't you either. I suspect you have things to tell me.'

Helena Justina wanted very badly to hurl a cushion in my direction, but she kept her dignity. Her long hands were clasped firmly in her lap, to stop herself. 'Did you find out what those women were doing in the street when they broke up your tussle with the brothel-keeper? Or were you too busy fooling with Chloris to ask any useful questions?'

I felt my teeth set. 'You, however, did ask them?'

'I managed a few enquiries while I was enduring their company.' She did not actually say coldly, *while you were frolicking in the love nest.* 'There is a businessman trying to take over their group. He is being too pushy and they do not welcome it. They work without a manager and they don't want to pay a cut to someone else.'

146

I wondered if this was the gangster Petronius was looking for. 'What's his name?'

'I never asked. All he wants is to exploit them. They know he runs brothels too,' Helena told me. 'So when you tried to help Albia escape they weighed in. They told me you needed them!'

'That's a cheap jibe, from you and them.'

Helena Justina had always been fair. She was silent for a moment, then agreed, 'Albia told me the old woman was horrible.'

'Right.'

'Albia is very upset by what happened. I still have to tice the full story out of her.'

A silence fell. Once Helena would have checked whether I had been hurt, looking me over for blood and bruising. No chance today.

'Anything else to tell me, fruit?'

She managed not to say *don't call me that!* Instead, she pretended not to notice.

'Why did you bring the children?'

'You didn't come home. We all went out to look for you.' Unsaid, was her panic. Rather than mention it to anyone at the residence, she had searched the streets herself. When she met Albia and heard I was in trouble, she must have clutched the children and ran.

'You're crazy, love. Next time tell your uncle and do it properly.'

'They were all still busy at dinner. We had a fascinating group of visitors.' I waited to hear more. 'Norbanus came again, clearly to moon around Maia. I think we all expected that to happen. Maia seemed rather distracted but he took it politely. He behaves like a nice man.'

'I make a distinction,' I observed drily, 'between when you say someone *is* nice – and when you phrase it that he only seems that way.'

'Norbanus appears to be genuine,' Helena said.

'If he's keen on Maia, I hope he is. But it's always possible *he* may be the big mover that Petronius is chasing.'

Helena was too intrigued to fight now. 'Surely Norbanus is too obvious. "Looking for property opportunities", as he claims to be, just shouts that here's a man who could be an extortionist. But if so, he would disguise his interest.'

'You would think so. But such types do like to show their faces at the highest functions. They hover in legitimate circles, fooling themselves that they get away with it. Well, often enough they do.'

'It's there they meet people who have influence,' Helena said.

'And important women! They don't all glue themselves to molls with bright hair and corn-bushels of jewellery. Some hanker for females with fortunes and grand pedigrees. The women seem to go for it. The more glorious a reputation their ancestors sweated for, the quicker it is thrown away. If the Emperor had a daughter alive, she'd be good prey.'

'I'd like to see Vespasian deal with that!' Helena rather admired him. I reckoned the outlook could be dirty.

'So who else came to present themselves to Frontinus and Uncle Gaius this fine evening?'

'More importers wondering if they should be wearing togas – and a lawyer hoping for new clients.'

'If Britain now attracts speculative barristers, it's all over. Civilisation has come – with its misery and expense.'

'He could be the criminal,' Helena insisted.

'He could indeed. Did he have gold rings made of solid nuggets? Was he protected by large men with cudgels? What's his name?'

'Popillius.'

'I must take a look at him.'

'Should that not be a job for Petronius?'

'Why should he have all the fun? If I think this partygoer looks promising, then I'll shove Petro in the right direction.'

'You know best.'

'Don't be like that.'

There seemed to be no more to say. I confessed that I was deeply weary and must go to bed. Though on the surface we had talked normally, Helena gave no sign that she was joining me.

When I reached the door I turned back and said quietly, 'I have never talked to anyone the way I do with you.' Helena said nothing. I had made it worse. 'I did nothing wrong. I'm sorry if you think I did.'

I had known how she felt. This was when she finally started showing it. 'Well, Falco. The point is, we both know that you might have done.'

I could say nothing. The matter had been settled by her presence. But if Helena had not intervened – who knows?

Alone in bed, for hours I barely slept. Eventually I roused groggily from light slumber and felt sure Helena had crept her way into the room. She had silently occupied a distant chair. Though it came with a footstool, a faint glimmer through the open shutters told me she was bunched up, hugging her knees. By now she must have realised how uncomfortable that was, but when my breathing changed she stopped fidgeting.

Well she was here. But that was unavoidable. We were staying in someone else's house. There were scores of rooms to go off to if you quarrelled with your husband, but also scores of gossipy slaves making forays everywhere. Helena would be embarrassed if anyone should know our current state.

'Come over here.' It sounded more angry than I meant. No answer. Was I surprised? Next time I judged the tone better: 'Come to bed, love . . . I'll have to come and get you then.'

She would not accept that. Slowly she shuffled over and climbed in. Relieved, I fell asleep momentarily. Luckily I woke again.

'Snuggle up with me.'

'No,' she said, on principle.

With a grunt I rolled over and captured her, folding her in a chaste, fully clothed embrace against my heart. 'This is all over nothing, love.'

Men might argue, such occasions always are. Women would say that arguments over nothing are in fact over everything.

So we lay there, Helena still rigid and resisting. She was right to some extent. Even then as I nursed her through her misery, I was thinking about another woman – so in one sense I did betray her. How could I not remember, though? Chloris and I had dallied in lust and it had ended badly, all before I ever dreamed of meeting anyone like Helena. Had I not then happened to come to Britain, when Helena Justina happened to be over here, she and I never would have met.

I was a man. When I encountered an old girlfriend, I became romantically nostalgic (do women not do this?) But it was Helena I was holding in my arms tonight and I had no wish to change that.

At last I stopped reminiscing. Before I drifted off to sleep, I thought about a woman fondly for a little longer. That time if anyone was betrayed, it was not Helena.

XXVII

In THE MORNING the fight still lay like heavy wet flock all around us. Helena rose by herself, made a brisk toilet, and ate breakfast in our room. That was to avoid prying questions at the communal buffet. She offered me nothing, but left enough on the tray if I wanted it. Sulking, I chose to go down to the dining room.

Maia had obviously heard about Chloris. She was on good form. 'I always thought she was an evil little cow. And now she's in the arena – that's a disgrace. You'd let a woman like that threaten all you have nowadays? So how would you feel, Marcus, if Helena Justina divorced you?'

'Dumb question!' The tray upstairs in private became increasingly alluring; too late. I plucked a roll from a basket and sank my teeth into it.

We were hardly heading for divorce. Mind you, all Helena and I had done in order to call ourselves married was to choose to live together; to end it, she only had to leave me. Roman law is extremely reasonable on these issues. Unreasonably so, many a client of mine would say.

My sister smirked self-righteously. 'I thought we were shot of that schemer years ago. Don't tell Mother that you saw her.'

'Get this straight. Chloris is past history, Maia. I'll leave you to break the news to Ma about your slimy new beau, the music lover!'

'He has invited me to his villa, down river.'

'What a terrible chatting-up line.'

'I may go.'

'You may regret it then.'

Helena entered the dining room, smart and ready for action. No glance passed between her and Maia; some women plunge into heart-searching with their girlfriends when they are distressed, but Helena shunned feminine conspiracy. That was why I liked her. She brought her problems to me: even when I was the problem. 'I have been thinking, Marcus. You ought to talk to Albia about how Verovolcus died. She was always hanging round bars; she may have seen something.'

'Good idea.'

'I shall come too.'

I knew when to accept matrimonial help. 'That will be nice.'

'Don't fool yourself,' she said, ever honest. 'I am watching what you are up to.'

I quirked up an eyebrow playfully. 'All day?'

'All day,' she confirmed soberly.

I smiled and turned back to Maia. 'By the way, I saw Petro yesterday.'

'Lucky you.'

I could tell that Helena thought I had just made it more likely my sister would be wafting down the River Thamesis for pastries and heavy seduction attempts at the Norbanus villa.

I now noticed that Maia's son Marius had been sitting under a side table feeding his dog. The look he gave me was inscrutable.

Where was my own dog?

'I gave Nux to Albia to comfort her last night,' Helena said.

'You read my thoughts, Helena. Better face it. We think the same way; we're a pair.'

'Oh I know that!' she roared. It caused consternation among the slaves mopping a corridor. I managed a good kick at their water bucket as we walked past. 'Marcus — try deciding what you want in life, so we can all get on with it.'

I stopped dead and spun her around to face me. The wet tiled floor made her skid slightly and I had to grab her hard. 'I was captured. Nothing happened. Don't waste effort wondering what I might have done. Here I am.'

Helena scowled. 'That's easy to say when you are safe here. What happens when you vanish into the stews and slums?'

'You have to take that on trust.'

'Trusting you is rather tiring, Marcus.'

She did look worn. She had two young children, one still being breast-fed. Our attempt at taking on a nursemaid had been more trouble than not having one. There had been some respite for her here at her aunt's house, where there was practical help, but all the time she knew – indeed I knew too – that we would be going home to Rome soon. Our endlessly demanding children would once again be all ours, and when I went out working she cared for them alone. If anything ever happened to me, Julia and Favonia would be her sole responsibility. Our mothers supported her – whilst causing more stress by bickering with each other. Ultimately, Helena spent a lot of time by herself, wondering where I was and what danger I was in.

Helena was worldly. She knew any man could stray. As soon as she saw Chloris she must have thought my day had come.

I did admit, it must have looked as if I thought that too. I could hardly blame Helena. How was I to foresee that M. Didius Falco, infamous lad about the metropolis, would end up being a good boy?

Albia was skulking nervously. Do not imagine that rescue from brutal prostitution had made the girl grateful. In the part of my life I never talked about, I had been an army scout. During close contact with the enemy, as the tribes were then, I had had a few dealings with the boot-faced element of British society. The don't-know, not-heard-of-that, never-saw-anything mob were as active here as in the criminal slums below the Esquiline in Rome and being a conquered people gave Britons special rights in unhelpfulness. Routinely, they made life awkward for anyone Roman, often in very subtle ways. Albia had absorbed all that.

'Albia, you and I need to talk.' As I tackled the girl, Helena was shooing away children. They had clustered defensively around their returned friend; I hoped these innocents had no idea of her adventure with the prostitution ring. Nux, convinced as ever that she was the joy of my heart, left Albia's side and climbed all over me. I had made the mistake of sitting down. I was trying to look non-threatening. When the dog saw I was accessible, she jumped straight up on me. A hot tongue busily licked anatomical crannies that might need a wash.

Albia said nothing.

'Now don't look so afraid.' Waste of breath. The girl crouched on a stool, expressionless. 'Stop it, Nux . . . down, stupid doggie! Albia, the other night –' It felt about two weeks ago, though it was only four days. 'A man was killed. It happened at the Shower of Gold. He was pushed down the well, upside down. He drowned.'

Albia still only gave me the wounded, empty stare of the destitute. Her face seemed whiter than ever, her spirit even more crushed.

'You are safe here,' Helena told her. Nux abandoned me and rushed over to Helena, clambering up on her lap. Helena subdued the dog with the competence she used to control our children. 'Albia, tell Didius Falco if you saw anything that night.'

'No.' Was that saw nothing, or wouldn't tell?

Nux looked from one to another of us, intrigued.

'Were you in the Shower of Gold, or anywhere near it, that night?' I repeated.

'No.' Useless. I was trying to net moonlight.

The more times she denied it, the more I doubted her word. Even if desperate people did not lie, they withheld information. But if they could get away with it, they lied. Truth was power. To keep it gave them a last shred of hope. To pass it on left them utterly exposed.

'Albia!' Even Helena sounded sharp. 'Nobody will harm you if you talk about this. Falco will arrest the men who did it.'

'I was not there.'

Even though Albia was so uncommunicative, I could tell one thing: she was absolutely terrified.

'Well, that was a dead loss.' I tried not to gloat.

'I'm really annoyed with her.' At least Helena did not blame me. 'Albia's a silly girl.'

'She's just scared. She's been scared all her life.'

'Well, haven't we all!' From Helena Justina that was a shock. I stared. She pretended she had not said it.

'Now can I go out to play?' I whined.

'Things to do, Marcus.'

'What things, beloved?'

'Have a look at the lawyer, say.'

'Your friend Popillius?' I hoped in vain for praise that I remembered his name.

'I don't feel friendly towards him, and he's not mine.'

'Good. I can put up with a lot,' I joked, 'but if you run off with a legal man, that's it, my girl!'

'Really?' she demanded in a light tone.

'Oh yes.' I frowned. 'Dearest, you know that I cannot stand lawyers.'

The day was looking up. Popillius was presumably slick – aren't they all in their business references? – but I found him in the act of being fleeced.

Helena had to let me out to conduct this next interview. She came with me, however. I waited patiently while she first fed Favonia; it gave me a chance to make snooty remarks about wishing my daughters to lead a quiet domestic life, not to be dragged out to unsuitable venues as they were last night. That enabled Helena to say she wished I could set them a good example then. Thus sniping, though cheerfully, we steamed off in a morning that was still good and hot, to a small rented house where the lawyer had set up in business. Despite a flamboyant chalked sign outside which promised the best prosecutions north of the Alps and tactful, cheap defence speeches, clients had yet to take advantage of the services he offered. I looked for a no-win, no-fee notice but of course failed to find it.

Popillius sat sunbathing in a courtyard, where he waited for all those people who wanted outrageous compensation for wrongs. While at a loose end, he had been found by a British entrepreneur. A shy-looking hopeful had wandered in from the street. He had tufty hair and wide-apart short legs, and had set out a big flat tray of carved jet jewellery and trifles.

There were more of these jet-sellers than fleas on a cat; there always had been. In reality the soldiers in the legions, wanting presents for their girlfriends, snapped up the best quality stuff while they were up on the frontier. In most parts of southern Britain there was as much chance of buying genuine sea-washed black stuff from Brigantia as of finding real turquoise scarabs beside the Pyramids in Alexandria.

I liked this seller's patter. He owned up that there was fakery in the trade. His cheeky premise was that the best fakes were so good it was worth buying them in their own right. He was promising to let the lawyer corner the market, in the hope he would later make a killing when the fake stuff became openly collectable.

Helena and I watched peacefully. As Popillius set about fetching the cash for his hoard, we parked under what would have been a fig tree if we were in the Mediterranean. Here it was some anonymous bush. Someone appeared to be aware of the concept of shady courtyards with cool pergolas, though if you looked more closely, the yard had been recently used for keeping draught animals. It must have been roughly cleaned up for the lawyer when he wanted to rent.

The jet salesman made a feeble attempt to interest us, indicating that I should buy a trinket for Helena. He could see what a mistake that was. She herself rebuffed him. I waved him away more gently. 'Sorry, pal; left my purse in the bedroom.' He knew I was lying, but he strolled off happily with his profits from the lawyer.

156

Popillius was a clean-cut sandy type. Thirties, maybe. Not quite too young to carry professional weight, but giving the impression he had energy and ambition, as well as his cynical greed for fees. He had a light, upper-crust voice, which was hard to place. A new man quite recently, I would say, maybe with grandparents who made it into the middle class, provincials even. Close enough for the infant Popillius to have heard their tales of backwoods life, and to be sufficiently enthralled to tackle a remote province himself. Either that, or he had absconded with a client's funds and had needed to leave Rome fast.

'This is my husband, Didius Falco,' Helena said. 'I mentioned him last night.' She had not told me I had been discussed. Now I was stuck, not knowing what role she had assigned to me. I grinned, sheepishly.

'Greetings, Falco.' Thank goodness, Popillius himself had no recollection of his chat at dinner with Helena. He was desperately trying to remember who and what I was, though he did remember Helena. Jealousy works two ways: I hoped he did not remember her too well. Lawyers womanise almost as hard as they drink. I knew; I had met plenty in my work.

We talked a bit about what Popillius hoped for in Britain. I suggested he was a slave-chaser, suing people for the return of runaways or for seducing someone else's human property. He reckoned British society was insufficiently slave-orientated to bring in much business of that type. 'There are slaves condemned to hard labour; they simply slog until they die, in remote locations. Domestically, if a household owns a couple of little kitchen workers, that's it. They are far too well treated – they end up marrying the master or mistress. No incentive to run away, and they don't even seem to get laid by the neighbours much.'

'Ah, what you need are big estates where the labour force is money; if a body goes missing, it's a commercial loss.'

'Better still, I need to be able to demand compensation for expensive Greek accountants, masseurs and musicians!' Popillius laughed.

'You have looked into the prospects, then?' I asked.

'Only joking,' he fibbed. 'Bringing a high-class legal service to the province is my mission. I want to do commercial and maritime case-work.'

I told him that was highly commendable. He seemed unused to irony.

'Sorry, Falco – I don't recall what your wife said you do?'

Sometimes I cannot be bothered to bluff. 'Government work. I'm looking into a suspicious death that seems to be gangster-related.'

Popillius raised his light-coloured eyebrows. 'That is surely not why you have come to visit me?' If he was offended, he was working out just how wronged, financially, he intended to be.

'I am looking at everyone,' I assured him gently. 'I hate to disappoint you, but letting me eliminate you from my enquiry won't lead to slander fees!'

Popillius gave me a level, warning stare. 'I don't bother with slander claims, Falco.'

The implication was that if I upset him, he would do for me in much more dangerous ways.

I smiled. 'How long have you been in the province?'

'Just a couple of days.' Not enough to be my suspect – if it was the truth.

'Ever found your way to a drinking dive called the Shower of Gold?'

'Never. I prefer to entertain myself at home, with a well-aged amphora.'

'Very wise,' I said. 'You can buy a good Italian variety, even this far north. Let it settle well. Then dribble it through a wine-strainer two or three times – and pour it down a drain. Table wines from Germany and Gaul seem to survive the route march better.'

'Thank you for the advice,' he replied.

'It's no trouble,' I said.

There was no point hanging around just to discuss his gustation habits. Lawyers are snobs. He was bound to believe in more expensive vintages than I ever thought worthwhile for home consumption with a pan-fried mullet. The grand wines of the Empire stood no chance of travelling well so far as this, but I deduced it would be hard to shake his prejudice.

I could see no sign that he had companions staying here, and if he had only just arrived, what new friends could he possibly have made? So the big question was, when Popillius poured the precious grape of an evening, who shared it with him?

We left, no better and no worse informed than when we came. Slowly we walked back towards the residence. Both Helena and I were mulling over what kind of man this lawyer seemed to be, and what his real quality was. I was paying little attention to our surroundings and less to passers-by.

But I was all there when a familiar voice hissed at me from a doorway: 'Marcus darling, come over here! I must have a little word with you –'

Chloris!

XXVIII

S HE WAS LEANING on a doorframe as if she had been there a long time waiting for me.

'Olympus, you made me jump, you fiend! Are you watching the lawyer's house?'

'What lawyer? I was looking for you, darling.'

Chloris ignored Helena. Helena's gaze was fixed on me.

'What's it about, Chloris?'

'The Briton in the well.'

Anything else could have been brushed aside. This I had to pursue. I turned to Helena, giving her the choice. With an angry shrug, she left me to it. As she strode off alone, a fool might have taken her departure for a sign of trust. Not me.

Chloris looked pleased with herself. 'That was easy!'

'Wrong. Make it quick.'

'We can't talk in the street.'

'Find a bar then.'

'My house is nearby.'

It was not that near 'We'll go to a bar,' I said tersely.

We walked to a food shop, fairly neat and tidy, called the Cradle in the Tree. I obtained the usual unappetising British cold snacks.

We sat on a bench in the street. This was some way from the wharves so I felt we were probably out of the extortionists' patch. Even so, by instinct I checked to see if the proprietor was leaning on the counter above, listening. He had gone inside.

'You look tired,' commented Chloris, who looked immaculate. Arena performers are fit and they know how to present themselves. 'Is your snooty goddess a goer? Rumpled bedclothes all night, was it?'

'Chloris, get on with it.'

'This is no way to approach a witness.'

'Witness to what?'

'The death scene.'

'Oh yes? Look, don't mess me about on this.'

'You just assume I know nothing,' she complained. She could have been nagging me for not paying her enough attention. Well, perhaps she was.

'Right.' I would do this properly. 'I am investigating the death of a Briton called Verovolcus, a visitor to Londinium from a tribe on the south coast. His body was discovered head-first down a well at a filthy mead kennel down towards the river, four days ago. It looks as if he was robbed. There could be more to it. So do you, Chloris, know anything that may help me find his killers?'

'How about, I know who did it?'

'Who?'

'Ask me questions. I'm a witness.'

'You'll be a suspect at this rate – and the questioning will done by the governor's horrible torture squad.'

'I won't talk to them.'

I opened my mouth to say that everyone talked to the *quaestiones*. Then I stopped. She was not boasting.

'They could even kill me,' sneered Chloris. 'But you know all I would say to them would be *Stuff you!*'

'So charming. In that case, they certainly would kill you . . . Tell me then. Were you there that night?'

'Close enough.'

'In the bar?'

'No, but right outside looking in.' There were windows, though I remembered they were small and barred.

'What brought you there?'

'Tailing a man who has been bothering us.'

'He's brave! Name?'

161

'That was one thing I was hoping to find out.'

'Helena Justina told me you are being pressured by an entrepreneur.'

'He won't get us.'

I sighed patiently. 'I know that, Chloris. But then I know you, while he's not so well informed. I'm sure you will make him quite aware of his mistake! He's a Roman?'

'He's a bastard.'

'I deduced that . . . Either help, or shut up. If you just want to tantalise me, I'm off.'

She grinned. 'I'll help. The tantalising comes later.'

'Oh please! Just get on with it.'

Chloris licked her fingers clean and stared up at the blue sky. 'I'll say this for the wife – she knows how to keep him skewered to the home bed!' I said nothing. My food lay uneaten alongside me on the bench. In this company I was not touching stuffed flatbread – or indeed, anything else; I felt a distinct lack of appetite. Chloris continued, as demurely as she did anything: 'The big punter – or he thinks he is – had been at our house nagging us again about letting him take over. We sent him off, then I slipped after. I followed him half across town to that dump, the Shower of Gold. Outside, he had a muffled meet with those other bastards, Pyro and Splice.'

'I've seen them.'

'Pigs,' Chloris denounced them, without much feeling. 'They held a confab then all went inside the joint. I sneaked up close. Soon the Briton came along. He took an interest –'

'In the place?'

'No, dummy.'

'In you? That's Verovolcus. He would.'

'You knew him then, Marcus?' She sounded surprised.

'We had met. That's how I came to be involved in the case afterwards. You shook him off, I take it?'

'He stood no chance.'

'Why not? He had a nice big torque.' That reminded me: I had

162

to find out what had happened to it.

'And a nice big opinion of himself. How could I fall for him, after I'd been with you, darling?' Chloris laughed. 'I may have moaned about you, Falco, but you show up well against a hairy Britunculus any day.'

'Thanks for nothing.'

'Pay me back later . . . He was going into the Shower of Gold, but there was no way I would join him there. I didn't want the big fellow to know I had come after him.'

'But it sounds as if the Briton may have had a pre-arrangement?'

She nodded. 'He said somebody was waiting.'

'What happened when Verovolcus went inside?'

'Not much, for some time. I couldn't see much anyway, the window was too small. I had decided to give up and leave. Then I overheard them all arguing.'

'Listen – would you say that they knew each other prior to that?'

'It seemed so. I could see them all sitting at the same table. Your Briton had gone straight up to them; they were definitely the people he had arranged to meet.'

'Could you tell what they were discussing?'

'No. But Verovolcus was getting the worst of it. There was a lot of talk, then it clearly got nasty. Looked as if Verovolcus was blustering – but he was out of his league. Our mighty would-be manager was running it. He did nothing – just sat at the table – but I saw him give the nod.'

'To Pyro and Splice?'

'Yes.' She paused. Chloris lived at the crude end of society; she had seen much envy and anger in action. Even so, she shuddered when she talked about murder. 'Pyro and Splice grabbed the Briton. It looked as if they had planned it. When their leader gave the signal they picked him straight up, turned him over, and dragged him off out the back. He must have known he couldn't trust that group, but he stood no chance.'

'Of course you couldn't see what went on out in the yard?'

'I didn't need to. They poked him in the well and left him there.

163

Everyone heard about it the next day – anyway, I saw the way they laughed when they came back into the bar.'

'Who took away the neck torque?'

'Pyro, I suppose. He is the swag-carrier.'

'But you're not sure?'

'No, I didn't see for certain.'

'Don't get clever then,' I warned. 'Tell me only what you saw yourself. What happened next?'

'What do you think happened, darling? The bar emptied like magic. Everyone knows what reputation Pyro and Splice have. I lit out of there just ahead of the crowd. I wasn't going to be found spying on that lot. If I didn't know you, I'd be making sure I forgot about it. I know what's good for me!'

I sat quiet.

Chloris had absorbed my mood. 'This is bad stuff.'

'The whole of Londinium seems to be full of bad stuff. Chloris, I need to know about this man, your would-be manager –'

'I knew you would ask.'

'Sorry to be predictable.'

'Ah, you don't change . . .' I had no idea what that meant. 'He's a mystery,' she said. 'He turns up out of nowhere when he wants to have a go at us. We don't know where he's staying, though we know he came from Rome. He has Rome written all over him, and I don't mean the pretty parts. He never even says his name. He demands to take us over – and makes it clear that he'll be very unpleasant if we keep saying no.'

'Can you describe him?'

'He's a nonentity.'

'That doesn't help, Chloris.'

'No – could be any man!' she giggled. 'Don't ask me. I only look at men I might go to bed with, darling.'

'Try, please.'

'He's nothing, Falco. If you passed him in the Via Flaminia you wouldn't look twice at him.'

'So how and why does this unobtrusive bastard get to worry you so much?'

'Silent threat. But I'll get him.'

'Be careful. Leave this to the professionals. I'm here to go after these gangsters – and as a matter of fact, so is my old friend Petronius.'

'Well, I'm chuffed to hear that,' Chloris muttered derisively.

'You remember Petro?'

'I remember the two of you, mucking about like idiots.'

I smiled, but I was thinking hard. 'Chloris, would you be prepared to make a statement about the killing?'

'Why not? For you, I can be a witness.'

'I warn you, if you give us a formal deposition, it will be dangerous.'

'Oh you'll take care of me!'

I would try.

'Is that it, darling?' she murmured. She sounded like a girl who had been let down by a man in bed.

'Unless you can think of anything else helpful?'

'No. So are you coming home with me now?'

'We've had our chat.'

'When was *chatting* any fun?'

'Sorry. I have other things to do.'

She stood up, not pushing it. 'I won't intrude then! Another time . . .'

Chloris could take a rebuff now, apparently. I remembered when my saying no would have been a challenge. But in those days she had known that I really wanted to be won over.

She marched off, swinging along the pavement with the easy stride of a trained athlete. I sat on for a moment.

Suddenly I had a witness. This was not all good news. I could arrest Pyro and Splice when I wanted, and interrogate the pair of them . . . That was all I could do. If they failed to crack, I was nowhere.

I had a witness, sure enough. At least she had described what happened that night. But I could never use her statement. Chloris

165

was a gladiator – legally infamous. Information from her was even worse than information from a slave. If she made us a hundred statements, she could not appear in court. Any good lawyer, especially a crooked one, would have a fine time in his speech for the defence, if someone of her low calling – and female too – was our only source of evidence.

I stood up to leave. The proprietor must have sensed it; he had appeared behind his counter. I wondered how long he had been there, but he did not look like a man who had overheard the story Chloris told. 'Anything else, sir?' he asked me deferentially.

'No thanks.' I had still not touched my food. 'The Cradle in the Tree,' I said, looking up at his sign, where a yellow crib among a few spindly twigs made its faded point. 'That's an unusual shop name!'

He just smiled and murmured, 'It was called that when I took over.'

Names given to food shops were starting to be of some interest to me.

XXIX

WANTING TO THINK, I sneaked back into the residence unobtrusively. Avoiding areas of the house where I might encounter people, I found my way to an upper reception room which had doors on to a long balcony over the formal garden. There I ensconced myself on a long, low sunbed in the shade. I could hear fountains below, and the occasional midday cheeps of hot little sparrows as they splashed in the half-evaporated fountain bowls. With a cool drink, this could have been a perfect way to pass the afternoon. Unfortunately, on my way up here I had not acquired a drink.

The day was so warm, I could have been in Rome. (If only!) You could feel the difference. Too much flower and tree pollen was thickening the air, the scent of August roses was rising from the garden below me, amidst hints of the countryside close by – yet no scent of pines. Too much sense of a big river estuary, with seagulls sometimes calling as they scavenged around the moored ships. Anyone could tell that Londinium was a port. And it felt a foreign one.

The sunbed on which I was lying had dampness in its thin pallet. It had been left in storage until this heatwave was well established, as if people feared the good weather would be fleeting. Garden furniture needed to be mobile in Britain; when people moved out among the flowerbeds below, I could hear the legs of chairs scraping the gravel as they brought equipment and arranged themselves.

It was Maia and Aelia Camilla. I would have slipped indoors, but

I could hear that they had been talking about how Maia found Petronius to tell him about his daughters' deaths. Perhaps that was what had improved their relationship; my sister and the procurator's wife were today gossiping more freely than before. Their voices rose clearly to where I was sitting. I refused to have a conscience about eavesdropping; they should have been more discreet.

'It was a bad moment, Maia – have a cushion, dear – don't blame him for being offhand.'

'Oh I don't. It just seems he deals more easily with my children than with me.'

'You should worry if he can *only* deal with you through your children.'

'Yes. Well, that's me – a mother!' Maia's crisp retort echoed around the enclosed garden. Her voice dropped. 'That is the only way anyone expects to treat me.'

'There speaks a noble matron.' It sounded as if Aelia Camilla had smiled sadly. 'Once we have the children . . . Of course, for a bride with her first husband at least there is a period when you deal with each other as adults. You never quite lose that.'

Aelia Camilla had a batch of children now; there was at least one set of twins. Maia must have done some arithmetic, because she demanded quizzically, 'Your first baby was a long time coming, wasn't she?'

'Flavia. Yes. We waited a few years to be blessed with Flavia.'

'And you never knew why . . .'

'It seemed inexplicable,' Aelia Camilla agreed. Something was going on here.

'So, were you making sure that you wanted to have them?' My sister could be so blunt it was rude.

To my surprise, the procurator's wife took it well. 'Maia Favonia, don't accuse me of devious practices!' She sounded amused.

'Oh I don't!' Maia was also laughing. 'Though I am wondering, does Gaius Flavius know?'

'You won't expect me to answer that.' Aelia Camilla was a clever woman. Her polite manner made her seem stuffy, though I had always thought it was a front. She was after all sister to Helena's father, and Decimus was a man I liked. His diffidence also hid a sharp intelligence. Brought up in our family, Maia had cruder social skills: nosiness, insults, accusations, rants, and that old favourite, flouncing off in a huff.

'So what about you?' the procurator's wife enquired directly. 'Your eldest –'

'My eldest died.' Like most bereaved mothers, Maia never forgot and she had never quite recovered from it. 'I suppose that's why I felt so much for the situation with Petronius . . . I was pregnant when I married. I was very young. Too young. Well caught out.'

They were silent for a while. A paragraph mark in the conversation.

'So now you have four, and you are widowed,' Aelia Camilla summed up. 'Your children are not helpless. I think you have a choice. You could be independent – make time for yourself in the way that you missed as a young girl. You are so attractive, you are surrounded by men who want to take you over – but, Maia, it's not for them to choose.'

'Ditch them all, you mean?' Maia laughed. I was beginning to realise that after Famia died she must have been very lonely. He was useless in many ways, but he had a large presence. Since he was gone, even Helena had probably not talked to Maia like this. Ma might have given her good advice, but what girl listens to her mother over men? 'Norbanus is very attentive,' mused my sister. Impossible to tell whether she was pleased by that.

'Will you visit his villa?'

'I haven't decided.'

'You could take my husband's river boat.' Maia must have looked puzzled, for Aelia Camilla added pointedly, 'Then if you wanted to leave, you would have your own transport.'

'Ah! I'm still not sure whether to go, but thanks . . . There have been others hovering. I got into a serious mess once, back at home.' I heard Maia's voice cloud. She was talking about Anacrites.

Aelia Camilla gave no hint of understanding that this was a reference to Maia being stalked by the Chief Spy. She could well know about it. I was under no illusions. Anyone of my rank arriving in a new province would be preceded by an intelligence brief. For all I knew, Anacrites himself had contributed to mine. My sister, having attracted his vindictiveness, must also be a special-category traveller.

Aelia Camilla was now talking about her husband. 'Gaius and I experienced problems at one time. I don't say we were publicly estranged, but I was very unhappy for a period.'

'It doesn't show now,' said Maia. 'You were a long way from home?'

'Yes, and I felt a very great void between us.'

'So what happened?'

'The usual — Gaius stayed out too much.'

'What — bars, or the Games?'

'Well, I knew there were neither available.'

'Oh, he said it was *work!*' Maia, chortling, knew all about that from Famia.

'Genuine.' Aelia Camilla was loyal. 'He had to travel long distances, sourcing precious minerals.'

'How did you solve it? I gather you *did* solve it?'

'Drastically. I forced him to see that the problem existed: I said I wanted a divorce.'

'That was a risk! Hilaris did not?'

'No. And *I* did not, Maia. Our marriage had been arranged for us by relatives, but it was right. We were in love. Sometimes more, sometimes less; but you feel it, don't you? When it is right.'

'So what are you telling me, Camilla?'

'It made me believe that you should speak out. You cannot trust a man to face up to things, you know. Maia, you could lose him before you even start. There is too much to lose if you drift, thinking everybody understands one another.'

A wicked note entered my sister's voice. 'Are you talking about Norbanus Murena?'

Aelia Camilla chuckled. 'No,' she said. 'Someone else – and you know it.'

Maia did not ask her who she meant.

XXX

THE NORBANUS HARPIST joined them. His twanging would have drowned out their conversation anyway, but they both stopped the gossip. They would certainly not discuss Norbanus Murena; anyone else male was also off-limits. If the tunesmith was meant to carry back news to his master, this shrewd pair had his measure. He was spoiling their fun too.

Helena arrived soon afterwards. I heard her dump a chair amidst the garden party. Annoyance could be detected in the angry scratch of its legs.

'Where's our boy?' scoffed Maia immediately. 'I thought you were guarding my brother all day!'

'He found a friend.'

'Anyone we know?'

Helena made no answer.

I waited a while then stood up. The others had their backs to me, but Helena looked up and saw me as I yawned and waved, making it plain I had been there on the balcony for hours. Perhaps she would feel guilty for doubting me. Perhaps not.

I went to our room and she joined me almost instantly. Nothing uncomfortable was said, and I quickly narrated all that Chloris had told me.

'I've acquired a witness, but one I can't use. Still, if she will make a formal statement, Frontinus may be prodded to make arrests. Maybe if word leaks out that the culprits are in custody, other people will feel safe enough to come forward.'

'King Togidubnus will want to know what that quarrel in the bar was about.'

'I need to know that myself. If Pyro and Splice just pretend they had an argument about a wine bill, that's not enough. I want to tie the Verovolcus killing to extortion. Then Frontinus can stamp on the racket.'

Helena frowned. 'Frontinus will support you, won't he?'

'Yes, though don't forget his initial reaction was to gloss over the problem. I have to prove beyond doubt what is going on.'

'And Petronius is working on the same lines?'

'He is – but Frontinus must not know. If he finds out, Petro will be in hot water.'

'You two!' she scoffed. 'Why can neither of you ever do anything the easy way?'

I grinned. 'Come here.'

'Don't mess about, Falco.' She sounded like me, coping with Chloris.

'No, come here.' I got hold of her. She was too interested in the Verovolcus story to resist. I held her nose to nose. We were peaceful with each other now. 'I love you very much, you know.'

'Don't change the subject,' said Helena Justina sternly, but by then I was kissing her.

I took my time. O reader, go and peruse a very long philosophical scroll for an hour. You damn well don't need to know about this.

Actually, you can come back now. What happened was fairly satisfactory to a man who had been fighting off jealousy all night and morning – but what *might* have happened never did. Instead, we were interrupted by a wary slave of the procurator's, who knocked on the bedroom door extremely shyly, looking for me. It was unclear whether he expected to find a vicious marital tempest or widescale pornography.

'Can I help you?' I asked sweetly. I was fully clad and hardly blushed at all. I had of course spent my youth being caught almost in the act by my mother. I could look innocent in no time. Chloris could vouch for that.

Forget Chloris. (I was now seriously trying to.)

'Message.' The slave chucked the tablet at me and fled.

It was from the customs officer, Firmus. He wanted me to come down to the ferry urgently. Somebody, the message said obliquely, had suggested that I would want to know they had found another corpse.

XXXI

THE BODY WAS still lying on the deck. They were waiting for me before moving it: Firmus, a couple of his juniors, and a man who rowed the ferryboat to and fro on call. A silence fell, as I absorbed the sight. The others, having seen it once, stared at me rather than at the dreadful corpse.

They had fished it out of the river this morning, Firmus said. None of us thought the man had drowned, however. That surprised me. Somehow after Verovolcus I had expected a pattern. But there was no parallel with the well-killing: this man had been battered to death. Someone had set about him with professional cruelty. To judge from the massive injuries he suffered, it would have taken a long time. The beating may even have continued after he had died. There was no foam around the lips, though being in the river would have washed it off. I looked in his mouth and still found no evidence to suggest he had been alive when he was tipped in the water. Firmus, and the ferryman, seemed to find that comforting.

The body had tangled in the ferry; I thought this had happened very soon after its being put into the Thamesis. Death, too, must have taken place quite recently. Only this morning, by the freshness of the corpse. He had had no time to sink properly and had not reached the bloated stage, full of gas. Though less hideous this way, the thought that he had so narrowly missed seeing the killers dispose of the body upset the ferryman more.

The last time I saw anyone murdered with such savagery, it was in Rome. Gangsters had inflicted the battering on one of their own.

This dead man was fifty or sixty, thereabouts. I cannot tell you about his features; the face had been too badly damaged. Of modest build in most respects, he had quite strong arms and shoulders. His skin was ruddy, with no dirt on his hands, which had noticeably clean cuticles and fingernails. Along the inner side of both his arms were old healed marks, which looked like minor burns, the sort you obtain from a brush against a trivet or an oven edge. He was dressed in British clothing, with the neck flap that is common to the northern provinces. Under the blood lay a faint trace of something, a fine grey sludge that had thickened in the seams and braids of his brown tunic. He wore no belt. I guessed his tormentors had removed it and used it as one of the weapons to thrash him, its buckle causing some of those short cuts among his heavy bruising.

'Know him, Falco?'

'Never seen him before –' I had to clear my throat. 'I can suggest who he may be, though. If this mucky deposit all over him was once flour-dust, that's a clue. A baker called Epaphroditus vanished and his shop burned down the other night. It's clear he had upset someone. Someone who must think that depriving him of his livelihood was not enough to punish him – or not enough to scare other people.'

I straightened up and walked over to the still-shocked ferryman. 'What did you see?'

'Nothing. I just felt something binding on the boat. I guessed we had a floater; I rowed in gently and Firmus helped me free it. I've seen plenty, but I've never seen . . .' He tailed off in distress.

'Were you rowing over with a fare?'

His eyes grew wide.

I said quietly, 'If it was the big man who is staying at the mansio, you can speak up.' I knew Petronius Longus must have seen the corpse at some time; the message from Firmus had hinted it was he who had advised fetching me. 'It's all right. He and I are a duo.'

Firmus had been listening. 'He's gone back over there,' he intervened.

I told the ferryman he would do better if he kept working, and persuaded him to take me across to the far side of the Thamesis. As we looped over slowly, first veering upstream and then drifting back, I looked down the wide grey river and thought black thoughts.

The great river marked a geographic boundary. Even the weather seemed different; when we landed on the southern bank, the heat we had felt in the town was less oppressive. Mind you, it was now early evening.

The mansio lay a short walk from the islands with their reeded banks, along the left fork of the big Roman highway. This was a decent full-width military road which went, I knew, far westwards beyond the chalky downs to the entry port at Rutupiae. It had been the first route prepared by the invasion force and still carried arriving armed forces and most goods that came into Londinium overland. The mansio was a brand new establishment; it only looked about a year old. A sign warned people LAST GOOD DRINK BEFORE THE COLONIA. I found Petro glumly sampling this beverage.

The landlord had been cagey, but must have been warned that I would be coming. I was led to a discreet table in a back garden where a second cup was standing ready. Petro quickly filled it for me.

'Thanks! I need a drink.'

'I warn you, Falco, it won't help.'

I drained the cup and started on a second one, this time adding water. 'That was a mess.' The baker's pulped flesh kept revisiting my memory. I set my beaker on the table, as nausea threatened.

'Familiar?'

'Took me right back to the Balbinus mob.'

Petronius let out a grunt. He had a bread roll alongside him. He had managed two bites, automatically. Now it just sat there. He would throw it away.

'Those were the days!' He sounded bitter. 'You took your time getting here.'

'Busy day. I had to go out and see a bastard lawyer, for one thing. Anyway, I'm staying at the residence. You can send a message which reaches there in a few minutes. Then the slaves spend all morning and afternoon passing it between themselves. Saying it is urgent slows them down.'

Petro lost interest in that. 'This is grim, Falco.' He must have been thinking for some hours. Now he plunged right in: 'With your man, the drowned Briton, his fight could have been spur of the moment. There was a flare-up and he copped it. End of story.'

'No, it was planned,' I broke in. 'Tell you in a minute. Go on.'

'This death was deliberate slow torture. Its aim was systematic terrorising of the whole community.'

'And the body was meant to be found?'

'Who knows? If they want secrecy they should have weighed it down. They should have dumped it further downriver, away from habitation. No, they intend it to look as though they discarded him like rubbish. They want the next victims they lean on to have heard all about this . . . Did you talk to the ferryman?'

'He's gone into shock.'

'Well, he told me the tide was on the turn. It looked as if the body had been chucked overboard to go downstream a bit, but it washed back unexpectedly.'

'Chucked overboard – from what?' I queried.

'A boat went down. The ferry had had to wait for it while he was coming to get me.'

'Why didn't you use the bridge?' I asked.

'Same reason as you, Falco. Hilaris warned me they don't maintain it.'

I grinned, then became serious again. 'When I asked him, the ferryman denied seeing anything.'

'Do you blame him? Suppose this was the Balbinus mob, would you pipe up, *"Oh officer! I saw the boat they threw this person off"*? You'd have your eyes very tightly closed.'

'So where were you at the crucial moment, Petro? Did you see this boat dumping him?'

'I was aware of the boat,' Petronius admitted angrily. 'Classic witness failure, Falco – I was paying no attention. I didn't think it was important at the time.'

'Big craft or small?' We had to drag it out of his memory while we could.

Petronius co-operated gloomily. He was disgruntled that he, the professional, had failed to take note of a vital scene. 'Smallish. Smart, a private river craft – pleasure not trade.'

'Sailed or rowed?'

He placed a wide palm on his forehead. 'Rowed.' He paused. 'There was a small sail too.'

'Nameboard? Flags? Interesting prow?'

He tried hard. 'Nothing that stuck.'

'Anyone visible?'

'Couldn't say.'

'Hear a suspicious splash?'

He grimaced. 'Don't be stupid. If I had, I'd have paid attention, wouldn't I?' Something struck him. 'There was somebody standing in the prow!'

'Good – what about him?'

It had gone. 'Don't know . . . nothing.'

I frowned. 'Why were you aware of the boat? Also, why did the ferry have to wait? The river's wide enough.'

Petronius thought. 'The boat was stationary for a while. Drifting.' He pulled a face. 'While they dropped him in, perhaps. They could have slid him over the side, the side away from me.'

'Hades . . . That was stupid – right by the bridge and the ferry crossing!'

'It was at the crack of dawn, but you're on the dot: it was stupid. Anybody could have seen them. These villains don't care.'

'Anyone else about?'

'Just me. I start early. I was here, squatting on the jetty.'

'Would they have seen you signalling to call the ferry?'

'No. I don't bother. I was just sitting still, listening to the marsh birds and thinking about –' He stopped. His lost daughters. I dropped a hand over his forearm, but he shook me off. 'I have a routine arrangement to be fetched at first light. The ferry was still moored opposite. If the people in the drop-boat were preoccupied, they may not have realised I was watching.'

'They were damned careless, all the same.' I thought about things. Life stank. 'I still say, this is a wide enough river. Why did the ferryman wait?'

Petro saw my point. 'Wonder if he knows who owns that boat?'

'And wanted to avoid them? Was he scared then? . . . All right – so what about the corpse?'

'Bumped up against us as we crossed. The ferryman would have pushed it away and hoped it sank. I made him hook it.'

'Did he know beforehand that it was death by violence?'

'I thought he just wanted to avoid trouble. He was horrified when he saw we had landed a corpse in that condition.'

'And Firmus? Firmus happened to be there?'

'Yes. He threw up in the drink.'

We sat quiet for a time. Dusk was falling; if I wanted to make it back across the river I would have to move. I would have liked to stay and give Petronius solace.

'I feel bad about leaving. I don't like you being alone over here.'

'I'm all right. Things to do, lad. Wrongs to right – villains to catch,' he assured me, his tone drab. Petronius had never been a pious hero. He was far too decent.

Before I set off, I told him what I had learned today about the circumstances of the Verovolcus death.

'It's clear Splice and Pyro did it – but I wish I knew what Verovolcus was talking to them about at the bar.'

'And *who* was the man giving them orders? What are you going to do?' asked Petro.

'Report it all to the governor, I reckon.'

'What will *he* do?' He managed to avoid sounding sceptical.

'What I tell him, I hope. Now I have to decide what that should be.'

'What do you think?' I knew he was dying to make suggestions. When we were lads out here in Britain he would have barged in, taking over if he could. But we were grown up now. If no wiser, we were both more sad and tired. He held back, leaving me to take the initiative in my aspect of the case.

'I think it's time we arrested Splice and Pyro. Are you happy? Will it cut across you?'

Petro thought quickly, then shook his head. 'No. Time to shake things up. So long as I know what's coming. But take care,' he warned. 'You may be pulling out a support that brings the whole damn edifice crashing down on us.'

'I see that.'

Petro was trying to prophesy: 'If you take out their main collectors, the group then has to reorganise. They'll need to do it fast, or the locals will start enjoying their freedom. Way out here, the gangsters are very far from their normal resources. If they lose a crucial operative, I doubt if they have back-up. They may make mistakes, become too visible. Then too, they have the worry of what Splice and Pyro may tell you.'

'Nothing, trust me on it.' I was a realist.

'Everyone has a weak spot. Everyone can be bought.' Bereavement, or something, was making Petronius sentimental. Gangsters' enforcers must be the hardest men in the criminal underworld and if Splice and Pyro had come from Rome, they were the worst of their type. 'This is the end of the world. It's frontier rules,' Petro insisted. 'Frontinus could sink them in a bog and no questions asked. If their masters place bail for them, we'll know exactly who their masters are. So they could be abandoned. They know they can be replaced; there is always some creep offering to become the gang's new bagman. Pyro and Splice know it, Falco: this is dead meat town for them if things start going wrong.'

'Oh yes! I'm taking notes,' I scoffed, 'for when we interrogate these babes! Cradle stories should frighten them witless. Whoever mashed Epaphroditus is obviously a nervous type –'

Petronius sighed. 'You suggest something then.'

'What can I say? Arrest Splice and Pyro – then watch what happens. That's as far as I can go, like you.'

'It's pathetic,' he said bleakly.

'Yes.'

We both knew it was all we had.

Before I left to go and see the governor, I said, 'Ask me who told me about the Verovolcus death.'

'Who told you?' Petronius demanded obediently.

'One of those gladiator girls.'

'Oh them!' Petronius gave a short mocking laugh. He had temporarily forgotten that he saw me being led off by the fighters in frocks. 'So they captured you outside the brothel. Now you're here, unscathed. How did you escape their clutches, lucky one?'

'Helena Justina came and fetched me safely home.'

He laughed again, though he could read the trouble in my face. 'So which one coughed?'

'She's calling herself Amazonia, but we know better. Remember Chloris?'

He looked blank, though not for long. He let out a shout. 'You are joking! That Chloris? *Chloris?*' He shuddered slightly. 'Does Helena know?'

I nodded. Then, like the two boys we had been years ago in Britain, we both sucked our teeth and winced.

XXXII

A SUNLIT STREET. Not much of a street by Roman standards, but feebly shaping up. It is morning, though not early. Whatever is happening has had to be approved, planned out, and put in hand.

A back alley bar has a portrait of a short-legged, punk-faced Ganymede offering his lop-sided ambrosia cup to some invisible sex-mad Jupiter. Waiters from the Ganymede stand halfway down the street, in conversation with a waiter from another place, the Swan. Its painted sign shows a huge randy duck pinning down a naked girl. All the waiters are talking about a dead baker. Everyone in the streets today is talking about him. By tomorrow he will be old news, but today on this fine morning, his grim fate is the main talking point.

Even so, the morning glows. There is little feeling of menace, just a faint lowing from a stable somewhere, the scent of eggs frying, a smooth-haired dog with a long snout, scratching herself. Between the pantiled roofs of the ramshackle properties is a narrow glimpse of clear blue sky, subtly more mellow than blue skies in Italy.

On the opposite side of the street from the two bars, a locksmith comes to his doorway to speak to a neighbour. They too are probably discussing the dead baker. They glance across at the group of gossiping waiters, but do not join them. After subdued words, the locksmith shakes his head. His neighbour does not linger.

The locksmith returns to his booth, and a man walks towards the Ganymede. He is confident and worldly, his pace jaunty. As he approaches the bar, a small group of soldiers appear out of nowhere. Swiftly they back the man against a wall, hands up. He submits to a search, laughing. He has done this before. He knows they cannot touch him. Even when they march him away, he is jaunty. The waiters, having watched what happened, return at once to their individual bars.

At the Ganymede, soldiers step out and arrest them. A man – tall, broad-shouldered, calm, brown-haired – goes in to search the joint. Another – sturdy, efficient, curly dark hair, handsome – identifies himself to the soldiers and follows the first inside the bar. Later they emerge, with nothing. Disappointed, they hold a short discussion, apparently about tactics. The bar is sealed. A soldier stays on guard.

The street is peaceful.

Elsewhere, at a barber's, a customer is in the chair half-shaved. Two men in plain clothes, though with military bearing, come up quietly and speak to him. He listens courteously. He removes the napkin from under his chin, apologising to the barber who steps back, looking anxious. The customer shrugs. He places coins in his barber's hand, waving away objections, then he goes with the two officers who have sought him out. He has the air of an influential person who has found himself the victim of a serious mistake. His pained demeanour shows that he is too sophisticated, and perhaps too important, to create a public fuss about this error. It will be sorted. Once his explanation has been accepted by people in authority, there will be trouble. There is a faint implication that some high-handed fool will pay dearly.

The disconcerted barber returns to his business. The next customer stands up quietly but does not take the shaving seat. He says a few words. The barber looks surprised, then scared; he goes away with the man, who has dark curly hair and a firm step. That shop too is closed up and sealed.

Another street lies peaceful now. The operation has gone well so far: Pyro and Splice, and some of their associates, have been lifted on the orders of the governor.

XXXIII

I HAD WATCHED the two men being picked up. Petronius and I had searched the Ganymede: no luck. If there had ever been money or anything else kept there, it had recently been removed. In the room where Splice and Pyro lodged we found only personal possessions of a meagre kind.

Cursing, we made plans. Petronius Longus would lean on the ferryman for information about the boat that had dropped the baker in the Thamesis. He would also enlist the help of Firmus to try to discover where the attack on the baker had occurred. We felt it must be near the river – in a warehouse, probably. There would be bloodstains.

I would see what happened about Splice and Pyro. The governor's men would supervise their interrogation, but I expected to deal with the ancillaries: waiters and barber, plus any other hangers-on the army brought in. Soldiers were picking up the staff at the bar where Verovolcus died. Word had also been sent to Chloris to come in and make her deposition to the governor.

I followed the arresting parties back to the residence. The enforcers were placed in separate cells. Neither was told the reason for his arrest. We left them to stew. They would be interviewed tomorrow. Neither knew the other had been detained – though they may have deduced it – and apart from the people who saw them being taken, nobody was informed by us that we had Pyro and Splice in custody. The waiters and the barber were put through preliminary interviews the same night. All refused to tell us anything. The barber may even have been innocent.

Word must have raced back to the gang leaders. The enforcers' lawyer came to importune the governor in mid-afternoon, only a few hours after the arrests. We already knew the lawyer: it was Popillius.

Frontinus had Hilaris with him for this confrontation; I made sure I was there too. I felt Popillius had arrived too quickly and overplayed it. Frontinus must have thought so too, and took him up on it: 'A couple of common criminals, aren't they? Why do you want to see me?'

'I am told they are held incommunicado, sir. I need to consult my clients.'

When I first knew Julius Frontinus, he seemed an amiable buffer with an interest in arcane branches of public engineering works. Given command of a province, and its army, he had grown into his role fast. 'Your clients are well housed; they will be fed and watered. They have to await the normal interview process.'

'May I know the charge?'

The governor shrugged. 'Not decided. Depends on what they have to say for themselves.'

'Why are they in detention, sir?'

'A witness has placed them at the scene of a serious crime.'

'What witness, please?'

'I shall tell you at the proper time.'

'Does the witness accuse them of committing this crime?'

'Afraid so.'

'Nonetheless, it is wrong to detain them overnight and they need an opportunity to prepare their defence. I am here to put up their bail, sir.'

Frontinus looked at the lawyer indulgently. 'Young man –' There was a decade between them – a decade in years and a century in authority. Julius Frontinus looked an efficient general and empire-builder, which meant he was equally impressive as a high-grade magistrate. 'Until I conduct an examination and evaluate the case, I can hardly set bail terms.'

'And when are you likely to conclude the examination?' Popillius tried to be crisp.

'As soon as the business of this province will permit,' Frontinus assured him calmly. 'We are among the barbarians. My priorities are to keep Rome's frontier secure and to found a decent infrastructure. Any civilian who interferes with that has to wait his turn.'

Popillius knew he had lost vital ground, but he had kept his big throw to the last shake of the canister: 'My clients are free Roman citizens.'

'Matter of security!' Frontinus rasped. I had not seen him in full cry before. He seemed to be enjoying it. 'Don't make an ass of yourself. These men stay in custody.'

'Governor, they have the right of appeal to the Emperor.'

'Correct.' Frontinus would not budge. 'If you assert the right, they go to Rome. But they go *after* I have interviewed them – and if I find a case to answer, then they go in chains.'

When Popillius had left, Hilaris broke his silence. He offered thoughtfully, 'He is inexperienced in these matters – but he will learn fast.'

'Do we think he is behind all this?' asked Frontinus.

'No, he seems to lack the depth to be running things alone.'

'There are *two* main operators, in partnership,' I put in. 'Though Popillius seems to have made himself too obvious to be one.'

Hilaris smiled. 'I take it you have conferred about the gang leaders with Lucius Petronius?' So Petro's cover had been blown.

'He is just the man you want for this,' I said loyally. Neither of the senior officials seemed upset. They both had the sense to see he was an asset. Pettiness about whether the vigiles had the right to send him here would be taken up later, if at all. If he made a significant contribution to the action, there would be no reprisal. Of course, if we failed to make headway, Petro's secret interference would be blamed.

Frontinus looked at me. 'Find out who hired Popillius, if you can.'

I hurried off to tail him as he left.

I kept my distance, following Popillius all the way back to his rented house near the forum. It had struck me that associates might have been waiting to meet up with him outside the residence, but he was not approached. On foot, walking steadily, he returned straight home. I strolled twice around the block, to give him time to relax, then I went in.

He was sitting alone in the courtyard at the same table as yesterday morning, busily writing on a scroll. 'Falco!'

I hauled a bench over to him, though he had not invited me to sit. 'We need to talk,' I said informally, like a barrister colleague who had come to bargain pleas. Popillius leaned his chin on one hand and listened. He was no young fool. I had yet to decide if Hilaris was right, that Popillius lacked presence. Looking lightweight could be a cover; he could be thoroughly corrupt.

I gazed at him. 'This is a new kind of venture for you. Am I right?' No acknowledgement. 'You're getting in deep. But do you know what the mire is?'

Popillius feigned mild surprise. 'Two clients, held in custody, without charge.'

'Shocking,' I answered. Then I stiffened. 'It's a routine situation. What's unusual is the speed with which you popped up screeching outrage. A pair of crooks have been pulled in. That's all. Anyone would think this was a grand political show trial involving famous men with big careers and full coffers.' Popillius opened his mouth to speak. 'Don't give me the sweet line,' I said, 'about all free Romans being entitled to the best representation they can afford. Your clients are two professional enforcers preying on society, in the pay of an organised gang.'

The lawyer's expression did not change. However, he moved his hand down from his chin.

'I don't exaggerate, Popillius. If you want a distressing view of their handiwork, there is a smashed-up corpse on the ferry jetty. Go and have a look. Find out what kind of people are employing you.' I kept my voice level. 'What I want to know is: when you took on Splice and Pyro, did you know their game?'

Popillius glanced down at his documents. Pyro and Splice must have proper formal names. He would be using those.

'Are you a salary hack, working full time for mobsters?' I demanded.

'That's a sick question, Falco!'

'You're in a sick situation. Let's suppose you really did come out to Britain to do harmless commercial case-law,' I chivvied him. 'Today somebody hired you, and you accepted the fee. This is a simple extrication from custody. Justice for the freeborn. Exemplary legal point; their morals don't come into it. Yours perhaps should. Because next time you are used by your principals – as you will be – the job will be more murky. After that, you will belong to them. I don't suggest they will have you working on perjury, perversion of justice and suborning witnesses in your very first month, but believe me, that will come.'

'These are wild accusations, Falco.'

'No. We have at least two really filthy murders here. Your banged-up clients are intimately linked to one killing; our witness saw them do the deed. I myself can place them at the premises of the second victim – a baker who had been harried by extortionists – just after he disappeared and while his building was being torched.'

Popillius gazed at me quietly, though I reckon he was thinking hard. My guess was, the killings were news to him.

He had had the full training. He was inscrutable. I would have liked to grab that scroll off him, to see what he had been writing. Notes on how Frontinus had rebuffed him? Suggestions of how the formal examination might turn out? Or simply listing his hourly charges to whatever cash-rich bastard would be paying for his time?

So was Popillius an amateur whom they had had to hire in a hurry, the best Britain could offer to a gangster who encountered an unexpected problem? Or had they brought him here and positioned him as their legal representative? Worst of all – and looking at the quiet swine, it still seemed an open question – was he one of the gang leaders himself?

'I have heard you out, Falco,' declared Popillius, his tone as steady as my own had been.

I stood up. 'Who is paying you to act for Pyro and Splice?'

His eyes, hazel behind light lashes, flickered slightly. 'Confidential, I'm afraid.'

'Criminals.'

'That is slander.'

'Only if it is untrue. There are more cells waiting for associates, remember.'

'Only if they have done something wrong, surely?' he sneered.

'I leave you to your conscience, then.'

I did as I said. It presupposed he had a conscience. I saw no sign of it.

XXXIV

ORGANISED CRIME LORDS HAVE most things working in
their favour. In the cynical world that Petro and I inhabited,
we knew that the crime lords would always win. They had money
on their side. In Rome, the vigiles and the Urban Cohorts
struggled constantly to maintain an uneasy peace. Without their
aid, even in the provinces, the governor did have one way to fight
back. He used it. Right at the start, Frontinus decided to bring in
the official torturer.

I knew these craftsmen existed on the staff of overseas embassies.
I had imagined they were a last resort. The speed with which the
decision was taken here did shock me.

'Amicus!' Hilaris named him to me, in a hollow tone. Frontinus
had formally approved using this man, but we had been charged
with briefing him.

'*The Befriender?* A nickname, I take it?'

'I never like to ask.' Hilaris chuckled briefly, though he seemed
serious. 'I always feel that involving him is like taking a wagon
with a broken spoke to the wheelwright. I expect Amicus to look
at the job – the suspects, I mean – then to shake his head and tell
me "Procurator, you have a real problem here".'

'Don't tell me he inspects the bugger waiting for him in the cell,
then vanishes for an hour, "gone to collect materials" . . . ?'

Hilaris shuddered. 'I leave him to it, at that stage.' He was a
kindly man. 'I always hope the mere threat of Amicus will make
them gasp and give in.'

'And do they?'

'Rarely. He is rather good.'

We needed him, then.

As soon as Amicus appeared, I saw exactly what Helena's tender-conscienced uncle meant. The torturer looked as if he had forced himself to leave another job – a more interesting job, one that had been properly booked into his schedule, unlike our last-minute, problematic one. His sleeves were rolled up and there were stains down his tunic (*what from?*.) He heard our request with the tired, slightly put-upon air of a man dealing with idiots. Had there been a fee, he would have overcharged. Since he was on the governor's payroll, that did not apply.

'Professional criminals can be difficult,' he remarked, wanting us to know how lucky we were to have his skills.

'Are you saying it cannot be done?' worried Hilaris, just as if he had a dodgy axle.

'Oh it can be done!' Amicus assured him, chillingly.

He had a long, thin, uncouth assistant who never spoke. This young man stared about with open curiosity and somehow gave the impression he might be extremely bright. Amicus himself was bound to be intelligent. Professional torture experts are among the Empire's men of subtlety. Their job requires them to be experienced in the world, and if possible well read. Trust me. I had worked with them before, during my time as an army scout. 'I bet he studies cosmography in his spare time,' I had suggested to Hilaris earlier.

'Nothing so frivolous as planets. I had a long conversation with him once about Democritean principles and whether deities experience pain or pleasure. He soon lost me!'

Now Amicus sniffed – his one expression of emotion, even that possibly caused by some summer allergy. 'I'll knock off the waiters; I'll get through them this afternoon.' I had intended to question the waiters myself, but deferred to him meekly. 'The barber may stick. I hate barbers. Measly runts and they're grizzlers, once they crack . . . Now as for your two enforcers, I would like them kept in solitary for a second night, if possible with little sleep. And no food, obviously. Then leave them with me. I'll send up Titus to let you know when it's time to come and watch.'

Hilaris and I tried to look appreciative.

'What do you want to know?' Amicus then asked as an afterthought.

'The truth,' said Hilaris, with a hint of a smile.

'Oh you're a case, procurator!'

'Someone has to have values,' I chided. 'Here's the list: we want to know about protection rackets; two murders – a Briton drowned in a well for unknown reasons and a baker beaten to death for resisting the rackets; and gang leaders.'

'There are thought to be two,' stated the procurator. 'Even one name would help.'

Amicus nodded. These trite tasks seemed to intrigue him much less than Democritean principles. He led off his assistant, the lank Titus, with the deathly catchphrase, 'Bring the bag, Titus!'

I should have mentioned the bag. It was enormous. Titus could hardly heave it up on to his shoulder as he swaggered after Amicus. It caught the doorframe a glancing blow as they went out, removing a chunk of architrave and emitting a resounding clank from heavy metal implements within.

Amicus popped his head back around the door. Flavius Hilaris, who had been inspecting the crunched joinery, dropped a fragment of architrave and stepped back, looking ashamed of himself for being annoyed at the damage.

'Do you want it done without leaving any marks?' enquired Amicus.

I thought Hilaris went pale. He found the right thing to say: 'The enforcers have a lawyer.'

'Oh!' replied the torturer, impressed. He looked pleased to hear of this challenge. 'I'll be *very* careful then!'

He went out again. Hilaris resumed his seat. Neither of us said anything. We were both subdued.

XXXV

ELENA DISCOVERED ME studying a street map. She leaned
over my shoulder, inspecting a note tablet on which I had
written down a list of names. 'Shower of Gold, Ganymede, Swan
– Swan must be as in Leda, seduced by Jupiter in the form of a big
white birdie. Shower of Gold would be his other conquest Danaë.
Ganymede is Jove's cup-bearer –'

'You follow my thinking,' I agreed.

'The wine shops your gangsters prey on all now have names
linked to Jupiter? It's a theme! How thrilling,' Helena exclaimed,
with her own brand of well-bred mockery. 'Some man thinks well
of himself for dreaming up this.'

'As an antique dealer's son, I do like things that come in sets,' I
confirmed drily. 'So helpful for their accountants too – bound to
be accountants plural, of course: "File all signed-up cauponae
under *Jove!*" Then again, proprietors who want to resist the
pressure will see just how powerful the enforcers are, as they notice
more and more Jupiter bars.'

'We could go for a walk,' Helena decided. 'We have time
before dinner. We could take the map and mark up places. See
how far the enforcement area extends.'

Nux was already chasing around us excitedly.

We spent a couple of hours crisscrossing the street grid from
near the river to the forum. It made us both depressed. The
permissive god's adulterous girlfriends were all featured: Io,
Europa, Danaë, Alcmene, Leda, Niobe and Semele. What a boy!
The ever-jealous Queen of Heaven, Hera, would *not* like to spend

a festival break in Londinium seeing all these rivals given prominence. For the safety of this town, I was myself wishing the Celestial King had kept his divine prick under wraps more. The beauteous bedmates were just the start. Thunderbolts adorned innocuous looking pot-of-pulse parlours and sceptres ruled over British beer gardens. Painters who could do attractive bolts of lightning must have been in heaven. Or rather, they were using up their fees swigging Lower German red at the Olympus Winery on the corner of downtown Fish Street. With hot or cold ambrosia served in gritty flatbread every lunchtime, no doubt.

Prices were very expensive. Well, they had to be. The people who ran these Jovian snack-counters needed to subsidise their payments to the heavy squad. Somebody somewhere was raking in money from this dead-end shantytown, hot money in huge quantities. This walk really brought it home to me that the gang leaders would be furious that Pyro and Splice, who collected the cash, had been locked up by the governor – at my suggestion.

Back home, Helena dismissed the slave who came to curl her hair and instead of primping she crouched beside a window to catch the evening light while she marked up our map with neat blobs of red ink. I came back from a lukewarm bathe, then saw how the map looked, and swore. The dots encroached on the commercial quarter to the east of the bridge, running right up across the Decumanus Maximus to the forum.

I sent the map along to Frontinus, to depress him while he was shaved. I sat in the wrap-around chair. Helena had a rapid sponge-wash, tweaked a gown from her clothes chest, clipped on jewellery. She touched my cheek. 'You look tired, Marcus.'

'I'm wondering what I have got myself into.'

She came across to me, combing her fine hair. After a vague attempt to pin it up, she let the whole swathe tumble. Knowing the comb would stick in my curls, she neatened them instead with her long fingers. 'You know this is vital.'

'I know it's dangerous.'

'You think it's right.'

'They need to be stopped by someone, yes.'

'But you wonder why you?' Helena knew that sometimes I relied on her to reassure me. 'Because you have the persistence, Marcus. You have the courage, the intellectual skills, the sheer anger that is needed to face up to such wickedness.'

I put my arms around her, hiding my face against her stomach. She stood, crouching a little over me, one hand running inside the neck of my tunic to massage my spine. I heard myself groan wearily. 'I want to go home!'

'Marcus, we can't go, not until you have finished here.'

'It never ends though, sweetheart.' I leaned back and looked up at her. 'Organised crime keeps coming. One success only quells it temporarily and opens possibilities for new rackets.'

'Don't be so disheartened.'

I smiled ruefully. 'I'm tired. I didn't sleep two nights ago. My girlfriend had a fight with me . . . Love me?'

Her thumb caressed my forehead. 'If I didn't love you, I would not have had the fight.'

That was when I chose to tell her – when I *had* to tell her – we were liable to see Chloris at the residence that night.

Helena released her hold on me, but when I caught her hands in mine she did not resist. 'Don't get this wrong, love. Chloris has to make her deposition for the governor and she has also been asked to look at our dinner guests. Both Norbanus and Popillius have been invited tonight, along with other newcomers who could be the gang leaders. This is business, Helena. I'm not playing about.'

Helena merely said quietly, 'What she is doing is perilous.'

'I know.' I was terse. 'She does not seem to know that her status makes the witness statement unusable in court.'

'She is doing it for you.'

'She's doing it because she likes stirring!' She always did. Women like that don't change. 'I am not sure she sees just what danger she courts.'

'Her career is based on physical risk,' Helena pointed out.

'Yes, but that's her choice. She enjoys the thrills and she earns a great deal of money. She and the other girls have come here to Britain because fighting in the new amphitheatre will make them independent for life – if they survive. But tangling with street criminals is different. The odds on survival are far worse. If I were an ethical person I would spell out the truth to her.'

'But you need what she tells you.'

'Well, I could myself report to Frontinus what she said, but he won't act on hearsay.'

'She saw what happened,' Helena insisted. 'Infamous or not, if Frontinus interviews her in private and he believes her, then she will give his actions validity.'

'Closed room verdicts are not my favourite scene, Helena.'

'You're a grumpy old republican! Oh I despise them too, Marcus, but if they have to happen I would rather it was in a cause like this.'

'Bad politics.' I hated this situation. The Claudian emperors were fond of it, subjecting their enemies to secret trials at the Palace, rather than facing them in the Senate or open court. I had hoped that with our Flavian dynasty the practice would die out. It was for panicking leaders, to remove imagined rivals after swift closet questioning – often based on trumped-up evidence. Informers, I regret to say, were often the filthy instruments of such private trials. I had never worked like that.

As we went to dinner, the procurator popped out of an office and signalled me. He had been lying in wait with Amicus. Helena went on ahead, while Hilaris and I held a hurried consultation with the torturer.

'Titus is just putting things away –' I caught Hilaris looking pale again as Amicus reported. 'I got the waiters' stories. They all match; it's nice and neat. Apparently, the two men you are holding run a helpful service. They deter troublemakers and sneak-thieves who might grab the takings. All the wine shops appreciate the extra security, and are happy to contribute modest sums to obtain it.'

Hilaris and I gazed at him in surprise.

'Well, that was today's silly story,' Amicus scoffed in a comfortable tone. 'Tomorrow I shall crank things up a bit. They think they've got away with it. When I reappear with the bag, they'll be ripe to tell me their life histories in ten volumes of fine poetry. Mind you, the barber stuck. I knew it. Bastards!' He then enquired anxiously, 'Is there any hurry?'

'Everything seems quiet currently,' Hilaris said, sounding cautious.

Amicus suddenly transferred his attention to me. 'Falco! Do you have a witness to any of the killings?'

I wondered why he asked. 'The murder of the Briton, probably. Do you want details?'

'No. I just like to warn the nasty fibbers that I can obtain corroboration.'

I was slightly shy of telling this professional I was using Chloris. Better for her sake, anyway, that I kept her name quiet.

Hilaris invited Amicus to dine with us. He refused gruffly. It seems torturers prefer not to socialise.

Tonight we had more guests than on other occasions; it had to be a buffet party rather than a formal dinner on couches. We spilled out from the dining room into the garden, with music from the Hilaris family's tibia-player and the Norbanus harpist. The tibia-player was excellent, he must have put in plenty of practice here in boring Britain; the harpist, presumably trained in Rome where there were more distractions, was simply adequate. The evening remained sedate. Anyone who hoped for half-naked gymnastic dancers hoped in vain.

Due to the plucking and tootling, conversation did not thrive. Norbanus himself hung around Maia as usual. However at one point he approached me rather deliberately; I was sitting with Helena, unfashionably conversing with my wife.

'I ought to have a word, Marcus Didius. About your sister –' I raised an eyebrow. His manner was open, friendly, even honest. He managed to avoid acting like a creep and although he was a businessman, clearly accustomed to his own way in most things, yet he was scrupulously polite over this. 'It cannot have escaped you that I enjoy Maia's company. But if my attentions offend you, then of course I shall withdraw.' (His sad smile, said Helena afterwards, was a delicate touch.)

I told Norbanus gruffly that my sister made her own decisions. He looked pleased, as if I had given him boarding rights. In fact I thought the only way she would see through him was if nobody interfered. Mind you, I had made that ridiculous assumption once before, over that swine Anacrites.

Norbanus Murena went back to my sister, who was staring across at me suspiciously. I watched him, keeping my face neutral; he was good looking, confident, and as the women kept saying, he seemed a nice man. I could see Maia was finding him welcome company. He was not being pushy. Perhaps this kind of courteous, well-heeled self-made man was just what she needed.

On his way around the gravel paths to the seat where Maia had placed herself, Norbanus had passed Popillius. They must have met before, the previous night when the lawyer first made himself known at the residence (when I was out, having my weak spots tested by darling Chloris). Now the two men exchanged brief nods. They did not speak. They looked like mere acquaintances.

Popillius was a typical off-duty lawyer. Socialising happily, he ignored the fact that his two clients were still incarcerated in this very house. He and Frontinus had chatted tonight as if their wrangle over Pyro and Splice had never occurred. By tomorrow Popillius would be back on the attack, while Frontinus would resist the lawyer's efforts as strongly as if he had never been tonight's genial host.

I hated that kind of hypocrisy. Helena said that in a province with a small social circle it was inevitable. She was justifying the system, though I could see she agreed with me. She had been brought up in a senatorial household, but since her father Camillus Verus had never sought public office, he had managed to avoid holding open house. Cash-starved and secluded, the Camilli kept their hospitality for family and friends.

'Life with your uncle and aunt may be comfortable,' I said, 'but I can't take to this constant diplomatic plate-pushing.'

Helena smiled — then showed sudden alarm as we were interrupted by a distant child yelling, 'Julia's got a bee!' We heard the sounds of other children scarpering. All but the teenagers ought to be in bed. I rose calmly and excused myself to investigate.

My elder daughter, deserted when the others ran off, was stark naked except for her little sandals as she crouched on her heels beside a pond. She had been *in* the pond at some stage. Her skin was cold and her dark curls were sticking together in wet clumps. I gulped, imagining the perils for a toddler who loved splashing about but who could not swim.

The bee, a large bumble, looked virtually dead. It was standing on the path, motionless, being stared at by my two-year-old from inches away. This was a fine clear night, with no need for lamps yet; I could see why the children had escaped from the nursery staff. I tried feeble remonstrations about water being off limits. Julia pointed her tiny finger and said firmly, *'Bee!'*

'Yes, sweetheart. He's not feeling very well.' I squatted down obediently and took a look. His pollen sacs were bulging; he was exhausted by the heat.

Julia waved her fist at the insect, while I tried to remove her gently from stinging range. 'Poorly bee!' she shrieked.

Time to inculcate a sense of kindness in my child, who could be violent. I tried putting water on a folded leaf. The bee expressed some interest, yet it was too feeble to drink. I would have just left it here, for the gardeners to sweep up tomorrow; by then it would undoubtedly be dead. Julia leaned up against me happily, trusting me to rescue it from its predicament. I left her to hold the leaf gently near the bee's head, while I went back to the food tables. I looked around for Helena but she had vanished somewhere. I dipped an olive spoon in honey from the wine waiter's equipment bench, then returned to Julia.

As soon as I put the spoon near the bee, it responded. Julia and I watched enthralled as its long black proboscis unravelled and dipped into the honey. I held the spoon steady with one hand, keeping Julia under control in my other arm. To be feeding a bee did feel rather wonderful. Visibly reviving right before our eyes, it began to shake its heavy wings. We sat back. The bee crawled about slowly, testing out its legs; it fluttered once or twice. Then it suddenly took off and zoomed away in powerful flight, high over the garden.

'He's gone home to his crib now. And you're going to yours!'

I picked up Julia and stood upright. As I turned towards the house, I noticed that Helena was now upstairs on the balcony. Someone was standing in the shadows with her, veiled and discreet: a woman. Julia and I waved to them.

My daughter insisted that I put her to bed. I managed to avoid story-telling; rescuing a bee was enough tonight apparently. I had a quick look at Favonia, who was sound asleep. Then I rushed to find Helena. She was back at the party, now alone.

We spoke in low tones. 'Did I see you with –'

'Amazonia.'

The blind harpist had strayed too near, insistently serenading us. I gestured to the boy who led him around to take him off elsewhere. Musicians have always irritated me. 'Where is she?'

'Gone home.'

'I would have spoken to her.'

'She watched you being a good father,' Helena murmured. 'Maybe it disconcerted her.'

For some reason I felt embarrassed. Informers are hard men; we don't generally go around rescuing weary bumblebees. We are famous for making women walk out on us and for expecting our children to be brought up as strangers. Still, doing it my way, I would never have some unknown fifteen-year-old who had quarrelled with Mummy turning up on my doorstep with her luggage and her bad habits. Julia and Favonia would have their quarrels direct with me.

'Well? What did Chloris have to say?'

'She has given her statement,' Helena said quietly. 'Then I showed her the visitors. It was no good. She could not recognise the man who was arguing with Verovolcus at the bar.'

So he was not Norbanus, not Popillius, not any of the entrepreneurs who had come to Londinium and approached the governor. While that fitted what I had said all along, that chief gangsters would keep a low profile, we now had no idea who they might be, nor where to look for them.

It seemed a quiet night, as Hilaris had said earlier. Too quiet.

XXXVI

I WAS CALLED away. In a private office I found Lucius Petronius,
wanting to see me.

'Ah! Reporting in?'

'Liaising, you big-headed bum.'

'Master of charm, as usual.'

'Shut up, Falco! Stop messing about – I've found a warehouse
where I think that baker must have been attacked.'

'Olympus! Out of all the hundreds –'

'We searched quite enough!' Petro said with feeling. 'Firmus
and the customs boys helped narrow it down. There's blood on
the floor, and crudely hidden outside were bloody staves and even
a belt.'

'Damned careless! What was in the store?'

'Not a lot. Firmus and his assistants will now watch the place.
People nearby say the warehouse has been in regular use – odd
boxes being taken away by boat almost every day.'

'Cash? There won't be much of that for a while, with Pyro and
Splice in custody.'

'Don't be so sure.' Petronius was grim. 'The gang has them
covered already. I saw an argument at the Swan that was almost
certainly about pay-offs. I reckon the owner there was always
lukewarm. Now he knows that the bagmen are in jail, he may
have tried to dodge his payments.'

'What happened?'

'Somebody reminded him about his instalment plan. That pimp
from the brothel, the Old Neighbour. I've been watching him.

The Old Neighbour is part of the Jupiter empire, you know.'

'How come?'

'When Zeus was courting Semele, his jealous wife Hera disguised herself as an old neighbour so she could advise the girl to question him about his true identity.'

'Good thing it doesn't happen to everyone,' I commented drily. 'I hate this mythical bosh. Shall we pull in the pimp?'

'I'm not keen, Falco. If he's put out of action too, we may not recognise the next replacement.' Petro looked thoughtful. 'He reminds me of someone. But I haven't placed him yet.'

'He should be tailed – find out where he's sending the money.'

'We know where it goes. First to a warehouse, then it's taken off by boat and shipped to Rome.'

We stopped bickering and brooded. 'I don't like this,' I confessed.

'Wise boy.'

'Listen – the governor's using his torturer. Amicus is taking his time with the hot pincers; it all seems too slow to me. You and I could shift things on much quicker with a little well-judged questioning.'

'Let him play,' Petronius soothed me. 'We have enough to do . . . A lawyer came to inspect the corpse, by the way. He said you sent him.'

'Popillius. He's here tonight. I had him down as a likely face for one of the gang. Or if he's innocent, what was done to Epaphroditus may make him back out. He's representing Pyro and Splice, he claims – or will be when the governor lets him talk to them.'

Petronius looked intrigued. 'Paid by?'

'He refuses to say.'

'He needs to be watched,' said Petro quickly. 'Tell Frontinus to keep a visitors list for him.'

'Tell him yourself. Come and eat with us. Frontinus and Hilaris know what you're doing in their province. I bet even the gang has noticed your fine presence. You may as well stop skulking in that dirty tunic.'

He joined the party, though he refused to change his outfit. It drew immediate comment from my sister, when she saw him come out into the garden alongside me. 'That's a disgraceful garment. You look like something the tide washed in.'

'I'm clean underneath,' Petronius reassured her, taking a sneaky squint at Norbanus, accompanied by a leer to emphasise that he and Maia were old acquaintances. 'I've been working at a public baths. Want to check?' he offered her, pretending to pull up his tunic.

'No, I have enough children to inspect at bath-time,' Maia retorted.

'We haven't met,' Norbanus introduced himself. 'Lucius Norbanus Murena – I'm in property.'

'Lucius Petronius Longus – I'm not.' It could be taken as rude, or merely playful. Norbanus chose to smile.

Apparently bored, Petronius wandered off to find himself a plate of food.

The company had thinned out. We were almost down to family, though Norbanus had decided to include himself. Popillius was still here too, talking intently to the governor by the ornamental pool. Maybe I did him wrong earlier. Maybe he had come tonight intending to stick up for his two clients.

I noticed Aelia Camilla looking towards Petro anxiously. She spoke to Gaius in an undertone; he nodded. Petronius was now munching, slightly by himself. Aelia Camilla waited until he had finished, then went and sat by him. Conversation had sunk to a murmur and I managed to overhear. 'I am so sorry for your loss. This is perhaps not the time, but I don't know whether you will stay with us tonight . . . We have tried to find out for you which of your children has survived. I just wanted you to know, my dear. Petronilla is alive and safe.'

Petronius said something, very briefly. Aelia Camilla rose quietly and left him. I caught Helena's eye. Tears started and she grabbed my hand. Even Maia seemed alert to the situation, though she was flirting with Norbanus, perhaps to distract him.

Petronius stood up. To go into the house he would have had to pass too close by too many people. He walked away to a bench where he could sit with his back to us. He slumped with his head in his hands. We all knew that he was overcome. I moved, to go to him. Aelia Camilla shook her head, suggesting I give him privacy.

Most of us were silent when Frontinus and Popillius approached, having completed a circuit of the garden. Petronius, who must have recovered a little, had just raised his head and was staring at the pool. Popillius noticed him. 'Is that the man who showed me the corpse this afternoon?' the lawyer demanded of me. I was ready to kick his feet from under him if he tried to go near Petronius; that was preferable to Petro himself lashing out.

'Friend of mine. Corpses are his hobby.' My tone was brusque.

'I thought he worked on the docks . . . What's his official role?' This time Popillius addressed the governor.

'Eyewitness,' snapped back Frontinus. 'He saw the corpse pulled out of the river.'

Popillius did not buy it. 'Is he working for you, sir?'

Frontinus was mild. 'He has excellent credentials, but other people own him.'

'People in Rome?'

'It is no secret.' Either Frontinus had drunk too much tonight, or he was angrier than we realised that an officer had been sent here without due clearance. Before I could stop him he came out with it: 'He's a member of the vigiles.'

'Then,' retorted the lawyer, as if he had scored a brilliant point, 'he has no jurisdiction here!'

'That's right,' agreed Frontinus, sorting out the best remaining almond cakes on a comport. He was calm, and said almost satirically, 'I am outraged to find him working in my province. If he discovers any dirty secrets I shall confiscate the evidence, and if he incriminates anyone, I shall claim all the credit.' Chin jutting, he leaned forwards from the seat on which he had plumped down. Before he popped an almond cake in his mouth he told Popillius in a much harder tone, '*Anyone* who enables me to stamp hard on criminal organisers is welcome in Londinium.'

Popillius could hardly rebuke Julius Frontinus, legate of Augustus, for wanting to run a clean town. The lawyer thanked Aelia Camilla for his dinner, then went home.

Norbanus had been watching with some amusement. 'A jurisdiction problem?' he enquired.

Frontinus felt the need to add to his earlier statement: 'I know Petronius Longus. I would bring him in on permanent secondment, but the Prefect of the Urban Cohorts won't release him; he's too good!'

'Oh so that's what he does,' exclaimed Norbanus in a silky tone. I felt uneasy, but he turned back to Maia.

Petronius stood up. He came back towards us, walking straight past Maia without looking at her. Aelia Camilla jumped to her feet, met him and hugged him briefly. She passed him on to Helena, who was still weeping for him so she too quickly embraced him and passed him straight to me. His face was drawn, and I could not help but notice that his cheeks were wet. He accepted our sympathy but was somewhere else, lost in suffering; he had different points of reference and different priorities.

He continued towards the house. 'Stay with us here, at least for tonight,' urged Aelia Camilla, calling out after him. He looked back and nodded once, then went indoors alone.

Norbanus must have watched this short scene with even more curiosity; I heard Maia explaining, 'A close friend of the family who has had a bereavement. We are all very fond of him.'

'Poor man.' We could not expect Norbanus to show real sympathy. For one thing, he must be wondering just how close a friend to Maia this friend she was very fond of might have been. It was clear that a good guest would take his leave at such a sad moment, so this Norbanus did. Maia found the grace to go along and see him out.

As soon as they were beyond earshot, I suggested to Hilaris that we have Norbanus tailed. I still viewed him with suspicion. It was impossible that he would return to his downriver villa after dark; taking a boat would be unsafe. So I wanted to discover where he stayed in town. A discreet observer set off after the Norbanus carrying-chair when he called for it; luckily he had dallied at the door for conversation with Maia, so our man was securely in place when Norbanus left the residence.

I went for a late-night drink with Hilaris in his study, while we compared notes and relaxed in private. We had always got on well. We talked for much longer than I realised. When I left him to join Helena in our room, all the corridors lay silent, dimly lit by earthenware oil lamps on side tables or spaced at intervals along the floor. The slaves had cleared up long ago.

Wearily I made my way to the suites where house guests were lodged. To my disgust even at that late hour, I ran into the damned harpist, loitering with his spotty boy. I told them to clear off, making a vow to have Maia return them to Norbanus next day. She could be polite about it, but we were overdue to shed the nosy pair.

I badly wanted to be with Helena, but first I went to check on Petronius. He and I had had fifteen years of seeing each other through troubles; Helena would expect me to offer him solace. That meant if he was drinking, I would either join in or stop him. If he wanted to talk I would listen. Hades, if the poor lad was sleeping, I would even tuck him in.

But another kind of comfort was on offer: I spotted Maia ahead of me. As I approached his door, I saw her knock quickly and go in. To reach my own room, I had to pass outside. Maia, stupidly, had left the door ajar. Maybe she thought she would be thrown out. Anyway, I could not carry on without them seeing me; once again I had been put in a position where I had to overhear my sister like a spy.

'Petronius.' Maia simply spoke his name. It was more to let him hear she was there than anything.

There was a faint light from an oil lamp that must be over by his bed. I could see Petro, stripped to bare feet and an unbleached undertunic; he was standing in front of a window, leaning on the sill, letting the night air fall on him. He did not turn around.

'This is no good,' Maia advised him. 'Sleep. You need to rest.'

'I can't.'

'What are you doing then?'

'Nothing.' He did turn. He showed her empty hands. But he had a full heart. 'Nothing at all. Remembering Silvana and Tadia. Waiting for the pain to end.'

'Some of it will pass,' my sister said.

Petronius swore coarsely.

'Well that ends the comforting part of the evening in good masculine style!' quipped Maia.

'I don't want people being bloody kind — I get upset.' He stepped towards her then, so in the small room they were standing close. 'I don't want pitying or chivvying — and I don't want your sniping wit. Either go, Maia — or damn well stay!'

'Which do you choose?' asked Maia, but the question was rhetorical for they had moved into each other's arms.

When they kissed it was neither young love blossoming nor established love reasserting itself. This was something much darker. They were both joyless and desperate. The way they had come together was deliberate and carnal; it struck me that nothing good would come of it for either of them.

Freed by their self-absorption, I walked past unnoticed. I even managed to hook the door to. I went on to my room, depressed.

Helena twined herself around me when I came into bed, her head falling on my shoulder in its accustomed place. I held her affectionately and stayed quiet so she fell asleep. I did not tell her what I had just seen.

XXXVII

IT WAS BARELY light when hectic knocking awoke me. Running footsteps sounded outside in the corridor. There were cries of alarm; then I heard a brief order and all the noises were cut off.

Rousing myself, I flung open the bedroom door. Helena murmured behind me sleepily as light from the corridor lamps came in. A scared slave was waiting. He told me anxiously that the soldiers who were guarding our prisoners thought something had gone wrong.

Hilaris appeared. Hair ruffled, and pulling on a long-sleeved robe like some barbaric Eastern potentate, he confirmed the worst: Pyro had been found dead.

An hour of frantic activity later we had worked out something of what had happened. Perusal of the body told us beyond question that it was an unnatural death. Pyro was the bristle-chinned enforcer, not heavily built and yet a muscular, tough-looking specimen. He was about thirty-five or forty, an age when many die, but he had been well nourished in his lifetime and was suffering from no obvious disease. He had not been told that the torturer was coming to work on him, but even if he guessed, none of us believed this hardened brute had died of fear or killed himself.

His lips and mouth showed faint indications of corrosion burn: poison. The soldiers admitted they had found him collapsed, though he was still living at that stage. When they tried to revive him, he suffered fits. He was unable to speak and appeared to be paralysed. Afraid of being disciplined for not watching him more closely, they had worked on him themselves – well, soldiers always believe they know better than doctors. He died. They then wasted what must have been a couple more hours debating what to do.

This was a private house. The only reason prisoners had been kept at the residence was to be closer to the governor when he put them through his magistrate's interview. They had been locked in windowless rooms that were normally stores. The soldiers were billeted in an improvised guardroom on the same corridor, but they admitted they had closed the door, probably so they could play illicit board games unobserved. This corridor was informally closed off with a rope but it was situated in the service area of the house. That put it near to the kitchen, essentially a public wing. Adjacent to the kitchen, as in many homes, was a lavatory.

Members of the procurator's private household mainly used the other facilities in the bath complex, but visitors would automatically seek out the kitchen, knowing there was bound to be a sit-down closet alongside. It had happened last night. All sorts of people had used that lavatory in fact, including the soldiers and a carrier bringing in late night deliveries of food for the dinner. Any of these could have noticed that the cook had prepared trays with basic meals for all the prisoners, and that two trays had remained on a side table after word went down that Pyro and Splice were to be deprived of sleep and food on the orders of the torturer.

Those two trays had stayed for hours, just outside the kitchen. Then somebody removed them. The cook, fully preoccupied with serving up a banquet, thought nothing of their disappearance. The soldiers told us they came across the trays in the prisoners' corridor; they supposed Amicus had changed his orders so they delivered the food. Pyro ate his.

The waiters and barber, who had been fed earlier, were all fine. Splice had refused to eat: he was frightened the governor would have him poisoned – not that the rest of us blamed Frontinus for what had befallen Pyro. But thanks to his fears, Splice remained alive. His foodbowl was now taken to be tested on some stray animal. It would die; I did not need to see the results.

Everyone in the kitchen had been working flat out last evening. Guests had come and gone. Beyond muttering 'It's that door there, sir!' several times, the staff had taken no notice.

Aelia Camilla swore by the probity of her cook. He was a big Trinovantian with a thick moustache, who looked more like a seaman than a gourmet chef, though someone had trained him well. He cannot have had traditional knowledge of rabbit richly stuffed with calves' brain and chicken, or even simple Roman custard or roasted dates Alexandrian. I suspect Aelia Camilla had taught him herself; she certainly rounded on her husband when angry questioning from Hilaris reduced the big cook to tears.

The governor turned up, naturally furious. Frontinus gave orders to have Splice transferred to the greater security of the fort. He was forgetting one important fact: Londinium did not have a secure fort. I pointed it out. Splice was sent to the military anyway.

There was nothing more to learn. I went to find Petronius. He needed to know that Pyro had been eliminated, presumably by an accomplice from the gang. I needed to discuss the implications.

I rapped on his bedroom door, intending to hover outside in the corridor to avoid embarrassment. The secretive Petronius had known since our army days how to keep his women to himself.

When there was no answer, I forced myself to open the door. As I had guessed by then, the room was deserted, its bed neatly made with smoothed pillow and covers. He had gone back on watch already.

Anxious, I decided I would pack in some breakfast; today was likely to be busy. I had forgotten that the cook was hysterical. So far there were only a couple of roughly chopped loaves and some rubbery eggs which must have sat in the pan on a racing boil for at least an hour. Even more annoying, I was joined for my grim repast by my sister.

I expect the worst from women but in contrast to our siblings (who were a bunch of hussies), I had always believed that my sister Maia was a virgin schoolgirl, a decent young woman, and a chaste wife. While it's true Famia had got her pregnant, she then married him. And they had stayed married.

Now I had seen her embarking on a night of savage physicality – yet she appeared the next morning looking the same as usual. She gave a grunt when she saw me and was soon eating a light breakfast in her accustomed grumpy silence. I found this troublesome. What was the point of any man expending himself on white-hot lovemaking, in the arms of a woman he had eyed up yearningly for years, if the experience only left her irritably picking stale crumbs from her teeth?

It raised another doubt. Petronius and I swore by that old line all bad boys believe: *you can always tell.* That was evidently untrue.

'What are you staring at?' demanded Maia.

'That egg's a bit black . . . I found your harpist lurking in a corridor very late last night. Get rid of him, sis. He's spying.'

'He's blind.'

'His boy is not.'

Maia fell silent. I could imagine her thoughts. The harpist was going back, no question. However, when I asked politely what plans she had today, she astonished me. 'Oh I think I'll take up Norbanus on his offer to go downriver to his country place.'

And I liked to think that juggling lovers was a male preserve.

'You would do better spending some time with your children,' I told her primly. My sister shot me yet another scathing glance.

I had been intending to go out to find Petro with the news about Pyro. But then we were joined at breakfast by another early-rising house guest: King Togidubnus.

'This is a first!' I joked politely.

'Yes, you're usually long gone when I trot along – old man's privilege. Today I heard the commotion.'

'I'm sorry that you were disturbed, sir. To tell the truth, since I hadn't seen you recently, I assumed you had gone back to Noviomagus.'

'Things to do,' replied the King, frowning at the meagre

supplies on the buffet. 'Does this prisoner's death mean you are losing your case, Falco? What about my commission to find who killed my man?'

'I am making progress.' Well, I knew how to lie.

'I heard the suspect was being tortured. Is that what killed him?'

'No, he had not yet been touched.'

'So you had no evidence out of him?' the King noted sourly.

'We'll get there . . . I may call up help from my nephew and brothers-in-law. I guess you would be glad if they stopped carousing around your district anyway?' Larius, my nephew from Stabiae, and Helena's two younger brothers were taking leisure time at Noviomagus – up to all the ghastly pursuits of young men. The Camilli were supposed to act as my assistants, though they were untrained and probably not safe to use in a case which involved professional criminals.

'We are managing to survive their presence,' said the King, commendably tolerant. The lads were rabid hitters of night-spots. If there was trouble around, they found their way straight into it. 'I want Larius to stay and paint for me.' My nephew was a fresco artist of great distinction. He had been brought to Britain to work on the King's palace. Maybe thinking about the project, on which Verovolcus had been his liaison officer, brought Togidubnus' mind back to the stalled investigation. 'My men have been pursuing enquiries, just like you, Falco.'

'Any luck?'

It was merely a polite question, but the King surprised me once again. This day was becoming stressful. All this time, the Atrebates had been in serious contention with Petro and me – and they had pulled off a coup. The King boasted genially: 'I think you will be impressed, Falco! We have persuaded the barmaid from the Shower of Gold to tell us all she knows.'

I choked on my beaker of goats milk. *'Oh?'*

'We have her in a safe house,' Togi told me, with a twinkle. 'In view of what has happened to your own witness, I think I had better make ours available, don't you?'

XXXVIII

THE ATREBATES MANAGED not to smirk. There were four of
the King's retainers, loose-limbed warriors with flyaway red
hair. In the summer heat they had cast off their colourful long-
sleeved tunics and were bare-chested (with sunburn). All boasted
gold bracelets and neck chains. A bunch of spears leaned against a
wall, while their owners lounged about in a yard. They were
hiding their prize at a farm in the northeast of the town. When I
was brought to see her at least it livened up a boring day for them.

'Obviously we have to protect her,' the King had said to me.
'Once she has given her evidence and helped to secure a
conviction, she will be set up in a wine shop of her own in my
tribal capital, away from here. You may not approve of the way
we have handled her,' Togidubnus suggested rather warily.

I grinned. 'When dealing with people who trade in vice and
extortion, it seems only fair to retaliate with bribery.'

He bridled. 'I am not paying her to lie, you know!'

'Of course not, sir.' Even if he was, so long as she piped up
boldly and stuck to her story with due diligence, my conscience
would cope.

She was still too stout, too ugly, and too slow on the uptake for
me. She was still four feet high. But they had provided her with
new clothes, so she looked like a middle-class shop-owner: a role
which, with the King's promise of the new wine bar in
Noviomagus, she intended to achieve.

The former waitress had already assumed an expression of great respectability. She reminded me of my mother, laying aside her working clothes for a festival, combing her hair in a fancy style (which did not suit her), and suddenly turning into a stranger. Ma used to drink too much and be indiscreet about the neighbours on such occasions. This one was sober at the moment, and certainly wanted to appear polite.

When I was taken to her by the slightly po-faced Atrebatan warriors, she did not exactly offer me cinnamon bread and borage tea, but she sat, with her knees close together and her hands firmly clasped in her lap, waiting to impress me with her new-found status. She was apparently looking forward to a life where she no longer had to sleep with customers; or at least, she said, *not unless she wanted to*. It almost sounded as if some sharp lawyer had been talking to her about the legal rights of tavern landladies. As such, I reckoned she would be a terror. She seemed extremely keen on the idea that she would be in charge. Of course most underlings reckon they can run places far better than the boss. (This was certainly true in the case of the legendary Flora's, a caupona run by my sister Junia who had all the public catering skills of a ten-year-old.)

'We meet again!' I challenged her. 'I don't suppose you remember me; I'm Falco. I like to think women find me looming large in the memory, but modesty is a fine Roman virtue.'

She giggled. That was a new and decidedly off-putting trait.

She was now being called Flavia Fronta. One of the weapons in the governor's armoury was to extend Roman citizenship to favoured barbarians. In return, he hoped to people his province with loyal little friends of the Emperor, obsequiously named after him. It had a knack of working. And it cost nothing.

'So Flavia Fronta!' I was trying hard not to remember her as the grimy purveyor of sex and bad temper that I had seen twice at the Shower of Gold. The Atrebatans were observing me. Access to their witness was only granted on condition they watched to see that I did not extract new clues from her unfairly. It put my methods under closer scrutiny than I liked. 'I understand you are now giving a statement about the death of Verovolcus?'

'Yes sir, that was terrible.' I nearly choked with laughter at her change of tune. She was quiet, dutiful and respectful. Frankly, I thought she was lying through her teeth.

'Tell me, please.'

Civilisation had a lot to answer for. She had come up with a painful new speaking accent. In these affected vowels, she recited the evidence as if tutored: 'A British man I had never seen before came to our bar that evening and sat down with Splice and Pyro.'

'Did you hear what they talked about?'

'Yes, sir. The British man wanted to join in their business – which is rather unpleasant, as you probably know. They did not want to let him in on it.'

'So they were not all friendly together?'

'No. They had met him to complain about his interest. He offered to work with them, but they laughed at him. He said, he was from this province and would do what he liked in Londinium. They soon showed him how wrong he was. You know what happened. They tipped him up and pushed him in the well.'

'Did none of you try to stop them?'

'I was too scared. The owner would not interfere.'

'Was he paying Pyro and Splice for protection?'

'Oh yes. He's terrified of them.'

'Pyro and Splice are well known at your bar? And you consider them violent?'

'Yes, sir. Very violent.'

'And what about the third man, their companion?'

'He comes in sometimes.'

'How do you regard him?'

'Someone to avoid very carefully.'

'And who is he?'

'I only know he comes from Rome, sir.'

'You think he is a leader of the gang?'

'Oh yes. Everybody knows he is; he brought Pyro and Splice and other people over to Britain. They have always worked for him. He runs everything.'

'And let's be quite sure – he was the man giving the orders, the night Verovolcus was killed? Did you yourself hear him do that?'

'Yes, he said: *"Do the deed, boys!"* And so they did.'

'Did he go out into the yard where the well was?'

'No, he just sat at the table where he was. And smiled,' shuddered Flavia Fronta. 'That was horrible . . .'

'I'm sorry I have to ask you to remember. Now when this man gave them that order, Pyro and Splice knew exactly what to do? They must have discussed it beforehand?'

'Yes. The man could not believe it was happening to him. I'll never forget the look in his eyes . . .' Her expression of pity for Verovolcus seemed genuine. The Atrebatans glanced at each other, nervous of the chilling, deliberate violence she described. They had all known Verovolcus, presumably.

I pursed my lips. 'This organiser is an evil man. We badly need to know who he is. It is a shame you have no idea of his name.'

'Oh don't I?' the woman asked, enjoying herself.

I paused. 'You told me all you know is that he comes from Rome.'

'That's right,' said Flavia Fronta. 'But I do know his name.'

For a blissful moment, I thought she was going to tell me. No such luck. Working in a downtown bar had taught the lady basic self-preservation. She gave me a whimsical smile. 'Now go on – you must think I'm daft! If you stick Pyro and Splice in court then yes, I'll give evidence. After I'm safe in my own little wine shop, far away down south, then I'll tell you who the big man is.'

I managed to keep my temper. I did wonder whether to hand over this self-satisfied baggage to Amicus. But I came from Rome; I knew how tough women could be. She was just the sort to become his first non-responsive victim and thwart us.

'You're very wise,' I told her with admiration. 'Let me give you a warning, however. Pyro is dead. He died last night; it seems this gang have a long reach, and they got to him even in the official residence.' She looked worried. 'If anything happens to Splice now – or if he confesses voluntarily when tortured – you will be left with no bargaining power.' She looked *really* worried. 'King Togidubnus will have no need for gratitude; there will be no wine bar in the south. If I were in your shoes . . .' I glanced down, and yes, the Atrebatans had bought the frowsty dame a pair of new patterned footgear in which to cram her misshapen hooves. 'Then I would co-operate at once.'

Flavia Fronta was watching me thoughtfully.

'We are going to find this man anyway,' I bragged. Maybe it was even true. 'But speed matters. That's where your help could be invaluable.' She was still silent. I shrugged. 'Of course, it is your choice.'

Never underrate the appeal of choice for those whose lives have, until then, lacked any chance of it. Flavia Fronta half covered her mouth with a nervous hand. Then she whispered, 'His name is Florius.'

XXXIX

FLORIUS! SO THIS was the Balbinus mob again.

Florius must be the second man Petronius was hunting, the one he had already chased for a long time. It had seemed personal: well, he and Florius certainly had reasons for a feud. Petro had slept with the little Florius wife – which led to the breakdown not of their marriage, but his own.

I racked my brains to remember what I knew. I had met Florius – back in the days when he seemed like a worthless and harmless hanger-on. His marriage to a gangster's daughter was incongruous; Florius, a shambling, feeble, untidy bundle who spent his days at the races, gave the impression that he had been chosen as Balbina Milvia's bridegroom simply because he was a soft pudding the family could push around. It had looked like a ploy to protect her father's money. If her papa were arrested, his property would be forfeit, but Roman law has a fine respect for marriage; if Milvia's dowry chests were labelled 'sheets and coverlets for the bride and her future children' they would probably be sacrosanct.

Petronius and I had chased down Balbinus, whose vicious gangs had been terrorising Rome. We eliminated him, incurring the hatred of his widow. Petro then complicated everything when he decided to bed dear little Milvia. She was ten years younger than him and thought he was serious; she even talked of them marrying. Florius cannot have taken that well – if he knew – which he probably did, because Milvia was dim enough to tell him everything. If she hadn't, her spiteful mother would have done. I had heard that the mother then made the married couple stick together (to protect the money) but life in their house must have been a strain ever since.

If Florius really had been a soft blob, there would have been no problem. But I could remember watching how he straightened up after his father-in-law died. His moment had come. Florius immediately started plotting to take over. Remnants of the Balbinus organisation still existed, though weakened. Florius would be welcomed. Underworld associates love crime lords' relatives; they have a big sense of history. His mother-in-law, Flaccida, was hoping to regenerate the family empire and when Petronius Longus rebuffed pretty Milvia, even Milvia may then have supported Florius' new career. Being married to the top enforcer would suit her. She had always claimed to be unaware of her late father's occupation – but she loved the money.

Florius threw himself into racketeering. His dead father-in-law had shown him how to do it. His rise must have been swift. The description of that third man ordering Pyro and Splice to dispose of Verovolcus, while he was callously sitting tight, showed a totally different character from the vague lump absorbed in his betting tokens whom I had first met. Florius was now a full villain.

I myself saved up tangling with crime lords for special occasions, days when I wished to toy with suicide. But Petronius presumably kept his eye on the reviving gang. He wanted to finish what he and I had started. He was planning to obliterate them. They probably knew his intentions.

I feared for him in Britain. Here, Petronius stood on his own. At least in Rome, with the seven vigiles cohorts in support, he had had some chance. The best back-up on offer in Londinium was me. And I had only just learned of the predicament. With the old Balbinus mob, a mere hour was enough for them to pounce and tear a victim apart.

So Florius was here. That meant Petronius Longus was virtually standing at the gateway to Hades, ready to tramp in after the guide with the downturned torch.

★

What was I to do? Find him. Tell him Florius was in Britain.

I guessed he knew. I hoped he did. That was probably why he had been sent here himself. So, find him and give him some cover – but where would he be?

I considered all our leads. The henchman, Splice, had been marched off to custody among the troops, awaiting the torturer. Top suspects Norbanus and Popillius were being watched by the governor's men. Florius would be Petro's priority. I crossed town, and headed for the wharves. I guessed Petro would be at the warehouse where the baker had been murdered. But he was not. I found Firmus, the customs man, who freely showed me what he and Petro thought had been the killing ground. He led me to one of many great stores that fringed the shore. Totally anonymous in the packed row of identical buildings, I could see why the gang chose it. It was sturdily constructed, fully secure for money or contraband. There was easy access, by water or even by road. All sorts of characters frequented the docks, too. Even hardened criminals from Rome – who tend to have distinctive habits and style – would merge in. Down here by the river, nobody would think twice if there were frequent movements in and out. And when they killed someone, nobody would hear the screams.

'Petronius was here at first light,' said Firmus. 'He wanted to talk to the ferryman – but the ferryman's gone sick.'

'What with?' I asked, knowing the answer.

'Fear.'

'Didn't Petronius try to find him?'

'I think he tried. No luck. After that Petro disappeared.'

I gazed at him. 'So how will you get in touch with him if something happens at this warehouse?'

'It's not my job,' Firmus demurred. 'We are only keeping watch, as a personal favour to Petronius.'

'His famous charm!'

'He's a good sort,' said Firmus. Well, I knew that. 'He's doing a good job, that none of us would like to tackle. Maybe he's stupid, but you can tell he's the kind who thinks somebody ought to do what he's doing, and if it's not him it will end up being nobody.'

'True.' I balked at following the logic, but his feelings were clear.

'The customs service doesn't have the manpower for this operation,' Firmus insisted. 'Nor any support from higher-up.' The pleasant, sunburned, roly-poly officer was sounding bitter now. 'They see us as petty clerks, just turning over tax. We know what happens. We tell the ones in charge. They just pay us cobnuts and won't even supply elementary weapons. We told the governor there is a large-scale operation working here, Falco. That poor sod the baker was murdered on my patch. But I've given up sticking my head over the fortress parapet.'

I gave him a look.

Firmus was unrepentant. 'I'm not being paid danger money,' he said baldly.

'Don't you get military support?'

'You are joking! So why should I and my men be stuffed, while the soldiers just play around and take backhanders from everyone?'

'Including from criminals?'

Firmus exploded. '*Especially* the criminals!'

I let him rave. If he told me any more I was liable to get wound up myself.

'I'll mention you, if I see Petro,' Firmus relented.

I nodded. 'Thanks. Now tell me something, Firmus. If the criminal action happens on the wharves, why is my friend Petronius Longus spending time at that bath house several streets up the hill?'

Firmus pursed his lips. 'It's a nice bath house . . . Excellent manicure girl. Blonde. Well, sort of.' He came clean. 'He's watching someone. Someone who uses that stinky brothel next to the baths.'

'What, as a customer?'

'No, no. He's a flesh peddler. It's his local office.'

I caught on. 'And this someone features big in the gang?'

A guarded look clouded the customs officer's normally open face. 'I believe so.'

I took a chance. 'We know who it is. I need to find Petro to warn him and to back him up. We are looking for a top man called Florius.'

'Well, good for you,' commented Firmus, in a distinctly quiet voice. He had known all along. I wondered how many others also knew, but were too scared to say.

XL

P ETRONIUS WAS NOT at the baths. The man in charge accepted
that I was a friend, and said he thought Petro had gone back
over to the residence. There, Helena told me I had missed him. 'I
may be wrong, Marcus, but I thought he was looking for Maia.'
Helena was watching me closely.

'Did he find her?' I asked in a non-committal tone.

'No, she had gone out.'

I checked both their rooms. Petro's was exactly as I had seen it
that morning when I wanted to tell him about Pyro's death.
Maia's looked as if a troop of wild monkeys had run through it;
still, that was usual for her. She kept a well-run home, but her
own quarters were always a tip. She had been the same since she
was a girl – clothes strewn everywhere, lids open on boxes, and
dried-up face paint mixed weeks ago in shells. Partly it was
because she never spent any time there. Until that bastard
Anacrites made her hunted and shrewish, she was too gregarious,
always out and about.

A potted plant, some feeble British thing, all leaves, stood on a
side table. 'Now I wonder where that came from?' Sharp-eyed,
Helena had noticed it. She had come up behind me, curious what
I was thinking.

'Is it new?'

'Some love gift to Maia from Norbanus?' Helena speculated.

'So it's gardening now. Will he stand more chance with foliage
than with his sinister harpist?'

'She sent the harpist back this morning,' said Helena, as if she thought I might have had something to do with it. 'The plant may be from someone else . . .'

'So where's she gone? I hope she's not playing at country life with Norbanus in his villa.'

'I doubt it.'

'She told me she would.'

Helena smiled. 'She tells you a lot of nonsense. This villa seems rather odd, in any case. Marcus, the man who tailed the carrying-chair, came back this morning and reported to Uncle Gaius.'

'And you just happened to be talking to your uncle at the right moment . . . ?' I grinned.

Helena smiled again, serenely. 'Norbanus lives in the northern part of town. According to the neighbours, he stays in Londinium every day. They were surprised even to hear he has a villa on the river. It sounds as if he never goes there.'

'Why is he so keen to show it off to Maia then?' Was it purely his love nest for seductions? I preferred not to think about that. 'What do these neighbours say of him?'

'A very ordinary man.'

'Informers know that no man is ordinary.'

'Well, all men think they are special,' Helena retorted.

I grinned. Luckily I liked her to be prejudiced. 'What about this one?'

'Norbanus lives quietly. Talks to people pleasantly. Speaks fondly and frequently of his widowed mother. Pats dogs. Eats lunch at a local food shop. Is respectful to local women and communicative with local men. He is generally liked, a good neighbour, they say.'

'I especially like the touch about the mother.' I then told Helena that the quiet ones always harbour dark secrets. When killers or world-beating fraudsters are apprehended, their neighbours invariably shriek with surprise. First they deny that such a sweet person could have done something terrible. Later they themselves hone up sensational tales of how he dragged a teenage girl down

an alley, and always had a weird look in his eyes ... Helena
commented on how cynical I was today.

Well, maybe Norbanus was full of antique nobility. Even so, I
did not want my sister cuddling up to him in some British bower.
I went into Maia's silent room and sat upon the bed, staring at the
plant. Helena remained in the doorway, watching me thoughtfully. I told her what I had discovered that morning about Florius.
'You never met him, did you?'

She shook her head. 'No. His relatives were bad enough. Petro
had a visitation from Milvia once, when he was staying with us.'
That would have been just after Petro's own wife threw him out.
Helena grimaced. 'And Marcus, wasn't it her horrid mother who
barged in another time, blustering that our Lucius must leave her
darling flower alone? As if we were not trying very hard to make
him do just that – for his own sake!'

'I wish Petro had taken the advice.'

'The mother was a fright,' Helena reminisced. 'All threats and
venom. And Balbina Milvia! One of those girls I hate – bright eyes
and loads of enviable jewellery. Much too pretty to bother with
good manners or brains.'

'Bad sex!' I exclaimed.

Helena looked shocked. 'How do you know that? Did
Petronius Longus tell you, during some evil drinking bout?'

'Actually no. He has never talked about his lovers.' He and I had
leered at plenty of women from wine bars over the years; I knew
how he thought. 'But you can see Milvia is only interested in
herself. She wanted Petronius because having a secret lover made
her feel important.'

Helena still felt she had stumbled on evidence of some boys'
lewd game. She had never entirely trusted me not to be off on
some affair. Chloris was the current suspect, of course. Frowning,
she went back to our original discussion. 'You thought Milvia was
trouble.'

'I was right.'

'As for the husband, he was ineffectual.'

228

'Not nowadays. It's all change in the Balbinus mob. The mother is showing her age. Who knows where the wilful wifey is? But Florius has transmogrified from a loose piece of gristle into one of the world's tight dealers. His treatment of Verovolcus shows he suffers nobody to stand in his way now.'

Helena was concerned. 'Florius had you attacked once. Then Petro was caught alone, and he was very badly hurt.'

'A warning.'

'Yet Petronius is still determined to get Florius? While Florius knows exactly who he is dealing with: Petronius Longus of the vigiles enquiry team, who turned Florius' sweet little, rich little wife into an adulteress — and then didn't even want her, but dumped her back at home.'

'I'm sure he gave Milvia a happy time first,' I said. It was automatic. Then I thought of him kissing my sister last night in that grim scenario, and I felt squeamish.

'What's wrong?' asked Helena. I shook my head. After a moment she let it go and said, 'These people want revenge.'

'That's right. And they won't quit.'

I stood up. I stopped wondering where my sister was. Off enjoying herself on some tryst with the suave and slimy Norbanus, while her last night's lover was in serious trouble.

I decided to retrace my steps to the baths. Petro would turn up some time. But first the hour was late enough to take in lunch here. Hilaris must be ravenous too, after our dawn start when the corpse was found, for we met him also guiltily scrounging in the dining room. That was how Helena and I happened to be with him when a confidential messenger arrived from the troops. In a great hurry, the man was looking for the governor. Hilaris knew Frontinus was still working diligently on dispatches, but before the messenger was passed to the right office, Hilaris made him tell us what the fuss was.

Splice had escaped.

We all rushed with the messenger to see the governor. Frontinus heard the news with that neutrality good officials learn. He must have been angry, but waited to think through the implications before shooting off.

'What exactly happened?'

'I only know what I was told to say, sir.' The messenger skilfully let blame slide on to others. 'The soldiers escorting the prisoner were somehow given the slip and they lost him.'

'That was first thing this morning. How come I only just have word of it?'

'They tried to recapture him, sir.'

Frontinus was speechless. Losing a vital prisoner was inexcusable. But to me it seemed typical; I could imagine some slack bunch of lags out here, laughing among themselves: *Oh just say sorry to the old man – he'll be all right about it . . .*

'I warned you about the troops.'

'You did.' Frontinus was terse. In a frontier province, dereliction of duty was a decimation crime: one man in ten, chosen by lot, would be bludgeoned to death by his disgraced colleagues. That would not be the end of it. The effect on morale would be grim, both here and up at the frontiers when the rumours raced there.

An aide was hovering. Frontinus rapped out orders, hardly pausing for reflection. 'Get me the commander. Before he comes over, I want that detail stripped of their weapons and armour, then held in chains. They are to be guarded by men from one of the other detachments, not their own legion. Disarm their centurion and bring him here to me. I want every on-duty legionary to go out in a search party. I want the troops put on permanent standby. It goes without saying, I want the prisoner back.'

Some hopes, I thought.

'Today!' he added. Julius Frontinus now saw his provincial capital slipping into anarchy. Luckily he was a practical man, and action helped him cope. Even so, I had rarely seen him so tight-lipped.

I was even more depressed. But then I had worked against the Balbinus mob before.

XLI

O N MY WAY out I was stopped by a message from the torturer. Amicus, the sardonically named Befriender, had made up for losing the chance to prick holes in Pyro and Splice. He had tackled the waiters with a heated manicure set, then turned the recalcitrant barber almost inside out with a contraption I tried not to look at.

'I am sorry not to have a crack at this Splice,' he grieved when I sought him out in the bowels of the residence. 'He sounds an interesting prospect. I hope they get him back for me. Do you know how he acquired the nickname, Falco?'

'I suspect you are about to tell me – and it will be unpleasant.'

He chortled. Maybe his happy manner helped unnerve his victims; the contrast with his pain-inflicting side certainly disturbed me. 'Splice wanted to punish two snackshop owners, cousins who shared a bar jointly, and who were refusing to pay up. He went in one night and hacked both men in two from top to bottom. Then he bound the left side of each body to the right-hand side of the other. He left the results propped up against the serving counter.'

'Jupiter!'

'That's apt. Jupiter is a favourite with this gang,' agreed Amicus warmly. 'Plenty of signboards with the same mythical theme. Apt, since the Best and Greatest is the patron god of grapes and wine. Also it lets everyone see just how many businesses have paid up.'

'Yes, I worked that out.'

'But you don't spot them all,' rebuked Amicus. 'I'll come to that

. . . First I shall tell you what I have.' He was pedantic in giving reports. 'The organisation works thus: there are two equal leaders, both currently engaged in setting up a British crime community. One takes the sporty premises – brothels, betting, and fixing fights for gladiators. The other collects neighbourhood food and drink shops. They have come from Rome, but are planning to leave when their empire here is established. Pyro and Splice were intended to run this section for them.'

'Do the gang have a tame lawyer, one Popillius?'

'Not mentioned. They do have storage, ships, safe houses, a safe *bath house* even, and large group of heavy fighters. Some thugs they brought here, mainly seasoned criminals who found Rome too hot for comfort. Some are being recruited locally. Bad boys are rushing to join them. That is how they met the man who died.'

'Verovolcus, you mean? Yes, he was on the run . . . How do they attract these local boys? Don't tell me they advertise for hired labour on a pillar in the forum – *free time, victuals and drink, plenty of beating up the populace?*'

Amicus shrugged. 'Word of mouth, bound to be. I can ask.'

'It's not important. Assuming we catch Splice again, what can he be charged with?'

'He beat the baker to death. Pyro had picked the baker up, he was drinking at a wine bar called the Semele.'

'One of Jupiter's favoured ladies.'

'But did the baker know the gang ran it, or was he caught off guard?' wondered Amicus. 'Pyro torched the bakery, of course; that was his job. He was then present for the killing at the warehouse, although Splice carried it out.'

'That's definite. Where's your evidence? Witnesses?'

Amicus shook his head. 'This is second hand, but I got it from the Ganymede waiters.'

'The waiters won't look good in court.'

'No, but now you can build on the information. If you ever apprehend them, some of the back-up bullyboys were in at the death. They also took the body on the boat and dumped it. The waiters heard all this when Splice reported to one of the two chiefs. The other didn't need telling; it was his boat. He was present at the warehouse where the killing happened. He came to take some money-chests away by river, then removed the dead baker at the same time. Good housekeeping. Better than a skip.' I shuddered; even the torturer pursed his lips disapprovingly. 'Now.' Amicus was coming to some special point. 'I was asked to obtain names.'

'Well let's compare,' I offered, knowing it would irritate him.

Amicus announced rather pompously, 'I was given Florius.'

My answer was calm. 'Gaius Florius Oppicus, to be precise.'

The torturer tutted, as though I was quite out of order in obtaining my own information – especially if mine was better than his. 'He is the vicious one, Falco. All agree he is vindictive, cruel and out to prevent any attempts by the authorities to interfere.'

'Sounds right. Florius gave the order for the Verovolcus killing.'

'No, hold it there, Falco!' Amicus held up a hand. 'My sources say different. They claim it was an accident.'

'Your sources sound insane!'

'According to them, Verovolcus was despised as a potential rival and not wanted as a colleague. He had tried to slither in on the market, and he thought he was tough – but the hard Roman gangsters simply regarded him as a clownish amateur. He was put down the well just to teach him a lesson.'

'Death's a hard lesson,' I commented.

'My sources dispute that,' Amicus insisted.

'Your sources are lying. I saw the corpse, remember.'

Amicus gave me a distasteful look; it was fine for him to haul men to the brink of death, screaming in agony, crippled for ever and mentally destroyed, but he disapproved of me for inspecting so many who had actually died.

He was starting to annoy me. 'Come on – "An accident"?' I scoffed. 'The lawyer must have tutored them! Verovolcus was shoved in and drowned.'

'The barber –'

233

I laughed harshly. 'Oh your strong-willed resistant razorman!'

The torturer grinned. He liked to think he was ascetic but he was showing intense enjoyment. 'The barber was a kitten once I found the right trick . . .'

'Don't tell me.'

'Ah, Falco, you are too sensitive. He overheard Florius and the other top man discussing the incident afterwards. Apparently, Florius goes for the shaved-head look, to fool people he's a hard bastard.'

'Not when I knew him,' I growled.

'Florius maintained what had happened was horseplay; he said they all went away laughing, expecting that the Briton would just climb out, embarrassed and wet. He was astonished later, when he heard that Verovolcus had been found dead.'

'*All a terrible mistake; my client is shocked* . . . You sound like his lawyer again.'

'Oh don't be cruel, Falco.'

'Sorry! I don't like insulting experts – but I'm on the Verovolcus murder for the old King. I cannot tell Togidubnus his retainer died as a result of a light-hearted game going wrong.'

'Just tell him Florius did it then.' Morality came in subtle shades among torturers. 'He must be guilty of other crimes, Falco. And you have a witness who says he ordered this one.'

'What do you know about my witness?' I asked apprehensively.

'You've been careless. You were given information by a female gladiator called Amazonia, at a bar called the Cradle in the Tree.'

I was horrified. 'Don't tell me it's one of the gang's establishments? But I thought of that; I checked the name. What has a rocking cradle to do with Jupiter?'

Amicus was literate, a reader and learner, more knowledgeable than me about myths. He liked showing off too: 'By ancient tradition, the god Jupiter was the son of a deity, Cronos. Cronos used to eat his children – a vicious way to avoid a prophecy that he would one day be displaced by his own son. Jupiter's mother hid the newborn baby in a golden cradle hung in a tree between the earth and sky, so he could not be found by his jealous father, anywhere on land or sea.'

'Oh shit!'

'You and the girl were overheard, Falco.'

'Then she is in danger . . .'

'Of course you could never produce a gladiatrix in court. Even so, Florius will want to wipe her out.' Amicus seemed to regard this outcome far more phlegmatically than I did.

'I have to warn her – fast!'

'One more thing.' The torturer's manner became as dour as I had seen it. 'This Florius also knows of a Roman officer who is tailing him. Falco, is that you?'

'No. It's a member of the vigiles.'

Amicus approved of the vigiles as much as he disapproved of me. Petronius was professional, a salaried paramilitary, on a par with the torturer himself; I was an informer, so just a low-class liability. My new equestrian ring just made me a jumped-up fake. 'Florius has sworn to get him.' Amicus had seen my face. 'Friend of yours, is he?'

'The best.'

I was rushing to fetch equipment when I met Helena. As if she had read my mind, she was hurrying towards me, carrying my sword. Behind her followed that distinctive member of the gladiator group, the girl who wanted to be a boy. Or whoever.

'Marcus! Chloris may be in difficulty –'

'We need your help,' said the flat-chested androgynous sprite with the limpid eyes.

'Tell me what's happened!' As I spoke, Helena was helping me buckle on the sword.

'That man who wants to take us over has asked for a meeting with Amazonia. She's getting nervous about him. She thinks he might turn violent.'

'She's right,' I replied grimly. 'He's called Florius. He leads one of Rome's worst criminal gangs – they are extremely dangerous.

What's more, Florius knows that she gave me a statement against him.'

The messenger squeaked. 'Well, she tried stalling him. But now he's saying he will lean on the arena programmers. We will never get billing again unless we co-operate. She had to do something about it. She arranged to meet him at the arena this afternoon.'

'Has she gone there? Did she go alone?'

'I don't know . . .'

'Fetch all your group! She will need anyone who can fight.' To Helena I muttered, 'Florius is likely to turn up mob-handed. Tell the governor and your uncle. We shall need troops. If they don't trust the garrison, ask them to send auxiliaries from their personal bodyguards.'

Helena was pale. 'What about Petronius?'

'Tell him what's up if you see him. But he has been on watch at that so-called office in the brothel by the baths. I bet Petro has known all along it was a regular haunt for Florius. If I know my boy, he'll see Florius leave and he'll tail him.'

'I'll go myself and tell Petro,' Helena decided.

I had no time to argue. 'Well be very careful. Take Albia; she knows where it is.'

XLII

T HE ARENA LAY in the northwestern sector of town. It was
brand new. Around it was a bare area where nobody yet lived
or worked. On rough land on the town side stood a row of
market-style stalls, their counters mostly covered at present,
though when there was a show they would undoubtedly all be
manned by conniving peddlers. One or two doggedly offered light
snacks and statuettes of gladiators, even though today there were
only a few casual sightseers milling about. A bear on a chain,
probably nothing to do with the arena beasts, was being sadly
paraded near an entrance gate. His teeth had been drawn. No self-
respecting organiser would put him in the ring. Deprived of his
fangs, he was starving to death.

A janitor was letting in the curious to 'see the arena' for a small
tip. Word must have circulated that the girl gladiators were
practising. The usual sex-mad men with no work to do and no
shame had ambled up for a squint at the muscles and short skirts.
It looked as if these oddballs came to drool on a daily basis.

Dear gods, there were even tourists. We needed to clear these
people. No chance. The strollers would refuse to leave, once they
sniffed out that an official operation was in train. People are nuts.
They forget their own safety and want to gawp. And it would be
obvious we had the place staked out. Oh Hades. Oh double
Hades. Florius wouldn't come anywhere near if he noticed a
reception party.

This Londinium amphitheatre was nothing compared with the
massive monument that Vespasian was creating as his personal gift

to the people of Rome. The Emperor had drained the lake of Nero's Golden House and was planning the largest place of entertainment in the world. At home, we had four teams of masons working flat out. A whole quarry had been opened on the road to Tibur; two hundred ox carts *every day* blocked the city highway as they hauled in the Travertine marble for cladding. The southern end of the forum was chaos, had been since the Emperor's accession, would be for years yet. All the slaves captured in the pacification of Judaea were being worked to death.

By contrast, Londinium's toy arena stood in a bleak spot and was made of wood. I expected it to look as if it had been knocked together by a couple of leisure-time carpenters, but it was an expert job. These sturdy hewn timbers were no doubt a treasure-house of the single dovetail corner and the spiked half lap joint. We Romans had taught Britain the concept of an organised timber trade; we introduced decent sawyers, but also brought pre-fabricated building frames that could be rapidly assembled on site. The army started it; some forts came as kits – pre-cut timbers and their fixing nails – ready to be thrown up in the face of the barbarians, seemingly overnight. A permanent armed force of any significance acquired its arena to keep the lads happy. This edifice signified that Londinium was now a legitimate part of the Empire and definitely on the up.

I had arrived from the forum direction. After crossing the stream, I picked my way through an approach road strewn with mule dung and stood in the shadow of the east entrance as I considered the locale. To my surprise, someone had imported and planted a Roman stone pine, twenty feet from the way in. So far from home, the tree had established itself and must provide cones for ritual purposes.

The smelly hangdog who was seeking gratuities from sightseers took one look at me, spat, and decided not to demand a ticket price. I glared at him anyway. He made to slink off. I called him back.

'Run to the barracks. Tell them to send a detail urgently. Tell them there's a riot.'

'What riot?'

'The bloody great big one that's going to start while you're running to the troops.'

I walked through the arch, passing into the dark passage below the seating tiers, ignoring the audience approaches. Pedestrians had their own stairs up to the seats and were denied access to the ring. I could see the arena ahead through great ceremonial double doors, which currently stood open. Alongside them to the right-hand side was a small wicket gate with a well-trodden approach, no doubt used discreetly by attendants when they stage-managed events. That was closed. The arena looked the standard oval shape. It was maybe a thousand paces long on this, the greater axis, which ran west to east. Before I went in, I checked around the gloomy entrance interior. To either side were antechambers, both empty. One, which was probably used as the fighters' rest-room prior to bouts, contained a small shrine, currently lit by a single oil lamp. The other must be the holding chamber for wild beasts; it had a massive sliding panel to give admittance to the ring. That was down. I tested its pulley, which moved with silken ease for rapid operation. Single-handedly, I raised it a few inches, then let it fall back.

I returned to the main passageway and passed through the huge open gates. They were set on a monumental wooden threshold, which I stepped over cautiously.

The central area must have been dug out for several feet, drainage installed, and a heavy layer of sand brought in; there would be a deep hard-rammed base, with a few inches of looser material on top which could be raked over. Around the ovoid, supported on massive wooden posts, ran maybe fifteen to twenty tiers of wood-planked seats. I didn't count. A crowd barrier held back spectators in the first row of seats. Below that ran a bare walkway all around the interior. Inside it stood a high square-cut wooden palisade. This entirely enclosed the centre, so neither raging beasts nor human fighters could escape and nor could show-off madmen from the crowd leap in.

The only access to the arena itself was here where I stood, or right opposite through the far end. That looked very far away. Its gates were closed, as far as I could tell. That was probably the way they dragged out the bodies. With no performance, the far end would not be in use today.

Above me now towered the eastern gateway. The fighters would parade into the arena through these two mighty gates which folded open inwards on great metal hinges and pivots. Nervous combatants, their stomachs churning, would pass through the dark entrance into a dazzle of light and noise.

A shiver ran through me. Last time I set foot in an amphitheatre had been on that dreadful day when I had watched my brother-in-law, Maia's hapless husband, being torn apart by the lions in Lepcis Magna. I did not want to remember. Standing here on the sand, I could hardly forget: the yells of the arena staff encouraging the animals, the lions' roars, the crowd baying, Famia's outrage and incomprehension, then his ghastly screams.

Today was hot, though not so hot as the North African sun beating on open countryside. That arena, bursting with colourful characters, had stood outside the city, on a baking, bright seashore against the glinting blue of the southern Mediterranean. Today, unusually, the atmosphere at Londinium was more uncomfortable and sultry, with a storm approaching to break the weather, probably this evening. Sweat trickled down inside my tunic, even while I stood in dense shade under the gatehouse. Three feet ahead of me the sand looked blistering hot. Forget the golden glint of mica; there were dark, sordid patches. Attendants may brush away the blood, but foul traces of the past always linger. Heavy sunlight brings out a rank smell of recent and not-so-recent butchery.

Far across the sand two figures moved. I turned my attention to the action.

The measured clash of swords echoed within the hollow oval. Without the roar of the crowd, any amphitheatre sounds odd. Here at ground level, looking straight down its full length to the closed gates at the other end, I was awestruck by the immense distance. You could shout to the other side at present, just about; if all the seats filled up, it would be impossible.

Amazonia and her friend were circling. They were dressed in a parody of male gladiatorial gear: high-sided short white skirts, with wide waist belts that came up right under the bust. With a full audience, they would probably be bare-breasted, for titillation. Today, legs, shoulders and forearms were armoured. Was it usual for practice? They must sometimes exercise in the full weight of greaves and a breastplate. I could not tell who one of the girls was; she had a full face-helm. Of the two remote figures, Chloris seemed unmistakable. I maintain that if I had been closer, and had she not been hidden behind a slit-eyed bronze face-mask, I would have checked her eye colour. (According to Helena, I would have noticed the size of her bust.) At any event, Chloris had that distinctive long dark plait. And I recognised the boots, I had seen being pulled off while she was threatening to ravish me.

They swung, clashed, and swung: with real blades, not wooden practice swords. Sometimes one turned her back. Waiting until she sensed a blow coming, she would swipe up at an angle behind her, or spin suddenly to parry full face, laughing. There was spirit out there in the practice. Those were genuine grunts of effort. I saw teeth bared with exultation after each successful manoeuvre. They were good, just as Chloris had boasted. They enjoyed the sport. They were operating as a team, of course. Professionals work for display. Programmed in pairs, their art looks more dangerous than it is. Their skill to choreograph enough for effect, while also improvising to cause excitement. Blood, but no death. In performance they know each other well enough to stay alive – on the whole.

I wondered if they had fought others for real. Must have done. They would be seen as second rate otherwise – and these girls were clearly popular. The public accepted them as professionals. I wondered if my light-footed, lithe ex-girlfriend had ever killed anyone. I wondered if anybody on her team had died.

Chloris had set Florius a task here. At present she was protected by sheer distance. The only way in to get to her would be by entering through a gate. Shinning up and over the safety barrier would be impossible; besides, there was no point. Out there in the centre, she would see anyone coming, whichever direction he chose. Had she noticed me? If she was looking out for Florius, she should have done. I could not tell. The two girls seemed completely absorbed in their practice and I knew better than to call out. Attracting their attention when they were working at that pace would be asking for a sword-stroke to shear accidentally into flesh.

There were too many people sitting in the tiers of seats. Apart from the men, there were couples and even a small group of silly school-age girls – eyeing up the men of course. High in the presidential box I spotted one woman entirely on her own, wrapped closely in a stole; she could not be cold in this baking weather so it must be for anonymity. She seemed intent on the couple in the centre – perhaps a would-be colleague longing to join their group, or maybe just lost in lesbian love for one of them.

I decided to move from the gates. If Florius should come in behind me, I did not want to put him off. Everything was quiet. I set off around the interior, and kept walking.

I caressed the pommel of my own sword reflectively. I wore it in the military way, high on the right, under the arm, ready to be extracted with a rapid wrist-swivel. The point was to keep free of your shield, but of course I was carrying no shield. Even coming overseas, I had not brought protection of that sort on what I thought was a trip to audit building works. Besides, a sword could be discreet but a shield was too obvious. In Rome going armed in the city would be illegal. Here in the provinces, personal weapons were tolerated by default (Mars Ultor, you try making a German or a Spaniard leave his hunting knife at home), though anyone acting suspiciously in the streets would be stopped by the legionaries and stripped of their blades, no questions asked.

Well, anyone except enforcers, who bully or bribe their way into tooling up without hindrance. If money talks, bad money sings.

It buys a lot of back-up too, as I was soon to find out.

Movement caught my eye. A far gate had partially swung open.

At first it was impossible to make out what was happening or how many newcomers stood in the shaded entrance. I speeded up, still on the perimeter, heading that way. The two girls in the centre continued their practice, but turned their stance slightly, so both could observe the far gate.

'Amazonia!' a man's voice yelled. The girls stood still; she of the plait made a welcoming gesture, encouraging him to join them out in the arena. There seemed to be no response. The two of them waited. I left the wall and started off gently towards them.

A male figure finally emerged from the gateway. I could see he was lean, tanned and shaven-headed. He wore natty dark brown leather trousers and navvy's boots; he had bare arms tightly tied with rope bracelets to make the muscles stand out. He looked like any tough nut from the Suburra, and that's a scary look.

He was nobody I recognised – or so I thought at first.

Behind him, by a few paces, came about five others. They strung out in a line sideways, walking casually. The odds seemed acceptable, so far. Two each, if I joined the women. The heavies were dressed up like anyone in the street, though even from this distance I could tell they carried an armoury. They had swords and daggers stuffed in their belts and a couple held staves in their fists. They sauntered in, behaving like some rich man's train of unruly slaves who would cause trouble just because they could get away with it. It did not fool me. These men knew exactly what they were about, and it was mean business.

I moved out fast across the ring. Chloris and her friend had shifted on light feet. They closed together, fully on guard and swords up, ready to make a stand.

The man in leather trousers stopped, within easy call. The heavies fanned out either side of him and moved up. They remained some distance from the two female gladiators, but if the girls made a run towards any part of the perimeter, they would be easily chased. I slowed down, not wanting to precipitate anything I could not control.

The nearest heavy was eyeing me up. He was about twenty strides from the couple at the centre, half that from me. No point attacking him; well, not yet. He was a snotty brute with thrusting calves who had never learned to bathe. I could see the dirt ingrained on his skin, and his lank hair was as thick with natural grease as some old sheep's stinking wool.

'Amazonia!' Repeating her name, the shaven-headed autocrat shouted a little more appeasingly. His accent labelled him: Rome. Born there and taught corruption there. It was a light, troublingly weak voice. It still sounded contemptuous and arrogant. This had to be Florius.

He had walked only as close as he needed, protected by his men. If the girls tried to reach him, they would certainly be stopped. They did not try. Nor did they answer. An intense silence filled the amphitheatre. Everything lay so still, I could hear a faint chink of ringed mail as one of the bodyguards shifted his weight unintentionally. The casual daywear was a disguise; the brute was professionally armoured beneath his tunic. The other men stood motionless.

'You fight well. I'm impressed by the demonstration. But you need organisation behind you and I want to supply it!' announced the hopeful manager. His tone stayed harsh, yet somehow unconvincing. Still, he had plenty of back-up. It would take courage to say no to him.

The helmeted figure with the dark plait took the risk, shaking her head. At her side, her friend showed by tiny movements that she was searching the heavies for any notice of surprise attack.

'Put down your weapons.'

Neither girl reacted.

'Time to talk —' With the pretence that this was still a business arrangement, he was wheedling. Then he spoiled it: 'You're outnumbered and outclassed —'

Not quite. The other girl touched Amazonia's arm and both glanced behind them. Through the gate where I had entered ran a small group of their colleagues, just three or four, but enough to even up the balance. Pausing only to drag closed the mighty gates, they raced across the sand, all wearing combat costume with either tridents or short swords. Soon they were fanning out either side of the central pair to give them cover.

Now we had a full stand-off.

The man who must be Florius toughened up. 'Oh let's stop the games, girls. Lay aside your arms!'

Then a new voice rang out, showing real authority: *'What – and be slaughtered, Florius?'*

The woman's cry had resounded around the arena from some high point. It surprised us all. Heads turned. Eyes sought the source. The voice had come from the President's box. Its owner was standing, feet astride, right up on the balcony rail where banners would be draped on ceremonial days. She balanced there effortlessly, far out of reach.

This must be the woman I had spotted earlier alone, tightly wrapped in a stole. Now she had shed her coverings and I knew her to be the real Chloris. With the showmanship she had used all her career, she sported bare, booted legs beneath a breathtakingly short skirt. She too had her hair scraped back tight, then braided in a long thin tail.

'You can speak your lies to me,' sneered the strong apparition.

'Oh what's this?' rasped Florius, looking angrily from the decoy to the real group leader and back.

'You tell me.' Chloris sounded coldly confident. She believed she had outmanoeuvred him. 'Why the troop of bullies? Why demand disarming? Why come heavy-handed and threaten my girls – if this is really a business meeting and you really want to work with us?'

He tried to bluff. 'Come down and we can discuss things.'

'I think not!' she scoffed. That was my Chloris. Succinct and resentful.

She was less safe up there than she had planned. There had been movement among the scattered spectators and now a couple of figures with evil intentions were weaving their way along the rows of seats towards the President's box. I waved madly to warn Chloris. She glanced quickly sideways, not too disconcerted.

'Oh send in your runners to snatch me,' she sneered, standing like the Winged Victory of Samothrace, but with better legs. Was she armed? I could not tell. She could have anything with her in the box. Being Chloris, it could be an ostrich feather fan and a couple of white doves. Mind you, in this new violent career, the doves might be trained to peck eyes out.

'Oh I want you,' retorted leather trousers. 'I'll get you too –'

'Have to catch me first!' cried Chloris.

She must have been well prepared for this. As the two came nearer, intent on entering the box, Chloris took a flying leap from the balcony. She had a rope, down which she slid with that swift chasing glide of a circus artiste concluding her trapeze act and returning to earth. Her feet were crossed to regulate her descent, and she held one gleaming arm high straight above her head, brandishing a sword.

The rope ran right down into the walkway, out of sight behind the safety barrier. Chloris disappeared.

Enraged, Florius muttered something to his men. I knew the fight was about to start. I readied myself to join it in support of the girls. The men closed with them. As the first clash of swords rang out, there were new developments.

Florius was intending to withdraw. I saw him pull back behind his men as they squared up to the gladiator girls. That coward was keeping out of it, even though he was armed. I slashed aside a heavy's weapon and stormed past to rush after Florius.

He was heading off back to the western gate through which he had arrived. But someone else was coming in that way: someone who yelled triumphantly. It was another voice I knew, and so did Florius. He pulled up short. Facing him now, the trousered gangster with the shaved head recognised the tall, brown-clad figure of Petronius Longus. That might not have stopped Florius, but Petro – unaware that I would be here as his fighting ally – had found himself another friend. Restlessly fretting at its heavy chain, it was rearing up even above Petro's height.

'Hold it right there, Florius – *or I loose the bear!*'

There were still fifteen strides between them, but Florius faltered then obeyed.

XLIII

M Y GOOD FRIEND Petronius Longus had many fine qualities. He was tough and shrewd, an amiable crony, a valued law and order officer, and a respected man in any neighbourhood he graced. He always sneered at my dog, but had himself harboured flea-bitten kittens for his children and I had heard him speak with devotion of an elderly three-legged tortoise called Trident, his own pet when a lad. Still, I had no reason to suppose he could handle a huge, bad-tempered, only partially tamed Caledonian bear. And I was right. He may have taken a swift lesson from the owner before he strode into the arena, but the bear had already seen a chance to assert its unpredictable character.

Petro encouraged the creature to advance on Florius. The shaggy mass, a close relation to the floor rugs Chloris strewed around her boudoir, made a short foray, grunted, then turned around and played with its chain, threatening to haul Petro off balance. Florius laughed, a loud and derisive cackle. That was a mistake. Petro muttered at the bear, which now turned and sprinted speedily towards the gangster. Petro let out more chain. Florius screamed at his bodyguard. Some of the heavies peeled off from fighting the gladiators and ran to save him. As I confronted them, I saw that the women were doing thoroughly good work, fencing with the other heavies. They did not need me. Just as well. I had my hands full as I stabbed at the gangster's supporters. One man yelled a warning. We all looked round. The bear took another run at Florius. Petro hauled back hard on its chain but it was damned fast. It had no teeth but as it swiped with a paw, now barely two strides from the gangster, it could do serious damage. Florius was hysterical with fear.

Then again the action changed. Through the western gate came the thunder of hooves. Mounted men galloped in, clearly Florius reinforcements0, two and three to a horse. The numbers of gangsters rose to a dangerous high – but now there were other movements on the edge of the arena: ropes shot down from the safety palisade, with figures sliding down them fast – more armed females who had materialised from among the apparent sightseers. They shimmied down their ropes at several points, loudly whooping a challenge.

Most of the riders sped past us to the centre. Fights broke out in all directions. There were almost as many combatants now as in the best ticketed displays. I tried to assess the situation. The day might still be containable. The women had skill and determination, and for some reason the newcomers were not attacking them. Instead, they were riding in circles, harrying the foot-soldier heavies who were already here. Petronius and his long-nosed hairy ally had stopped Florius leaving; I was tackling the bodyguards closest to him, so Petro could make him a prisoner. Two events destroyed that hopeful plan. First, a lone horseman rode up behind Florius. Florius turned, hoping for rescue from the angry bear. Then he went pale. He was facing me, so I saw what had alarmed him: wide-shouldered, warty and scowling, the rider was Splice.

I began to run towards them, yelling to Petronius. Under my feet the sand was packed hard enough to run on, but it's an odd surface for those not arena-trained. Slow going. Your feet soon tire and drag. It allowed time for Splice to rein in his mount so hard it reared up right above Florius. Splice, knowing that his leader had intended to kill him with poison, obviously meant to retaliate. It explained why the new arrivals were fighting their supposed allies – we now had a gang war to contend with.

Florius scrabbled away desperately. The bear roared and came at him. This time Petronius was pulled over, though instinctively he clung on to the chain. I was trying to attack Splice, but a man on foot is no match for cavalry.

Through the open western gate then raced a new contender. This would be a big thrill for a watching crowd: a girl fighting from a light, rapid two-horse British chariot. It was Chloris. She had a driver, while she herself leaned out over the wicker side, one arm raised with her drawn sword. She went straight for Florius. Splice had to avoid the chariot. He leapt from his horse, cursing, but reached Florius, and grappled him. Torn between avoiding Splice and dodging the maddened bear's needle claws, Florius ended up with his back to Splice, who gripped him with one arm across his chest while pummelling him with his free fist. The driver wheeled the chariot around them in a tight circle, looking for a chance to get close. Then in the chaos, she made the mistake of driving too fast over the bear's chain. A wheel jerked violently and left the ground. The chariot skewed, flew up, and nearly went over. Chloris, unprepared, was flung out. She lost her sword but scrambled after it. Finding itself free, the bear leapt and clambered on to the horses. The terrified girl driver screamed and threw herself off the side, landing on Petronius and temporarily flooring him. The chariot careered on into the main fight at the centre of the arena, now looking as if the great black bear was riding in a circus act.

Apart from this mad scene, there was a sudden tense pause. Florius was being dragged backwards by Splice. Petro, Chloris and I were regrouping to tackle him.

Then the light changed. The heavens closed and it grew dark as a portent.

Dry in the mouth, I saw no way this could end well. In the eerie new half-light, fighting would be even more dangerous.

As I struggled towards Splice and Florius, Petro pounded after them too, in an easy style, on his long legs. Many a thief had been caught out and brought down, thinking Petro was putting no effort into a chase. He was gaining, but Splice was aware he had trouble. He turned, using Florius as a human shield, ready to fight Petro for possession of the gang leader.

In the main battle, heavies still appeared to be fighting each other, though some broke away from the pack to support their leader. It split the action nicely but there was still work for the girls. A hasty glance told me those honeypots were excellent. What they lacked in weight they made up in training and bladework. A stamp and a flick brought a man down before he had even started fighting them. They were not squeamish: if a slashed artery would stop an opponent, they wasted no energy with a death blow – which takes strength – but sliced into an accessible limb, then leapt away as the blood spurted. Those I could see were methodically working through anyone who came at them.

Petro and I would have made short work of Splice, and if Florius was killed, well, no complaints. We were thwarted, however: the loose chariot swerved back at us, its horses crazed with fear of the slavering bear. Out of control, it rattled between us and our quarry. We tried leaping for the horses' heads but were knocked aside. I heard Petro curse.

'You brought the hairy boy racer!' I complained.

'I didn't know he was chariot-mad.'

Some of the bodyguards now rushed us. Not sure even if they were for Florius or Splice, I took on two of them. Without armour, this was no fun. I had put one man down before Petro joined me. Close by, Splice and Chloris were hard at it. Florius was on the ground, Splice holding him down with his foot. Other thugs were there in support. Chloris was labouring. The heavies had no scruples about attacking women. They were pressing in on Chloris; I was losing sight of her. Petro and I made a big effort, finishing off our opponents with savage sword strokes.

Chloris had no intention of letting us in on the fight against Splice. She was letting out high-pitched grunts of effort every time she struck a blow. Even that hard nut Splice looked anxious.

More thugs were arriving. The chariot veered back towards us and turned over on its axle, cutting them off. The bear sprang off, sideswiping me with a hot, heavy flank and pouncing on one of the bodyguards. I smelt its rank odours and heard a scream. The man was down. There were shouts, jeers, frantic growls.

A female voice shrieked, then I saw Splice fall. Chloris stabbed him again hard; he was done for. Miserably wriggling from under them, Florius escaped the pack and made a run for it. The heavies were fighting the bear. It was overcome by weight and numbers. They kicked and slashed at the creature, which fought back viciously. Chloris raced after Florius. Petro and I burst through the mob and took off after her.

Chloris and Florius were already halfway to the eastern gate. They attracted attention, so when Petro and I reached the centre of the arena, men ran out to intercept us. In the lead, I raised my sword and let out a tremendous shout. There were more than I could handle, but I was fighting mad.

'Falco!' Petronius could see the odds.

I took the head half off the nearest brute while he stood with his mouth open. I still don't know how I did that. It felt good though. In my next onslaught I went for two at once. Now the thugs scattered away. I was on my own for half a minute, then I was aware of Petronius alongside.

Other things were happening.

Rattling chains signalled the opening of the huge hatch for animals at the eastern gate. It shot up; new figures raced out, amid the frantic noise of baying dogs.

'Watch out!' Petronius called to me. If these were arena-trained, they were killers. We made a run for the outskirts. Some of the heavies were less lucky. The pack of hounds were on them, hot for blood. To my astonishment, in among the dogs I saw the slight, pale form of our rescued girl, Albia, wild-eyed and cheering them on. Running in behind in a flash of blue came my own Helena. After her lumbered the dogman, waving his arms, puffing with effort, protesting in a way that said he had not parted with his dogs willingly. Helena turned to remonstrate, defending the hijack.

Petronius and I had lost Chloris and Florius in the mêlée. Petro

spotted them first. Almost at the gate, Florius kept going, unaware
how closely he was being chased by Chloris. He thought he was
safe. Then Chloris leapt on him from behind. We heard him gasp.
He went flat, swallowing sand.

Chloris was up again. Merciless, she hauled Florius to his feet,
her sword at his throat. She was angry. 'Get up, you bastard!'

A grumble of thunder disturbed the summer afternoon. It
seemed to be darker than ever.

'We'll take him —' commanded Petronius as we two ran up,
breathless. He thought himself the gallant type, which meant never
subservient to women.

'Stuff you!' growled Chloris. I bent double, getting my breath.
We had run almost the length of the arena, after fighting hard.

'This rat is mine —' Petro would never learn. Sweating hard in
the sultry temperature, he drew a forearm across his brow.

'No, I want him,' Chloris insisted.

'I've been after him for years!'

'And now *I've* got him!' Chloris backed away, dragging the
gangster like a barley sack. White-faced in her grip, he now looked
like the old bundle of gibbering nonentity. Leather trousers don't
turn a wimp into a demi-god. He may have shaved his head but
he still had all the personality of a dirty rag. He was so scared he
was dribbling.

'How's the wife, Florius?' Petronius taunted.

'I'll have you for this, vigilis!'

Out in the arena the female gladiators were now sporting with
the Florius bullies. Blades flashed and women laughed harshly.
Maddened horses ran free. The dogs were chasing around,
showing themselves to have no pedigree as mastiffs, but to be
simple-hearted British curs with mange and fleas and a love of fun.
They fastened their teeth in the gangsters' garments and swung in
the air, like Nux tugging a rope end as a game.

Helena was coming towards us, pulling Albia away from the
area of danger. Even in this weird light I could see the little
scavenger, bright-eyed with excitement, clearly relishing life in the

adventurous Falco household. Then she spotted and recognised Florius. He must have been at the brothel while she was a prisoner. He must have done something to her. Albia stood stock still and began to scream.

Her piercing shrieks caught us all out. I covered my ears briefly. Florius ignored the girl. Seizing his moment, he bucked and broke free. Chloris reacted instantly, but he slashed her with a brutal fist across the face, and snatched her sword. Her wrist was sliced as she tried instinctively to grab it back. Before anyone could stop him, he had stabbed her in the belly with a wild, circular stroke. Florius, who normally let others do his killing, staggered and looked startled.

With a murmur of surprise, Chloris collapsed to the ground. There was blood everywhere. I fell on my knees beside her and fumbled to staunch it, but he had ripped her open fatally and no one could push back the unravelling gut. The task was hopeless. I still knelt there, disbelieving and sick.

'She's dying,' said Petronius Longus harshly. He was wrong for once and I knew it. She was dead.

XLIV

A HUGE CRACK of thunder scared all Hades out of everyone. Ferocious lightning split the skies. Torrential rain ruined visibility and left us gasping – just as Florius seized his chance and made a bolt for it.

'Leave her!' Helena commanded. She pulled off her stole, its fabric already soaked in patches, and laid the blue material over Chloris as I wiped my hands and forearms on the sand. Out in the arena there were plenty of bodies, most of them male. The women were starting to look over here; one or two began to run. At the far gate I could see a few red tunics: soldiers had arrived, at least in small numbers. Some were talking with the heavies; most were casually examining the dark corpse of the dead bear.

'Marcus!' urged Petro.

'Leave her to us,' Helena repeated, giving me a shove. 'Go! Go after Florius!'

Petronius was already going, so as if in a dream I followed him.

Now we knew we were in Britain. Dear gods, any softness I was feeling for this province was wiped out by that first tremendous onslaught of rain. Storms in the Mediterranean have the grace to come at night. Why, when the weather broke in northern climes, did always it happen in the afternoon?

No building in town was likely to be so well drained as the amphitheatre, but the sheer quantity of water pelting down earthwards had us splashing through torrents even in the shelter of the gateway. The drainage gullies were already thundering with water. Above, sheets of rain careered off every tier of seats. The passageway between the public barrier on the first row and the safety palisade had flooded almost instantly.

Outside the amphitheatre we could not have been more exposed, anywhere in Londinium, except on the river. Petronius and I staggered from the gateway, with our clothes plastered to our bodies and our hair stuck down, while rivulets cascaded from all parts of us. I felt I could drown in what was streaming off my nose. My eyes were filled with water. My feet stuck to my dead-weight boots, which I could hardly lift from the sodden ground.

We peered about but Florius had vanished. Dim figures, hunched, covering their heads as best they could, scurried away in different directions through the rain and mist. Petro tried asking them, but they shook him off. If Florius had found or grabbed a cloak from someone, we would never pick him out.

Lightning still careered across the pitch-dark skies, illuminating our stark faces. Petronius flung an arm in one direction, then he hared off. I turned right. I would be heading towards open country, a fool's errand. Another appalling roll of thunder cracked all around. If there had been a doorway, I would have rushed for shelter and abandoned everything.

The track that led from the arena hit a road. I jarred my knee when I first pounded on the metalled surface, but I limped on, as the rain increased. I hated this place. I hated the weather. I hated the damned badly run, vulnerable society that had let Florius in, and the administration that did nothing to control his antics. I hated the planners who positioned arenas in remote locations. I hated life.

Didius Falco, ever the cheery one in a gathering.

I turned south, making for a built-up area. The first place I reached seemed to be industrial premises, with what sounded like machinery working. I half opened a door. There must be a treadmill. It was pitch dark but I could hear the rackety clatter of its paddles, with the dribbling kiss of the water being raised then sloshed into a collection chamber. It sounded rather tentative.

I could have sheltered, but it might be hours before the rain let up. I still entertained faint hopes of catching up with Florius. I called out, but nobody answered, so I plunged back outside into the storm again.

Exhausted by the effort of running through such weather, I then found somewhere more promising: glimpsed through the darkness stood a cluster of buildings. As I approached, head down against the storm, fortune for once smiled. The place had a commercial look. Someone was standing in the open doorway, staring out, but he drew aside to let me in. Warmth hit me. Civilisation awaited. I understood: visitors to the arena had been provided with a set of public baths.

Ever cautious, I searched for a nameboard. There was a pale fresco above the table where they took the entrance fees. It was called Caesar's. Well, that sounded just fine.

XLV

'No swords!'

'In the name of the governor; I have to search this place!'

I wanted to bathe. I wanted to shed my drenched garments, drop my weapon from my wet fist, peel off my leaden, sodden boots, then sit on a hot ledge, letting insidious steam wrap around me while I drowsed off. If my conscience allowed me to give up, I could happily stay here for days.

'Is this official? Got a warrant?' No one had warrants in the provinces. Hades, no one had warrants in Rome. If the vigiles banged on anybody's door, anxious to have a look around, the proprietor would let the roughnecks in and start saving up to pay for breakages.

I waved my sword angrily. 'This is my warrant. You want to argue, you can send a runner to the procurator's residence.'

'What — in this weather?'

'Then shut up and show me round like a bath keeper who wants to retain his licence.'

They were probably so keen to have bath houses built in Britain that no licence system operated either. Who would police it, if there were no vigiles? Legislation without enforcement is a bad principle.

Licensing of commercial premises was something we did have at home, with pompous baby senators prancing around as aediles, deadly keen to shift their togate backsides upwards on the *cursus honorum*, and meanwhile concerning themselves with nosy checks on opening hours, plebeian licentiousness and fire precautions. A bribe to their escort usually moved the irritation up the street to the next victim.

Here, where bureaucracy had yet to grow taproots, the simple power of language seemed to impress. I can't say I was led around like a hygiene inspector, but I was allowed to wander through the hot and cold rooms undisturbed.

My life as an informer seemed to be spent in constant searches of wet-floored baths; they were treacherous when in a hurry, wearing boots. It was hard to concentrate while skidding across slippery tiles face-first into a ridged wall which was shot through with hot air tubes. At least the din of thunder from outside was muffled by thick masonry roofs. Here, apart from routine tricklings and gurgles, was a cocoon of warmth and silence.

Silence was not what I expected. This was a spacious suite of hot rooms, yet there were no customers. This dark establishment lacked the sociability the Roman baths are intended to offer. Nobody at all was debating philosophy, discussing the Games, swapping gossip, or biffing beanbags for exercise. It was another failure for the British judicial legate's citizenship lessons. Come to that, the body oils smelt rancid.

'Are you always deserted? This is a big place!'

'There is supposed to be a new fort coming.'

'Who knows when! How do you make a living? Who uses your baths?'

'Soldiers mainly. They like the bar next door. They were in earlier. They all got called out on an exercise.' That would be the governor, ordering the troops to search for Splice.

A thought struck me. The barkeeper who had helped me entertain the centurion, Silvanus – it felt about six weeks ago – had talked about fetching his water from a bath house. 'Does a military drinking den use your water?'

The owner nodded. 'We have a well with a treadmill and a waterwheel,' he informed me proudly. 'There is nothing like our system anywhere north of Gaul –'

'Indoors?'

He gestured in the direction I had come from. 'We had to build the well where the water is.'

'Oh I saw your well-head premises.' That was behind me in the storm; I lost interest. 'So which way is the bar?' I demanded.

'Right next door,' replied the bath keeper, as if surprised I did not know. 'Caesar's. Same as us.' Well, that saved the drunks having to remember two names.

I left Caesar's Baths and hurried a few strides through a large, spreading puddle, to Caesar's Bar. When I walked in, who should I see gloomily supping a flagon, but my dear pal Lucius Petronius.

He half rose, looking anxious. Immediately all my pain over Chloris resurfaced. 'You all right, Falco?'

'No.'

He called for another beaker and pushed me on to a bench. 'Grieve. Do it now.' He meant, while I was here with him, not with Helena. Bad enough that she had seen me distraught, red to the elbows with the blood and intestines of a past lover. I glanced down at my clothing. At least the rain had washed away some of the mess. As for grief, that decides its own timing.

Petronius had his elbows on a table, his boots off on the floor to dry, and his big bare feet in a towel. He looked depressed, yet oddly comfortable. He had lost his quarry in the teeming wet, and he had bunked off. I couldn't argue, because so had I.

'You found him, of course?' I challenged, shaking water from my hair.

'I will,' Petro croaked: he was obsessive.

I drank, then wiped my mouth. 'He looked a bit different! That was a shock. I remember him as a soggy lump with hangnails and lanky hair, dreaming he would open his own racing stable – which he never would have done.'

'Power sharpened him up,' growled Petro. 'Now he goes for snappy clothes.'

'Those bloody Parthian trousers!'

Petronius allowed himself a wry smile. If anything he had more conservative taste than me. 'The leg casings had a raffish style. They'd look quite good on a smelly muleteer in Bruttium.'

'So would a goatbell round his neck . . . I noticed his equestrian ring was three times the size of mine.' I spread my hand and looked at the slim gold band that signified I had been dragged into the middle class. Florius had worn a bar that covered a whole finger joint.

'The difference is,' said Petro, 'you wouldn't even wear one, from choice. Helena bought yours. She wants the world to know you are entitled to the honour and you go along with her out of guilt.'

'Guilt?'

'Being a scruff when she deserves better. But Florius –' Petro stopped; he did not bother to express his full contempt. I had seen Petronius once take the ring owned by Florius' gangster father-in-law and flatten it under the heel of his boot.

Glumly he poured more wine.

'Is Florius the brothel pimp?' I asked suddenly.

Petro leaned back. I could see this was no new proposition. 'You mean "the Collector"? Yes, that's him. The old gang always ran whores in Rome, don't forget. They had brothels both for their own sake, and for the crime that goes on in them. Not just manicure girls who talk to their friends all day and fortune tellers who can't tell Cancer from Capricorn. I mean theft. Hustling. Illegal gambling. Contract killing. All on top of the usual depravity.'

'And Florius rounds up new talent himself?'

'Then he gets first go,' stated Petronius. We had both stopped drinking. 'Every filly in the Florius stable has been personally deflowered by him.'

'Raped?'

'Repeatedly, if needs be. To terrorise them, so they do as they are told.'

'That girl of ours he grabbed is about fourteen.'

'Some are younger.'

'You've been watching and not doing anything to stop it?' I glared at him. 'Did you realise you were directly watching Florius?'

'Not at first. As you say, he looks quite different.'

'Your customs pal told me he uses the brothel as an office when he comes into town. So he hangs his boots up properly somewhere else?'

'I assumed the Old Neighbour rented out space to him,' Petro confirmed. 'He came and went right in front of me a few times, before I even realised that it was him. Then I soon worked out that he owned the place, that he was closely bound up in its activities.'

'So where else does he hang out?'

'Downriver. He has a boat,' Petro told me. 'It was the boat that alerted me. Remember, I saw someone standing in the prow that morning when the baker's corpse was being dumped?'

'You said something was bothering you.'

'I couldn't work out what. I yelled out loud when I realised it was him. The way he was stationed there, doing not a lot . . .' Petro scowled. 'He must have been watching his men dump the body over the side. Typical Florius. He enjoys observing. All the family are like that. They gloat over suffering, knowing they've caused it.'

'The sense of power and the secrecy. I bet Florius spies on customers when they are with the brothel girls.'

'Bound to.'

We fell silent. We had lost Florius and the weather was too grim to endure. It would do no harm to sit quietly to reflect.

We were still considering things when the door blew in. After the newcomers managed to slam it shut again on the blast, the barkeeper told them helpfully, 'No women.'

Since it was Helena and Albia who had stumbled inside, Petronius grinned and told him these bedraggled mites were with us. The barman assumed they were drabs and we were buying their services, but we treated them courteously anyway. As soon as she saw me, Helena came over with the same concern that Petronius had shown. 'Oh Marcus!'

'I'm fine,' I lied. Still standing, Helena put her arms around me; that nearly did for me. I choked back tears.

'Her friends have taken her. There was nothing anyone could do. You know that.'

When she released me, I steadied myself. She sat alongside.

Albia had calmed down from her hysteria, and was now completely silent. Helena wrung out her hair, then her skirts. The girl just sat. Helena tucked Albia's straggling hair behind her ears and dried her face as best she could on Petro's towel.

'Florius?' asked Helena quietly.

Petronius topped up his beaker, looking bad-tempered. 'We lost him. But this is a dead end province at the end of the world. He has nowhere to go.'

That was optimistic, in my opinion.

We all sat lethargically, wearied in our bones by the weather. If we stayed too long, we would all be chilled. Our soaked clothes were not drying, only becoming heavier and colder on us.

We did stay, because Helena Justina had an urgent project. She put her arm around Albia and spoke gently. 'You were very upset when you recognised that man. I want you to tell me – now would be best, my dear – what you know about him.'

'We know he runs that brothel called the Old Neighbour,' Petronius supplied in a quiet tone, to get the girl started.

'Did you want to go there, in the first place?' asked Helena.

'I don't know.' Albia sounded as if she feared being in trouble whatever she said or did. 'I didn't know where he was taking me.'

'Did you know who the man was?'

'No.'

'You had never met him before?'

'No.'

'So how did he approach you?'

'He came up and was nice when I was sitting where Falco left me.' Albia paused, then admitted shamefacedly, 'He said something to me, because I was crying.'

I cleared my throat. 'That was my fault. I had been angry. Albia may have thought that I had left her there and that I was not coming back.'

'But you were of course,' said Helena, more to reassure the girl than to applaud my honest intentions.

'Maybe she didn't know me well enough to be sure.'

'So Albia looked like a miserable young girl who had run away from home.'

'The man asked me that,' Albia piped up intensely. 'I said I didn't have a home.'

Helena pursed her lips. Strong feelings were affecting her. 'Well, let's get this clear: I am offering you a home, if you want it, Albia.'

Tears welled in the girl's blue eyes. Petronius dug me in the ribs, but I ignored it. Helena and I had held no private debate on the issue. Taking a wild child to Rome, and exposing our own daughters to an unknown influence, required thought. Even the impetuous Helena Justina was an advocate of traditional family councils. However, every Roman matron knows that domestic councils were devised by our foremothers purely so the views of the matron of a household may prevail.

I just went along with it. I knew how to be a patriarchal Roman male.

Helena leaned towards the girl: 'Tell me what happened to you, after you went to the Old Neighbour with Florius.'

There was a long silence. Then Albia spoke, surprisingly strongly, 'The fat woman told me I had to work for them. I never thought I would come back to you and Marcus Didius. I thought I had to do what they said.'

Helena managed not to react angrily, but I saw the muscles tighten around her mouth. 'And what about the man?'

'He made me do what you have to do.'

Helena was now holding the girl, half turned away from me.

Petronius was gripping his hands, lest he smash something. I put my palm against Helena's back.

'Did you know about that already, Albia?' she murmured.

'I knew what people did.'

'But it had not happened to you before?'

'No.' The young girl suddenly began crying. Tears fell, almost without sobs. Her grief and desolation were heart-rending. 'I made it happen –'

'No. Never believe that!' Helena exclaimed. 'I cannot change what has been done to you, but you are now safe with us. I will help you tell this story to the governor. Then the man and the old woman can be stopped from hurting other girls like you. You will know – and it may help you, Albia – that you have fought back against him. Him and his kind.' After a moment Helena added in a hard voice, 'Men are not all like that, I promise you.'

Albia looked up. She was gazing from Helena to me.

'Men and women can be happy together,' Helena said. 'Never forget that.'

Albia stared at me. This was the longest communication any of us had had with her, so what came next was understandable. She must have been brooding over it most of the time she had been with us: 'You find people. Will you find my family?'

It was always the most painful question an informer could be asked. Either you cannot trace the missing ones, and you never stood a chance of doing so, or you do find them and it all goes badly wrong. I had never known a good outcome. I refused to handle such requests from clients any more.

'I can only tell you the truth, Albia. I don't think that I can do it,' I said.

She let out a cry of protest.

Stopping her, I went on steadily, 'I have thought about it for you. I believe that your family must all have died in the fighting and the fire when Queen Boudicca attacked Londinium. You must have been a baby then. If anyone had lived, they would have looked for you.' Probably that was true. If they had run away and

265

just abandoned the baby, it was best she never knew.

'They were lost, Albia,' said Helena. 'Love them – but you have to let them go. If you choose to come with us, we take you far away, and you can forget all that has happened in between.'

Her words made little impression. Albia was at her lowest ebb.

Petronius and I left Helena to take care of the girl as best she could. We went to the door, staring out at the rainstorm. He hopped on one foot, strapping back a boot.

'She will be scarred for ever. You'll have your work cut out to save her.'

'I know!' And that was even if Florius had not given her disease or pregnancy to contend with. Only time would tell us that. Helena would have to watch her carefully and tactfully.

Petronius Longus was lost in silence now. I had my own misery to preoccupy me. He, I knew, was thinking that somehow, somewhere, he would get Florius.

XLVI

T IME HAD BROUGHT an abrupt halt to the storm.
The landlord or waiter came out to stare at the clearing
skies. He was not the man I remembered. That one had been a
bald Gaul in a blue tunic with a stupid belt. He had been self-
composed and professional. This was a wiry scruff who had taken
an eternity to attend to us and who seemed ignorant of the stock.

The change in staff had been bothering me. In my mind I had
been waiting for my acquaintance to reappear, but it was not going
to happen. I had disliked him but the thought that he had been
usurped by this inadequate gave me a bad taste. I forced myself to
take notice. 'Someone else was serving, the last time I came here.'

This man's eyes glazed slightly. 'He left.'

'Itchy feet?' That was not the impression I had had at the time.
That other man, who had helped me try to sober up Silvanus, had
come over to Britain to make a success of himself. He had seemed
settled in the soldiers' bar, ready to stay as a long-term resident. So
where was he now? Who drove him out?

The new man shrugged. That was when I noticed that the old
signboard with the hook-nosed general's head had been taken
down. Somebody was repainting it.

'Changing your name? What are you calling yourself now?'

'I haven't decided,' he hedged, as if he hated my close scrutiny.
Then I knew what all this meant.

'Plenty to choose from,' I retorted grimly. 'Day like today, the
Lightning Bolt would be a good one.'

'That's right,' joined in Petronius, who took the point; he spoke with menace. 'Anything to do with Jupiter is always popular.' To me he muttered, 'If they've spread this far north in the city, Frontinus has to take account!'

If this really was a new manager installed by the Florius gang, he knew we were on to the take-over, but simply gave us a contemptuous look.

I called to Helena that we should all leave. She was cold and uncomfortable, and suggested we should warm up at the baths next door. If we struggled back to the residence there would be hot water and dry clothing, but we were all too chilled to pass up this opportunity. It was not entirely self-indulgent. Petronius and I could plan what to do next.

We waded through the flooded street; the drains were so full of water they had backed up. Our party was silent. I was already thinking.

Florius would not return to the brothel. Not if he reasoned that Petronius must be watching the place. The governor could safely raid it and haul in the old hag, with any hangers-on. We could then search the river for the Florius boat and discover whatever other haunts he had.

For the time being, Florius would lie low.

Maybe.

When we entered the baths, I winked at the manager, who then found himself haggling. Petronius Longus had taken charge; he wanted a party discount, which was pushing it for a mere four people. Still, the vigiles expect respect for their position, just as gangsters like Pyro and Splice do. All the manager could do was mutter feebly about their high quality service and how they had plenty of hot water . . .

'They have a waterwheel!' I exclaimed cheerily. 'And a very tired slave who trundles it.'

'Myron!' retorted the bath-keeper. 'Nothing wrong with Myron's legs! He rattles it along.'

That wasn't what I remembered. I tried to ignore it, but the comment niggled. I sighed. 'Save a strigil for me – I want to check something . . .' I did not tell Petro, but I suddenly realised I might have missed Florius by a hair's breadth.

It took no time to hop back to that building where I had looked in at the waterwheel. In fine weather, it seemed pretty close. Outside the shack, I paused. This was stupid. I was chasing someone dangerous; I should have brought Petronius with me. I drew my sword. Very gently I pushed open the door and stepped inside.

I noticed immediately that the waterwheel was chuntering much more robustly than before. The man on the treadmill must have extra energy. The light was dim even now that the storm had abated, but I could make out the works. The raising system was spectacular. It had been installed inside a huge wood-lined well that was so wide two men could have stood in it with their arms outstretched. They might have drowned if they tried it, however; I could not see how deep the shaft went. Remembering past terrors, I felt sick just looking down it. If Verovolcus had been pitched in here, he would have vanished from view and nobody would ever have found him. That would have spared me a lot of grief.

A looped iron chain, operated by a wheel, dropped into the pitch dark depths below, bringing water up in a long line of rectangular wooden buckets. A human treadmill alongside kept the upper wheel rotating and the buckets churning. I found the treadmill, grabbed a rung, and hung on. The mechanism was about ten feet high, worked by a man inside who kept walking doggedly all day, presumably. Jarred by the pressure as I braked his wheel, he now stopped. He was a stick-insect slave in a headband who looked offended that I broke in on his solitude.

'You must be Myron. Having a bad day, are you? I'm sorry to intrude again. Tell me, Myron, who made you take a rest from your work, earlier?'

Myron eyed up my sword. Still, he was game. 'Are you going to pay me to tell you?'

'No. I'm going to kill you if you don't confess.'

'Fair enough!' A pragmatist.

'He's a racketeer,' I warned. 'You're lucky to be still alive. Shaved head and ridiculous trousers, am I right?'

Myron nodded and sighed. 'I didn't even get a rest – he just jumped right in with me. Was it you who opened the door? He was squashed here, with his hand over my mouth.'

'Better than up your bum.'

'Oh I get no fun! He kicked me and made me keep on walking so it would sound normal.'

'You weren't going at your normal pace.'

'He was getting in my bloody way.'

'Where did he go afterwards?'

'I don't know and I don't care. He gave me a belting and told me to keep my mouth shut about seeing him. Why should I? You'll just belt me again . . . If you catch him, do give him a wallop for me. I do a good job, without all this.'

'Did you know him? He's called Florius.'

'Seen him before. He came round with some other fellow, wanting to invest in the bath house. They know there's going to be a fort, I dare say. I'll be flogging along at a fast pace then.' This gang's tentacles were extending everywhere – and they were quick to find investment opportunities. Myron added, 'They call themselves the Jupiter Company. Nice ring!'

'Heavenly! Who was the other man?'

'Don't know. Perfectly decent stiff. He was actually polite to me.'

'Don't be fooled, Myron. Either of them would slit your gullet.'

'Ah yes,' exclaimed Myron, who must be a bit of a character. 'But the one who was not Florius would apologise nicely first!'

I returned to the baths and picked up my companions. There was no point depressing them by revealing that Florius had fooled me. I told them it was time to go. I was too upset myself to bathe.

We were all tired out, and on the way home human error

brought us away from the direct route and to the area near the forum. Shivering now, we pressed on as the skies cleared more and the rain left only a faint haze. No sun came out. Instead, a breeze blustered around us. The air, which should have cleared, was heavy with moisture, humidity clogging the atmosphere. It clogged the lungs too. We were all wheezing.

As our road climbed, we soon realised we were at the rear of the civic centre.

'That's the lawyer's house,' said Helena. I nodded. I could not care less. 'You should tackle him,' she instructed me.

'What, now? What about?'

'His clients. Pyro and Splice. He may not know their fates – or if he does, you could ask him how he found out.'

I was tired, cold, wet and miserable. I would have liked to be the slapdash kind of informer who ignored loose ends. No chance. I had often told Helena that flair and intuition were all I needed, but she forced me to use dogged sleuthing. For her, being wet through and weary was no excuse. She dragged me into the Popillius house. We had to take Albia, and Petro came too out of curiosity.

Popillius looked pleased to have company. Well, lawyers are gregarious.

'I'm Falco and you know Helena; we have Albia with us. Albia in fact is contemplating a claim for damages against your employers –' Popillius' sandy eyebrows shot up. I bet he was now wondering if Albia would hire him; he would not wonder for long, once he worked out that she had no money. 'And this is Petronius Longus, a member of the Roman vigiles.'

He had blinked slightly as I reeled off the introductions. Clearly remembering that Frontinus had revealed what Petro did, Popillius looked hard at him. Petro just glared back. The vigiles are used to being despised. They are rude, brutal, and proud of it. 'May I offer refreshments?'

'No, don't put yourself out.'

'The young girl seems troubled . . .'

271

But Helena drew Albia aside and sat with her. Petronius looked on caustically, while I braced up to Popillius.

'Popillius, a question: have you managed to see your two clients yet?'

'I have not. In fact, I may have to get angry with the governor, if this delay continues –'

Petronius barked with laughter. 'I wouldn't try it!'

I kinked up an eyebrow at Popillius. 'No one has told you?'

The lawyer was on the alert now. He gave me an enquiring look, not speaking.

'Pyro is dead,' I told him bluntly. 'He collapsed last night. Apparently poison.'

He considered this very briefly. 'I am shocked.'

'If you're going suggest that the governor arranged the death,' I added, 'don't even think of it.'

Popillius' gaze was shadowed with caution. 'Why should I suspect the governor? Why ever would Frontinus –' He was a persistent cross-examiner.

'For an easy life. Remove an awkward criminal without the need for evidence, or the risk of trying him.'

Popillius seemed to be genuinely baffled. 'I find that out of character. And what *risk* of trial?' he demanded.

'The risk that the criminal might get off.'

He laughed. 'Is that a compliment to my speech-making? So –' Popillius abandoned that line. 'The man you know as "Splice" – what has happened to him? I must see him.'

'You'll have to find him first,' scoffed Petro.

'What has happened?'

'He escaped from custody,' I acknowledged sombrely.

'Pyro was probably wiped out by the gang,' Petro added, being professional. 'To stop him talking. Splice may have reckoned *he* had lost his value for them too, so once on the loose he turned on them.'

'Wait, wait –' Popillius broke in. 'Go back a stage. You are telling me my client escaped?'

'Fixed up by you, Popillius?' I enquired satirically.

Popillius retaliated, 'Just be professional and tell me what is going on.'

We sat either side of him and talked to him like schoolteachers. 'One of your imprisoned clients has been relieved of his life while in custody –'

'Splice saved his skin by not eating the tainted trayful –'

'Then while being removed to a safer place, somehow the troops managed to "lose" him.'

'Bribes were used,' decided Petro flatly.

'And who is the prime suspect for paying them?' I asked him.

'Falco, I'd say, look for a crooked lawyer.'

'Face it,' I advised Popillius. 'If you work for gangsters you are assumed to be their fixer.'

Popillius growled. 'I merely accepted clients, in a case where legal intervention was justified.'

'Well, you've lost them both now.' I was grim. 'Pyro was poisoned – and Splice has been killed in a fight.'

'Are you sure, or is this hearsay?'

'I saw it. How exactly were you first approached to take them on?'

Popillius replied openly: 'Somebody's slave brought me a letter. It outlined their position as prisoners and asked what my fee would be.'

'Who signed the letter?' Petronius demanded.

'Anonymous. The proverbial "Friends of the Accused". It happens. Usually the reason is, they don't want the man in question to feel obligated and embarrassed afterwards.'

'So how did you answer?' Petro snapped back. 'Was that by letter too?'

Popillius nodded. Cynically, I then asked, 'How could you be certain that you would be paid?'

He smiled slightly. 'My terms were payment in advance.'

'Oh smart! The upfront cash arrived, I take it?' Again he nodded. 'So,' I summed up, 'you never had any direct dealings, and you still don't know who your principals are?'

Popillius gazed at me. That was when he chose to surprise us. He leaned back, with his hands linked on his belt. 'Not quite,' he retorted. 'I do know who commissioned me. And more important to you, perhaps – *he* does not know yet that I traced him.'

Petronius and I looked at each other. Even before Popillius continued, we understood what he was going to do. It appalled us that he was about to undermine our prejudice – but his last speech warned us: he would tell us the name.

We were lads of tradition; we were shocked. But it was true: we were staring at an honest lawyer.

XLVII

EVEN HELENA HAD stopped murmuring to Albia. Helena had wonderful ears. Those shapely shells were perfect for pearl earrings, tempting to nibble – and they could single out whispered words of scandal from right across a humming banquet hall. She held up a finger to keep the girl silent.

Petronius Longus placed his hands flat on his thighs, breathing slowly. 'You are about to do something noble, Popillius?'

'I am not as stupid as you seem to think,' returned the lawyer peacefully.

A half-grin fixed itself on Petro's face. *'You tailed the slave!'*

'Of course,' confirmed Popillius with a light inflection. 'When the legal profession are offered anonymous clients, it is regular practice.'

Petronius winced. 'And to whose house did the slave return?'

'That of Norbanus Murena.'

Petronius and I leaned back and slowly whistled. Popillius looked reflective. His voice was low, almost sorrowful, as he contemplated the devious world. 'The perfect neighbour, I am told. A decent man, with an elderly mother upon whom he dotes. She is not with him in Britain, if the lady really exists. Which I regard as unproven, incidentally.'

Petronius and I both shook our heads in amazement.

'So why are you telling us?' I queried.

'That should be obvious,' the lawyer replied piously.

'You hate and despise gangsters?'

'As much as anyone.'

'But you take their money?'

'If there is a justification legally.'

'Then why give Norbanus away?'

Now Popillius did look slightly embarrassed, but the mood was fleeting. 'I was hired. I took the case.'

I still did not see the point.

'You told me Pyro was poisoned by these gangsters,' explained Popillius. Then he showed us that a lawyer's conscience is a tender thing: 'I have been paid for my services and I will defend his interests. What has happened to Pyro is an outrage. I cannot allow anyone to kill my client and get away with it.'

XLVIII

So FLORIUS WAS in partnership with Norbanus Murena.

There was a sensible course of action (go home; inform governor; change into dry tunics and put feet up while governor took risks). Then there was the course Petronius and I chose.

I blame Helena Justina. She reminded me that Norbanus also lived in the northern part of town, nearby. Popillius told us the address. He lent his carrying chair to take Helena and Albia back to the residence. When he offered to escort them himself, I refused.

'So I may be an honest lawyer – but you don't trust me!' he twinkled.

'Not with my wife,' I replied.

The lawyer's directions took us to a neat house on the bank of the main stream. There stood several shrines to the Three Mother Goddesses, bulging British deities sitting among fruit and baskets of wool and looking as if they would clout anyone disrespectful rather hard around the ears. A couple of other buildings in the vicinity were using the water supply for light industry, among them a pottery and a decorative metal works. These must be where those neighbours lived who thought Norbanus such a nice man.

Petronius and I approached quietly. We walked discreetly all around the boundary. It was quiet. Nobody was about, that we could see. But if this was the headquarters of a major gang of criminals, armed personnel could be all over the ground, waiting to ambush us.

'You knock on the door,' I said. 'He knows me.'

'He's met me too.'

We were behaving like naughty schoolboys who planned to disturb the porter then run away. We did not make a move, however. We were taking stock. For one thing, while Norbanus had no reason yet to suppose we were on to him, this house lay close to the arena, and not far from the waterwheel hut. There was a possibility that Florius had hidden up here. If we had only associated him with Norbanus before this, we could have searched this house in time.

Now however, the question was not did Florius come here after the fight – we both thought it almost certain – but was he still on the premises?

'I think he would bolt to his associate, get his breath, then move on fast,' Petronius said. I agreed. But we still needed to approach the joint with care. If Florius and Norbanus were both there, this operation really needed more than two of us. Even Norbanus must be far more dangerous than he had always seemed.

We had already made plans to cover the worst contingency. Helena Justina was to ask the governor to send troops. But would they ever come? I had requested support earlier, when I first left to join Chloris at the amphitheatre: the riot was all over before a few desultory soldiers turned up. Petro and I could be sitting here all day waiting for reinforcements.

We chose to investigate by ourselves. We would certainly do that without thinking if we were back home on the Aventine.

We did wait for some time. It gave us a feel for the place. We stood against the wall of the next door house and dutifully watched the Norbanus residence. Nobody went in or out. Most houses are like that except at certain times of day. This was not one of the busy times. There was no activity.

In the end, I was sent in. Petronius lay in wait outside, watching to see if anybody legged it out the back way. He told me reassuringly that if anyone jumped me he would see who did it. I made a rather short reply.

The door was answered, fairly swiftly, by a perfectly innocuous household slave.

'Greetings. I am Didius Falco. Is my sister here?'

Why did I still feel like a schoolboy? Perhaps because I had asked that question numerous times in the distant past, when my mother sent me out on vain errands to round up my horrid siblings. At least now the rest of my story had changed: 'My sister is Maia Favonia. She and your master are on friendly terms.' I really did feel quite anxious that Maia might be with the crook.

'She is not here.'

'You know her?'

'Never seen her.'

'Is Norbanus at home?'

'He's out.'

'When are you expecting him back?'

'Later.'

'Well look – I don't know if you would like to do this, but he very kindly promised to show me around his house. I am thinking of renting a similar place and I wanted to see what they are like. To save me a wasted journey, is there any chance . . .'

Of course there was. The slave, a Briton who came with the rented property, I guessed, was perfectly willing to show me everything. But then his master would not object, would he? Everyone said Norbanus Murena was such a pleasant man.

'Can I ask my friend to come in too?' Petronius Longus was just as welcome as me. I winked at him triumphantly. He kicked my ankle.

We searched the whole place. We even looked in the out-buildings. Well, you need to know what stabling and workshop facilities are available when you take on a lease. We were feeling pretty proud of ourselves. The slave had no idea we were fishy specimens.

The house was small by Mediterranean standards, set around a tiny courtyard which could never see much sun. Wattle and daub in some parts; elsewhere brick built, with a decent pantiled roof.

The best rooms actually had sheets of translucent talc on the windows and were frescoed in a basic way. Painted panels were divided by finely traced candelabra and urns; long-beaked birds of only slightly uncertain parentage bowed to each other in pairs on mottled ochre friezework. The furnishings were spare but adequate, less masculine and more fussy in style than I expected. Everywhere was clean and well-kept.

As a gangster's palace this lacked ostentation. That was wise. Londinium had not grown much since its days as a traders' camp among the marshes. To install grandiose marble and exquisite artwork, when even the governor so far had only a few building-trenches in place for his headquarters, would be indiscreet.

'Norbanus has a villa downstream too, hasn't he? Do you know if he rents or owns?'

'The villa is being built just for him.' So that was where some of his profits were invested.

'Is it across on the south bank?' asked Petro.

'Yes sir. Close to the religious sanctuary on a hill just outside town.'

Petronius knew it; his expression was sardonic. 'That's the new complex for the temples of the Imperial Cult, Falco. Our friend Norbanus has pitched his tent to be all cosy with the Emperor!'

'No, he's down by the river,' the slave corrected him snootily. 'The imperial estate owns all the high ground.'

Instead, Norbanus would have access to the water and its amenities. I bet that suited him. He could make a quick getaway, in case of trouble.

'So where is he today?' I asked innocently. 'His villa?'

'I'm afraid I cannot say, but we keep the house in readiness; he sleeps here most nights.'

By now we had been led back to the exit and were poised to leave. 'What about his friend?' asked Petronius. I saw he intended to take a chance. 'Do you see much of Florius?'

The slave did pause, though it was imperceptible. Perhaps his gaze sharpened, but he replied smoothly. 'Yes, he has been known to visit, but I've not seen him for some days.'

Well, that confirmed the gangsters' partnership. But it would also tell them we were on to both of them. The slave was bound to report back what we had said.

Petronius was keen for results now. He had taken a bloody-minded risk; this was his field of expertise, but I felt uneasy. Abandoning secrecy might get him more than he bargained for.

The door was open. We were being shunted out.

As we walked outside, we both stepped wide to allow entry to newcomers. This pair was familiar: the blind harpist and his boy. The boy scowled at me, then gave Petronius an even filthier look.

Petro and I walked around them, nodded coolly, then strode on. After a few steps I looked back and saw that the boy with the unpleasant stare was now watching us; Petronius in particular seemed to excite his interest. That did bother me. 'Our presence will be reported. Norbanus may feel we have encroached too closely.'

'Good!' snarled Petro.

I did not admit that I'd seen the harpist spying on Maia last night as she went to his room. My own role in that incident would be difficult to explain. But I did say, 'I'm worried about Maia. Need to warn her about Norbanus.'

'Good thinking.'

After a while I asked him straight out: 'Is something going on between my sister and you?'

Petronius looked at me sideways. Then he shrugged. His voice was hard. 'You had better ask her. And if she does happen to tell you her intentions, you could pass on her answer to me!'

'Oh, so she's being herself,' I remarked bluntly. Then I risked it: 'Are you in love with Maia?'

Petronius Longus slapped me on the shoulder. 'Don't you worry about it,' was his strained response. 'Whatever I feel has been there for a long time. It never mattered to anyone before. There seems no reason why it has to matter now.'

But I found that on behalf of both of them, it did matter to me.

★

We walked on in silence through the rain-sodden streets of this unformed, unfilled, vulnerable town. Evening had fallen. More rain was lowering in the dark skies. The immigrant wild people, entrepreneurs and crazy freaks who wanted to make their fortunes, were cowering at home. The pudding-faced Britons who originated here were sitting at their smoky firesides, trying to work out how to buckle a sandal strap. I hoped the judicial legate had taught these new citizens that very wet leather needs to be dried slowly, while stuffed with rags to preserve its shape . . .

When Petronius and I were almost at the procurator's house, we finally heard marching boots. Legionaries were coming towards us. They had failed to help us when we needed them. We glanced at each other then with one accord stepped under an awning outside an olive oil shop, where we remained unseen until the soldiers passed.

XLIX

THE DAY SEEMED long enough to me. Hours before, I had been roused at early light on Pyro's death and since then I had been constantly active. We had made progress. Both chief villains had been identified. All we had to do was painstakingly track them down. Petro might convince himself we were at the world's end where they had nowhere to hide, but I felt less confident. The brief conflict with Splice had ended with his death in the amphitheatre. But Florius and Norbanus could command enormous resources. Our task from now on could be demanding. So when I returned to the residence, I was determined to rest. I found Helena in our room. She sent for food trays, and we stayed private together with our children all that evening. No one bothered us. I did think of tackling Maia over Norbanus, but I was too tired. It would lead to a row. Tomorrow, I decided, I might manage to be more tactful.

Petronius had volunteered to report on the situation to the governor. Since Petro had his own clandestine position in Britain to discuss with Frontinus, I let him go alone. He would describe the gangsters' identities and our abortive reconnaissance and if he wrangled with Frontinus about further action – which was quite likely, knowing the vigiles – that was their own grief.

The only gripe *I* wanted to tackle with the high-ups was their failure to provide military support. As with Maia, I was too angry to broach the subject now – well, too spent physically to be polite. Helena said she had mentioned the problem to her uncle, who had been surprised. According to him, prompt orders had been given for troops to attend the arena and then later, when Helena returned home with Albia, more cover was supposed to have been sent to the Norbanus house. When I told her nobody turned up, Helena was furious. After I fell asleep, I am sure she slipped out and berated Hilaris about me being left in danger.

It may have helped Petronius Longus. His discussion with the governor must have been fairly forceful, and he obtained a decent escort for a plan he still had. I learned next morning that at nearly nightfall Petro crossed the river and rode out to the Norbanus villa. He was convinced it must be searched that night, so he chinked off on horseback in the eerie light of torches. I knew why: he had decided that Florius – not Norbanus – had been secretly staying there.

Much later, Petronius returned to Londinium, disappointed. His search party had failed to find any evidence. The villa seemed to have been stripped. A guard was left, with orders to conduct a meticulous search the following morning in the light and then to wait in case either gangster should return. Petronius rode most of the way back to town, but it was too dark to cross the river so he stopped off at the mansio on the south bank where he had been lodging, and slept there. That was good because if he had been given next morning's message in person, I know he would have sneaked off and dealt with it alone. I mean the message that Popillius brought for Petro from the two gang leaders.

Popillius arrived at breakfast time. He looked embarrassed. Since Petronius was absent, the governor ordered the lawyer to speak up. Anxiously Popillius repeated the message from Norbanus and Florius. When we heard it, we accepted that he had acted as a go-between from decent motives. Popillius had realised the situation was desperate. So did we.

The text was brutal. It was a ransom demand, though not for money. The gang said they had Maia. They were offering to return her – in exchange for Petronius.

L

THERE WAS PANIC. A swift search revealed that my sister was nowhere at the residence. Nobody had seen her for at least a day. The residence was large and people came and went at will. Then in the excitement over identifying the gangsters, she had not been missed. Her room looked the same as when Helena and I went in there yesterday morning; Maia had not slept here last night. Worse, although the gangsters had not mentioned them, none of her children could be found.

All anyone could remember was that Maia had considered accepting the invitation to visit the Norbanus villa. I now wondered if Petronius had been anxious last night over more than the hunt for Florius. Had he gone chasing off there in the dark because he was afraid Maia might have been lured to the gang's hideout? Of course, she did not know Norbanus was a villain. Maia had shared the general opinion that her admirer was 'a nice man'.

Aelia Camilla anxiously admitted she had given Maia permission to use the procurator's boat. This vessel, which I knew to be a substantial flat-bottomed barge capable of plying up the coast, was now missing from its mooring. Its crew were gone too.

Petronius was found. His immediate response was to rage at me for 'allowing' my sister so much freedom.

'Oh don't be ridiculous.' Terrified for her, I flared up myself. 'Maia does what she wants. She never answers to me, or anyone. If I tried to stop her, on the pathetic grounds of being her male guardian, she would behave even more defiantly – and probably sock me in the eye first.'

'She's unwittingly put herself in the wrong place,' murmured Helena. 'She doesn't know who she is dealing with.'

'I'm afraid of her reaction,' Petro growled. 'Maia will speak out, and feisty confrontations with violent criminals are damned dangerous. If they knock her about . . .' He checked.

'Norbanus may still be charming,' Helena tried to reassure him. The thought of Maia enjoying a lovers' tryst with Norbanus produced no happy reactions in Petro and me. 'Anyway, Lucius, you didn't find them at the villa. Tell yourself she's safe. Maybe Norbanus really does like her.'

'He set it up.' Petro's reaction was darker. 'Right from the start he was using her as bait.'

'Florius.' I was ahead of him. Well, it was obvious. 'Norbanus approached her, because he was a stranger. Florius had to keep away; he might have been recognised. But Florius is behind this scam. Norbanus could visit the governor in safety. At first it was to find out what Frontinus knew about the Jupiter protection gang, but once you were identified as one of the vigiles, Petro –'

'Bloody governor should have kept quiet! Florius would have known at once that if their British operation was to flourish they had to get me out of the way.'

I agreed. 'Florius carefully planned this as a means to get to you. From the moment they knew you were affectionate with Maia, she was a marked woman.'

'The harpist,' said Helena. 'He was put here to spy – and it won't have taken him long to know Petronius was very close to Maia and her family. The children were always talking about you, Lucius.'

'One of the children's most vocal worries was why you had vanished, when you went under cover,' I groaned. 'The gang would have seen immediately why. They may have bought off the half-baked Londinium troops, but you were a different proposition.'

'And they could get to you through Maia,' Helena said.

Petronius shook his head. 'I don't see why they would think that.'

'Don't fool yourself,' I said tersely.

'She treats me like —'

'Oh stop being dense! We all know what's up. Anyway, the harpist saw her go to your room that night.'

'What?' Helena riveted me with accusing eyes. Petronius himself, normally so relaxed, bit back any comment, but his annoyance was plain. Now they both knew that I had been a witness. My discretion over the incident won me no laurel crowns.

Restraining his anger, Petronius still tried to gloss it over: 'Just a fling . . .'

It was Helena's turn to lose her temper. 'Juno! Lucius Petronius, how can you be so hopeless? It's plain to everyone what Maia feels.'

He glared. 'Not to me.'

'Oh let me tell you then!' Helena prowled the room. She was edgy and desperately worried about Maia. 'You drink too much, you flirt too much, you do dangerous work,' she rattled off. 'You are a risk to a woman who wants a good life — but Maia Favonia is aching to take that risk. You must be the most exciting man who ever courted her.' Petronius looked startled. Helena brought him down to earth: 'And there have been plenty! Maia wants you — but she doesn't want to be deceived by you. Her children love you — she doesn't want them to be let down. And now if you don't do something,' said Helena more quietly, stopping in her tracks, 'she will die because of you.'

'That won't happen.'

'So why,' demanded Helena furiously, 'are you just sitting here?'

'Because this is the game,' Petronius said baldly. He was indeed sitting (in a chair Maia herself had often used). His face was strained, but he must have slept last night and I had seen him look worse on many other occasions. He explained in a grim tone: 'They will give her back and take me instead — but first Florius has to toy with me.' He was right. Florius would humiliate him and torture him with fear for Maia. Only then would Florius reel him in. 'It's no fun unless I suffer. I am sitting here because I now have to wait until the bastard sends instructions.'

Petronius was very quiet and still. He knew exactly what fate awaited him if he gave himself up to the Florius gang. With Maia at stake, he would make the sacrifice.

LI

THEY GAVE US a day and another night to suffer.
While he waited for his next message, Petronius stayed at
the residence. He ate sparingly, rested, occasionally sharpened his
sword. He would not be allowed to use it. They would want him
unarmed. This obsessive routine was just the old legionary's way
of keeping sane before an action. I was doing the same.

I had my own tensions. From the moment Helena understood
how serious the position was for Petronius, she made me
responsible for saving him. Her dark eyes beseeched me to do
something. I had to look away. If there had been anything I could
have done, it would have been in hand.

Officialdom had finally swung into action. I could not decide if
I approved, but it was reassuring to have some movement that was
independent of the gangsters. The governor took personal control.
He had men very quietly searching every known place connected
to the Jupiter empire. Unlike the usual noisy raids conducted by
government agencies, the troops went in in small groups, lacking
only fur slippers to deaden their footfall. One at a time, they picked
through all the bars and other premises that had overt links with
the enforcers. The Norbanus house and the villa downstream had
already been gone over and sealed.

Piecing together evidence for the gang's past routine, Frontinus
now reckoned they used to collect their gains in the warehouse
on the wharf for security, then Florius would come from the villa
to transport it downstream in his small boat. A larger oceangoing
craft probably nosed up the estuary and took moneychests on

board from the villa's landing stage, before making for Italy. Since Petro's search party yesterday evening had found nothing at the villa, it must all have been sent overseas quite recently and would not yet have reached Rome. The navy, the grandly named British Fleet which patrolled the northern waters, had been alerted, though it might be too late to intercept the latest consignment. A cordon was now in place between Britain and Gaul, though realistically the gang might yet slip through. A message was signalled back home to the vigiles. Both Rome and Ostia would be on the alert. It would be a pleasant irony if Florius and Norbanus were brought down through charges relating to import tax. But the penalty would only be a heavy fine, so that would not suit Petronius.

We knew Florius was still in Britain. We assumed Norbanus was. Petro's most favoured venue for apprehending them was the warehouse where the baker had been killed. His customs contacts said it had been deserted, but he clung to his theory. The governor believed he could apprehend the fly-by-nights at the brothel. That was his bet as the place where, at the very last minute, my sister would be exchanged for Petronius.

'Seems fair,' agreed Petronius, in his dry tone. He looked at me, with an expression I remembered from when centurions gave us information we distrusted, back in the legions years ago. He thought the governor was way off. Florius would know now that Petronius had had the brothel under surveillance; he was unlikely ever to reappear there.

Petronius and I continued to wait at the residence. We had stopped honing our swords.

The next message arrived in the early evening. This time they did not use Popillius, but a driver who jumped off a passing delivery cart and grabbed the residence steward by the neck of his tunic. In a hoarse whisper, the slave was told, 'The swap will be at Caesar's Baths! Longus is to come in an hour. Tell him – alone and unarmed. Try anything, and the woman gets it!' The man vanished, leaving the steward almost uncertain that anything happened. Luckily he still had the sense to report it straight away.

There was no question of Petronius going solo. Nor could he go unarmed. He was a big lad, with a distinctive build; we had ruled out sending in a decoy. This was it.

Provincial governors do not jump to attention just because some lowlife makes the call. Julius Frontinus surveyed the evidence cautiously, before he too decided this was genuine. 'It's right away from the river if they intend making a getaway. But it is near the Norbanus house; maybe they hid Maia Favonia somewhere we missed.' He drew himself up. 'Maybe she was at these baths, or at the bar adjacent to them, all along.'

Petro and I let it pass. We knew we would not be sent directly to the place where they were holding Maia. Petronius would be drawn to a meet, probably via several staging posts, then Maia would be brought to the last spot – if the gang believed the situation safe.

'I'd like to put a search party into those baths.' Luckily Frontinus worked out for himself that that would jeopardise everything. 'We just have time to assemble the support team at the venue,' he told us. 'We shall be in place ready, before you two arrive.'

We nodded. We both still wore our old sceptical expression. I saw Helena gazing at us curiously.

When almost an hour had passed, Petronius and I combed our hair like boys going out to a party, checked our belts and bootstraps, and solemnly gave each other the legionaries' salute. We set off together, side by side. Behind us at a safe distance came Helena in her aunt's carrying chair, which would bring Maia home if we achieved the exchange. My role was to watch what happened – and find some way to rescue Petronius straight after the swap.

We walked steadily, shoulder to shoulder. We paid no great attention to whether we were followed or observed; we knew we would be tailed by the governor's men and we expected the gang to have lookouts too. We travelled at a pace that gave messengers time to nobble us. This happened as soon as we turned left on the Decumanus, heading for the bridge over the stream.

It was the dogman who stepped out in our way. With his group of skinny, mangy hunting curs careering around his legs, he was unmistakable. 'Is one of you Petronius?'

We stopped and Petro acknowledged his name courteously.

'Listen to this then.' His long-nosed hounds nuzzled us, gently slobbering on our tunics and bootstraps. 'I was told to tell you, "The meet has been changed. Go to the Shower of Gold". Does it make sense?'

'Oh yes.' Petronius was almost cheerful. He had bet me the first assignation was a bluff. Luckily I had agreed, so I lost no money. We had enough at stake.

The governor and his men would sit around outside Caesar's Baths, trying to hide behind bollards and drinking troughs. Petronius would be forced to abandon their support and walk into trouble at some other location.

We executed an infantry turn in two smart stages. Anyone watching should have been impressed by our precision marching. Now instead of heading northwest we were heading southeast. We walked back past the chair, dividing one each side, and nodded politely to Helena as she stared out at us anxiously.

'New venue. Don't worry. We expected it.'

We then passed a troubled fellow, the governor's tail, who was trying to make himself invisible in a doorway while he panicked about our change of plan.

'Shower of Gold next!' announced Petronius loudly, hoping the man would realise we were not just going back home for a forgotten neckerchief: someone ought to inform the governor that things were more complicated than he had hoped. There could be several of these redirections yet.

We reached the narrow side road where we had to turn off, then all too soon we halted at the entrance to the tavern's own filthy byway. It was unlit and lying silent. We could see the Shower of Gold halfway along, its door outlined by a faint gleam of lamplight.

We stood there, observing. Nothing moved.

Now we were in a predicament we both dreaded: stuck at one end of a deserted alley, with dusk falling rapidly, in the certain knowledge that someone was waiting somewhere down that alley, intending to surprise and kill us. This was an ambush. It had to be. These situations always are.

LII

I
T WAS A still evening, with a pervasive cloud cover. It felt cool.
The storm had reduced the sultry temperature, but you could
still go without a cloak and be comfortable. Dampness was taking
over, however. Mist from the nearby river and marshes made our
skin and hair sticky. In Britain in late August nightfall varies with
the weather. Had it been fine, we would still have had plenty of
light. But rain was hovering nearby. In the narrow entry we
peered through murk at shadows which could be hiding any kind
of trouble.

Petronius sucked his teeth and swore. 'Classic!'

The alley looked like a dead end. I could not remember. I had
only ever come and gone one way. 'I'm twitchy.'

'Me too.'

'It's your call.'

He thought for a moment. 'You'll have to wait here and cover
this junction. If we both go in, there's no way out behind us.'

'Stay in sight as long as you can then.'

'They'll make me go inside the bar.'

'No, don't go in unless they send Maia out.' I knew he would
ignore that if he believed she was inside.

We made no move.

Adjacent buildings lay in darkness. It was difficult to tell if they
were houses or commercial premises. In the absence of sun terraces
or balconies with windowboxes to laze on, the population had
vanished like razor shells in sand. None of the scents I would
expect in Rome were present. No resins, or fragrant herbs, or

flower garlands, or subtle bath oils pervaded these chilly streets. They seemed to have neither public bakery ovens nor apartment griddles on the go. Peering at the roofline, all I could see were pantiles and ridge tiles. Windows were closely latched with dense wooden shutters. I glanced behind. Some distance away down the wider cart track I could see Helena's chair. Its discreetly armed bearers stood in position, motionless. Following instructions, Helena remained hidden behind drawn curtains.

'If they stuff you in the bloody well, remember – hold your breath until I come and pull you out.'

'Thanks for the advice, Falco. I never would have thought of that.'

This was a quiet city. No one else seemed to be in the vicinity. No late night cobblers or copper-beaters worked in their artisan booths. Pedestrians were missing. Where Rome would have had a cacophony of delivery carts after sunset, with their wheels trundling, their loads crashing and their drivers famously cursing, Londinium operated no curfew and lay still.

Silence. Silence and now a fine drift of miserable rain. Londinium, where Petronius and I as earnest young men had seen the worst of human grief. Once a desert of ashes and blood, now a city of small ambitions and great terror.

'Well, here we are again. Londinium. This bloody place.'

'Next time we'll know to stay away.'

'I'll just be happy if there is a next time for anything.'

'You optimist!' grinned Petronius. Then all at once some hidden device in his soul triggered him; he squared his wide shoulders, touched my elbow in an informal farewell, and set off.

He walked on light feet, constantly looking everywhere. He kept moving, but he made a gentle pace. Halfway to the bar, he crossed from left to right and paused, turning sideways to scrutinise the house walls opposite. I saw the pale gleam of his face as he glanced my way, then it changed and I knew he was staring down to the far end of the alley. I moved to the corner, intending to scan the other street side.

Something exploded from a ledge beside me. Brushing my face, I felt air, heard noise, knew abject fear. An old, squalid, horrible grey pigeon had flown up, disturbed, from a window ledge.

Petronius and I stayed motionless until our panic died.

I raised my arm. He signalled back. If they were going to rush us in the alley, it had to happen now. But nothing moved.

Petronius walked silently to right outside the bar. He paused again. He tried the door handle. It must have given. He pushed gently, so the door swung open. A dim light flowed out around him. Still nobody aimed a spear or threw a knife.

'*Florius!*' Petro had let out an enormous bellow. It must have been heard three streets away, but nobody dared peer out to see who was challenging the mobster. 'Florius, this is Petronius Longus. I'm coming in. I have a sword but I won't use it if you keep faith.'

Desperately nervous, I kept my eyes swivelling everywhere for trouble. Now, I thought, now they will emerge from cover, trapping him. I waited for the thonk of an arrow or the streak of a shadow as some unseen watcher jumped. Nothing moved.

The door to the wine shop had begun to swing closed. Petronius pushed it open again with his foot. He looked back at me. He was going in. This could be the last I would ever see of him. Stuff that. Keeping close to the wall, I set off down the alley after him.

Petro had disappeared inside. Suddenly he was back again, outlined in the doorway, close enough to see me coming. 'There's no one here. Absolutely nobody. I bet Maia's never even been here. We've been set up like idiots –'

Hardly had he spoken when he knew how true that was. Like me, he must have heard that sound we knew so well from the old days: the well-oiled hiss of many sword blades, drawn from their scabbards simultaneously.

Neither of us supposed for a moment that this was a convenient rescue.

LIII

I F THERE'S ONE thing I enjoy, it's being stuck up a blind alley in
a grim province on a gloomy evening, while an unknown
number of the military prepare to disembowel me.

'Shit,' muttered Petronius succinctly.

'Shit on a stick,' I qualified. We were in big trouble. No doubt
of it.

I wondered where in Hades they were hiding. Then I didn't
bother. They came swarming out of nowhere until they filled the
alley. The big boys in red raced up in at least two directions.
Others piled in on us through the back of the bar. Some leapt over
barrels showily. A few squirmed around on their bellies. None of
these tough lads felt it necessary to drop from the eaves or swing
on a lintel, though to my mind it would have made the picture
prettier. Why be restrained? With only two targets – both of us
caught out and startled – their officer had had scope for dramatic
effects. Properly stage-managed, the demise of M. D. Falco and
L. P. Longus could have been a feast of theatre.

Instead of which, lazily, the soldiers just flung us back against the
wall, yelled at us, and made us keep still by applying swords to
places we preferred not to have cut. I mean, all over us. Petronius
and I endured it patiently. For one thing, we knew this was a big
mistake on their part, and for another there was not much choice.
The legionaries were menacing; they all clearly hoped for an
excuse to kill us.

'Steady on, lads.' I cleared my throat. 'You're making asses of
your whole damned cohort!'

'What legion?' Petro asked the nearest one.

'Second Adiutrix.' He should have been told not to communicate with us. If he had, he was shamefully forgetful. Still, every cohort carries some dopey boy who spends his entire service on punishment, eating barley bread.

'Very nice.' Now Petro was being sarcastic. They were amateurs. Amateurs can be very dangerous.

Whatever their outfit, they knew how to invest a quiet night in a dead end town with the urgency factor. Petronius and I watched and felt like jaded old men.

Our back-up arrived. Helena Justina had emerged angrily from her chair and was demanding to speak to the officer in charge. Helena did not need to mount a tribunal to sound like a general in a purple cloak. Petronius turned to me and raised his eyebrows. She weighed straight in: 'I insist you let these two men go at once!'

A centurion emerged from the scurrying mass: Crixus. Just our luck. 'Move along there, madam, or I shall have to arrest you.'

'I think not!' Helena was so definite I saw him backstep slightly. 'I am Helena Justina, daughter of the senator Camillus and niece to the procurator Hilaris. Not that this entitles me to interfere with military business – but I advise you to be cautious, centurion! These are Didius Falco and Petronius Longus, engaged on vital work for the governor.'

'Move along,' repeated Crixus. He failed to note that *she* had noted his rank. His career meant nothing, apparently. 'My men are searching for two dangerous criminals.'

'Florius and Norbanus,' Helena sneered. 'These are not them – and you know it!'

'I'll be the judge of that.' Cheap power makes for obnoxious clichés.

'He knows damn well,' drawled Petronius loudly. 'Don't worry about us, sweetheart. This is men's business. Falco, tell your bossy wife to hurry along home.'

'That's right, love,' I agreed meekly.

'Then I'll just go and feed the baby, like a dutiful matriarch!'

sniffed Helena. 'Don't be late home, darling,' she added
sarcastically.

As if huffiness was in her nature, she stormed off. Disposing of
a senator's daughter was a problem the soldiers had not pre-
considered and even these renegades balked at it. They let her go.
More fool them.

They were waiting until she was off the scene before they dealt
with us. I watched her leaving. Tall, haughty, and apparently self-
possessed. No one would know how much anxiety she felt. The
soldiers had now brought up torches, so light gleamed on her fine,
dark hair as she stormed past them, with a toss of her head, flinging
one end of a light stole back over her shoulder. An ear-ring
glinted, her garnet and gold drop. It had caught in the delicate
fabric; impatiently she freed it with those long, sensitive fingers
that our daughters had inherited.

My own stomach was in a brutal knot until she left safely. If this
was the last time I ever saw her, our life together had been good.
But my heart ached for the grief she would feel if she lost me now.
If I were taken from Helena, my ghost would come raging back
from the Underworld. We had too much living left to do.

It was never going to happen. Petro and I were finished. The
mood had turned even more ugly. Young faces, dark with fright
and false bravado, stared at us. These troops knew they were in the
wrong. They could not meet our eyes. Crixus, the mad bastard in
charge, must realise that if Petro and I survived and told the
governor what went down here tonight, the game was up. He
came and stood in front of us, baring his ugly teeth. 'You're dead!'

'If you're going to kill us, Crixus,' Petronius said quietly, 'at
least tell us why. You're doing this for the Jupiter gang?'

'You're sharp!'

'Paid or pressured by Florius? So did he tell you to kill us? I
thought that he wanted to finish me himself.'

'He won't object.' I reckoned Crixus was making up his mind
as he went along. That meant rash decisions. Decisions that could
only be bad for us.

It was no use consoling ourselves that if he killed us, he could never get away with it. Helena had gone to fetch assistance. In a moment even Crixus would work out that letting her go was a fatal error.

The centurion was crazy, and his youthful, inexperienced men were becoming hysterical. The Second Adiutrix were a new legion, cobbled together from scratch using naval ratings; they were a Flavian creation rushed into service to fill urgent gaps in the army after other, older legions had been massacred or corrupted to the point where they were past saving. These raw, mad boys were now jostling each other in what they mistook for camaraderie; then they barged forward and started pushing us around. We tried not to retaliate. They laughed at us. Disarmed, we stood no chance. They were taunting us to make a move so they could tear us to pieces.

We knew better than to hope for escape now. Sure enough, the situation grew a great deal worse. We heard the measured approach of yet more soldiers, and lest it raise our spirits, the Second Adiutrix greeted these newcomers cheerily. Crixus swore affectionately at that other lag of a centurion, Silvanus. Silvanus and his men scowled at Petronius and me.

And then the unexpected happened. I never heard an order given, but the new boys all whipped out their swords and fell on the careless bastards who were holding us. Next moment, we were being grabbed once again, but this time to be thrown from hand to hand up the alley, until we were clear of the conflict.

The fight was disciplined and dirty. The Crixus century gathered their wits and fought back. It all took longer than it should have done. Slowly, however, the Crixus men were rounded up and stripped of their weapons. Crixus himself, fighting like a beer-crazed barbarian, was overcome, grounded, and placed under arrest. Silvanus read him the order, which came straight from the governor. Crixus was the defaulter who had 'lost' Splice. He had been on the loose ever since, carefully avoiding barracks, but his good times were over. There are centurions who survive for years, famous for corruption and bribe-taking, but he had overstepped the mark by a mile.

Whether Silvanus himself had ever been on the take was unclear. He had made a choice today. We could only see it as a good one.

There seemed to be a reason for it. He came up and spoke to us. 'I hear you were in the Second, Falco.'

I took a breath. This was the big question, the embarrassment I had avoided when I first met him. Owning up to service in the Second Augusta, during the Rebellion, could lead to bitter accusations. 'Yes,' I said levelly.

But Silvanus gave me a rueful grin, full of shared grief. Wearily he put out an arm to grasp wrists in the soldiers' salute first with me, then with Petronius. This was something I had not allowed for: Silvanus was in the Second Augusta too.

It was one of those moments when all you want to do is collapse with relief. Petronius and I could not even consider it. We still had to find and rescue Maia.

Petronius marched up to the prostrate Crixus. 'Do yourself a favour. Tell me what you were told to do. I am supposed to be a hostage exchange for Falco's sister. The whole point was for Florius to capture me and make me suffer – so why did he send you to do the job?'

'He knows I'm more competent!' sneered the centurion.

I elbowed Petro aside. He was too angry; he was losing control. 'You're so competent you're now in chains, Crixus,' I pointed out. 'So what was the intention here tonight?'

'I don't know.' I stared him out. He lowered his voice. 'I don't know,' he repeated.

I believed him.

LIV

WE PAUSED TO reconsider. 'So where now?'
'Caesar's Bar, after all?' Petro suggested.

'They are not at Caesar's,' Silvanus broke in. 'I just got
dispatched from there by the governor after Falco's wife rushed
up.'

Petronius grinned. 'Falco knows how to pick a woman with
character.'

Silvanus pulled a face that told me the high style of speech my
girl had addressed to Frontinus. 'What's she like if you fart in the
bedroom or leave muddy boots on the table, Falco?'

'I've no idea. I don't try it. So where to?' I reiterated to
Petronius.

The choice was decided for us. A soldier rushed up to tell Silvanus
of urgent developments at the wharf. The customs men had spotted
activity by the warehouse they were watching, the one where the
baker was beaten to death. It had looked as if loot had been hastily
assembled, ready to be shipped out, and they reckoned the gang
were planning to flit. When they investigated, the gang had
panicked and rushed them, seriously wounding Firmus. Then the
gang had invaded the customs house, which was now under siege.

We went the way I knew, so we never did find out if that alley by
the Shower of Gold really was a dead end. I wasn't going back
there. Places where I have so nearly been killed repel me.

It was a short step. I wished we had come here first.

Down on the river, soldiers quickly took over from the

embattled customs force. A long stretch of dockside was made off-limits to the public. They started moving ships out from their berths. Stores were searched. The ferries were beached. The bridge was cleared. Little boats in daily use for nipping about were taken upstream and moored. In streets all around the wharves, more troops arrived and waited patiently for orders.

Petronius and I stood on the heavily piled and banked wooden quay. We had our backs to the dark rippling water of the great river, facing the long row of packed stores. Soon there was no shipping moored; it had all been moved off, both from the deep water docking points where cargoes were unloaded, and even from out in the channel. We were staring at the customs house, a handsome stone building. Nothing there moved.

Silvanus was deploying men, some along the warehouse frontages, some on the forum road, some shinning up and clambering all over the roofs. They were silent and quick. Once on position they froze. The Second had always deserved better than their recent reputation. They were the Emperor's old legion, and it showed.

Now we had the place surrounded, every exit covered.

'Something bothering you?' I nudged Petro as he stood in a reverie.

'We were set up at the Shower of Gold,' he answered warily. 'I'm still wondering why.'

'You think there was more to it than Florius paying the Adiutrix to do for us?'

'Not their style, Falco. Florius knows I'm after him, and *he* wants *me*. But it's personal. He needs to see me suffer. Then he wants to finish me himself. He had Maia; he could have taken me. This doesn't make sense.'

Petro was too good an officer to brush aside his qualms. I trusted his instincts.

'Another thing,' I warned him. 'If he did lean on Crixus to finish us off, Florius won't now be expecting to go through with the handover. He thinks we're dead . . .' I tailed off. If he thought Petronius was dead, holding Maia served no purpose.

Unable to face the thought of what they might do to her, Petro found himself some action. Firmus was lying on the walkway being tended by a doctor. He had a deep gash in the side, from which he had lost too much blood. We did not ask whether he would make it; he was conscious, so we tried to seem optimistic.

Petro knelt beside him. 'Don't talk much. Just tell me who went into the building, if you can.'

'About fifteen or twenty,' Firmus croaked. Someone passed Petro a water flask, which he held to the injured man's lips. 'Thanks . . . Heavy weapons . . .'

'Were there women with them, did you see?'

Firmus was passing out. From the look of him, that might be the last he knew of anything. 'Firmus!'

'Couple of camp followers,' croaked Firmus, fading fast.

Petronius stood up.

Silvanus came to report. 'We've staked out the whole locale. We can pin them down for weeks. There's a bivvy set up, two blocks along, if you need a hot drink.' He glanced down at the customs officer, then swore under his breath.

Petronius seemed remote. Silvanus – wide, slow, and now oddly respectful – was watching him. Petro started walking up towards the customs house. I quickly informed Silvanus that the hostage situation had to be resolved. He knew about it from the governor. All the men must be aware that Petronius Longus had volunteered to hand himself over to Florius. They had worked this patch. They knew what the Jupiter gang was like. They knew what fate Florius must be planning for Petronius.

Darkness had set in. The troops assembled torches, flooding the wharf with mellow light for a long stretch in either direction. It flickered out across the nearside of the river. A crane sent a long distended shadow straight across the boards. We were aware sometimes of faces in the pools of darkness beyond our ground. A crowd must have gathered.

Petronius was now standing in shadow on the opposite side of the road from the customs house, across from the entrance. No point in delay. Silvanus signalled his men to the alert, then himself marched openly to the heavy panelled door. He beat on it with his dagger pommel.

'You inside! This is the centurion Silvanus. We have the building surrounded. If Florius is in there, he can parley with Petronius.'

After a silence, someone inside spoke.

Silvanus turned to us. 'They are telling me to get back.'

'Do it!' Slight impatience coloured Petro's order.

Silvanus moved back out of range. 'All right!'

For what seemed an age, nothing happened. Then people inside opened the great door a crack. A head, attached to the man who was holding the door, checked the exterior. Various muscular types ran out into the road, covering the space outside. They had an armoury none of us expected: two full-sized ballistae which they pushed quickly over the threshold and set up to guard the entrance, plus several rare, hand-held crossbows. I heard soldiers gasp. This was staggering firepower. Most legionary footsloggers had seldom been so close to artillery, and never when it was in opposition hands.

'Nobody move!' Their centurion's warning was hardly needed.

A quick-thinking soldier passed Petronius a shield. I doubted that even triple laminate would protect him from ballista bolts at short range. But it reassured the rest of us. In theory.

There was a balcony at second storey height above the customs house entrance. A figure had appeared there. Petronius walked straight out to a central point, about twelve strides in front of the door, looking up. The two fixed ballistae continued to sweep the whole area; they had the usual heavy iron frames, manoeuvred on wheels, and were easily aimed by swinging their sliders around on universal joints. That was bad enough. Meanwhile the men with the tension-sprung manual crossbows threatened Petro. If they let fire, he would be killed instantly.

'Florius!' His voice was strong, virile, and seemed fearless. 'I'm still here, you see. Crixus let you down and he's in custody.'

'You're hard to kill!' jeered Florius, his voice unmistakable. The balcony was in darkness, but our men were bringing torches closer, so his figure and shaven head became eerily outlined against an open doorway.

'I'm not ready to go,' answered Petro. 'Not while you're alive. We had an agreement about an exchange.'

Florius half turned and muttered something to an invisible companion behind him.

'Stop messing me about!' yelled Petro. 'Hand her over!'

'Wait there.' Florius went back inside.

We waited.

Florius reappeared. 'We'll go ahead.'

'I'll come in,' Petro volunteered, 'but I want to see Maia Favonia first.'

Florius was curt. 'The centurion can come up.'

'He doesn't know her. Her brother will identify her.'

'The centurion!'

Silvanus courageously marched forwards to do it. They let him approach almost as far as the entrance, where he was told to halt. Something went on inside the building. We heard Silvanus speak to someone out of sight indoors. There was no audible answer. Immediately he was motioned away. He came back to Petronius, and I joined them.

'They've got a woman there all right.' The centurion spoke rapidly, in a low voice. 'She's bound, and had a cloak or something over her head. They took it off for a moment. Dark hair, her face is bruised –' He looked at us anxiously. 'I'd say they've beaten her, but don't fret; I've seen worse when the lads lose their tempers with their girlfriends after a party night . . . I asked her if she's Maia and she nodded. Red dress. She looks all in; you'd better get her out as soon as possible.'

'How many?' I muttered.

'Enough,' Silvanus growled.

I wanted to move closer, but they had thought of that. Those two ballistae were angled so they covered a wide arc. No one could approach.

Up on the balcony, safe from a sudden assault, of course, Florius was brandishing one of their crossbows. Clearly it made him feel good. He waved it at Petronius, showing off, then pointed it straight at him and slowly wound the ratchet. Now the bolt would fire any time he pulled the pin. Set-faced, Petronius did not move.

'I'm ready. So send her out.'

'You have to come in.'

'Send out Maia and I'll come in past her.'

Florius spoke to somebody below him. In the doorway at ground level two figures appeared. One – slick dark hair and handsome bearing – was Norbanus Murena. He was leading a woman, who half collapsed against him. A short, neat figure, wearing a crimson dress, she had her head and shoulders wrapped in material as a blindfold. I could see that her arms were tightly bound behind her.

'Where are the children?' Petronius rasped hoarsely.

There was a very slight pause. 'We sent them back,' Norbanus claimed silkily. It seemed a long time since I had heard that urbane voice. 'We sent them to the residence.'

'Maia!' Petronius insisted. 'Are they telling me the truth?'

Norbanus tugged at her arm, at the same time hauling her more upright. She nodded. With her head covered that way, she must feel disorientated. It was a slow movement; I could deduce little from it except that, as Silvanus said, she needed our help urgently.

It was now two days since I last saw my sister. Anything could have happened to her. From her state now – and remembering how Florius treated Albia – it probably had.

'We'll let her go now,' Florius announced. 'Falco, move to the crane. She'll come over to you. Longus! You move the other way, then come in.'

I touched Petro slightly on the shoulder, then we moved quickly apart. I could see what they were aiming at. Maia and

Petronius would now cross paths at an angle, some distance apart. He had no chance to grab at her. If he tried anything, both Maia and he could be shot.

I reached a position away from Petronius. Norbanus muttered something then pushed the red-clad figure towards me. He seemed to instruct her to walk forward. She did so, with faltering footsteps, unable to tell where she was going or what was underfoot. Instinctively, I started towards her, but Florius swung his weapon so it covered me. I stopped. He laughed. Maybe he was jumpy, but certainly he enjoyed the power.

'Come on, now!' Florius yelled at Petro. 'Don't try anything, Longus. Get in here.'

Petronius advanced, watching the hostage. The woman kept coming across the roadway, small feet testing the ground ahead of her uncertainly. Petronius matched his advance to her pace. Eventually they were level, equidistant from the building, a few strides apart. Petronius stopped and said something.

'Don't speak!' bawled Florius frantically. 'Mind it – or I'll do you both!'

The hostage walked on. I began to step towards her. Florius had the bolt-shooter aimed on Petro, who remained halted: he seemed to be thinking. Florius urged him on with wild movements of the weapon, finally swinging around to train it on the hostage. Petronius walked forwards again. The men at ground level began backing towards the doorway, some ahead of him but others closing in behind.

They were drawing into a tight predatory group. Florius ordered Petronius to put down the shield. He did so, stooping to lay it on the road. As he straightened, Florius barked out another instruction; Petro, using both hands simultaneously, unslung and dropped both his sword and his dagger. Head up and in silence, he had turned to stare back after Maia while Florius angrily motioned him into the customs house.

The door was being opened wider. Outside, I was two strides from the slight-figured woman in red and reaching out for her.

Suddenly, Petronius started and yelled something to me. At the same moment he was rushed. Gangsters snatched him and dragged him inside. The heavy door slammed shut. Petronius was gone.

I ripped off the woman's blindfold and understood what he had said.

'That's not Maia!'

LV

T HE WOMAN TURNED out to be a pallid prostitute, half starved, and shaking with nerves. She said they had forced her to do the impersonation. Well, she would. Luckily for her, Silvanus yanked her back out of reach as I lashed out.

As she blinked in the torchlight, I cursed my stupidity. Petronius knew my sister better than I did. He had seen – too late maybe – that this was a decoy: right height, but wrong shape and wrong build. The dress she wore was a tawdry, ill-dyed shade and of coarse-weave material. Even allowing for some distress, her walk was quite wrong.

I raged at this hollow-eyed travesty to tell me where my sister was. She claimed she did not know. She claimed she had never seen Maia. She knew nothing about the children. None of them had been at the warehouse; none were at the customs house.

She was led off.

Someone slipped through the military cordon and joined us: Helena. She stood beside me in silence, carrying a cloak that I knew belonged to my sister – not that we had any use for it.

If the decoy was right, the gang never had Maia so no exchange had ever been possible. They would have lost nothing if Crixus had killed Petro at the Shower of Gold and by believing they had power, we had let them get their hands on him unnecessarily. So where in Hades was Maia? And how could we extract Petronius before Florius killed him?

The soldiers were itching to act. I agreed. My one thought now was to rescue Petronius. Already it could be too late.

Florius knew what he had achieved. He appeared once more on that balcony, this time triumphantly showing us two of his men holding Petro between them. Now he had new demands. He wanted a ship, and safe passage for his men and himself to go aboard.

It was at this moment that we were joined by the governor.

Decisions were no longer mine to make. Frontinus must already have been briefed. He took stock very quickly. The life of a Roman officer was at risk, but a public building had been taken over and if he allowed criminals to do as they liked in this way, his provincial capital would reach a state of anarchy. 'I can't have this. We'll go in.'

I kept myself under control as best I could. 'If you attack the building, they will kill Petronius.'

'Don't fool yourself,' Frontinus warned. 'They intend to kill him anyway.'

We were taking too long. Frontinus left me and went into a huddle with his staff officers.

'You could have kept him off the scene,' I muttered to Silvanus.

'He's no slouch. He wouldn't hear of going home for borage tea and waiting for a report later. I don't want him here, Falco, believe me. Can't risk losing him to a bloody ballista bolt.'

'Oh such consideration for an imperial legate!'

'It's consideration for myself,' Silvanus grinned. 'Just think of the reports to write if we let a legate of Augustus get wiped out!'

Now I definitely knew that he was a member of the canny Second.

While the governor brooded bureaucratically, the gang lost patience. Maybe they spotted Frontinus and guessed his hard attitude. Maybe the numbers of soldiers now arriving made them give up hope of negotiating their way out. A shutter smashed open; a ballista shot through the opening nearly killed Silvanus.

We all fled for cover. Silvanus was desperately ordering men to remove Frontinus from the danger zone. There was nothing for it. The legionaries would fight to regain the customs house.

'We can burn them out or batter them.'

'Try to save the building,' Frontinus said drily. 'I have enough demands on my works budget.'

We had no idea what was going on inside. I could only hope that the distraction of an attack would deter Florius from any plans to put Petronius through torture.

I wanted to help but was rebuffed. 'Keep out of the way. You're not in the damned army now. Leave this to us, Falco.'

Silvanus called the order. Timbers appeared out of nowhere; in a hail of missiles, men rushed the main entrance and started beating in the door. Forming a classic testudo, under walls and a roof of shields, they managed to approach close enough to pile in though windows and shin up to the balcony. Ballistae were fired, but they are long-range weapons. Once the legionaries ran up close, they were more than a match for the gangsters. The speed of their reaction to the first shot seemed to take the mobsters by surprise, and the boys in red soon burst in on them.

There was a sharp bout of fighting inside. Silvanus and his men were ruthless. Ten or so heavies, some bleeding copiously, were taken into custody. A handful had been killed. Norbanus was captured. Soldiers swarmed through the offices, searching for Petro as a priority. Uniformed men ran in all directions. But in the chaos, our quarries escaped. I searched the building myself; I scanned all the prisoners and lines of bodies and wounded to make sure: unbelievably, Florius had given us the slip. There was no sign of him. No sign of Maia. No sign of Petronius.

The legions do not mess about. A systematic beating of one captured gangster, with the others watching, soon produced information.

'Where – is – Florius?'

'The warehouse –'

'You're lying!'

'No – he's got a load of stuff there, going to Rome.'

It was hard to believe. How could he have got past us? We had had men all along the wharf, and others in the backstreets. Silvanus and I pelted along there, followed by pounding legionaries. The wooden boards reverberated dangerously as we hared up to the store.

The wide doors opened outwards as they do in most stores to save making useless space inside. That made it difficult to break in. Silvanus pointed upwards with one finger: on the warehouse roof a group of soldiers were hastily removing tiles. Leaning forwards to listen, a rooftop legionary let us know in sign language that everything below was very quiet. He and his colleagues then continued lifting tiles.

I frowned. 'Something's up – I'm worried. We have to get this right. Why seal themselves in, with us crawling all over the exterior? The longer they stay inside, the worse it gets. They can't withstand a siege. Trust me, they are not intending to.'

'There are no windows and no other doors – and we're on the roof. Unless they've spirited themselves off in a cloud, they have to be still in there.' Silvanus was a literal man and he was obstinate. I remembered when he first showed us the Verovolcus corpse. He was helpful as far as he had to be, but he took no initiatives.

Fortunately initiative was not needed here. Sheer force broke through the doors. The huge place was empty.

Helena Justina came up and touched my arm. 'Listen – how could Florius have travelled along this part of the wharves with all the soldiers on guard?'

'This is the gang's warehouse, love. They killed that baker here –'

'And they know the customs men were watching it! They would be daft to come back here. Marcus, they had plenty of money. Why would they stick to one warehouse? I bet they have others – and while you are all searching this area, have you noticed that the warehouses also extend further upriver? The gang could just as well be using one on the far side, beyond the ferry landing stage.'

Helena was right. The ferryman had known about Florius.

I pelted back along the wharf. I crossed the road by the customs house, shouting to the legionaries to help. There was a landing-stage for the ferry, beyond the forum road. Beyond that were more lines of warehouses, packed along yet another wharf. While Silvanus and I had run in the wrong direction, his men must have continued to threaten the prisoners, and we found a group of soldiers breaking through various warehouse doors. The next part of our search took longer than I can bear to think about. One after another the stores were broken open. Eventually, with new information screwed out of the prisoners, the soldiers converged on what they thought was the right place. With Helena at my heels I pushed through, heedless of splinters. It was pitch dark. Someone handed in a torch.

'Petro!'

There was no answer.

'Petronius!'

This place was crammed with loot. I started forcing my way past chests and bales. More slender, Helena grabbed the torch and slipped past me through the piles of stuff, rushing ahead into the darkness, also calling out. Behind us soldiers were still breaking in.

Helena found Petronius first. Her scream chilled my blood. 'Marcus, Marcus, help him – *quick!*'

LVI

H E HAD NOT answered because he could not do so. Every ounce of his being was under stress. At the limit of his endurance, even our arrival almost caused him to waver. Hope was the last distraction he needed.

Florius had left him absolutely stuck. He had taken his time to set this up. Petronius was tied by the waist with several long ropes lashed in a star-shaped pattern so he could not change position. Arms above his head, he was desperately holding on to a ring at the end of a long chain. It went up and over a pulley on a loading arm. To the other end Florius had attached a great crate of ballast. You know what ballast is – rocks, big enough to hold an empty ship steady in a storm. I could see the rocks piled high on top. It was perilously balanced immediately above Petro, jutting out over the edge of a walkway. An iron bar supported it halfway along. If Petro let go of the chain – or even loosed it a few inches – the crate would tip off its supports and crash straight down on him. The game was, Petronius had to last as long as possible, knowing that when his strength gave out, he would be crushed to death.

Sinews were standing out in his forehead. Beads of sweat shone on his face. His mouth was a tight line, his eyes were squeezed shut; he was close to the limit.

Helena and I flung ourselves beside him, and dragged on the chain. I got one hand through the ring; there was no room for more. It was almost impossible to grip the cold slippery metal of the chain itself. Petronius breathed, but dared not give up. I carried less weight than him, though I did know how to use it; Helena was

315

no feather, but she had never been the type of tomboy who did training at a gym. We all three clung on. The soldiers behind us must have been distracted by the chests of loot. I yelled for help, but we couldn't wait.

'Helena, fetch that coil of rope –' She obeyed, though when she loosed her grip on the chain, I felt it nearly jerk free. I could hardly talk to give instructions; luckily she was sharp. At my strained nod, she forced the rope through the ring we were holding then ran to secure it. The upper walkway was supported on huge timber posts. Helena was able to wind the rope around the nearest. She had the sense to turn both ends several times, then tried to knot them.

Men were now up on the walkway, running. A soldier appeared alongside us. Those above were seeking ways to take the strain on the balanced crate. Petro and I still clung on, scared to believe we were safe. We were not, yet. The nearest soldier desperately slashed his sword through the ropes holding Petronius. More men arrived. Nervously, Petro and I let go of the chain. Despite our alarm, Helena's rope held. Arms caught Petro as he staggered. A soldier and I dragged him sideways as half his ties were released. Almost fainting, Petronius sank to the ground. Then the timber post creaked ominously. Suddenly the rope gave way.

The crate crashed down in a hail of dust and rock. Amidst tremendous noise, huge chunks of debris missed us all by inches. Petronius lay groaning open mouthed, as the blood returned to his arms and hands. Coughing, Helena and I held him, massaging his stricken limbs and aching spine. His tunic was soaked, his brown hair plastered to his head with sweat.

'Dear gods. That was too close, my lad.' I waited for him to say *what kept you?* but he was too shocked to speak. He leaned his head against my arm, eyes closed but gradually breathing more easily. A soldier brought a water bottle. We got some into him.

Above his head, my eyes met Helena's. She reached over and touched my cheek. I turned and kissed her palm as she withdrew it. Petronius forced himself to revive enough to smile at her.

He looked at me, searchingly. I reported the best and worst.

'We caught most of the gang. We've got Norbanus, but Florius was somehow missed. How in Hades did you and he get out?'

'Uniforms,' croaked Petro. He waved his arm and I saw familiar crimson material lying discarded by a bale. 'Red tunics.'

'Crixus!' The bad centurion had supplied the one disguise that would take Florius unnoticed almost anywhere if there was enough chaos going on around him.

'He's taking a boat.' Petro was still mithering. 'He had one hidden upriver. They've loaded more loot –'

'Don't talk,' murmured Helena.

'Never mind me – where's Maia?'

'We still don't know. But not here.'

Petronius squirmed into a more upright position. He held his head in his hands, elbows on his knees. He moaned with frustration and misery. 'I don't think they ever had her.'

'They said they did,' I reminded him.

'They said a lot of things.'

Long before he should have done, he was dragging himself upright. I gave him a shoulder to lean on. Once we brought him outside, Helena tried to wrap him in Maia's cloak; he would have none of it, but when she told him whose it was, he took the garment and kept it over one shoulder, nuzzling his cheek against the woollen folds.

We walked up the quay back to the prisoners at the customs house. Petronius took note of all of them. He knew some of them from Rome. Silvanus was organising search parties for Florius and any other missed gang members. The wharf was still sealed, on the off-chance we would roust them out. Men were searching all the warehouses. A bunch of the troops had huddled around one of the abandoned full-size ballistae, exclaiming over its sophisticated design. 'It's a damned automatic repeater – look, you can fill this barrel and it fires off a whole load of bolts without having to reload –' I was amused to see Frontinus among them.

Eventually the governor tore himself away and arranged to

remove the prisoners to safe custody, all except Norbanus. Petro wanted him.

As soon as the customs house was cleared for use, we took Norbanus in there. Petro picked up his sword as we went in. He first kicked aside but then gathered up another weapon, one of the vicious hand-held crossbows. 'I've always wanted one of these!'

'Look, it's got a top-speed ratchet and a perfect trigger – and some kind person has primed it. That must have been helpful Florius. Let's try it out,' I said, menacing our charge with a snarl. We had not even tied him up. Why bother? Norbanus seemed to accept his fate, and the wharf outside was still full of legionaries. Some had remained inside here, but Petronius dismissed them; clearing away witnesses is always ominous for a prisoner.

'I'll have you here in the dark, out of public view,' Petronius told Norbanus pleasantly. 'Just in case I forget my manners.' The vigiles were known for their harsh enquiry methods.

'You could truss him up under some ballast,' I suggested. 'Like Florius did to you – or is that too good?' I kicked Norbanus unexpectedly. I kicked him *very* hard. 'Where's Maia?'

'I've no idea.' The businessman still sounded the same. Learning he was a master criminal should have altered our perception. Now we knew that the slick tongue and amiable smile were treacherous, yet he remained in character. It was real. That's how some gang leaders succeed in holding authority: apart from occasional lapses into murder, they have winning ways.

'Did you ever hold her?' Petronius demanded. He was the professional; I let him take the lead.

'A small deception.' Norbanus was rubbing his leg where I had lashed out. I don't normally resort to brutality, but my sister was still missing and I felt no regret.

'Did she come to your villa?'

'I wouldn't know.'

'Florius was there. Did he see her?'

'I believe not.'

318

'Where is he now?'

'You will have to find him for yourself.'

'You admit you were partners?'

'I admit *nothing.*'

Petronius caught my eye. This was going to be a long business. We might never extract any useful information.

Helena appeared in a doorway. Petronius paused, unwilling to let her watch the dark actions afoot.

'Marcus —' She seemed unwilling to be in the vicinity of Norbanus, or else unwilling to see how we dealt with him.

'Unless it's urgent, I can't come.'

I had told her to go back to the residence along with the governor, but she was always clingy after I had been in danger.

'Never mind,' Helena said quickly.

'No, wait, What is it?'

'A boat.'

'Leaving?'

'No, arriving. Limping up with a broken mast.' It seemed irrelevant.

'So long as it's not Florius fleeing.'

'No, don't worry,' Helena assured me, and she withdrew.

I thought I heard excitable voices outside, but the heavy doors blocked out most sound. Petronius and I resumed our interrogation.

'Jupiter was a nice touch,' I said to Norbanus admiringly. 'The patron of wine, women and weather. Symbol of power too . . . But now you find out, Norbanus — thinking *you* had any power was the myth.'

Petronius laid down the crossbow and with the flat of his palm pushed Norbanus across the office where we were holding him. It was soft, encouraging movement; there was no need yet for drama.

'I want to know —' Petro's voice was quiet. That made it worse. 'I want to know everything about your sordid empire — here, and back in Ostia, and Rome. Norbanus, you are going to tell me every fiddle, every threat backed up with violence, every wretched, dirty scam. I'll have the endless property portfolio, the seamy food shop take-overs, the obscene child brothels, the pitiless beating up of innocents, and the deaths.'

A draught caused the torches to flicker. I felt cold air momentarily. I did not look round.

'I have nothing to say,' smiled Norbanus, still the handsome, urbane man of affairs. 'Your accusations won't hold up in court once my lawyers get involved. You don't have any evidence against me –'

'I will,' said Petronius. I had seen him in action on plenty of occasions, but never so impressive as this. 'Tell me about Maia Favonia.'

'What for? You know her well enough.'

'Enough to care if she falls into the hands of men like you.' Petronius was utterly controlled. 'But let's hear about your interest, Norbanus. Or was it all a ploy to help Florius get at me? You were simpering at Maia's feet, regaling her with music and offering trips to your country bower – but did you really give a damn for her?'

The man shrugged and smiled. Then he stopped smiling.

'He's a bachelor, a loner who reveres his mother,' I jeered. 'No other woman interests him. The pressing seduction attempt was all false.'

I had heard someone come into the room behind me. Light increased, as Helena Justina rejoined us, holding high a tar-soaked brand. At her side, when I turned to see who it was, stood my sister Maia.

She looked fine. A little tired, but vibrant. With her spirits up, she was glorious. Her crimson gown was bedraggled, as if she had worn it for days, yet it glowed with a richness the red rag on the prostitute decoy had lacked. Her dark curls tumbled freely. Her eyes blazed.

Her eyes went straight to Petronius. 'What happened to you?'

'A small adventure. Where,' asked Petro, enunciating carefully, 'have you been, Maia?'

Maia glanced at Norbanus briefly. 'I took my children sailing on the river. We borrowed the procurator's boat. We went downstream and that terrible storm struck; lightning hit the mast. The children thought it was wonderful. We spent a day patching up the damage, then when we struggled back, we were not allowed to land here for ages because of some secret exercise. That's you and Marcus playing about, I gather?'

'Where are the children?'

'Gone home with the governor.' Maia. with unaccustomed delicacy, paused. 'I seem to have missed something.'

Some of us were dumbstruck.

Helena took charge. 'Listen, Maia! Norbanus is a leader of the criminals Petronius is pursuing. The other is called Florius and *he* lived at the villa to which they were trying to lure you. The point was to use you, Maia darling, as a hostage, to get to Petro. They claimed they had you – and Lucius thought it was true. So he surrendered himself in your place and was nearly killed horribly –'

Maia gasped. 'You *gave* yourself up?'

'It's an old army trick,' Petronius said defensively. 'The manoeuvre that is so stupid, you hope you'll get away with it.'

'You were nearly killed?'

'Ah, Maia, you think me a hero!'

'You are an idiot,' said Maia.

'She means that fondly,' Helena mediated, wincing.

'No, she means it,' returned Petronius. He sounded cheerful. It was as if my fractious sister's presence had lifted his spirits.

Norbanus made the mistake of laughing to himself.

'*You!*' Maia stabbed her finger in his direction furiously. 'You can answer to me!' She pushed past Helena to get to him. 'Is it true then? What I heard my brother say? You lied to them? You threatened them? You tried to kill Petronius? All the time you were hanging around, you were just using me?'

I tried to hold her back: no use. Petro just stood aside with his admiring look.

'I am sick of men like you!' Maia beat Norbanus on his chest

321

with her fists. They were real blows, swinging from the shoulder with both fists locked together, as if she was chopping at a dusty carpet hung on a line. She was a sturdy woman, used to physical toil around the house. If she had had a stick, she would have broken his ribs.

Norbanus was taken completely by surprise. Well, nice men who put their old mothers on mental pedestals don't know about real women. The closest they get are dolled up glamour-hungry floozies who pretend such men are wonderful. 'I am sick of being used –' A beat from left to right. 'Sick of being played with –' A beat from right to left. 'Sick of evil, manipulating swine ruining my life –'

'Leave it, Maia,' I protested uselessly.

Norbanus was taking the punishment now for all the men in her previous life – for her husband even, and certainly for Anacrites whose harassment had driven her here to Britain. As he staggered under the rain of blows, I stepped in, pulling my sister backwards away from him. Petronius made no attempt to calm her down. I think he was laughing.

'He's getting away!' shrieked Helena, as Norbanus seized his moment.

Petro and I let go of Maia. Norbanus made a lunge at Helena. She brandished the torch at him. He sent the fiery brand flying. In trying to save it, Helena cursed uncharacteristically, then wailed again, 'He'll get away!'

'Not from me!' Maia had found and raised the ready-primed crossbow. Then she lifted the safety claw, snapped up the trigger pin, and shot Norbanus in the back.

LVII

THE RECOIL SENT her spinning, but somehow she stayed upright. Open-mouthed, she gasped with horror. She was still holding the weapon, keeping it away from her, as if terrified it would fire another bolt. For a moment no one else could move.

Norbanus was on the floor. Hundreds of defeated tribesmen in this province could testify that it only takes one direct hit from a Roman artillery bolt. We didn't even check for signs of life.

'Oh!' whispered Maia.

'Put it down,' Helena murmured. 'It won't go off again.'

Maia hesitantly lowered the weapon. Petronius walked to her side. He looked more shocked than anyone. Well, if we were right about his feelings, the light of his life had just demonstrated a frightening personality. He took the weapon from her limp grasp, passing on the deadly thing to me.

'It's all right,' he said gently. He knew she was in shock. 'Everything is all right.'

Maia was trembling. For once her voice was barely audible. 'Is it?'

Petronius smiled a little, gazing down at her ruefully. 'I'm here, aren't I?'

That was when Maia let out a choking sob and collapsed into his arms. I think it was the first time, at least since she reached womanhood, that I had ever seen my sister allow someone else to comfort her. He wrapped her in her own cloak with tender hands, then held her.

Helena met my eyes and wiped away a tear. Then she pointed at the corpse and mouthed, '*What are we going to do?*'

'Tell the governor a gangster's body needs to be cleared away.'

She took a deep breath. Helena always tackled a crisis with logistical thought. 'We must tell nobody, ever, who killed him.'

'Wey-hey, why not? I'm proud of her!'

'No, no.' Petronius joined in. 'The children already have to cope with their father's death. They don't want to know their darling mama makes stiffs of professional mobsters on her evenings out.'

The darling mama struggled to free herself from his enfolding grasp. 'Give up,' he said. 'I'm not letting go.' Maia stilled. Their eyes locked on to each other. Petro's voice dropped. 'I thought I had lost you, Maia.'

'Would it have mattered?' she asked him.

'Hardly at all,' remarked Petronius Longus, who was not normally given to poetic conceits. 'Well – maybe just enough to break my heart.'

LVIII

H E STARED AT her. She said nothing. That was Maia. 'And what about you?' Petronius dared to ask. 'Suppose *I* had been lost –'

'Shut up,' said Maia. Then she buried her face against his chest and held him tight, sobbing. Petronius bent his head over her so they were close when she looked up again.

Maia had clearly prepared this speech some time before: 'I took the children out on the river to have time with them and talk about going home,' she said. 'And now I need to talk to you.'

'I am ready to listen,' replied Petronius. This was not strictly true. Instead, that rascal's way of listening was to demonstrate to Maia that he was keen on kissing.

Helena thumped me in the ribs, as if she thought that I was laughing. No chance. I had just seen my best friend throw himself into a life fraught with risk, and my sister agreeing to it. On both counts I was too shaken to mock.

We went outside eventually. The legionaries were clearing up. The prisoners had left. I muttered to Silvanus that Norbanus Murena was dead. We discussed what to do with the body. 'Which way is the tide flowing?'

'Going out,' he said.

'The ebb? That will do fine.'

Silvanus took the point. He lent a couple of lads for the business. Petronius and I went back in the warehouse with them, and we carried out Norbanus, one man to each arm and leg. We brought the corpse to the edge of the wharf, just below what Hilaris had once called the temporary permanent bridge. We swung together a few times to get up a rhythm, then we let fly. Norbanus Murena sailed out a short distance over the Thamesis, then splashed in. We had not weighed him down. Nobody wanted him to hang about in the port area then one day come bobbing up again. Let him be washed well down the estuary and beached in the mud or the marshes.

If this town ever became a great metropolis, plenty of corpses would wind up in the river. Londinium would be a draw for drownings, through grisly foul play or tragedy. Some would even end up as floaters by accident. Over the coming centuries this great river would see many – the newly dead, the long dead, and the living sometimes, drunk or distraught or maybe merely careless, all pulled to oblivion by the strong dark currents. Norbanus could set a precedent.

As we watched him lurch and vanish, the procurator Hilaris arrived, anxious to inspect his damaged boat. He had had it for years (I had borrowed it myself); he used it for trawling along the south coast to his houses at Noviomagus and Durnovaria. Maia rushed up, to explain what had happened in the storm. Petronius glued himself to her. I saw her hand wind into his. They could hardly bear to be apart.

We brought Hilaris up to date on the gangsters. He made no comment on what had happened to Norbanus, though he must have seen our disposal measures.

'Well, you've cleaned up the town for us, Marcus! I knew I could rely on you.' The words sounded flippant, but anyone who thought it would underestimate him. 'And thanks, Petronius.'

'We lost Florius,' said Petro glumly. 'He slipped the net somehow.'

'We can search for him. Any ideas?'

'He may change his plans now we have been so close to him, but he spoke of going back to Italy. We had the river sealed tonight. Nothing was allowed to move on the water. He cannot have sailed yet.'

Maia looked surprised. 'Oh a ship did go downstream, Lucius, just before ours landed here. It was carrying no lights, but showed up in the flares we had. The captain cursed because he nearly ran into it.'

Petronius swore and Flavius Hilaris growled. 'These gangsters have both cheek and incredible influence —'

'Money,' stated Petro, explaining how they managed it.

Hilaris considered whether to order a pursuit, but it was too late and too dark. Every creek, beach and landing-stage from here to the great northern ocean would be scoured tomorrow.

'One ship?' Petro checked with Maia. She nodded. 'Can you describe it?'

'Just a ship. Quite big. Loads of cargo lashed on its deck, as far as I could see in the dark. It had oars and a mast, but just came gliding silently.'

'No chance you know what the vessel was called?'

My sister smiled at her heart-throb teasingly. 'No. But you should talk to Marius. My elder son,' she explained blithely to the procurator, 'so loved the experience of sailing. I am very grateful that you made it possible. Marius has been collecting ships' names in a special note-tablet . . .'

Petronius biffed her for stringing him along, then he and the procurator smiled hopefully. 'I'll signal across to Gaul,' chuckled Flavius Hilaris. 'He may berth there and go overland, or he may go around Iberia by sea. But by the time that ship hits Italy, every port on the coast will be on notice.'

'Good luck then.' Petronius was sanguine. 'But I'm afraid you need to alert every harbour in the Mediterranean. Florius has to maintain his links with Italy; his real fortune is tied up in his wife. But he'll have made enough here to survive as a renegade for a long time . . . He could go anywhere.' Petro was taking it fairly well. 'One day he will come back to us, and I'll be there waiting.'

'I have every faith in that,' Hilaris assured him quietly.

Petronius Longus gazed down river. 'He is out there. I'll get him in the end.'

★

As a courtesy we had to wait while Flavius Hilaris checked the condition of his damaged boat then spoke to the soldiers. Petro and Maia sat together on a bollard, intertwined.

I grumbled to Helena, 'I'm not sure I can face a thousand mile journey home, with those two acting like star-struck teenagers.'

'Be glad for them. Anyway, they'll have to be discreet with four nosy children watching.'

I was none too sure. They were lost in each other; they didn't care.

The soldiers had now removed the barriers, so members of the public could come and go at will. Numbers had been attracted here by the military activity. A vagrant, one of the wide-eyed hopefuls who congregated in this frontier province, wandered up and decided I was a suitable friend for a man of his mad status. 'Where are you from, legate?'

'Rome.'

He gazed at me, from some vague world of his own.

'Italy,' I said. The need for explanation grated, even though I knew he was a derelict. He was filthy and showed signs of disease, but acted as if he recognised a like soul in me.

'That Rome!' murmured the vagrant wistfully. 'I could go to Rome.' He would never go to Rome. He had never wanted to.

'The best,' I agreed.

He had made me think of Italy. I went across to Helena and hugged her. I wanted to go back to the residence and see my two daughters. Then, as soon as possible, I wanted to go home.

LIX

A NY GOOD INFORMER learns: never relax. You fight to create a workable case. It has flaws; they always do. In ours there was a gaping hole: we had one target dead in the Thamesis, but the other chief suspect had escaped.

Petronius Longus was anxious to leave Britain on the next available boat from Rutupiae. He had personal reasons to call him back to Ostia, but naturally intended to put himself where Florius might reappear. In view of the Florius angle, the governor allowed him a pass for the imperial post service. In recognition of the demands of love, he extended that to Maia and the children, and then he felt obliged to include Helena and me. Fine. A quick journey suited all of us.

Just as we prepared to leave for Rome, however, a key witness let us down. We were doing well in some respects. The very public success of the attack on the gang at the customs house had impressed the locals. As a result, Frontinus was able to draw depositions about the extortion from some tavern-keepers, and these were with Petro to take back and use in any trial. A formal statement from Julius Frontinus himself might also be read out in court, if ever Florius was brought to justice. That would sound good. But we had already lost Chloris. Her companions could testify only that Florius had pressurised them, which — apart from their dubious status as gladiators — a good lawyer would demolish by calling it 'legitimate business practice'. Any Roman jury would envy the ability to make money. As the jurors struggled to stay afloat amidst their mortgages and creditors, Florius would seem to them an ideal citizen. He would walk.

Our one damning piece of evidence against him was the waitress' claim that at the Shower of Gold Florius had deliberately ordered Pyro and Splice to shove Verovolcus down the well. *I could say I saw him kill Chloris* – but accuse him of murdering a gladiatrix, in the arena? Excuse me. Case dismissed!

I wanted to persuade Frontinus that the waitress' evidence was so important he should order her transportation to Rome. With her smart new name and newly refined accent, Flavia Fronta could be tricked out as a nearly honest woman, even though the profession of waitress ranked very close to gladiating socially and legally. I was ready to prime a barrister to blacken Florius by suggesting that the low venue for the killing had been his choice, symptomatic of a despicable man who frequented filthy dives. Verovolcus was in effect British aristocracy, so with the King's closeness to the Emperor there was a scandal factor in killing him.

I first became uneasy while discussing whether Frontinus would agree to a Rome trip for the waitress. King Togidubnus had returned to his tribal capital; I assumed he was still saddened by the fate of his renegade retainer, yet comforted by the fact that the issue had been resolved. But instead of being taken to Noviomagus with the King, to be installed in the promised new wine bar, Flavia Fronta was still in Londinium.

'So where is she?' I demanded of the governor. 'There is a security angle.'

'She is safe,' Frontinus assured me. 'Her evidence is being reassessed by Amicus.'

Reassessed? By the torturer?

I went to see Amicus.

'What's going on? The waitress said Florius ordered the well-drowning. That alone will send him to the lions if he ever stands trial. Giving the statement makes her our one strong witness – but, with due respect to your art, it has to be seen that she made this statement voluntarily!'

'There is doubt,' replied Amicus dourly.

'Well, we cannot have doubt! So what is the problem?' I tried not to rage too fiercely. I was irritated, but concerned to ring-fence our case.

Amicus then told me one of the arrested men he had been allowed to work on was the owner of the Shower of Gold. I remembered him from the night I took Helena there for a drink: he had been an unwelcoming, stubborn piece of truculence.

'He sticks with what others had told me,' said Amicus. 'Verovolcus was a nuisance to the gang, and Florius wanted to humiliate him – but putting him in the well was just a game. That barber said the same. But the bar owner actually saw what happened.'

'He denied that before.'

'Well, I loosened his tongue.'

'That's your job. But under torture people say what they think you want to hear –' Amicus looked put out. 'If he admits it was murder, he may be scared that we'll charge him as an accessory.'

'He has been assured we won't punish him for the truth. Oh go and see the procurator, Falco!' Amicus burst out. 'Ask him to show you the evidence. You won't argue with that.'

I found Hilaris, who looked depressed. He confirmed that the bar owner had croaked out a clue, which had caused a new search to be made of his premises. Hilaris then unlocked a small panelled wall-cupboard. With two hands he removed an object which he dropped on a table with a loud thump. I picked it up: a torque of truly regal weight. It was a wonderful snaky thing of interlinked thick gold wires that must have made its wearer's neck ache. I wished I could ask my father's advice, but it seemed to me to be of some age, maybe dating back to Caesar's time. The techniques of weaving the wires and the granulated filigree that patterned the fastener were Mediterranean.

I sighed. 'Tell me this was found among the loot we took from the gang, Gaius.'

'Afraid not. We found it hidden in a wattle wall panel at the Shower of Gold.'

'And that's why Amicus is trying out his best skills on the waitress?'

'He has done it. She won't talk to him. The woman is being brought before the governor now, if you want to come.'

Flavia Fronta, as the informant now called herself, was dragged before a strict tribunal: Julius Frontinus, Flavius Hilaris and me. We sat in a line on folding stools, the Roman symbol of authority. Where we went, our power to adjudicate went too. That did not mean we could persuade an intransigent waitress to talk.

There were some signs of damage on her, though I had seen women look far more battered. The soldiers who brought her in were holding her up, but when they stood her in front of the governor, she stayed upright stoically. She still had breath to complain loudly about her handling by Amicus.

'All you have to do is tell the truth,' Frontinus pronounced.

I thought she now looked like a liar who was losing her nerve.

'Let us go through your story,' said Hilaris. I had seen him in this situation before. For a quiet man, he had a terse and very effective interrogation style. 'You are the only person – the only free citizen whose word counts legally – who claims that Pyro and Splice killed Verovolcus on the tavern well.'

Flavia Fronta nodded unhappily.

'You say you heard the Roman called Florius order them to do it?' Another, even weaker nod. 'And when Florius left the bar with his two associates, the Briton was dead?'

'He must have been.'

'Oh bull's balls! That's not good enough.' Everybody looked at me. I stood up slowly. I paced closer to the woman. I had noted the new weakness in the way she told her story. Amicus was not the only professional involved here. Even when it is inconvenient, a good informer continues to test everything. 'Pyro told us Verovolcus was still alive.'

'You'd better ask Pyro about it then!' she jeered.

'Pyro is dead. The gang had him killed.' I lowered my voice: 'Before you think it lets you off, you have something very serious to explain.'

I nodded to Hilaris. He produced the torque.

'Flavia Fronta, we believe you hid this at the bar.'

'It's been planted!'

'Oh, I don't think so. Now, as the governor told you, we are going to go through your story. You can tell us now, or you can be sent back to the official torturer – who believe me, has not even started on you yet. Let's begin: You say Florius told Pyro and Splice *Do it, lads!* Then, you say, they shoved poor Verovolcus in the well. You described it; you told me his expression was horrible . . . You say Pyro and Splice held him down – but if they did that, how exactly were you able to see his expression?'

'Oh . . . it must have been while they were dunking him.'

'I see.' I pretended to accept it. The woman could tell I had not done so. 'So he was there dead, and everybody fled in fear?'

'Yes. They all ran.'

'What did the three men do? Florius, Pyro and Splice?'

'They left too.'

'Straight away?'

'Yes.'

'Someone told us they were laughing?'

'Yes.'

'So behind them in the yard was Verovolcus in the well – where was the bar owner?'

'Inside the bar. Whenever there was trouble he found something else to do.'

'Well, that's typical of a landlord, isn't it? And what about you? You went out into the yard to have a look? Then let me guess – you stood there staring at Verovolcus and – am I right? – you told us next morning that his feet were waggling?'

On his magistrate's stool, Hilaris moved very slightly. He too remembered that the woman had mentioned this when we inspected the corpse.

Flavia Fronta made her mistake: she nodded.

I pierced her with a furious gaze. 'And then you did – what?'

She faltered, unwilling to explain.

'*You* took his torque, didn't you?' I knew now. 'Pyro had not removed it, as people thought he must have done. You were alone with the Briton. He was half drowned and at your mercy. You could see this beautiful, very costly torque around his neck. It was too much to resist.'

Flavia Fronta nodded again. I cannot say she looked crestfallen. She was aggrieved that I had forced this out of her, and she seemed to believe that stealing the precious neck collar had been her right.

'Explain now how it happened. You must have pulled Verovolcus at least partially out of the well to get at it?'

'That's right.' She was bolder now. We had the torque. Deception was pointless. Women are such realists.

'Verovolcus was still alive. He must have been heavy, and weakened perhaps. I dare say he was struggling. Pulling him out just enough must have taken some effort.'

'I may be short but I'm strong,' the waitress boasted. 'I spend half my life shifting full barrels and amphorae. I dragged him up and hauled the torque off his neck.'

'He was still alive. You admit that?'

'He damn well was. He made a big fuss about me wrenching off his gold.'

I tried to moderate my distaste for her. 'Verovolcus was meant to survive being dunked in the water. But you had stolen his torque and he saw you; so then –'

'I had no choice,' responded the waitress, as if I were an idiot to ask. 'I shoved him down the well again. And *I* held him there until he stopped kicking.'

I turned to the governor and procurator. 'Always a good feeling when you charge the right suspect with murder, don't you think?' They looked rueful.

Flavia Fronta's confession had destroyed our viable case against Florius. On murder we would have had him. Putting him before

334

a jury on charges of racketeering would be messier, and with clever lawyers to confuse the issues, the outcome would be much more unpredictable.

'I suppose I should have hidden the torque better,' the woman groaned.

'No, you should never have taken it. King Togidubnus gave that torque as a present to his retainer. The King will be pleased to have it returned. But I don't hold out much hopes for your nice little wine shop in the south.'

The waitress would go to the arena. The death of an unrepentant murderess in the jaws of bears or big wild cats would be a huge draw for an audience. She did not seem to have realised her fate. I left it for the governor and his staff to bring that home to her.

To Petronius Longus I broke the bitter news that we had solved a crime but lost his witness.

LX

THERE WAS ONE sad task remaining: Helena, Petronius and I attended the funeral of Chloris. Maia, still shaky after her bout with Norbanus, refused to come with us. She had harsh words for all female fighters and worse for my old girlfriend. She even blamed Helena for attending.

'This is noble, Helena – but nobility stinks!'

'She died at my feet,' Helena Justina reproved her quietly.

Gladiators are outcast from society. Their infamy means their graves lie not just beyond the town, as happens with all adult interments, but outside the public cemetery too. Established and wealthy groups of fighters may buy their own tombs, but Londinium so far possessed no townships of elaborate mausoleums for the dead. So her friends chose to bury Chloris in open ground, with an antique and peculiarly northern ritual.

It was a familiar walk to the site. We went westwards along the Decumanus Maximus, crossing the central stream and then out past the arena and the bath house. Londinium had no walls and no formally ploughed *pomerium* to mark its boundary, but we knew we were at the town limits. Beyond the military area, we reached a cemetery, one which contained some grand memorials. We walked through it, noticing a massive inscription, set up by his wife, to Julius Classicianus, the previous procurator of finance, from whom Hilaris had taken over after he died in service. Up and over the hill, we came to sloping ground that looked out across another tributary of the Thamesis. There, separate from the official tombs and monuments and facing the empty countryside, the funeral party met.

Chloris was the founder and leader of her group, cut down in unfair combat. It called for particular honour. Her body was brought at daybreak, the bier carried slowly by women. Her companions formed a sombre ceremonial escort. Other mourners, mainly women also, had come from all parts of town. They included a priestess of Isis, to whose cult many gladiators are attached. There was a temple of the Egyptian goddess on the south bank of the river in Londinium, incongruously. I knew Chloris had barely honoured her own Tripolitanian gods, but some of her companions found the attendance of the priestess appropriate. Anubis, the dog-headed Egyptian guide to the Underworld, equates to Rhadamanthus or Mercury, those messengers of the gods who officiate over deaths in the arena. So it was in a heavy fug of pine incense, and accompanied by the rattle of a sistrum, that the bier reached the burial site.

Outside the perimeter of the cemetery we found a carefully dug, straight-sided grave pit. Above this had been constructed an elaborate pyre of crossed logs, built up in rectangles. The timbers were meticulously laid. They would burn hot and they would burn long.

Deep in the pit were placed new lamps and incense burners, symbols of light and ritual. There were a few personal treasures and gifts from her friends too. Someone had washed Helena's blue stole and Chloris lay upon it. If Helena noticed, she gave no sign of approval or otherwise.

Chloris looked older than I wanted to remember her. A fit woman in the prime of life who had chosen a harsh but spectacular career. However desperate it seemed, she might have hoped to win her fights and be acclaimed, with wealth and fame. Instead, she had been cut down for her independent spirit. Today she had been carefully robed, her ghastly wounds concealed. She wore a long dark gown, crossed on the breast with a costly gold body chain, bejewelled at its centre. Even in death, she looked expensive, honed, sexually dangerous, troubling. I had not wished her dead, yet I was half relieved to be leaving her here.

'Who bought her the jewel?' I wondered.

'Nobody.' Helena glanced at me. 'She will have bought it for herself. Don't you see, Marcus – that was the point for her?'

As the flames were lit, her colleagues stood around her, beautiful and disciplined. Some wept, but most were still and grim. They knew they all faced death in the life they had chosen. Yet this death had been untimely; it demanded a special requiem. Heraclea, statuesque and blonde, took the torch first and fired a corner of the pyre. The sweet, aromatic scent of pine cones intensified. A thin trail of smoke curled upwards, then the flames began to take. She handed on the torch. One by one the women touched the logs, circling the pyre. A low moan filled the air. Brief farewells were spoken. Even Helena moved away from Petronius and me and took her turn with the brand. He and I did not. It would have been unwelcome. We just stood with the smoke gusting around us, winding its way into our lungs, our hair and our clothes.

The flames would burn all day and night. Slowly the layers of logs would fragment and sink into one another. At the end, the charred remains would fall into the pit, flesh melted, bones burned to fragility yet virtually intact. No one would collect the ashes and bones. This would be her perpetual resting place.

Eventually I went forward alone to say my farewells. After a while, the woman called Heraclea attended me like a hostess.

'Thank you for coming, Falco.'

I did not want to talk but politeness forced it. 'This is a sad day. What will happen to your group now?'

Lowering her voice, Heraclea nodded to the priestess of Isis. 'See her with the priestess?' There was a richly clad young matron alongside, one of those holy hangers-on whom temples attract, all dangling silver jewellery. 'New patron. There were always several on the sidelines, widows or wealthy wives of merchants. They want the thrill of the blood but if they sponsor us, they can avoid being thought to lust after men. Amazonia said –'

I guessed. 'Accepting their support would be no different from taking on Florius.'

'You knew her well.'

'Yes, I knew her.' I stared at the pyre. 'I knew her, but it was a long time ago.'

Heraclea was also subdued. 'Amazonia was right. I'm giving up on Britain. I'm going home.'

'Where's that?'

'Halicarnassus.'

'Well, that's the right place!' Halicarnassus is the spiritual homeland of the Amazons in myth. I glanced behind. Helena was talking to Petronius. From the stark expression on his face, this funeral was affecting him. He was thinking too much about that other in Ostia, when his two daughters were sent to the gods in his absence. Helena would comfort him. It would take her concentration off me for a moment. I took a chance. 'Heraclea, did Chloris say anything about me?'

The tall blonde turned and gazed at me for a moment. I don't know what I was hoping to hear, but she could not or would not supply it. 'No, Falco. No. She never said anything.'

So that was it. I left her amidst the sweet scent of burning pine cones and the avid flames.

Sometimes in the ensuing years I would remember her, trying not to dwell too much on the times we had spent together. I could cope with the memory.

'You were always trouble.'

'And you were always –'

'What?'

'I'll tell you next time we're alone . . .'

I returned to Petronius and Helena. They seemed to be waiting, as if they thought I had had something to finish.

We would not stay to the end, but for some time longer stood watching the flames in silence. The evil that had caused the death we mourned had been averted, at least temporarily. Londinium would fall prey to worse gangsters eventually, and for Petronius the task of hunting Florius remained. This woman who had died and her friends, whose grieving faces were lit by the fire, were outcasts – just like the criminals; they, however, stood for skill, talent, comradeship and good faith. They represented the best of those who came here to the end of the world in hope. Chloris had been destroyed, yet it was on her own ground, using her skills, defiant, admired, and, I thought, holding no regrets.

Who could say that was uncivilised? It depends what you mean by civilisation, as the procurator said.

ARCHAEOLOGICAL NOTE

WHEN I DECIDED to bring Falco and Helena to Roman London, it was partly because they were already in Britain after their previous adventure, and the problems of ancient world travel would not permit them to return too soon. This timing was good, however. There have been spectacular finds in recent years, greatly improving our knowledge of the Roman town. Sometimes it has seemed that the Museum of London Archaeology Service and the Museum's exhibition curators have been working flat out to find background material for a Falco plot. I am grateful particularly to Nick Bateman and Jenny Hall for their help, especially where dates and building locations are uncertain.

But my portrait of Londinium is personal. Fiction authors are allowed to invent. (Yes we are!) So, the wine-cask well is inspired by one found near the Decumanus, which featured in the exhibition 'High Street, Londinium', but mine is in a different location. The Shower of Gold, and all the other bars named in this story, are my creations.

Likewise, the burial in the final chapter is *not* the 'bustum' burial in Southwark which caused much media excitement as the possible dis-covery of a female gladiator (a conclusion which is probably wrong); my burial takes place at the known Roman cemetery around Warwick Square, the area where the famous monument to Julius Classicianus may originally have stood before its stones were re-used near the Tower. Had my lass existed, she would lie under the Central Criminal Courts (the Old Bailey). Don't expect her to be found!

The stone-built Roman fort by the Barbican dates to the AD 80s. Evidence for earlier defences with turf ramparts, perhaps hastily thrown up in the aftermath of the Boudiccan Rebellion, has been found at Fenchurch Street but it seems most likely that at this date the soldiery occupied the western hill in a haphazard way (waiting perhaps for some government agent to suggest building them a decent fort . . .) The amphitheatre, identified only recently, is under Guildhall Yard. There was a military-style baths nearby in Cheapside, and Myron's waterworks were recently discovered on a corner of Gresham Street.

The forum lay above what is now Gracechurch Street, north of Lombard Street. The Decumanus Maximus ran across town there, following the modern Cheapside and Newgate Street. Another major road lay under Cannon Street and the road from the forum to the river was aligned with Fish Street Hill.

The Thames in this period was much wider than now. It was bridged from an island in Southwark, just downstream of the present London Bridge, and what evidence we have suggests that several versions existed between the Invasion and the second century, developing from wooden ones to the permanent stone one, which did come ashore at an extensive wharf system. There may have been a ferry landing to one side, and on the other there is evidence of a grand stone building, possibly with a colonnade, which has been identified as a possible customs house for the port.

The governor's palace, built in the last decades of the century, lies partly under Cannon Street Station. Who knows where the procurator lived? Somewhere decent, given that he ran the works budget!

Southwark did have a mansio, which would have been new, and a Temple of Isis.

Greenwich Park had a Vespasianic temple complex, re-investigated by 'The Time Team', which would just have been visible on its hilltop from the house where I finished this novel . . . I do not believe Roman villa developers failed to exploit Greenwich, but the 'love nest' with the landing-stage is invented.

Lindsey Davis
London, 2002